Hesitant Hearts *and*
the Wrestling of Goats

Ballydoonan Days

Ivan McKeown

Ivan McKeown

BALLYHAY BOOKS

Published by Ballyhay Books,
an imprint of Laurel Cottage Ltd.
Donaghadee, N. Ireland 2010.
Copyrights Reserved.
© Ivan McKeown 2010
Contributed texts are copyright of individual contributors.
Photographs are reproduced by permisssion.
Printed by Gutenberg Press Ltd., Malta.

ISBN 978 1 900935 83 8

"Whoso findeth a wife findeth a good thing." Proverbs 18:22

I would like to dedicate this book to my wife. Now, before you say, 'How unoriginal, how trite, that's who just about every author dedicates their work to,' let me just stop you and say, no, there you are quite wrong. I know, I checked. I have read hundreds of books of all types, genres and authors. Many have dedications, some to children, parents, fellow authors, Napoleon and the recently deceased pet hamster, but not one of them was dedicated to my wife. It is about time that this was put right. She is an amazing person.

25 years ago, when she vowed to 'love, honour and obey' me she never mentioned that she would also remain totally gorgeous and lovely.

And she has. She has been my inspiration, encouragement and best friend. She has laughed at my stories, pointed out the flaws, made suggestions and stayed gorgeous.

So, to Gillian, the best wife a man could ever hope to be blessed with, I dedicate this book.

1.

THE TROUBLE WITH GOATS

Nathan McCutcheon lived with his family just outside the village of Ballydoonan. He was sixteen and he lived in a house that was not. The house sat squat upon a hill; an edifice of brick and mortar planted on a soft rising curve of green. The house was not actually that old, but the roof made no great efforts at keeping out the rain and the builder hadn't seen fit to install any kind of a damp proof course in the brick. Any pride he had in leaving a memorial of his work in the world was overcome by the greater incentive of how much he would leave it with in his pocket. Mould grew up the single-brick walls as nature tried, with surprising ease, to reclaim the single-storey building and restore it to its rightful origins of the stuff of Earth. The small steel-framed windows cracked at every rumour of wind and frost and the howling wolves of the ever-present wind prowled the halls and bedrooms carrying away their prey of heat and warmth.

For all that, the McCutcheons liked the damp and chilly place. In the summer the views over the Irish Sea to the Mull of Galloway and the Isle of Man were worth the trials of winter, and the isolation at night when stars beamed down in their twinkled billions was a life far removed from the wearisome noise and bustle of community.

There had always been a goat at the place. Nathan could not remember a time when there had not been a goat. At times they had had no dog, now in fact was one of them, but a goat was always around in one form or another. A curly-horned goat. A small, skinny goat. A dubious eyed goat with a remarkably long beard. Probably before the house had been raised a goat had chewed its cud, sitting on its gnarled knees on the green hill as it pondered the coasts twenty miles away and entertained goat-type thoughts about Scotland and waiting for the house to be built below its stomach.

All the goats had been given names and all those names began with a 'g'. Gertie Goat, Gruffy Goat and Gracie Goat. There was a Gus Goat too, though Gus was actually somebody else's. The 'somebody else' had made no effort to recover the goat when it wandered across the fields into the McCutcheon's garden and proceed to eat every edible plant in the flowerbeds along with every inedible one for completeness' sake. So it stayed and Mrs McCutcheon – Ellie – christened it Gus: it was 'g'reedy and it ended up with 'us' and that was that.

Gertie Goat was a girl goat. She was a nanny goat without anyone to nanny. Not having a billy about the place, she was a young single female and without the trials of female friends, quite equable in manner and demeanour. This would have been a fine mix of goatly attributes had Nathan seen fit to leave it at that but Nathan was sixteen and had no brother. He had sisters of course, but everybody had sisters and they didn't count. Not unless of course they were somebody else's sister, somebody else's sister was a completely different creature altogether. No, Nathan had been badly let down by thoughtless parents who had not engineered to produce a brother for him and that left instead a goat and two sisters. The sisters expressed no great enthusiasm for wrestling, which of course is one of the prime purposes of a brother, but the goat had nothing to say about it. Not that it might not have said a great deal about it had it been granted the gift of speech but like all goats before and after it, this was a gift denied.

Thus encouraged by the goat's silence on the matter, Nathan proceeded after a moment of some enlightenment to engage the goat in a series of wrestling bouts.

The realisation that a goat was an excellent proposition for hand-to-hand combat came to him one day in Maths. The teacher happened to mention during something to do with sines and cosines that she was afraid of goats. There was also some talk about tangents and coalmen having soot on them but that was lost in the sudden epiphany that burst upon Nathan's wandering thoughts. A goat was an object of fear to some people and thus by a simple matter of deduction, an opponent worthy of challenge. A goat could be faced up to and its terror defied. A veritable championship of defiance in fact that began that very day when Nathan returned from school and got changed into clothes more suited to goat wrestling.

At first it was a fairly straightforward affair. Nathan would approach the goat and the goat, being equable of manner and demeanour would allow itself to be thus approached and wrestled to the ground. The goat, it must be said, initially found the experience somewhat shocking and made every effort to inform her assailant of his misdirected exertions. She bleated and complained loudly about the daily topples but found little in the way of understanding or sympathy from Nathan who made himself ignorant of the goat's protestations. Nathan had found in the wrestling of the animal the brother who for sixteen years had eluded his physical endeavours of Olympic performance. His skills in bringing down the goat were applauded from far and wide as invisible crowds of thrilled onlookers roared with applause at the mighty feats of strength and Herculean muscle.

Finally, Gertie's gentle and disinterested manner had had enough and the worm turned.

Having her horns grabbed was bad enough, but having her horns grabbed and her head twisted so that she fell to the ground was simply more than any self-respecting goat should have been expected to forbear. In that the best form of defence was attack, Gertie, now wise to Nathan's intentions, initiated her defence as soon as the boy made any move in her direction. As soon as Nathan entered the fenced off garden, the goat charged, head down at her opponent and got her six bob's worth in first. A long chain tethered Gertie to a stake driven in to the ground but the chain gave her a full range of the garden which had long since lost its flower-beds and shrubs. At first her attacks were somewhat tentative and made only half-hearted connection with Nathan as he warmed to the upping in the goat wrestling skill department. As her opponent was clearly unperturbed by her lunges, she became much more energetic and developed an ability to ram into his legs with all the force she could from as short a run-up as possible.

Nathan now realised his opponent was in the game to win and this produced within him a sudden disinterest in the sport. Unfortunately for him, Gertie was only getting going.

Nathan had limited his wrestling bouts to the goat; Gertie had no such inhibitions. All that had been equable and reserved was now replaced by a set of attitudes so bent on visiting violence on the nearest victim as to be positively maniacal. The boy soon learned after receiving no small number of green and blue bruises on his legs and thighs that the goat was no longer to be messed with. He avoided the garden and avoided too the stares of the creature as it dared him enter her ring. The very sight of him crunching up the gravel path was enough to have the goat drop her head, straighten her fore-legs and cast an aimed bead on the approaching target.

"There's something odd about that goat," said Mr McCutcheon one day on returning from work at the depot and entering the kitchen at home. Mrs McCutcheon was stirring a large pot of homemade vegetable soup and only half heard her husband.

"Oh, hello dear, what did you say?"

"The goat – there's something different about her. Is she all right?"

Ellie knifed the scallions into the bubbling pot and replaced the lid.

"Gertie?" she asked again. "What's wrong with her?"

"She stamps about that garden as if she's upset about something. She used to just lie about and eat; now she prowls about pulling at her chain and rearing back on her hind legs every time I see her. Do you think she needs something?"

"Needs something?" smiled Ellie, "like what, Bob? You mean a billy?"

"No, one goat's quite enough, I'm not having a stinking billy-goat around the place. Maybe she needs a bit more room or something. Where's Nathan? I'll get him to stake her into the back garden for a while, she can keep the grass down there instead."

"Sure I've been saying that for ages, I want to get some flowers back in the front again and if Gertie was in the back I could work at the front again. Nathan's out across the fields somewhere; he said he'd be a couple of hours." She lifted the lid and began slowly stirring the soup.

"I'll move her then; Nathan's forgotten to move her for over a week," said Bob as he hung up his Ulsterbus jacket. "I'll have to speak to him about that," he added heading back out.

Gertie watched Bob approach and saw him lift the latch on the gate. He entered the garden and headed for the long iron spike with the chain running to the goat's collar. The spike was embedded into the grass at the far side. It was Nathan's job to move the spike about so that the goat had access to new grass every other day. Mr McCutcheon noted with some annoyance again that the spike hadn't been moved in some time and the circle of nibbled grass was like a billiard table. Leaning down, he grasped the flattened head and began to wiggle the spike to loosen its hold in the soil.

The goat looked up and saw the large grey target beckon as it wobbled temptingly from twelve feet away. It looked soft and therefore capable of receiving a butt of a velocity that could be delivered without any serious consequences on her head.

There was no warning. One second he was in the process of pulling the loosened spike from the garden, the next Bob McCutcheon received a blow to his backside that was along the lines of being rammed by a motorcycle with a log tied in front. He fell forward, the spike in his hand and landed on his hands and knees on the grass. Somewhere in the back of his head he was aware that the goat was in the garden and that there was a possibility that the immense wallop to his rear was somehow connected to its presence. Before he had time to join the dots the goat struck again.

This time the target was even more perfectly placed. Where before the goat had not been fully able to exploit the situation as the proffered rear was at a height that did not allow her to get her head fully down into the optimum ram position, now all was wonderful. It was a shorter run up sure enough, but still, with all of her might she smashed her horns into the trousered bottom staring back at her.

Now Bob got the message; he was under attack and his attacker was preparing to strike again. Still on his knees he spun and threw his hands up just in time to grab the goat's horns as she tried for her hat trick.

"Get off you brute!" he shouted as the goat stared at him with her large slit pupils and grunted ominously. The brute had no intention of getting off anybody. Not knowing the trick of twisting the goat's head to get her to fall over, Bob slipped farther and farther back as the heavily breathing animal pressed her head hard against him. She was enjoying herself. Bob was not.

Nathan had been out with his air rifle. It was a Diana .177 calibre with telescopic sights and he had been shooting in the woods at the old quarry. The woods were filled with rooks and magpies and the encircling Whin bushes thrived with rabbits. None of these were in any danger from Nathan's gun however. He had only ever shot two creatures since getting the gun for his birthday and one of those had been an accident. It had been a sparrow that was perched on the telephone wires leading to the gable wall the very day that Nathan got his rifle. Putting his very first pellet into the breech of the weapon, Nathan aimed carelessly in the general direction of the bird and pulled the trigger. Just what he thought he was trying to achieve was lost in the sudden shock of seeing the little sparrow fall in a flurry of uncoordinated flaps to the lane. Still shocked, he watched as the hapless creature gave a few disjointed struggles and then lay still. He had killed it.

Walking slowly over, his conscience twanging away on his heart strings like a violin orchestra tuning up, he came to a guilty stand beside the expired bird.

There was a full burial complete with a twig cross and sermon from Nathan directed at himself. He was the only one at the service in the corner of the field – he was the only one invited, or aware of the recent decease come to that, and so he was able to be quite blunt.

"You twit!" he preached to himself. "Since when did God give you a right to go around killing poor innocent sparrows? I hope you're ashamed of yourself." He was. He opened his pocket Gideon's Bible given to him in first form and read where it fell open. He wanted to give God the choice.

God chose Matthew Chapter ten. 'Are not two sparrows sold for a farthing? And not one of them shall not fall on the ground without your Father.' He cringed and cast his eyes heavenward. He decided to try again; this time he steered the Bible in the direction of the Psalms – they were more typical funeral material. It was Psalm 51 and verse 4. He cleared his throat and read aloud. 'Against thee, thee only, have I sinned, and done this evil in thy sight.' There was obviously no escape. He bowed his head and earnestly vowed never to go around shooting birds again… not unless he meant to eat them in the event of the Third World War. The second creature had been a rabbit, but he *had* thoroughly intended to eat it. After bloodily skinning it in his mother's dish basin whilst fixedly thinking brave manly thoughts of wilderness survival however, he fed it to the cat.

The only things Nathan shot now were things like knots in trees or puffball mushrooms whilst lurking commando style behind rocks or furze bushes. It was whilst returning from just such an expedition that he came up the yard and saw his dad wrestling with the goat. His dad didn't see him and since he was at that moment rolling about under the goat it wasn't altogether surprising. It was quite a wrestle. The goat seemed to be winning.

Nathan hesitated as he decided what to do. He had never admitted to anyone that the change in the goat's character was entirely down to him. His mum had liked the friendly animal and he didn't want her to be made intelligent of the fact that the animal's recent conversion from nice to nasty was all his own work. It seemed however that his dad had taken up where he had left off. If he showed himself he might embarrass his father who was obviously reliving a part of his youth in the front garden. Dad had had several brothers and who knew? Perhaps he was having a wrestle with one of his childhood siblings. Imagination was a wonderful thing; it was nice to know it didn't die when you passed forty. Instead, he took a left and headed around the back of the house to the back door.

"Hello dear," said his mother as he entered, "did you see your dad?"

Nathan's eyebrows lifted. Did his mum know?

"Er, yes… he's out the front."

"With the goat?"

Life could take some very surprising turns.

"Yes, he seems to be enjoying himself," said Nathan baffled. "I didn't think Dad and I were both doing the same thing. I gave it up a week ago."

"Yes, I think your father is a bit annoyed about that. That's why he's having to do it. He'll probably mention it when he comes in."

"Oh," replied Nathan confused, "uhh…why does he *have* to do it?" He was becoming increasingly puzzled.

Ellie looked at her son. Sometimes sons were a mystery to a mother. You bore them into the world, you nursed and coddled them, fed and clothed them and still the workings of their minds were often a closed book.

"Because you didn't. Do you want the poor thing to starve Nathan?"

"No, I… *starve?*"

Mrs McCutcheon simply shook her head and began to set the table.

"Tea's almost ready. Tell Liz will you? She's in her room."

Nathan walked out of the kitchen and headed down the hall to Liz's bedroom. Liz was fourteen and spent most of her awakened life doing homework. It was a sore point since Nathan's suspicious parents reckoned he spent precious little of his life doing any of his. That sister was a pain. Why couldn't she just do her homework in the bus like him? He saw homework as a collective thing. In the bus he and his friends could whiz through a physics sheet in ten minutes if enough of them piled in. It didn't take a genius to so word the answers as to avoid any accusation of copying. The way he saw it, in his future in an office or whatever, working together was what you did. Why leave it till he was nineteen or twenty to find out how to do it? His other sister was a nurse. He missed Pam around the house. She was good at helping him with his homework.

As he went to shout Liz's name outside her room, a knock at the door suddenly redirected his thoughts. He turned and headed to answer the door and at the same time his mother walked in from the kitchen.

"I'll get that," she said. "Did you tell Liz? Have you done your homework yet?"

He spun again as his mum opened the door to the visitor standing in the lobby. Looking back he saw Mr Hamilton, the Presbyterian minister. He had an odd look on his face.

"Oh, hello Mr Hamilton, come on in, how are you?" he heard his mother say. As she shut the door behind the visitor, Nathan caught a brief glimpse of his dad's legs waggling about on the grass and Gertie's hooves stamping around like a one-fingered typist. He forgot about Liz and stood at the door of the living room where his mother had taken the minister.

"Would you like a wee bowl of soup, Mr Hamilton? We're just about to have tea, we'd love to have you join us."

"Is, ahm… is Bob about?" asked the minister in an oddly quizzical voice. "I was wanting to ask him about the choir outing… is he… is he here at all?" Nathan could see him glance toward the window looking out onto the front garden. His mother spied him standing at the door.

"Nathan," she said. "Tell Liz to set the table for five will you?"

As he turned again he heard his mother reply to the minister. "Oh he's out with the goat. Didn't you see him in the garden?"

Liz frowned and set down her book. Maths was such an interesting subject; the way numbers all came together in equations and formulae was as exciting as anything else she knew. Why others didn't share her enthusiasm was beyond her understanding.

"Who's here?" she asked.

"Reverend Hamilton," Nathan replied, heading back to the living room. His mother was talking as he paused at the door.

"I can't understand how he didn't see you. It only takes a minute to sort out Gertie, Nathan normally does it; didn't you let him know you were here?"

The minister replied with a fixed grin. He knew that words were required but he was at a momentary loss as to which ones. Bob Mc-Cutcheon was usually a serious, sober individual and the last person in the world he might have expected to see engaging in some kind of a macho goat-wrestling episode. When he saw him he had his arms wrapped around the animal's neck and appeared to be trying to bite its ear. Mrs McCutcheon seemed to be very unconcerned about it all. That was one of the awkward things about being a pastor; nothing was supposed to shock – everything was to be taken in its stride and discussed calmly and reasonably. Sitting with a woman while her husband was outside rolling about in the garden trying to bite or wrestle or Lord knew what, a goat was stretching it a bit. He was rescued by the sudden appearance of Bob at the window. He looked somewhat agitated.

"The ruddy goat's gone mad!" he shouted through the glass, his hair jagged about like he had been electrocuted. "It tried to kill me!"

'Ruddy' was Bob's worst word. Ellie could not remember the last time he had used it. Hearing it in the presence of such a pinnacle of Presbyterianism was no small shock. Ellie reddened.

"Bob, come in, Mr Ham…"

"I said the ruddy goat's just tried to murder me, Ellie! Phone the police or something, get me the poker!"

Mrs McCutcheon adjusted her hair and tried again.

"The Reverend Hamilton's he…"

"No, not him, what use is he for pity's sake! I need a farmer and a ruddy big shotgun!

"Mr Hamilton's *here*!" said Ellie frantically pointing at the seat opposite. "To see *you*!"

Bob's face at the window froze into a portrait of a man who looked like he's been shot at and missed. The portrait turned ninety degrees and disappeared.

It reappeared fifteen seconds later at the living room door. Nathan was hiding in the back hall.

"Ah… hello John… I didn't hear you arrive. I was just…I suppose you're wondering… well, you see the goat… it must have…" A look of resigned desperation fell across his face like a slammed door. "Oh *fart* it all!" he exclaimed as he gave up the hope of explaining anything. Having burned his boats by swearing in the worst way he knew possible he promptly turned and left the room. The minister and Ellie remained staring at the spot just vacated by the inexplicable Mr McCutcheon, neither wanting to have to face the embarrassment of conversation after such an outburst.

"Well, I… I think that…" began Mr Hamilton as Ellie took one look at his face and fled out into the hallway leaving him in his unfinished sentence – which was just as well since he had no idea in the slightest as to what it was he had been about to say.

Nathan, feeling the duty of family honour weigh suddenly around his neck ventured into the room and sat down facing the minister.

"Do you think there might be sparrows in heaven, Mr Hamilton?"

2.

MESSING ABOUT WITH BOATS

Kirkie's real name was William Mungo Kirkpatrick. The Mungo was bestowed upon him by an overzealous father who, as a boy, had thrilled at the stories about the famous Scottish explorer Mungo Park and felt he had to mark it in some way. Fortunately for the boy his mother managed to suppress any use of the name and it languished away on his birth certificate and nowhere else. In school the 'William' likewise was also rejected and was replaced by 'Kirkie'. It suited better and it stuck. Parents could save a lot of bother by waiting and asking their children's friends what to call their kids.

Kirkie had many plans in life. His job as a night watchman at the local Newtownards hospital gave him time to concoct them during long spells sitting in a wooden sanger in the casualty car park. Surrounded by flickering ten-inch monitors and clipboards with names and extension numbers, he would formulate schemes that transformed the slowly dribbling hours into priceless episodes of brain-storming inventiveness.

Kirkie's shed at home was no ordinary outhouse. It was his own private domain of creative engineering. It measured twenty feet by thirty and had been built in the rear garden by Kirkie himself. He had not bothered with a spirit level or any other level when building the breeze-block walls. Kirkie believed in the supreme accuracy of the 'Mark 1 eyeball.' Obviously Kirkie's Mark 1 needed a bit of adjustment. The unstable looking walls were topped by a corrugated iron roof, which had initially leaked profusely where holes liberally spotted the tin in the places where Kirkie had drilled and missed the joist. The maxim 'measure twice and cut once' was practised in reverse by the indomitable Kirkie and most usually without the 'measure' at all. After caulking the holes with mastic and painting the tin with Hammerite paint, it looked almost all right. Unfortunately 'Watson's Haberdashery and Hardware' only sold 250ml tins of the stuff and it took a lot of them to do the job. Kirkie would never have guessed paint colour batches could vary so markedly. His long suffering wife Wilma guessed it would have been cheaper to get a man to do it but whenever she ever suggested such things Kirkie always said if you wanted a job done right, then do it yourself. Wilma agreed, but only if the words had been uttered by a professional painter and not her husband.

Inside the shed Kirkie had amassed a substantial plethora of tools and equipment. The crooked walls were lined with saws and spanners, pliers and planes. Welders and air compressors, spray guns and torque wrenches – if there was a tool for it, Kirkie had it. Having the tool and having the skill to use it however were not always possessions enjoyed simultaneously by William Mungo Kirkpatrick. When allied to his somewhat optimistic plans it gave him the capability, but not always the ability, to realise his imaginative ideas.

Kirkie had often toyed with the idea of submarines. He had always had an interest in the sea and living on the eastern coast, south of Ballydoonan, gave him the opportunity to see it. It was right outside his front door, he could hardly have missed it. Apart from a quiet single-lane road that ran by the front of the house, all that spread before the front of his house was the Irish Sea. Sometimes after a heavy night with a high tide and a southeasterly gale, a fair bit of it ended up cluttering his front garden. Alan Titchmarsh said seaweed was good for plants but he obviously wasn't thinking of it mixed up with stones, plastic milk bottles, Castrol gear oil containers and dead guillemots.

Kirkie's long-suffering wife listened patiently to his latest proposal and 'yes dear'ed in the appropriate gaps. Lying on his back in the bed, his head facing the ceiling, he outlined his latest project.

"Two old steel baths welded together, one upside down on top. An electric motor with a car battery for power and your father's periscope. It would be easy. I could take underwater photographs and make a bit of money at it."

"That's nice dear."

"Of course, there wouldn't actually be much room, but later on I could build a bigger one after ironing out any design issues with the first."

"Yes, that would be good," said Wilma Kirkpatrick as she continued reading her story in the *People's Friend* magazine. It was about a young airman who washed up on the Isle of Skye during the Second World War and was found by Maggie McTavish, the redheaded harbourmaster's daughter. He had lost his memory and she was young and beautiful. It wasn't hard to tell where this story was going, but that was why she liked the magazine; there were no nasty surprises lurking in the *People's Friend*. Kirkie was as easy to read to Wilma. Sometimes he came up with zany ideas but he always had and, mostly, they worked out O.K.

At least, he hadn't died yet.

The old steel baths weren't that hard to come by. People were all into nice new coloured bathroom suites now and old baths littered the countryside like so many plastic bags. He did actually find one in the countryside. It was in a field where a farmer had been using it as a cattle trough. A nice new concrete one sat primly beside the old one and Kirkie correctly guessed it was a redundant item. The farmer took three pounds for it as giving anything away was outside of his experience but Kirkie's submarine had commenced. The second cost him ten pounds from a salvage yard in Newtownards but it was a small price to pay if a working submersible was going to be the result.

The shed sparked and flashed as Wilma watched dispassionately from the kitchen window. She had forgotten most of the submarine conversation but vaguely remembered something about the sea and a lost pilot. Kirkie had lots of friends. Maybe the pilot one was helping him make a boat or something in the shed. Kirkie had placed one bath on top of the other and was in the process of welding both together. The welder was an electric one and tended to either blast holes in the metal or kept getting the rods fizzingly stuck to the steel baths. When that happened the lights dimmed and the television in the house blinked and stuttered. Wilma frowned and waited for *Emmerdale* to return to normal. For that to happen a new scriptwriter would have been required but Wilma waited patiently all the same.

Electric welding was not proving to be one of Kirkie's strong points. It wasn't helped by the enamel on the baths pinging off in slivers and dropping, hot, down his collar and Wellington boots. Still, he was a trier and perseverance and an angle-grinder paid off as eventually and after two nights of flashes and smoke the two baths were as one. It was about now that Kirkie realised he had now no access to the inside of his deep-sea voyager. In his enthusiasm for the project he had done the last part of the job first and omitted all the little jobs, like the installation of the electric motor, the batteries, the fireman's air cylinder, the seats, the periscope and a hundred other engineering aspects that required access to the inside of the baths. Undoing all the hours of welding were out of the question and instead he drew a chalk square on top of his vessel and put a new disc in the angle-grinder. It needed a door anyway.

The chalk line had been pretty much a square but the newly cut hole was pretty much not. The angle-grinder had insisted on skidding about all over the place and Kirkie had used up a fair few words that young boys sometimes seek out in their dictionaries in English class and get in trouble for sniggering over. In any case, Kirkie could get his head and shoulders into his creation now and as he looked about in the upside-down innards he pondered what task ought to come next. He decided on the creation of three portholes. One on each side and one in front.

Wilma wondered what Kirkie wanted the plates for but didn't ask as an explanation was not really what she was looking for. She handed him one of her good willow pattern ones immediately wishing she had thought about it first but didn't ask for it back. She had been brought up to believe a wife should show confidence in her husband's leader-ship and ability. Faith could bring about miraculous effects and one day she hoped to live to see it.

The plate was used as a template to draw a circle on the submarine where the three portholes would be cut. The experience learned in cut-ting the square had shown him he was pretty good at circles so thus encouraged, Kirkie got to work. After more skittering about on the metal surface, Kirkie tried a different tack. Taking the plate from the workbench he taped it onto the chalk circle with an X of silver duct tape and started again. The plate would act as a guide and allow him to cut a perfect round hole in the metal. Kirkie had heard of people called 'Polymaths' – people who were multi-talented and capable of great ability in almost any discipline. As the plate cracked and shattered in a pile on the concrete floor it occurred briefly to Kirkie that he might actually not be one of those people. It was a brief thought and quickly subsumed by the knowledge that the spider in the cave didn't give up just because of a broken plate. 'If at first you don't succeed, try, try again.' Four or five tries later he began to have immense respect for that spider. Broken plates lay in shards around a submarine with three very uneven and shapeless holes not including the one on the roof. The Lexar Plexiglas was easier to cut and using nuts and bolts along with liberal applications of clear silicon, Kirkie took another day to fasten the windows over the portholes. The unsightly openings were disguised quite satisfactorily by the Lexar and all in all Kirkie was beginning to be pleased about himself.

"How's it going?" asked Wilma who hadn't asked about the missing plates. "Are you getting on O.K. with your thing dear?" She was feeding little David his liquidized dinner and going through the motions of eating and chewing in encouragement to the eight month old as the mush plopped back out of his mouth and ran down his chin.

"Good, it's going really well," replied Kirkie cheerily. "The superstructure is all in place and I'm working on the electrics now. It's a bit tight for space but I'll need a backup battery just in case. It doesn't leave much room what with the air cylinder and all that."

"No, I'm sure it doesn't," said Wilma distantly. It was amazing how babies grew at all. They seemed to swallow nothing and yet spew without ceasing.

"And then there's the problem of steering. I can't go putting too many holes in it in case it creates a weakness. Do you have any idea what pressures it'll have to deal with? I need to think about some way of fitting a rudder. Did you ask your father about the periscope? It's not like he's going to be needing it."

"That's great dear," replied Wilma, aware there was a silence and it was her turn to fill it. "Would you pass the fennel water?"

"What is that stuff anyway?" asked her husband studying the small bottle and its light brown liquid. "Some kind of medicine?"

"Hmmm? No, that's the baby's drink. He likes it."

As Kirkie watched the contents of the bottle pour first into, then immediately out of his son's mouth and mix in with the soggy paste on his bib and babygrow, he wondered how she would know if he didn't like it.

"Well, I might take it down to the harbour anyway just to see how it goes so far," said Kirkie as he finished off his tea. "This Saturday. Are your folks coming down this weekend?"

They weren't and that made things happier for Kirkie. Wilma's dad had this thing about safety. He never turned the key in his car until he checked the oil, fuel and water. The tyre pressures were measured with a little gauge he had attached to his keys and after giving the tyres a kick which checked Kirkie could never guess what, he got into the vehicle, adjusted the seat – which no-one else had been in and fastened his seatbelt. "Clunk-click every trip!" he always said as he gave a final tweak to his rear-view mirror and 'entered the road-system'. The man was a robot.

The first thing Kirkie noticed was that the battery heated up very quickly. He had converted an old Vauxhall Viva starter into the propulsion motor and made a brass bush to allow the shaft to pass out through the drilled hole in the rear of his invention. Aghast at the price of an actual propeller, he made his own out of mild steel and simply welded it on to the end of the shaft. Over-design was the curse of the modern world. Simplicity was the key. Not only did the battery heat up, it also gave off acrid fumes that made Kirkie's eyes water when he squeezed into his vessel in the shed to give it a trial spin. Turning on the valve in the old fireman's cylinder helped clear the air but he did wonder what he would do when he had made a door for the roof opening and took it underwater. Still, that was a problem for later. Today was the seaworthy trial.

Getting the thing on to the trailer would have been impossible but for the fact that the two Nathans called by. Nathan McCutcheon and Nathan McFadzean were two local lads who had struck up a friendship with the Kirkpatricks. To help others they had agreed that the McFadzean Nathan would use his shortened name of 'Nate' to help avoid confusion. They knew who they were but others seemed to have a problem. They liked Kirkie's derring-do and were persuaded that his plans were proof of a man ahead of his time. Things happened with Kirkie and it was good to be close enough to see it when they did. Nate McFadzean had heard about the submarine and had brought round his friend to see the project. All the better that they were going to be a part of the first launch.

"It's not finished yet," explained Kirkie as the boys looked curiously at the large object on the shed floor. Kirkie had fastened small wheels to the bottom bath's legs and it was not quite what either had expected.

"Won't the water come in the top?" asked Nathan. "What do you do there?"

"Today's only a seaworthy trial," explained Kirkie walking around the black painted hull. "I'll not be going underwater yet. Just out in the harbour and a bit of a sail about. It's all about hull integrity. Water pressures, things like that."

"How will you steer it, Kirkie?" asked Nate. Kirkie reached up and brought down a paddle from where it hung below the roof joists.

"I'll just use this. The rudder's still in the development stage. It's not required for the trials."

It was actually quite heavy and the trailer sagged as Kirkie and his two young friends struggled to hoist it aboard the single-axled home-made affair. A large plank was set in and after smiling at Wilma, the two boys jumped into the back of Kirkie's old Fiat. The tyres rubbed the whole way to the harbour, which was fortunately only half a mile away, although a little less fortunately the harbour had quite a few visitors strolling about on the wall, enjoying the early morning September sunshine. Kirkie hadn't planned on an audience. Not that he was embarrassed with onlookers, he just hadn't wanted to reveal too much of his hand at such an early stage. Who knew, counterfeiters could be lurking amongst the crowd, waiting to replicate what he had spent so much time devising through his own brainpower. Brilliance is unique but its products easily copied.

Reversing a trailer was not one of Kirkie's many talents and after ten minutes of reversing all over the beach, a good bit of the grass at the roadside but not the slipway, Nate took over. He was a farmer's son and reversing was in his genes. The ability to reverse trailers came shortly after the nurse wrapped the little blue name-band around his wrist when he was born. All farmers' sons were the same. Less than a minute later the trailer's wheels were in the tide and Kirkie was untying the ropes that held the submarine. At the slip the water rapidly became deep – fifteen feet out was near enough the continental shelf. On the harbour wall a small knot of onlookers began to gather. Ballydoonan was not Faslane but what was this, a mini-submarine?

Getting the submarine into the water and yet maintaining an air of scientific detachment was not easy – especially since Kirkie managed to get his hand stuck between the trailer and the prototype as it careered out onto the water's edge. "OW!" he yelled, the shock of the yell momentarily causing the two young men to let go their sides of the invention so permitting it to fall heavily onto Kirkie's foot. There were more yells, some of them a little more descriptive. Eventually the black slug reposed in the water and Nate drove the car and trailer back up the slipway to the car park. Nathan stood holding a rope connected to a lug welded onto the back of the strange contraption. Kirkie was speaking as Nate returned.

"Right, when I get in I'll give the nod and you let go the rope," he said to Nathan. "I'll head out a bit a see if there are any leaks or design issues. If all's well then you lads can have a go too." Nathan smiled weakly. It was one thing watching a lifetime event, it was another taking part in it. The first Apollo mission to the moon was absolutely captivating, he remembered seeing it as a young boy on a fuzzy black and white television late one night when his father had dragged him out of bed to see it. "You'll tell this to your children one day," his dad had said to his sister Pam and himself. It seemed too far away to consider a possibility. The 'One step for man' was unbelievably exciting but he was glad he was not that man. Actually, there had been little chance of him being that man since seven year olds were self-evidently exempt from such endeavours. Being one of the first three people in the world to sail in Kirkie's bath submarine gave him mixed emotions – dread *and* fear.

Up on the wall someone had brought out a camera. Kirkie spotted it immediately and gave a polite frown in the direction of the photographer. The camera slowly came down again. Kirkie knelt down into the machine so that only his head and shoulders were showing. A faint stirring of water eddied from the stern.

"O.K. Nathan," called Kirkie, "you can let go now."

As Nathan let go the rope, Nate looked around as if looking for something. "Have you got your paddle?" he asked. The look on Kirkie's face said that he hadn't but in the hearing of so many on-looking faces he declined to reply.

The submarine was still resting on the beach below the water and although Kirkie was applying power to the motor, the pathetic effort was not enough to move the thing. Behind him water was freely flowing in at his feet as the brass bushing proved its utter uselessness in the water-tightness department. The portholes were also letting their fair share in, but Kirkie was not dismayed – this was what sea-trials were for – to find the minor flaws and iron them out.

"Will we push you Kirkie?" asked Nate. It seemed the obvious thing.

"Yep, just push straight out... watch the propeller."

Nate and Nathan stood in the water either side of the mini-sub, sacrificing dry shoes for the cause of innovation. An almighty push and Kirkie sailed out into the sea that separated the Scot from the Ulsterman and Kirkie's face beamed with the buoyant sensation of floating in a vessel hand-crafted; at sea on a labour of love.

It was not a long-lived sensation. In fact, it lasted somewhere between two and three seconds, certainly not more. Maybe it was a matter of balance, perhaps there was already more water in the sub than Kirkie was prepared to admit; either way, fifteen feet out the black slug promptly turned over and sank without even the good grace to bob about stricken on the surface. It just went straight down. There was an audible gasp from the audience and Nate shot a shocked grin at his friend.

"Can Kirkie swim?"

Although the submarine proved conclusively that it could not, thankfully Kirkie could. Arriving back at the slip he looked surprisingly unshaken and he merely shrugged as the lads went to help him out.

"No harm done. I've had worse happen. I'll get it back at low tide."

Behind them the audience clapped and the man with the camera took a picture.

"Turn round lads, the gentleman wants a picture," said Kirkie inexplicably content to have the moment photographed. Nathan reckoned anyone looking at the photo after it was processed was going to have to have a pretty good imagination. The only thing visible in the water behind them was the Isle of Man. The submarine was truly Sub-Marine.

As they hooked up a small hunched-over man came over and stood at the car. It was Jacob Cully the harbour-master.

"That'll be fafty pence Mr Kirkpatrick."

"Fifty pence? What'll be fifty pence?" Kirkie had no idea what the old man was on about.

"A boat launchin' on a Saturday 'afore noon. The launch fees are fafty pence. Unless you've got a mooring in the harbour, which as it 'appens ye don't."

It was too much for Nate. He bent over double at the sight of Kirkie's face. Losing his creation was one thing, having to pay for it was another.

"Does that include bringing it back in again?"

The old man frowned as he considered the question. He supposed it did.

"Well then," said Kirkie, his eyes narrowing. "It'll be twenty five pence then since I only went one way."

On the way back Kirkie called in to the bakery and bought four cream buns.

"You know," he said as they headed back to his house for a cup of consolatory tea, "you can buy an aeroplane kit in Exchange and Mart. I think that would be more my kind of thing."

They all laughed and snorted at the idea, though Kirkie with less reason than the others.

He was quite serious.

3.

THE HORSE DOCTORS

Sarah-Jane Thompson lived pretty much on her own in a small cottage up the Tubbernacreevey road. Not only was the name of the road a long one, so was the road. Its length however was not reciprocated in either its width or condition. It was a dead-end and grassily ran up from Ballydoonan, through an old quarry, and eventually fizzled out in Sarah-Jane's yard. She was thin and wiry, a mop of suspiciously black hair sat atop her head, tight curls giving her an almost North African appearance from behind. She was eternally good natured and pottered about her smallholding whistling or humming tunes of no fixed abode to herself as she went about her daily business on her small farm.

There she lived with no husband or children, a spinster all her days – but not from the want of trying. Strangers out on a day trip would often find themselves driving into the yard only to find a middle-aged woman throwing bales onto ancient unpainted trailers or digging potatoes out of a weedy half-acre field. Just excusing themselves and driving back down the lane was not an alternative when Sarah-Jane was at large. Sarah-Jane was pretty much on her own and when the Good Lord sent a visitor for a wee natter, who was that visitor to argue otherwise? Single male accidental tourists were in mortal danger. Sarah-Jane had an amazing capacity for opening passenger doors and sitting down on spotless velour seats in her enormously oversized working overalls before the driver had time to perform two consecutive blinks. The man who found himself in a sudden forced tête-à-tête with Miss Thompson was in for a demonstration of all of her feminine charms and captivating guile. 'Captivate' was exactly the right word for it. Many an escapee finally screeched into Ballydoonan in search of something stronger than Barr's brown lemonade to calm rattled nerves and celebrate escape from the closest thing in their lives to an arranged marriage.

'Pretty much on her own' was true when speaking of her human company, but as far as non-human presence went, the cottage was a menagerie. Sheep and goats wandered about freely in the yard and a donkey seemed to spend as much time in the house as out of it. Geese hissed, ducks quacked, dogs barked, calves mooed and a tired looking horse stood eternally statuesque in a paddock beside the cottage, one back leg propping the other.

The animals on Sarah-Jane's smallholding were a lucky bunch. No mass-produced, hormone induced mush of genes this lot. Living with Miss Thompson gave a pretty unique experience to a farm animal – the opportunity to die of old age. Occasionally a chicken would have its neck wrung and once a pig even ended up being on the menu – a menu that took the single woman ten jaw aching months to eat her way through. That though was rare, usually – normally, an animal on the Tubbernacreevey road got to draw its pension.

Old Trigger had been drawing his for some time. The Lone Ranger's version was bright, white and full of galloping energy – old Trigger was just tired. His once white coat got an occasional brush through from Sarah-Jane, but Sarah-Jane was an impulsive woman – brushing a horse just didn't lend itself to reckless spontaneity. He might have been tired

BALLYDOONAN DAYS

of eating pills actually. His owner was a great believer in Alternative Medicine. She was in fact a great believer in a great many alternative things but Homeopathy was her specialism. It has been said that a generalist is one who learns less and less about more and more until he knows nothing about everything whilst a specialist is one who learns more and more about less and less until he knows everything about nothing. Sarah-Jane was a mixture of both. She had whittled down her impressive knowledge of all things homeopathic until it came down to one thing – Arnica. It didn't matter what the complaint was, bruising, depression, bad blood, intestinal worms, itching in the places not talked about, it made little difference – Arnica was the supreme answer to it all. She also suspected it would sort out the problem of bad starting on her old open-cabbed Massey Ferguson tractor, but she had yet to get around to how to apply it. With so many animals, a casual observer might have wondered how the lady up the lane managed to afford the vet's bills. It was easy for Sarah Jane. She never called one. Why waste good money on some quack umbilically linked to the false god of chemical solutions when there was that wonder of the natural world… Arnica?

Sarah-Jane had a sister who had met a Canadian in the café where she worked. Maggie must have been an impressive worker, certainly impressive enough for the Canadian to end up marrying her and taking her home to Sault-Saint Marie in Ontario. Canada was a big country, certainly bigger than Ballydoonan and in the rarefied atmosphere of forests and lakes, Sarah-Jane's sister missed the small-scale familiarity of home and especially her sister up the lane with her pigs and chickens. Letters crossed the North Atlantic and over the frozen Baffin Bay on a weekly basis until eventually one Saturday morning Sarah-Jane knifed open a letter from her sister and an airline ticket fell out. Written correspondence had run its course – Maggie wanted Sarah-Jane over and the ticket was the summons.

Leaving home for a few weeks was no bother to Sarah-Jane but leaving her animals was. She was going to need someone to check on the fences, feed the chickens and keep an eye on all the others. Especially old Trigger.

From time to time, Sarah-Jane would give a few lads in the village a bit of pocket money to help around the farm. It was very occasional and so was the money – Sarah-Jane could forget some particular things with great alacrity but Lennie McClurg and 'Bisto' Gillespie were two guys who didn't mind.

Lennie was a big lad, in fact six feet seven and a half and Bisto was not small, but ten inches smaller than his big mate made him feel it. He had swarthy skin and Bisto had been his nickname ever since he could remember. Even his mother called him it and most had forgotten his real name if they ever knew it. Lennie was nearly twenty and Bisto was eighteen and both had been in the Boy's Brigade. Being helpful to others in their hour of need they saw as a Christian duty and Miss Thompson had many hours of need to offer.

Actually, they enjoyed her company and giving the old girl a bit of a hand now and then was a bit of fun in any case. Whether it was helping fill a gap in the hedge with her old clapped-out Toyota or clambering onto her roof at Christmas in order to point the TV aerial in the direction of London in a misguided attempt to improve the picture quality of the Queen's speech, Lennie and Bisto were happy to help. When it came to asking someone to keep an eye on things when she was gone, Lennie and Bisto were the obvious choices.

"Now the sheep only need kept in the field," said Sarah-Jane, explaining the details to the two. "The chickens need locked up each night and the feed trays filled every other day. Watch out for cluckers, I don't have a rooster, not since the fox got him and the stupid old things haven't worked out yet why their eggs aren't hatching. Willie Drysdale will take whatever eggs you collect – don't worry about the money, I'll sort that out when I come back."

She had a list of things to do, many of which the young men doubted she actually ever did herself, but they nodded away as each hoped the other was paying attention and taking it all in.

"Listen, this is the most important thing," she said holding up a large bottle of yellow pills. "Trigger hasn't been too well recently and this is his medicine. One pill morning and night and it'll keep the old darling as right as rain." Lennie looked at the name on the side of the bottle. 'Arnica'. He hadn't heard of that one before but then, how many horse-medicines was the average person supposed to be aware of? It was probably one of Sarah-Jane's herbally-things anyway. The horse looked stoically over the fence and stared at the ground at Lennie's feet as Sarah-Jane scratched behind its ear and told it how much she loved it. Neither Lennie nor Bisto had ever heard a horse called 'My Big Handsome Honey-bunny-wunny' before.

It all began well enough. That's to say, as far as looking after the sheep went it all began well enough. The chickens were more difficult.

"I doubt if these stupid things have *ever* been in the hut!" exclaimed Bisto. "How does Sarah-Jane do it?"

"Probably keeps them in the house along with the donkey," sighed Lennie who had developed a sore back from running around bent double, flapping his arms in a chicken-catching fashion. Only in fashion, the chickens were uncaught.

"Here, where's the horse?" said Bisto suddenly looking at an apparently empty paddock. "Wasn't it there this morning?"

Johnny Patterson was Will Patterson's older brother. Will was still at school thinking often about Liz McCutcheon but Johnny was newly married and living in the village with his young wife. As young marrieds often discover, they were often visited by their many younger friends who were magnetised by the mystery and maturity of friends who had entered the marvellous and inscrutable estate of marriage. Young marrieds are known to be the possessors of all human knowledge and wisdom – it is simply a universal fact – even the happy couple believe it – for a month or two anyway.

When the door knocked on a fine Saturday early afternoon, Johnny was therefore not surprised to see Lennie and Bisto standing on the doorstep.

"We have something to ask you," said Lennie before Johnny had a chance to ask them in. "Do horses sleep standing up or lying down?"

"What?"

"Can we come in?" asked Bisto.

"I think you'd better," agreed the puzzled Johnny.

"Well, do they or don't they?" asked Lennie again when they were seated opposite Johnny and his pretty young wife.

"The guys want to know if horses sleep standing up," explained Johnny. "Though why I should know is beyond me."

"Just say what you reckon," pressed Lennie, "this burke has no clue!"

"Yes I do!" retorted his friend, "you're the one whose head is full of sweetie-mice!" They began arguing and Johnny had to cut in to quieten them.

"Alright, alright, let me see. I suppose they can do either maybe? Probably they lie down at night though."

"Told you!" cried Bisto, stubbing a finger into the bigger man's chest.

"He said 'probably' you deaf twit!" replied Lennie angrily. "Not 'definitely'!" He turned again to the couple on the chairs opposite.

"Well, answer this one then. Do horses die standing up?"

"Do horses die standing up?" repeated Johnny looking at his wife Beth. "What, and stay standing?" he added quizzically.

"I think they are dead when they are lying down," said Lennie. "Thickhead here thinks it's only sleeping!"

"Is there a horse about here somewhere that this is all about?" asked Johnny. "Or is this just a mental exercise?"

"The only *mental* around here is Lennie who thinks everything that lies down for a sleep is dead just because it's not snoring!"

"It's Sarah-Jane Thompson's horse," explained Lennie, shooting his friend an evil glare on the sofa. "I think it's died on us."

"Just sleeping," intoned Bisto.

"Yeah, with its legs in the air… I don't think so!"

"We couldn't get its medicine into it last night," explained Bisto more reasonably. "I think it was too tired."

"Too dead, you mean," corrected Lennie. "I think we've killed it." This time Bisto didn't argue back. He was considering the possibility that the animal was in fact deceased. The legs in the air were a persuasive argument. He hit upon an idea.

"Would you come up and take a look with us?"

The dead horse lay dead in the field. Nothing about it looked alive or even remotely asleep. The tongue lolling out of its mouth was a pretty good clue, as were the four legs sticking out and hanging stiff and horizontal from its swollen stomach.

"It's dead," was all Johnny said. Additional comment seemed unnecessary. Lennie gave Bisto an 'I told you so' look.

"Do *you* think we killed it?" asked Bisto, a worried look on his face. 'Horse killer' was not an epithet he was particularly keen to have hanging around his neck. Johnny shrugged and took another look at the horse corpse lying inert in the paddock. Trigger never moved much at the best of times but at least he was normally vertical. It looked slightly surreal.

"Hardly," replied Johnny. "It's not like those pills of Sarah-Jane's are any more than pure sugar anyway. I don't think any vet's going to write 'cause of death – lack of sugar cube'. The old horse just reached the end of the road." he paused and then added, "Glad I wasn't looking after it though."

Lennie would have said something except he was prevented by the outside bell to Miss Thompson's phone suddenly ringing on the gable wall.

"I better get that," glared Lennie at the other two. "I told my Dad where I was. Probably him looking me for something."

As Bisto and Johnny climbed the fence and circled the horse, Lennie disappeared into the house. Neither Johnny nor Bisto said anything, Bisto out of worry and respect for the dead creature, Johnny because he was afraid he would laugh out loud. It wasn't that it wasn't sad, after all, poor Sarah-Jane would be heartbroken; but the idea of Lennie and Bisto sorting out what to do with a dead horse was too much.

"You do know you'll have to bury it?" said Johnny, his voice cracking ever so slightly as Lennie approached them from the house.

"What! Us?" It obviously hadn't occurred to Bisto. Lennie made no response.

"Was it your dad?" asked Johnny. Lennie's dad hadn't been all that well. He hoped everything was all right.

"No."

"Oh," replied Johnny. He wondered why he seemed to have suddenly gone so quiet.

"Well? Who was it then?" asked Bisto.

"Umm… It was Sarah-Jane."

"What, from Canada?" asked Bisto surprised.

"No, from Mars. Yes of course Canada, where else?" shot back Lennie.
"What did she want?"

"She just wanted to know how Trigger was doing."

Bisto's eyes bulged. Johnny burst into laughter. Lennie and Bisto glared at him.

"Oh very funny, it's all right for you!" said Bisto crossly. Johnny just laughed all the more.

"What did she say?" asked Bisto turning to Lennie who seemed strangely unforthcoming.

"About what?"

"Very funny… about the horse!"

"Well, actually… I ahm…"

"He didn't tell her!" guffawed Johnny who was struggling to maintain any self-control. "I bet you told her he was fine."

Lennie smiled weakly. Bisto looked in shocked accusation at the taller man.

"I just said he was in the paddock… I didn't tell a lie."

Lennie and Bisto were relieved when the chortling Johnny left. He did offer to help but his comfortable detachment was too unsettling. There was a serious job to be done and a giggling gravedigger did not fit in to it. The first decision was where to dig the hole. There was a low bit of ground at the bottom of the back field behind the house and, after agreeing that it was well enough out of the way and soft enough to dig, the two friends tracked down a spade and a pick and began to dig. They took turns at digging and using the pickaxe but it was hard work. Very hard work. Soon they were stripped down to their waists and sweat glistened on their faces and backs.

"Flip!" exclaimed Bisto. "remind me never to become a grave-digger – this is mustard!"

Lennie straightened up and rubbed his back. Being a big man, no tools were ever the right size. He felt like his back was broken.

"Another fifteen minutes and we'll take a break. Stupid horse!"

They worked for twenty minutes and rested for five, continuing on and digging till four and a half hours had dragged painfully by. Eventually Lennie clambered out of the depths and the both of them peered into the hole.

"Never again!" complained Lennie. "I'm knackered."

The hole was certainly big enough and a pile of soil and stones towered beside the pit, the soil and clay musty and earthy. It was a smell that reminded Bisto of the time he mitched off school because he had forgotten to do his maths homework and instead sat all day watching diggers excavate foundations for the new council homes on Fowler Crescent. He might have been better advised to do his maths, which he still didn't have the next day when that obvious solution had occurred to him in class. The maths homework would have been infinitely preferable to digging a horse-grave. His mother had always told him he should have worked harder at school. Once again she was proved right. It was only when they stood at opposite sides of the horse that the unspoken problem made itself glaringly apparent. It was Bisto who needlessly mouthed the words.

"How do we move the horse?"

It was a badly timed map-reading error that brought the old couple up the Tubbernacreevey road just as Lennie and Bisto were hauling on the rope attached to Trigger's back legs. Such was the effort and concentration the two were exerting at that moment that they completely missed the car as it came to a staggered halt part-way up Sarah-Jane's lane.

Seeing two gasping and grunting young men tugging and pulling at a dead horse was not a sight Ernie and Sadie Armstrong had been prepared for that day. As they watched from the confines of the small motor, the tall one began leaping backward, pulling and heaving like a man possessed. He was also doing a fair bit of yelling. Sadie pushed down her door lock – Ernie did the same. When the smaller one began kicking the horse in the stomach Ernie looked for reverse gear and quietly crunched back over the stony road the way he had come.

"Will we just go back to Bangor instead dear?"

Sadie nodded. She had always suspected the peninsula folk anyway… inbred you know.

Bisto collapsed onto the horse and put his head in his hands. The horse hadn't moved so much as an inch. Actually, an inch might have been nice – the lump of deadweight that had once been Trigger hadn't budged one atom. Lennie lay flat on his back, his long legs pointed in the direction of the horse, the rope cast down across his stomach.

"Should we try again?" he gasped. He didn't know why he said it. He doubted he had the strength to ever again stand erect. Bisto peered through rope-burned fingers and sighed. The reply was in his head, he just didn't have the energy to say it. In the cause of non-violence it was probably just as well.

After some five or six minutes, the two stood and looked again at the body on the ground. After a long silence Bisto spoke.

"So now what?"

The obvious answer was to dig another hole, but this time right beside the horse but the renewed exertions required for this solution were so daunting as to make it an unspeakable proposition. Lennie decided a whole new exercise was worth exploring.

"I was wondering about the hole we've dug?"

"What? What do you mean?"

41

"Well we can't leave it open like that, one of the sheep will fall in. Let's forget about the horse in the meantime and sort the hole out. It'll have to be done sooner or later."

After they struggled to extract the sheep that had fallen into the hole, Bisto and Lennie began to shovel the soil they had so painstakingly dug back into the hole. It was nothing like as hard as digging and in less than an hour the hole was filled and level. Beside them a pile of soil lay in a mysterious heap.

"What happened there?" asked Lennie. There was as much soil left over as they had shoved back in.

"I dunno, must be denser or something until you dig it up." A thought suddenly struck him. "Here, I've an idea!"

They took turns at using the wheelbarrow. Soon the extra earth had been removed and taken to the front paddock. In what they hoped was their last digging exercise, Bisto and Lennie shovelled the soil onto the dead Trigger. As the animal slowly became covered, Lennie attempted to bring some reverence into the scene.

"Earth to earth, ashes to ashes," he intoned. "Poor old Trigger."

At last all the soil covered the horse and a great brown mound of earth rose like a massive, monster cowpat in the paddock.

"It's a bit obvious though don't you think?" suggested Bisto, squinting and imagining what it might look like to a fresh set of eyes. It looked like a massive, monster cowpat.

"Naw, it'll all decay down. By the time Sarah-Jane gets back it'll be almost flat… possibly… maybe. Sarah-Jane will be so busy in Canada she'll have forgotten she even had a horse by the time she gets back."

Sarah-Jane phoned every day. Every day she asked about Trigger. Was he taking his Arnica? Did he seem all right? Was he drinking plenty? Was he warm enough? Did he need covered? At least to the last question Lennie was able to be honest. Yes, the horse was well covered.

Bisto bought some grass seed and sprinkled it liberally over the brown mountain. Anything to take the bad look off it. To both their disappointments the mound did not shrink each day. In fact, Lennie was convinced that for a few days the thing was growing.

The day before Sarah-Jane was due to arrive home, the much avoided question of how she was going to be told was brought up. Lennie and Bisto were at Johnny and Beth's and Beth asked the question.

"How are you going to tell her?" she asked as she brought in a tray of toasted pancakes for supper. "You know she loves that old horse."

Lennie shook his head seriously. He wished he knew. He wished he had told her when she had asked. He wished he had thought of something. He wished he was dead.

The pancakes stuck in his throat as he tried to speak.

"I don't know... it's wick!"

Bisto had his head in his hands again.

"If only the stupid thing hadn't died. Do you know I dream about horses every night? Horses leaping about in green fields, horses jumping over hedges, horses running... and what do I waken to? Dead Trigger! I still think it was because we missed the medicine."

"You'll just have to be there to tell her when she arrives home," suggested Johnny's wife softly. "You'll have to do it."

Lennie and Bisto both nodded. She was quite right of course but it didn't make it any easier.

The night before Sarah-Jane's return, Lennie and Bisto took a last look around the farm. They felt like condemned prisoners taking their last breath of free air before the long walk.

"I think you should be the one," said Bisto without prefacing his remark. He didn't need to.

"Why me? You're the one she explained the pills to!"

"You're the one told her the lies!" retorted Bisto.

"Oh, like and you'd have been Mr 'let me spoil your holiday by telling you your horse is dead'?"

"Well, one of us has to do it and you're the oldest," countered Bisto.

Lennie thought for a moment. Something was forming in his mind.

"You know Beth was right, we do have to tell her, but she didn't say we had to actually *speak* to her to do it did she?"

Bisto looked up and made the connection.

"Brill! I'll get paint, you find a brush!"

Sarah-Jane had had a lovely time in Ontario, but there was nowhere like home. The wide open spaces of Canada, the great wandering forests and towering impossible mountain wildernesses were a sight for the eyes, but home was smaller, warmer, familiar.

As the taxi turned into Tubbernacreevey road and trundled up the hedge-rowed track, she caught sight of something large and white fluttering on a pole at the gate to her lane.

The taxi-driver evidently saw it too, for he came to a halt at the large block lettered message, hand-painted onto an old white bed sheet.

'Welcome home,' it said. 'P.S. The horse is dead.'

4.

THE HAPPIEST DAYS OF YOUR LIFE

Looking around, Nathan guessed that he was the only ex-pupil at the funeral. He watched as the coffin was lowered along with quiet grey heads in the leafless grey graveyard. A solitary secret shared and a lesson that is all that it seems is rarely how it is…

At seventeen Nathan didn't believe the line he had heard repeated so often - 'School – the best days of your life.' School was all right, but if it was true that the days spent there were the best days of his life he reckoned he hadn't much to look forward to. School was all right in the same way that a visit to the dentist was all right. You sort of had to go in order to stave off any problems in the future but, given the choice, the dentist was someone he was quite prepared to know only by vague rumour. School was not a vague rumour however, it was a daily reality and it slapped him hard in the face like a sodden towel every weekday morning.

How he had ever ended up in a grammar school was beyond him anyway. Liz deserved to be there alright. She actually woke up early most mornings in some kind of excited anticipation. She had long ago learned not to pass on her latest thrilling discoveries in maths to her brother but for her, school did indeed seem to be a place she wanted to skip merrily into. She was fifteen now and Nathan had thought that that was the age girl's brains died at and got replaced by a head full of nail-varnish and boys. Liz must have taken some pills against it.

No, he had worked out now what had happened. Some poor enormous foreheaded primary seven's eleven-plus paper had obviously been inadvertently swapped for his. While he was staring open-mouthed at results that were no more his than the man in the moon's, some potential neurosurgeon got a mark that sent him to a school that specialised in woodwork and lessons in how to survive borstal.

All the same, if it meant he missed Mrs Keeble's maths class, maybe Nathan had done him a favour.

Mrs Keeble wasn't the worst but she had to be darn well close to it. Somewhere out in the universe there might have been a teacher whose over-whelming control of a class was even more awesome, but Nathan doubted it. Mrs Keeble was simply breath-taking.

One of the ways she was breath-taking was the way she came up unexpectedly from behind and grabbed a misbehaving boy's throat and squeezed. In the days before parents believed their children got educated other than by fear, threats and good old violence, Mrs Keeble shone like a star in her own galaxy. Although she had no qualms about laying hands suddenly upon unsuspecting necks, that was actually not her normal *modus operandi*. Pure fear was her speciality. Not the fear engendered by a system of loud shouts and slamming rulers – it was a fear of cold, lurking danger. She just exuded it. As she sat erect at her desk and calmly trained her guns across the deck of her class, the message was clear. 'I am Supreme – you are the ground on which I walk'. A look brought to bear upon some guilty soul cowering behind a desk before her intimidating personage was enough to physically shrink that pupil so that they left the class ten inches smaller. Small was what you felt in Mrs Keeble's class. She wasn't a large woman – she was normally proportioned, but her formidable personality dominated the room.

If Nathan had been good at maths it might not have been so bad. If he even knew what maths was all about it might have been good. The trouble was that all the maths brains in the McCutcheon household had been dropped exclusively into the head of Liz. It had all missed Nathan by several light years. He hadn't much liked physics either, but at least he hadn't had to do that at O level – maths was compulsory. Apparently in later life it was going to be crucially important that he knew how to discover the value of x in an inverse equation. In that his current idea of a future career was to be a policeman he wasn't sure how this was going to come about. Maybe it had something to do with traffic law.

"Excuse me sir, but did you calculate the fractional value of x over y as you overtook that lorry on the brow of a hill? No, I thought not. Would you step out of the vehicle while I give you a quick calculus test?" Not likely.

Nathan, having got the neurosurgeon's eleven-plus exam mark, had not been given any further help. The school expected him to do twenty hours of homework a night and swot like a professor on obsessive pills every study break in school. Thankfully Nathan's parents trusted him to get on with his own work and do what needed to be done. Nathan guessed they weren't fully conversant with all things academic them-selves anyway and were just happy he was going to a nice school. Liz was a threat to the status quo, but luckily his mum and dad had not quite made the comparison between her four hours' homework each night and his.

His was about twenty minutes. On a good night he could stretch it to thirty but concentration just blew up after that. Outside the window the woods beckoned, waving their woody limbs in welcoming gestures. The call of nature was a strong one and, besides, the air cleared his mind and left space to ponder his homework in surroundings God had made him for.

Ponder, but not *do* unfortunately. The twenty-five minute journey on the bus was always awaiting next day as far as Nathan was concerned. Twenty-five minutes in which to tidy up any loose ends of his maths homework and check it over.

It was while bumping up the country roads to Newtownards that Nathan would remember why the bus option was not a good one. As school-bags flew by overhead and soggy cheese and tomato sandwiches landed on his lap from some clown two rows back, he got about two minutes of shaky numbers written into his graph-papered jotter. Numbers that bore little relationship to the questions and required answers. The loose ends that needed tidied up weren't all that loose. In fact they were still in their packaging and there were an awful lot of them. As he feverishly scribbled he looked over in mid panic and watched Liz sit quietly in the seat across the aisle, her long dark hair framing her face as she peacefully watched the fields and farms pass by. She was probably adopted. A mix up in the labour ward, maybe an alien in a human skin.

People who didn't bring in homeworks or got consistently low marks were put on report in Nathan's school. A report card was a small blue folder about the size of a postcard, the outside bearing the words 'Report Card' and space below for the criminal's name. Inside, rows and columns marked off two weeks and room for up to ten subjects. Each day each subject teacher had to initial a box for that subject to indicate that the work that day had been satisfactory and homeworks had been handed in on time. Initials written in red signalled a failure and a week's extension of the report card.

To be put on report was a shameful thing. In that the reportee had to stand at the teacher's desk and wait while it was signed towards the end of class, there was also no hiding it. If there was one thing in school Nathan hated the most, it was being put on report. Wisdom would dictate that if doing homework in time avoided such a penalty, then surely the homework ought to be done in time. Unluckily for Nathan, he had a remarkable capacity for forgetting all about the dread when facing the wayward woods out of his bedroom window. The dread only started in the bus.

So it was that the report card and Nathan were reasonably well acquainted. Extensions were not unusual, in fact any time he had been awarded a report card, he was certain to get another week out of it. So lacking in rarity was the card that when Nathan's parents signed it at the end of the week, as was compulsory, they imagined every other parent was doing the same thing.

Nathan told them Liz was too stupid to get one.

Mrs Keeble had chosen education as her vocation. It was lucky for the enemy she had not chosen the army – Mrs Keeble did not take prisoners. A boy or girl who dared to whisper in class – no-one ever dared speak – was alerted by the voice of Mrs Keeble announcing their name in voice that was loaded with accusation and assured condemnation.

"David Harvey! And just what do you think you are doing?"

"Nothing, Mrs Keeble." Never a good answer.

"Am I blind, Master Harvey?"

"Uh… no, Mrs Keeble."

"Am I deaf young man?"

"N…no."

"Am I a liar?"

"No, Mrs Keeble."

"So, let us try again. What do you think you are doing in *my* maths class David Harvey?" The repeat of the name made the individual cringe. She wielded names like Visigoths wielded severed heads.

"Talking, Mrs Keeble." There. It was said. Judgement would follow.

"Write this down Master Harvey. 'I will not waste time in idle chitter-chatter in Mrs Keeble's maths class. I am an ignorant boy.' Now, how many times do you think you should write that out?"

That was always the killer blow. Too small a number and the disdainful Mrs Keeble would simply double, or even treble it. Too large a one and you agonised all that wrist-aching night that she might have accepted less. One thing was for sure; you never won.

The lines were for the fortunate. More usually it was double homeworks for a week and a desk up at the front for as long. In Mrs Keeble's class, Mrs Keeble ruled with a rod of iron. Double homeworks were against school rules, but who was going to complain? And to whom? The principal? She would just give him double homework too – and he would surely do it.

For all that, Mrs Keeble wasn't actually particularly disliked. In a list of hated teachers, Mrs Keeble's name was unlikely to be mentioned. Teachers who were unfair were high on that kind of a list. Teachers who picked on someone just because of a snotty nose or pimply face were the ones who were hated, not Mrs Keeble. She was, for all her prim severity, completely fair. Pretty, fat, spotty, untidy, ginger, blonde, tall, rich or poor; it made no difference. The only crime in her class was when high standards of maths were not applied and the subject was treated with careless recklessness. Then it mattered not one whit what or who you were. Rugby captain? Death by applied algebra. Head girl? Drowning in a sea of equations. Mrs Keeble may not have been much loved, her class not one on the 'oh I can't wait to get there' list, but it was at least a plateau of balance and impartiality in a world of uneven playing fields.

Which was what made it all the odder for Nathan McCutcheon.

At first he wondered if he imagined it. It wasn't like anyone else seemed to notice, but there was something about the way she looked at him that was definitely... different.

Everyone else got the same indifferent attention – she treated the class as a whole – as one animal. The way to get noticed was to upset her class, but Nathan gradually became aware that she would watch him. It wasn't much, not as if she would stare at him and examine what he was up to; it was a discreet glance, a look that would stray in his direction and loiter for the slightest second before moving on. It wasn't a look of reproach or a frown of concentration – it was a fleeting warmth of regard, a moment of softness that was gone and drawn back into a closed face before Nathan was sure he had seen it.

It wasn't often; Nathan had seen it maybe only three or four times and it was only because he had the habit of looking up into space from his page to work out answers in his head that he saw it at all. Then he would catch her face and see for a brief second a different maths teacher behind her desk – a secret Mrs Keeble.

Unfortunately the public Mrs Keeble was very much there whenever he was late with maths homework, or with a homework that had 'I was written on the bus this morning and, yes, that scribble is actually supposed to be numbers' written all over it. When that happened, Mrs Keeble would set down whatever she was holding, take off her half-moon spectacles and fold her fingers under her chin. Looking straight and unblinking into Nathan's face, she would present him with one simple fact.

"This will not do, Nathan." No-one else commented, but Nathan had noticed he was the only one she addressed by his first name solely. "What do you have to say for yourself?"

What he would have liked to say was something along the lines of 'stuff the maths, this is only a dream!' That actually worked sometimes, like when he was actually having a dream. He had one where he was in a car trying to escape from a pursuing crowd of black cartoon cats with red top hats on their heads. The cats were clawing the car door and the car couldn't go fast enough. He hated that stupid dream, but sometimes he knew he was dreaming it and was able to tell himself to wake up. Maths was a different kind of nightmare and there was no release of awakening.

Usually he muttered something along the lines of 'Sorry Miss' and took the resultant lecture on the chin. The double homework he had to take home ruined a whole weekend by having to slave away in his bedroom over a list of stinking equations – or would have ruined it if the trees hadn't waved at him expectantly and made him forget.

The amazing thing was that it wasn't his mathematical failures that had awarded him his latest report; that was another disaster altogether.

The fume cupboard in lecture room number 23 didn't work. That was to say, the extraction fan didn't and that meant that the interesting part of chemistry was always passed over whenever demonstrations could not be performed due to its inability to extract.

Not that Nathan was doing chemistry, but once an officer from the fire-brigade had come in to take a period on fire safety. His interesting bit where he showed just how combustible a small vial of petrol could be was thwarted and instead all they got was death by over-head.

"You know it's just a fuse," said Peter Johnston.

"What, the fume cupboard?" asked Nathan. Pete and he were last out of the lecture room and Pete had been referring to the failed experiment.

"Yeah, it's just the fuse is missing. No-one could be bothered to put a new fuse in. What do the teachers care? They've seen the flashes and bangs a hundred times before."

Nathan thought for a second and as he did so, caught sight of something lying on the teacher's desk. It was a paper-clip.

"I could get it going again. Watch this."

Picking up the clip he went over to the fume cupboard and looked at the switch. It was one of those ones with a switch, a little red light and a fuse compartment. A bit of a twiddle with the point of a compass and it was open. Sure enough there was an empty gap where the fuse ought to have been.

It was a simple matter of folding over the paper-clip so that it could be pushed into the small opening. Pushing home the fuse cover, Nathan flicked the switch to hear the fan sucking high in the cupboard.

Except that it didn't. Instead the lights went out.

"Oh," he said.

"I'm out of here," said Peter as Nathan watched his electrical advisor flee like a crook from the scene of a bungled burglary.

"Rats!" said Nathan.

The lights to the lecture room had indeed been tripped by Nathan's completing of a short circuited fan motor. As had the lights in the entire school; and the power sockets, including one powering a brand new top-loading Ferguson Video Star video recorder which had been showing a tape of human reproductive biology to a class of first formers. It actually sparked in a blue flash and spewed out black smoke – which added considerably to the shock already being experienced by the young innocents as they had all ideas of storks and birds and bees shot out of the clear blue skies of their previous convictions. Parents were in for some funny looks that night.

Nathan hoped Pete could keep a secret. It was a secret that lasted until next period when the Vice-Principal, an office particularly well named, stormed into English class.

"Who in this class was in room 23 last period?" He didn't sound very happy. About eight pairs of hands tentatively rose into the air.

"Who short-circuited the fume cupboard?" Six blank faces looked up at the Vice.

"Johnston!" barked the man, holding up a blackened piece of wire between his fingers. "What do you know about this?" Nathan hoped Peter would hold the ground of honour. The secret was in sticking together.

"Nathan McCutcheon did it sir. I don't know what he was at."

As Nathan left the room in the truly Vice-like grip of the successful pupil prosecutor, he mentally scored off the name of Peter Johnston from the list of 'people I most admire' list. Not that he was ever on it, but he had blown for ever any chance of ever making it.

And so he was on report. At least a report card never said what the victim was guilty of; just that he had to be signed as being satisfactory each day in all classes and subjects, which when Nathan thought about it, was a little unfair. He hadn't done anything wrong in art, or history. It wasn't like he had made a total mash-up of understanding what the dickens D. H. Lawrence was on about in *Bavarian Gentians* in english class. He had a fair idea actually what he was on about at when he said 'not every man has gentians in his house'. Not having a big blue flower in your front room seemed fair enough.

The embarrassment of handing in the report card to each teacher as the rest of the class thought things like 'what a plonker' was of course how the system worked. If you didn't like it you sorted yourself out.

Mrs Keeble looked up as Nathan set the report card on her desk. Her eyebrows lifted as she looked first at the card, then at Nathan.

"Ah!" she said as she remembered the discussion in the staff room, "The fume cupboard." Nathan's attempt to blow up the whole school had spread like wildfire. Even teachers like a bit of drama now and again.

It was just Nathan's luck that it was also a day in which he had a homework that resembled a car accident in a number factory. Dead numbers lay upon the page, their lifeless little forms totally detached from any connection with an actual answer. There certainly were plenty of them. Nathan had hoped that the multiplicity of apparent workings-out would give the impression of effort. Everything would point to time spent adding, subtracting, multiplying – right up to the point where the answer would appear. Unfortunately that was the one bit that never made it onto the page.

"Right class, you may hand in your homeworks at the conclusion of class. Turn to page fifty-five; *Pythagoras theorem*."

At the end, and as the others were filling in homework diaries and packing bags, Nathan stepped forward and set his homework fiasco onto the teacher's desk. Mrs Keeble looked at the aimless groupings of numbers crowding around the set questions on the page. She looked at the report card – she looked at Nathan. Pulling out the class register from below the text-books crowding her desk she ran her finger along until it stopped at 'Nathan McCutcheon.' She looked up again at Nathan.

"You find maths hard, Nathan?" Her voice was quiet, soft in tone. Only Nathan could hear her, the rest of the class was finishing copying down the prepared equations homework on the blackboard and leaving in dribs and drabs.

"Uh… yes Miss. I'm not sure about where I use π in working out the area of a circle."

Mrs Keeble glanced again at the various attempts on Nathan's page. 'Not sure' was putting it very optimistically.

"It was a bitter February," she said, so quietly Nathan had to strain to hear her. Nathan thought he had misheard.

"Sorry, Mrs Keeble?"

"The day you were born… the eighth of February. It was bitter – the hardest winter in thirty years."

Nathan saw that she was pointing to his date of birth in the class register. He had no idea what the weather had been like – it wasn't like he could remember. She was still speaking, half to him, half to herself.

"Schools were closed and roads were snowed in all over the North. For two days nothing moved." Nathan listened. He had never heard this before, pictures of swirling snow and arctic storms whirled in his head. Mrs Keeble gently rubbed her cheek.

"The ambulance managed to get to the house, but a blizzard prevented it from getting to the hospital. We were snowed in and couldn't move forwards or back. How those lovely ambulance men tried! But it was hopeless. It was a little boy, but they just couldn't get us to hospital. I held him in my arms as his little heart just faded and ebbed away. As I looked into his perfect little face he opened his sweet eyes and left me behind. He was gone and I couldn't keep him."

Tears glistened in her eyes and she looked deep into Nathan's face as if seeing someone long loved and lost. "Your age, he would be exactly your age now."

For what seemed like the longest moment in his life, Nathan looked with dawning understanding into the face of a woman whose hopes and dreams had been forever changed in one storm filled night, a night that lived with her in painful echoes the rest of her life.

Nathan didn't know what to say, what to do. Mrs Keeble discreetly wiped the tears and handed back the report card. As she did, Nathan's fingers rested for a moment on hers. She smiled and closed her eyes. When she opened them again, Nathan took his card and silently returned to his desk in the now empty room. He packed his bag and headed out the door.

"Goodbye, Mrs Keeble."

"Goodbye, Nathan."

At home that night Nathan handed his mother the blue wrinkled card to sign.

"What's this?" she said.

"My report card," replied Nathan. "I told you about it before."

"No, I mean in the maths column, isn't that where the teacher signs?"

Nathan took the card and looked at the box beside the maths subject.

Mrs Keeble hadn't signed her name; in the box was a single word, lightly written…'Mother'.

As the graveyard emptied only Nathan remained behind in the leaf-blown paths. Years had passed since his days at school and he stood for a long time at the grave just thinking and remembering. Mrs Keeble had never mentioned it again, never spoke another word about the events she had softly recounted that day, but she had shared with him her hidden story, its fragile secret one he would always keep. As he watched the crisp brown beech leaves scurry and chase one another around the head-stones, Nathan thought of his own mother and the life of sacrifice and love she had given and still gave to him. He saw that within every heart lay unknown secrets, unfathomable love, untold hopes and for some they lay silent and still, forever beyond fond and tender grasp. He stepped forward and set the little bundle of flowers beside the earth at the headstone. It was a family one and Mrs Keeble was not the first to lay her head to final rest below its cold stone. Above where her name would soon be marked in granite chiselled letters, he read another inscription.

Nathan Keeble
Died in infancy, only beloved son of John and Elizabeth Keeble.
'Jesus loves the little children'

He knelt down and in misty-eyed silence wrote with his finger on the dust swathing the grey marble.

'Mummy's home.'

5.

THE STORY-TELLER

Bob McCutcheon's brother was a washing-machine repair man. His job took him all around the peninsula answering the distressed calls of women whose machines had ground to a halt right in the middle of a huge wash. What was a minor disaster to them was run of the mill to Thomas McCutcheon and after the usual repair of replacement brushes in the motor and a new main bearing, life returned to relieved normality to a family suddenly redeemed from a life of grime and another call for Tom.

Tom and his wife had three children. Willie-Joe Mehaffy was the middle one, though that was not actually his name – his real name was lost in the mists of birth certificates and health records. It was vaguely half-remembered as Mark – but Isobel McCutcheon had called him the pet name Willie-Joe Mehaffy in a fit of playful warm-hearted tenderness in the van, on the way home from the hospital, and the Willie-Joe just stuck. When she was in a particularly fond mood, tickling his chin or snuggling him up against her warm cheek, she would add the Mehaffy at the end. That, however, was just Isobel's motherly teasing – to everyone else it was just Willie-Joe

Willie-Joe at nine years old was giving his parents a bit of bother. Not the sort of bother that had them worrying about his bad behaviour

59

or capacity for getting into fights, Willie-Joe was never in that sort of trouble; it was his stories.

Willie-Joe never saw his stories as lies – he was just making things more *interesting*. He liked interesting, he was sure others did too. People did such boring things, talking about boring things was what everybody else did – he talked about *interesting* things. Willie-Joe was at that very minute talking to his teacher who was wanting to get home. All the other children had left and were glad to have left; this incessant boy was insisting on finishing off his story. She still had a short interview with the headmistress to squeeze in and Willie-Joe was holding everything up. She knew it was a chief tenet of teaching to listen to a child when he felt he had something important to say but if he had much more of it to say, she was going to miss her lift.

"So Dad says if Uncle Fred can just make it to the cabin, he'll be alright. There's bears and all in the forests you know… and snakes. Uncle Fred is strong and he has a gun. Dad says he can shoot bears and eat them until the Mounties come and rescue him. If he finds enough gold he will send some home and then we'll be rich. But not if the bears eat Uncle Fred of course."

Miss Carlisle smiled at the boy. She heard he had an uncle and aunt in Canada, but this story? Being a new addition to the school she had only been teaching him for a month now, but either he had a tremendous imagination or he had some very remarkable events to relate. At least this story seemed to have come to some kind of a conclusion.

"Well, thank you for telling me that Willie-Joe, and I'm quite sure that your uncle will get to his cabin before the snow or, or the, em… bears, so don't you worry any more about it. Now, I'm sure your mother will be waiting for you, so why don't you run along now and I'll see you on Monday?" She gave him a pat on the head and a slightly over-enthusiastic steering push from behind. The boy skittered out through the classroom door and she gave a sigh of relief. She made a mental note to ask the Headmistress if Willie-Joe had ever related such stories to her.

Outside, Willie-Joe's mother was beginning to worry when her son suddenly appeared, his school bag thrown casually over one shoulder. She got out of the old Morris Minor, holding the door up to prevent it falling onto the ground. Along with its other many ailments it had no top hinge in the driver's door and it tended to swing about when left to its own devices.

"Is everything all right, Willie-Joe?" she asked, immediately wishing she had stayed in the car. Her hair was up in rollers with a home perm' and was covered in a plastic bag. She had looked better. The perfectly presented Miss Carlisle waved from across the school yard, checking the playground was empty before locking the gate. Isobel waved back and felt a frump. It wasn't fair. Teachers should come to school in floury pinnys and messy hair. It made mothers look bad.

"Miss Carlisle had a problem, mum," replied Willie-Joe as he clambered in through the passenger window. Mrs McCutcheon wished he wouldn't do that in public. The passenger door was welded permanently shut but he could have got in through the open driver's door.

"Oh, what kind of a problem, dear?" she asked getting in and slamming the door a number of times until it finally connected with something that kept it shut.

"Police trouble – she has policemen hiding in the bushes around her house at night. She is a bit worried about it."

"Hiding in bushes? Whatever would the police be hiding in her bushes for? Don't be silly, Willie-Joe. Is your indicator up?" The old Morris had indicators that popped out from behind the front doors – half the time they weren't working.

"Nope. She thinks they think she's a spy. Do you think she could be a spy? She speaks funny sometimes."

"She speaks politely – she's from Bangor. Give your side a thump, dear." Willie-Joe thumped the side of the car behind the door – the indicator flicked up.

"Yip, that's it. Well, she was worried about it and asked me to phone the Prime Minister if she goes missing. I said I would. Do you know the Prime Minister's phone number?"

Their house was only three miles from the school and soon they were turning into the lane. Isobel had only been half listening to her son and all the stuff about police and spies was mixed up with trying to remember how long her hair had been up for.

The headmistress pursed her lips crossly as the new young teacher mentioned in passing the ridiculous story about snowed-in rich uncles, snakes and bears. What kind of education were they giving children that they could come out with such muddle-headed nonsense. Mrs Ferguson was a teacher firmly embedded into the school of thinking that encouraged children to act as adults. The unfortunate childishness of children was something school was designed to educate out of the young malleable mind. It was the teacher's job to curb fanciful woolly thinking and engender a capacity to ingest. To ingest education; that was what young brains were for – not to be allowed to run off into the deserts of aimless imagination.

"Of course it's a lot of nonsense!" she exclaimed with a sigh. She still found it hard to believe that any adult could be so gullible – especially one University trained. Willie-Joe had spun another one of his preposterous tales and found in Miss Carlisle a fish easily hooked. It was about time she curtailed his poaching.

"Miss Carlisle, I can assure you Willie-Joe has no more a gold prospecting uncle than you have. His uncle lives somewhere in Canada and sells cars as far as I know. Everything else is a total fabrication – a little

made-up world that Willie-Joe sometimes invites the naïve and unsuspecting to enter into. The silly boy will spend his entire life in make-believe if you let him. We are here to educate the boy, not humour his wild imagination. No, if you hear any more such nonsense, either stop him right away or send him to me. Willie-Joe's stories will not live long in the cold light of *my* clear-headed reason!"

Miss Carlisle felt chastened and left the room feeling foolish. To think she had listened to all that stuff about shooting and eating bears! No, the headmistress would not be required; if Willie-Joe tried to tell any more of his tales she would be ready for him. The headmistress would see – but now she had a lift to get and she was going to have to run to catch it.

As Willie-Joe told the dog that he was to be the Nazi guard in the next game of 'hunt the escaped soldier', he saw Joyce come out of the back door to the house. The house was a single brick two storied post war building and had corrugated-iron roofed outhouses across a stony yard. The gap between acted as a wind-tunnel and in an attempt to thwart the blasts of air rushing in through the open door, years previously an eight foot high slab of slate had been erected as a wind break up against the right side of the doorway. Joyce peered around the slate and saw Willie-Joe sitting face to face with the dog on the grass at the bottom of the yard. The dog was a border collie called Tessa and it was looking up into the face of her brother. It seemed interested. Willie-Joe looked at the dog and then back at his sister.

"Do you want to play a game?"

"What sort of a game?" asked Joyce suspiciously. "Is it one of your soldier games?"

"No," lied Willie-Joe as Joyce approached, the wind tossing her skirts about like washing on a line. "It's a game where we pretend to be, ahm… lost in a remote island and Tessa is out looking for us."

"Why are we lost?"

"What?"

"Why are we lost? Are we lost soldiers? I'm thirteen now you know, I'm almost a woman and I don't want to play lost soldiers."

Willie-Joe looked up at his sister. What was it with girls anyway? Usually they acted stupid; as if their brains were made of marshmallows and stuff. Suddenly, when you weren't expecting it they looked at you at read your mind. Girls were tricky.

Willie-Joe scowled and shook his head.

"Forget it. I'll just play with the dog."

"Suit yourself!" shrugged Joyce, flicking her eyelashes dismissively and turning away. "Play your stupid games with the dog then. At least your I.Q. and hers will be the same." She marched off and swung nonchalantly back up the yard. As she re-entered the house like a scornful debutante, Willie-Joe threw back his head in a sigh of disgust.

Joyce had done an I.Q. test in school and got a score of 128. Apparently this meant she was a genius. Mum and Dad thought it was brilliant. Joyce liked to remind Willie-Joe of it frequently. He couldn't see how you could be a genius and still not be able to tell the difference between what was a good exciting game and one that made you sick. And how could a genius read *Mandy*? It was the biggest load of rubbish he had ever read in his whole life.

He became aware that Tessa was still looking expectantly up into his face, her mouth open, her tongue thin and pink.

"Right, so you're the German then? You wait here till I whistle and then try and find me." He got up and beckoned for the dog to stay where she was. The animal's muscles tightened and her panting speeded up. She liked chasing games.

Willie-Joe decided on the sycamore tree at the top of the lane. If he could hide among the branches, Tessa would have a job of finding him and when she was poking about in the front garden, he would drop down and dash to the chicken house. Once in, he was over the Swiss border and into the wonderful air of freedom.

Getting well tucked in amongst the upper branches, he gave out a single loud whistle and waited to execute his plan.

Two seconds later Tessa had her paws up on the trunk of the tree and was panting excitedly and barking in victorious German.

That was the trouble with playing hide and seek with a border collie – something that was born and bred to hunt, find and herd was a difficult opponent. He was going to have to find a different game – one that didn't involve your nose.

It was as he was descending out of the tree that he heard it. At first he thought it was a tractor but from his vantage point he saw that there was none in the field from where he heard the noise. It was definitely the sound of an engine – an engine spluttering and coughing and sounding not at all well. Landing on the ground at the bottom of the tree he realised the sound was coming from above his head. Looking up, he was just in time to duck as a bi-plane staggered over the house, missing the chimney by inches and swooping in irregular hops down the lane. Tessa cowered with her tail between her legs and as soon as the noise faded, shot off with a whine into her dog-house at the back door.

Willie-Joe stood staring in unbelief in the direction the plane had gone, his breath held as he awaited the crash and exploding fireball. There was neither. Looking at the area where the plane had vanished into he listened hard, expecting to hear the engine rising as the plane soared back up from its low swoop. Nothing.

Already beginning to doubt what he had seen with his own two eyes,

Willie-Joe ran flat-out down the grass strip in the middle of the long lane. The lane ran straight down to the quiet country road and as he arrived panting at the bottom he jumped up onto the wooden-barred gate that led into the field opposite.

Sitting in the field with cows scattered to its hedges was an aeroplane. A cream coloured two-seater biplane with one man already out and one in the back seat holding his helmeted head in his hands. The plane was quiet and still and the man on the ground was leaning on one of the bottom wings face down. Neither was speaking.

Willie-Joe climbed the gate and walked quickly across the field. He tried to look as if he was just out for a walk, albeit a very fast one.

"Hello," he said breathlessly, approaching the plane. "That was scary."

The men looked at the small boy and the one still in the plane shook his head as he took off his goggles and helmet.

"No son, that wasn't scary, that was the worst two minutes of my life. Did you see us land?" He was getting out of the plane as the man at the wing turned around to take in their surroundings.

"Yip. Are you just visiting or something? I could get my mum to make you a cup of tea if you like?" The man at the wing gave a silent laugh and muttered.

"Whiskey more like. In fact make that a whole bottle."

The two men walked around the plane pulling at strings and feeling the struts and wheels. Willie-Joe watched quietly and spoke again.

"Didn't you mean to land here then? You nearly hit my dad's chimney."

"No son," said the first man who Willie-Joe could see now had a very large and bushy moustache. "We did not mean to land here, we had to. The engine died and I just had to put her down anywhere flat." Willie-Joe looked at the humpy field. It was a small field, no more than three acres and it was far from flat. The ground around about was very rocky underneath – a small slate quarry was at one end. At the far side the field faded away into a bulrush filled bog and a steep little hillock dominated the right-hand side near the quarry. At the far left a herd of Friesians began slowly ambling through the rough grass in the direction of the aircraft.

"Does your dad own this field, son?" asked the baldy-lipped one. "Is he about?"

Willie-Joe shook his head.

"No, dad owns a van. The farmer owns this field. He owns all these fields. He owns those cows too." He pointed towards the oncoming inquisitive herd. They were heifers and naturally curious. It wasn't every day they got to see aeroplanes landing in their field and they were coming to take a closer look.

"Oh," said Mr Baldy-lip. "I see… um… so where does the farmer live?" he was speaking and watching the cows at the same time. He was obviously not from the country; he was looking at the heifers the way townies looked at all animals in fields – the 'I wonder how safe those things are?' look.

"That's his house over there," said Willie-Joe pointing towards the cows. Beyond the advancing black and white puffing and huffing beasts was a large grey house, across two sets of hedges – about four hundred yards distant.

The two men talked together for a minute and then Mr Moustache spoke.

"Do you think you could look after our plane while we went to speak to the farmer son?"

Willie-Joe nodded.

"Yip, sure. What do you want me to do, just watch it?"

"No, it's those cows. The plane's made of Irish linen covered in a kind of paint that the cows might like. I want you to stop the cows eating it.

We'll not be long."

Willie-Joe had never heard of cows eating aeroplanes before. He had never read that in *Look and Learn.* He supposed even they didn't know everything.

The cows were very interested in the aircraft indeed. Willie-Joe had to continually shoo them away as they kept approaching, their large nostrils spewing out steamy breath and their necks straining as they stretched forward tentatively inspecting the strange object in their field. Willie-Joe had wondered before if the reason cows breathed all over the field as they were grazing was to heat up the grass for eating. They looked as if they were trying to cook the aeroplane.

"Away!" he cried as one almost got its big wet nose onto the far wing. "Go on! Away home!"

In that the heifers *were* at home, he hoped their grasp of English wasn't good.

After about ten minutes of 'shooing' and 'awaying' he was beginning to think that the increasingly bold animals were going to succeed in having a diet supplement very unnatural to the bovine world. No sooner did he chase a couple of sneaks off the tail than a couple more were heavily breathing all over the propeller. He hoped the pilots were going to come back soon.

Just then Willie-Joe heard his name being called. It was Joyce's distant voice.

"Willie-Joe! Willie-Joe!"

Willie-Joe ran to the gate and let out a shout.

"Here!" he cried and immediately ran back to shoo away the plane-eating cows. Joyce caught sight of her brother at the bottom of the lane darting about in the field across the road. What was he at? It was almost tea-time and Mum had asked her to fetch him. She jumped as the dog brushed by her legs and raced down the lane in the direction of

Willie-Joe's voice. Now she had a brother *and* a dog to fetch.

Joyce looked in amazement at what she saw in the field. Sitting as large as life in the field was an aeroplane with Willie-Joe running around it chasing cows. Tessa had joined in and was dashing at the lowered heads of the creatures as they crowded around the aeroplane. The cows seemed to be enjoying it all. Willie-Joe looked flustered. The cows looked extremely interested in the aircraft – she had never seen cows look so interested.

"Come on and give me a hand!" he shouted to her. "These cows are trying to eat the aeroplane!" She clambered over the gate and stood looking at the rough grass. She had light shoes on and the place was a minefield of cow pats.

"What on earth are you doing? Whose is that?" She pointed at the plane.

"Quickly!" shouted her brother, "you keep them off the back, and I'll watch the front!"

Ten minutes later Mr Moustache and Mr Baldy-lip arrived in an old beaten up land-rover driven by Mr Woods, the farmer. He looked at the plane as the pilots got out of the vehicle and climbed over the gate. Seeing Willie-Joe and Joyce, he came over and stood beside them as the pilots negotiated their way through the cows.

"Thought it was a joke," he said pushing his flat cap back on his head and scratching all his four strands of hair at once. "An aeroplane! Lucky they didn't kill themselves."

"They asked me to keep your cows off the plane Mr Woods," said Willie-Joe. "Joyce was helping." They looked over at Joyce who paid them scant attention. She was frowning at her shoes.

"Your cows like aeroplanes, Mr Woods," said Willie-Joe. "They like this one especially."

As the farmer moved the heifers into an adjacent field and shut them in, Willie-Joe and Joyce waited as the men opened up a large panel at the front of the plane. The baldy-lipped one had borrowed some tools from Mr Woods and was stripping something out of the engine.

"Dirt in the carburettor," he declared after a few minutes. "That's why she stalled – fuel starvation."

Willie-Joe nodded knowingly. "Ah," he said knowing nothing. Hearing the word 'starvation' reminded Joyce of something.

"Oh, Mum sent me to get you for tea," she said remembering. The man with the big moustache looked up.

"Oh, do you have to go right now, if you could manage another five minutes you could do one last thing for us." He looked hopefully at Willie-Joe and his sister.

"Oh, we'll stay as long as you like," replied Willie-Joe. "I never go for tea on time. Mum always has it ready fifteen minutes after she says it is."

The man with no moustache had finished and had screwed the bits back on that he had screwed off. Willie-Joe had watched mechanics before and reckoned being a mechanic seemed a good job. As far as he could see, all you did was to screw things off and then screw them on again. Also you got to get your hands dirty and no-one seemed to mind. He thought he might like to be a mechanic some day. His dad did things like that – he had lots of bits for washing machines hanging about in the shed – bits waiting to be screwed on to something. Maybe some day his dad would take him on one of his big jobs and he would get to screw something off and on again.

"What we need to do is to get the plane to the far side of the field," said Mr Moustache. If we can get enough space and Danny here stays off to reduce weight, I should be able to get her up before those hedges." He pointed over towards Mr Wood's farm-house. Mr Woods shook his head but said nothing. He was having images of aeroplanes sticking out of bedroom windows running about in his head. Danny Baldy-lip didn't complain about not being taken back up in the plane. Willie-Joe reckoned he had had enough flying for a while.

The engine coughed into life and Mr Moustache steered the plane as his colleague Danny Baldy-lip, Mr Woods, Joyce and Willie-Joe pushed the wings. The plane bumped slowly over the field as the wind from the propeller blew into their faces and whipped Joyce's skirt like a flag in a storm. The noise of the engine drowned out the words of the pilot as he encouraged them to push. Willie-Joe thought his job looked the easiest.

He taxied the plane around the back of the hillock and brought it around so that it came to a stop at the summit. Willie-Joe's legs were sore with the pushing and his ears rang with the noise of the engine. Danny baldy-lip man came over and shouted in Willie-Joe's ear.

"You and I will push at this wing, the farmer and your sister on the other. When he winds up the engine, just push as hard as you can until you can't keep up. You're a good lad. Thanks!"

Willie-Joe only thought the engine had been noisy and windy before. Mr Moustache put both his thumbs up, pulled down his goggles and pressed forward the throttle. The rumble of the engine became a roaring, deafening thunder of brutal noise and the violence of the wind from the propeller pushed back the skin on his face. He had to shut his mouth to stop his cheeks turning into balloons. He couldn't see Joyce on the other side – he wondered if she was having as much fun as him.

The plane jerked and jumped like a living thing as they pushed with all their might. At the bottom of the hill, Willie-Joe's legs ran out of speed. The men managed a few seconds more and then they let go, bent over gasping for breath as the plane accelerated and bumped and bucked across the field.

It wasn't going all that fast for all the pushing. It was half-way across the field now and not looking like it was going anywhere but into the hedge at the far side. Danny Baldy-lip was willing it to take off.

"Go on! Get up! Get up!" The plane didn't appear to be listening.

At last, with only yards left, the back wheel lifted and the plane seemed to suddenly gather more speed. Willie-Joe glanced at Joyce and saw her put her hands to her mouth in shock. The plane was about to crash!

Almost too late, it seemed, the aeroplane broke free from the grip of the field and lurched heavily toward the hedge. It seemed it was going to clear the hedge all right, but two large ash trees stood in the way and Willie-Joe watched absolutely fascinated as the plane gave a final stagger and struggled over the branches and clipped the top sending leaves and twigs flying.

"Wow!" exclaimed Willie-Joe, "did he know that would happen?" Danny Baldy-lip shook his head and gave a nervous laugh.

"That was as close as it gets folks, and if hadn't been for you all giving a hand he'd never have made it. Thanks again."

Mr Woods ended up taking the man all the way up to Newtownards where the airfield was. Willie-Joe and Joyce returned back up the lane. Joyce had forgotten about being thirteen, dignified and reserved. She chatted animatedly with her brother.

"That was amazing! Imagine us helping a plane to take off! How did you know it was there anyway?"

Mum found it hard to believe and if Joyce hadn't assured her she would just have put it down as another of Willie-Joe's tales.

"You could have been hurt," she said, the thought suddenly occurring to her. "If any more planes crash in the field I don't want you going near them – it's dangerous."

Monday morning was a bit of a disaster. Tom's van wouldn't start and he ended up having to take the Morris-Minor. Mrs McCutcheon had arranged to meet her sister in law at ten and Tom had a washing machine refusing to wash Mrs Moore's sheets at ten-thirty. Everybody ended up bundling into the car along with Dad's tools and spare parts, making Willie-Joe late for school since Joyce had to be got to her bus first. He was itching to get to school, every second late was a second less he had to tell his friends and Miss Carlisle about the aeroplane. Did Dad always drive this slow?

When Willie-Joe finally arrived it was just after ten and the class were sitting at their desks listening to Miss Carlisle explain something.

"Sorry I'm late Miss," explained Willie-Joe apologetically. "Dad's van broke down and Mum has to see Auntie Ellie to get her hair fixed."

Having seen Mrs McCutcheon on Friday afternoon, Miss Carlisle accepted the excuse and got everyone to pay attention. Willie-Joe opened his mouth to tell her about the plane.

"All right Willie-Joe, just take your seat," she interrupted before he got a word out. She turned to the class and gently steered Willie-Joe down the aisle. "Now, I want you all to write an essay. Here is the title, ready?" Just at that the door knocked and the headmistress walked in. She scanned the class and after frying everyone to a crisp where they sat with her dreaded eye-ball death-ray, she went over and spoke briefly to Miss Carlisle.

"Class!" called the teacher after a few seconds. "The headmistress is going to inspect the class for half an hour this morning. Mrs Ferguson may walk around class checking your work; just carry on unless she says otherwise. Now the essay title is, *What I did this weekend.* Just write about what you did, shopping, helping around the house. I don't expect anything extraordinary – just write about whatever you did. All right, children?" The class shook its collective head and bent to the task.

Willie-Joe couldn't believe it. What an opportunity! Now he could write all about it – the aeroplane, the cows, the man with the big moustache, the helping push the aeroplane so that it could fly again, how it almost didn't make it – there was so much! He didn't need to add to any of it, he had no need to exaggerate or make anything up to make it more interesting. He was fit to burst with the excitement of what he would write. Suddenly Mrs Ferguson's voice broke into his thoughts. She was addressing the class and looking directly at him.

"And class, let's not have any silly stories, just write what Miss Carlisle has instructed you to write." Her eye sharpened to a lance and pinned Willie-Joe to his chair. As she spoke she slowly made her way down the classroom.

"So no ridiculous stories about Canadian bears, lost gold or silly things like… like…" she paused as she thought of something totally unlikely, "like planes crashing beside your houses or some such equally ludicrous nonsense." Now she was looming right over Willie-Joe, her deadly gaze pouring vertically onto his withering head. "Any silly tales and you'll give me a hundred lines each day this week." The eye narrowed. "Understand Willie-Joe?"

Willie-Joe's heart gave a thump and his stomach fell into his schoolbag at his feet. He couldn't believe it! But he had *such* a story to tell, and it was *true*! He was devastated, a hundred lines? For telling the *truth*?!

Suddenly he had a thought. He put up his hand.

"Miss?" he said looking at the headmistress.

"Yes Willie-Joe?" Her eyes narrowed to slits. The boy was flying close to the wind. Whatever he said next had better not be wild and bizarre. Willie-Joe beamed a face full of innocence and simplicity.

"Can I write a story about what cows like to eat?"

6.

THE UNDEAD

"What do you mean, like selling cabbages and stuff?"

Lennie McClurg had been outlining his idea to his friend Bisto Gillespie. In wondering how he could make a bit of serious money, he had hit upon his brilliant masterstroke – a fruit and veg van.

"Yes of course selling cabbages and stuff. What else does a fruit and veg man sell? A van around the doors is just what this place needs. Fruit and veg needs to be got while it's fresh – I could buy it from the local farms and sell it directly to people at their homes the same day – how much fresher can you get?"

"You know as much about veg as my dog," dismissed Bisto, "so how are you going to sell them?"

"You know nothing," retorted Lennie. "It's all about market research – it doesn't matter what you're selling as long as you know you can sell it. I'm telling you, it's a cert" He saw his argument was beginning to impress his friend with its undeniable logic.

Bisto was remaining unimpressed. "Market research? What are you on about? What market research have you done? I doubt if you even know what it means."

"Look," said Lennie patiently. He was on the brink of something great, something that was going to change the direction of his life and his friend's clearly defective brain had obviously not got it at all. "It's about time I made my mark in the world – I'm not a young man anymore and…"

Bisto snorted. "You're not even twenty for goodness sake!"

"Exactly!" glared Lennie. "It's not like *I'm* eighteen. I'm in my twentieth year of life; my teenage years are gone. When you're a teenager you think different – you wouldn't understand, one day you'll see I'm right."

The eighteen year old Bisto sighed and tried another tack.

"So where are you going to get a van? Or didn't it occur to you that a fruit and veg van business kind of needs the van?"

Lennie shook his head in pitying disdain. "Of course I know that. That's why I'm heading up to McGurke's timber yard – he's selling an estate car and it sounds exactly the thing – are you coming or not?"

Lennie had indeed heard that McGurke was selling an estate car. In fact, McGurke was capable of selling anything; although officially he ran a timber yard, he also sold compost, pet-food, corrugated iron, plaster-cast statues, reconditioned freezers and sheep. This was not an exhaustive list – McGurke sold whatever came to rest long enough in his yard. Regular customers knew not to stay too long, or at least to keep a watchful eye on their cars – it wouldn't be the first time McGurke had tried to sell a vehicle that had, to his judgement, become his to sell merely by staying long enough for him to lay title to.

McGurke's timber yard did not resemble so much a timber yard as the aftermath of an earthquake, a tidal wave and what's left after a visit by a squadron of B52 bombers – the place was a mess.

"This place is a mess!" exclaimed Bisto when they arrived in Nate McFadzean's old Ford Zephyr. Bisto was already in a bit of a twist about being involved in a venture which began by being picked up by a car that had no actual brakes to speak of, no actual tax or insurance and being driven by a guy with no actual licence.

McGurke saw them coming and recognised Nate from previous visits. Although he was only seventeen, Nate McFadzean was a regular customer, coming over to pick up fence posts and barbed wire spools for work around his father's farm.

"I see you've got your licence now then, young McFadzean," he said as the three lads got out of the purple Zephyr. He dusted his hands and pushed back the cap on his dusty head.

"Nearly," said Nate, "I'm getting very close now to applying for the test – I'm still practising away though." He didn't add that he had also nearly got around to applying for his provisional licence. He patted his overalls' pocket. A licence application lay within, signed and addressed by him, it gave him a sense of legality. At least he had some kind of intent, some vague intention of doing the right thing sometime. His conscience was easily pacified.

"Hmmm," grunted McGurke, "so I see. Well, what can I do for you lads?"

Lennie raised a finger as if he was about to ask a question and spoke up.

"We're here about the estate."

"The estate?"

"Yes, the estate car you have for sale. I was actually looking for a van for my business, but I thought I could paint out the windows of an old estate and have a good sized van."

McGurke pulled his cap back onto his forehead and scratched his stubbly cheek.

"Ah!" he exclaimed, "the old Wolsey? Yes, she's down at the back, just follow me down and I'll show her to you. Mind how you go."

He led them through a labyrinth of piled timber and scrap metal. As they followed behind, the three friends privately wondered how far back into his yard McGurke was taking them. They were getting deeper and deeper into the depths of amassed possessions, it was like going back in time. They passed ancient boilers, brass radiators, metal telegraph poles, and megalithic lorry axles. At the very extreme recess of his yard was a corrugated shed, hidden from every angle by mountains of wooden pallets and moss covered car doors.

"She's in here," said McGurke, pulling back a screeching door. Light flooded into the gloomy shed. "There, what do you think?"

It was Bisto who spoke first.

"It's a hearse!"

The big black vehicle's front grille grinned back at them grimly from the murky darkness. It was a hearse all right – an old split screen model with great curving mudguards and broad running boards. The tyres looked flat in the semi-light and the roof was green with algae. Impressive it wasn't.

"Aluminium body, walnut dash and leather seats all round," said McGurke slapping the driver's wing. "You'll not find another like this anywhere."

Lennie struggled for something to say as Nate turned away to hide his face. Bisto looked disgusted.

"Well, what do you say, big lad?" said McGurke looking up to Lennie. "I'd say with a bit of TLC she's exactly what you'd want. What was your business again?"

"Uh… fruit and veg" stammered Lennie.

"Perfect!" exclaimed the older man. "Sure look at this." He took them around the back and hauled open the rear door. "Look, shelves already in place. You could put your fruit up on those racks and here," he opened a small door below the high floor, "here is a great spot for keeping spuds and the like."

The racks still had a couple of tattered wreaths in place and the raised floor sported runners for sliding coffins in and out. Lennie was still having problems knowing what to say.

"How does it go?" asked Nate. He was fiddling with the side opening bonnet catches and, being mechanically minded, wanted to have a look at the engine.

"Ah, now there's a problem with the engine right enough," said McGurke quickly as Nate sprung the bonnet open. The problem became immediately obvious. There was no engine.

"I can't believe this," muttered Bisto under his breath so that only Lennie could hear. "What kind of an idiot would want a second-hand hearse? Especially with no engine?"

"How much?" asked Nate. Bisto looked up surprised – Nate actually looked serious!

"Well now, she's a great body – she'll never rust you know – and that's genuine walnut, not your rubbish laminated stuff. I'd need a hundred and fifty for her just to cover myself"

"Fifty quid," said Nate.

"Seventy five," shot back McGurke.

"I'll buy it," said Lennie.

"Good grief!" said Bisto.

Getting the hearse out of the yard took considerably longer than the buying of it. Once he had the money, McGurke's involvement in the process evaporated like so much morning mist and he left it to the three lads to conjure up some way of getting the hearse out of the shed and across the Armageddon that was the yard.

In the end Nate had to bring over his dad's David-Browne tractor the following Saturday and use the front fork to lift pallets and scrap metal out of the way to make a passage for the car. They had arranged to tow it over to Nate's farm where an old barn had been cleared as a place to work at it. What Nate had known but had not shared with McGurke was that by coincidence, an old abandoned Wolsey saloon car of the same vintage had lain for years in one of the air-raid shelters at the McFadzean farm. The vehicle was a wreck but the engine appeared to be intact. Nate was up for an engine transplant, after all what was a mechanic's job but a matter of making sure you put the right nuts on the right bolts?

Lennie and Bisto turned out to be useless mechanics. Neither could tell the wiper motor from the fuel pump and the help they gave Nate as he spent long nights underneath the hearse was mostly of the advisory sort.

"Do you think you should hit that so hard with the hammer?" asked Lennie as he watched Nate wallop at his investment.

"It's an impact driver, you're supposed to use a hammer," said Nate.

"Oh."

"Would 'three in one oil' help that squeak?" asked Lennie swinging the passenger door as Nate struggled with separating the lower engine mountings.

"Yes, probably," grunted Nate from below the car.

"Do you have any? Will you get it or will I?"

" Do you think... ughh... that it can... agggggghh... maybe wait?"

Lennie swung the door a few more times.

"Mmm, I suppose so – do you want me to hold a spanner or something?"

As Nate attempted to release the engine from the saloon car, Bisto was in the hearse sitting behind the wheel. He had never driven before and the feel of an actual steering wheel in the grip of his hands was quite an exhilarating thing. He shot a quick glance across the barn and saw Lennie kneeling down talking to the prone Nate. He grabbed the wheel with both hands and narrowed his eyes.

"And here comes Stirling Moss," he mumbled under his breath, "he holds the corner at one hundred and fifty miles an hour and controls the vehicle with astounding skill." He made a rumbling engine noise and changed gear. "Britain's greatest motor-racing ace has taken the lead – watch him go folks, he's like a flash of lightening, he's untouchable, he's uncatchable, he's..." he caught a sight of himself in the rear-view mirror, "he's a handsome devil, watch as the girls scream as he waves out the window!" Bisto leaned out the driver's window and grinned widely at his adoring fans.

"Hi," said Nathan McCutcheon who was standing at the car door. Bisto's face froze.

"Oh... hi Nathan... I was just... I was just... just testing the steering wheel for Nate... that's O.K. now Nate!" he called out the window.

"What?" came back the disembodied voice from below the other car.

"Or what about the ash-trays? Does it matter that they're full of sweet-ie papers?" Lennie was asking the legs below the car as Nathan walked over.

With Nathan there to help the task became somewhat easier. Nathan wasn't a great expert on car engines either, but he could work a spanner. With Lennie and Bisto bringing crisps and Coke, Nate and Nathan had the big straight four engine out in two nights. It took all four of them hauling on the make-shift pulley chained to the roof beams to lift the engine out of the engine compartment.

After four days of late-night engine transplanting Bisto had had enough. He didn't want to let his friend down by appearing disinter-ested but watching mechanics was a job he had firmly decided was not for him. His current job of stacking shelves in the local Stewart's Super-market wasn't for him either, but it was nonetheless what he was doing until something better came up.

On the fourth night he brought over an old set of walkie-talkies his older brother had got from somewhere and left lying around. In the days before mobile phones and mass communications, walkie-talkies were an exciting piece of technology. As Nate and Nathan sweated away with solenoids and constant velocity joints, Bisto and Lennie messed about in the yard and outhouses sending one another radio messages.

"Bisto to Lennie, over."

"Ten-four good buddy. What's the situation report, over."

"Can you read me, over."

"Roger that. Do you copy? Over."

"That's a ten-four Lennie, over."

"You're loud and clear, over."

"So are you, over."

All very exciting stuff, though a bit repetitive.

Lennie decided to give his future business vehicle a bit of a clean as the two Nathans did their thing with the engine. Bisto joined in for want of something to do. It was Bisto who discovered the dummy.

"Hey, look at what's in here!" He was at the back of the vehicle with the rear door wide open. Lennie came around to see, a peaked cap on his head.

"I found this in the front glove compartment; it's a chauffeur's cap," said Lennie.

"I found this," said Bisto, pulling out a life-sized mannequin from the storage compartment below the raised floor. "It was stuffed right up in. What do you reckon it's for?"

"Probably for when they're training hearse drivers," suggested Lennie. Bisto gave him a curious look.

"What are you on about?"

"Well, you know, maybe when you're learning to drive a hearse you have to have a body in the back to pass the test or something."

"Maybe you're not used to being up late," said Bisto shaking his head. Suddenly he stopped. "Here, I've an idea!"

The McFadzean farm was just outside Ballydoonan, up a road that led across the peninsula to the villages on the western side. It was a quiet road but one that folk sometimes used for a quiet evening's stroll. Lennie and Bisto took the mannequin out to the road, Bisto leading with the legs and Lennie following behind with the head. Bisto sniggered the whole way as he thought of the implementation of his plan.

"Down the road a bit," he said, "a bit closer to the village."

It was dark and the lights of the village glimmered from half a mile down the road. After walking a hundred yards Bisto stopped and set down his end of the dummy. Before leaving the two Nathans working away at the hearse, Bisto had found a pair of overalls hanging on the back of the shed door. They were probably Nate's but he wouldn't miss them for a while. He and Lennie stuffed the dummy into them. In the dim light of the evening, it looked very life-like.

"Half in the hedge, half out," sniggered Bisto. Lennie set the head up against the dark shadow of the hedge and gave a snort himself.

"I'll stuff my walkie-talkie into the top here," he said as he turned on the radio and tucked it into the overalls at the chest. "Where'll we hide?"

They squeezed through a hole in the hedge ten feet from the mannequin and settled down into a dyke on the other side. The two of them began to chortle and gurgle as Bisto turned on the other walkie-talkie and tried a test call.

"You crawl over to the hedge behind the dummy," he laughed quietly, "see if you can hear this."

Lennie crawled in the darkness until he was at the reverse side of the hedge with the dummy just on the other side.

"Urghhh!" crackled the radio, "help me, I'm sick, over."

Lennie crawled back to where in the darkness he left Bisto.

"You twit," he said, "don't say 'over' at the end."

"Oh yes, forgot. Is anybody coming?"

"I didn't look," replied Lennie, "do you want me to check?"

"Yes, I'll stay here, you crawl out and look down the road, if anyone comes, crawl back."

"Right!" said Lennie as he crawled off again in the darkness to squirm through the hole in the hedge. This was going to be some good joke!

Old Widow Donnan took her dog out for its nightly walk at ten every evening. She didn't go far, just out of the village and out towards the McFadzean farm, but it was something she did as regularly as clockwork. Friends tried telling her that she was too old to be out so late, but Widow Donnan paid no heed. She had spent a lifetime outliving a succession of dogs that she took up that road at night and she wasn't about to change her ways at this stage in her life. It was while walking a long-gone dog and lifetime ago that she had met her first husband. Other memories followed and for Rosie Donnan, each evening's walk was a journey down a familiar memory lane.

Actually, memory was probably too distinct a word for what went on in the old woman's head. Although filled with the fragrances of a life lived, the detail was very hazily outlined. Mrs Donnan had a memory like a fish, and a not particularly *compos mentis* one at that. The chances of her dog, for example, ever getting called the same name twice in a row would have been nice, especially for the identity befuddled dogs.

She had been a muddled old lady for as long as anyone could remember – apart for old Jacob Cully, who had a memory that went back to before the Battle of the Boyne and remembered even Rosie Donnan as a young girl. The old lady was well liked though, a kindly and gentle old biddy. Even her fragile grasp on reality was actually quite endearing. No-one minded her one flaw – her nosiness – that much; it wasn't as if she was going to remember anything.

So it was that after a half an hour of waiting for a passer-by on a dark country road at half ten at night, and wondering why they weren't passing by every few minutes, Lennie eventually saw the light from a torch coming up from the village. He crawled back quickly to where Bisto lay, all sniggering long gone in the long cold wait in the ditch.

"Someone's coming!" he whispered into Bisto's ear.

"What?" said Bisto feeling something at his left foot.

Discovering that he had missed Bisto's ear by five foot nine inches, Lennie crept up to where he heard Bisto's voice.

"A torch, there's someone coming, about fifty feet away."

"Right, listen, when they're about fifteen feet off give me a nudge."

Rosie Donnan suddenly stopped and spoke to her dog.

"What's that, Rex?" she said in her thin and warbley voice.

The dog stopped and listened. He wasn't called Rex, but then neither was he called Tiddles, which is what he had got the day before.

"Listen, there it is again, noise in the hedge… listen!"

"Urgghh," crackled the radio in the dummy's chest. "Help me, I'm not well. Urghhh!…over… no, not over." Behind the hedge Bisto and Lennie held their breaths and waited for the sounds of offered help and sympathetic assistance.

"It's a drunk!" exclaimed Rosie aloud. Lennie raised his eyebrows: the dog lowered his.

"You silly old man!" pronounced the old woman waggling her stick.

The dog nodded in agreement.

"You know, it's people like you who give this place a bad name," she continued, shining her torch toward the dummy. "Silly old fools like you lying about in hedges are a disgrace! I suppose you thought you were having a great time and now you're lying about like an old mattress in the ditch – you deserve a kick in the backside!"

Lennie and Bisto had expected a slightly softer approach and Bisto hardly knew what to say into the radio in reply.

"Urrghh, I'm not drunk," he tried, "I'm not well." Suddenly they heard a loud clunk.

"There! How do you like that? That's all you deserve you silly old man! You see, Rover, that's why I keep warning you about the booze."

She went to move off but turned and, shaking her stick again, gave a final parting shot.

"And if a car will drive over your legs and that'll show you!"

Lennie and Bisto listened in amazement as Rosie walked off, complaining and muttering as she went.

"She kicked it!" exclaimed Lennie after a while. "She was my mum's Sunday School teacher I can't believe it, she actually kicked it!"

"So much for that great idea," said Bisto, "I thought we could have had a laugh, I feel sorry for that poor old dummy now. What if it had been a real person in trouble? Grab it and we'll take it back to Nate's. We can see how your hearse is doing. Come on before she comes back and gives it another kicking!"

In the darkness Lennie shook his head.

"Grab it yourself!" he complained, "it was your big fat idea anyway!"

Aware that Widow Donnan might still be within earshot, Lennie did not speak much above a whisper. A little bit louder and Bisto might have heard him. As it was neither was able to see much more than a vague shadow of one another as they made their way up to the farm.

Unknown to both, the mannequin did not accompany them.

"Where's Lennie and Bisto?" asked Nate when he emerged from beneath the hearse. They were nowhere to be seen.

"They must have gone out for a walk or something," replied Nathan. "Do you know what time it is? The eleven bus will be passing in a few minutes – do you mind if I leave my bike here and get the bus? It goes right by our house on the way back to Ards."

"O.K." replied Nate, "I'm wrecked anyway – that clampet Lennie isn't much use at helping with his own car is he? Maybe they've gone on home." He wiped his hands on an oily rag and looked at the hearse propped up on axle stands. "A couple more hours will do it anyway, have you a car battery charger?"

"Yip, I'll bring it over on Saturday – see you about."

As Nathan left his friend to turn off the lights and tidy away his tools he headed down the short lane to the road. The bus would be here in two minutes.

Lennie and Bisto skidded into the shed just as Nate was about to turn out the light.

"Oh, I thought you guys had gone home – what were you up to?" asked Nate.

Lennie quickly explained about the dummy and the walkie-talkies. Nate laughed and shook his head.

"You're mad – where's the dummy now?"

"Talking to you," muttered Bisto.

Nate was tired.

"Do you two mind walloping one another about your heads as you walk home? I'm off to bed. Come on round on Saturday and we'll get the car finished – Nathan's bringing a charger. Can you bring a couple of gallons of petrol?"

Lennie stared at Bisto. Bisto glared back.

"Yes, I'll bring some," said Lennie. "Will I bring paint to block out the back windows?"

"Whatever," yawned Nate flicking the switch and plunging them all into darkness. "See you later."

Bisto and Lennie headed down the lane and turned to walk the mile and a half to Ballydoonan.

"It's dark though isn't it?" said Lennie after walking a few yards. The sky had clouded over and obliterated the moon and stars. Bisto felt the hairs on the back of his neck begin to tingle.

"Lennie?" he whispered as quietly as he could.

"What?" whispered back the tall black form walking at his side.

"Did you hear something?"

"No… I don't…"

Suddenly there was a crackle in the hedge and at the same moment the clouds parted for a second to allow a dim beam of moonlight to fall onto the roadside. Right beside them, not three feet away a pale face appeared in the hedge.

"RUN!" screamed Bisto. Lennie didn't need to be told twice – he galloped off, his longer legs soon passing the frantically puffing Bisto and propelling him down the road, expecting every moment to feel a strong hand grab his throat from behind.

They didn't stop until they reached the village. The orange street lights illuminated the empty streets and the two friends glanced at one another's yellow faces.

"Split now and head home!" said Bisto. "Make sure he doesn't see what house you live in!"

They ran different directions and were both soon in their homes. In Lennie's house everyone had already gone to bed. He sat in the darkness of the living room peering out through a gap in the curtains. In his own home, Bisto lay wakefully in bed listening to every noise in the street outside.

It was about three in the morning that Lennie first began to wonder what had happened to the dummy and the walkie-talkies.

Not actually getting to sleep until some time after four in the morning left Bisto with very little enthusiasm for getting up just to stand around watching someone poke about under an old hearse. In that it was Saturday, no-one in the house bothered him and he was able to sleep on.

Lennie never went to bed at all. His mind stayed active all night and he ended up tuning into the Russian shortwave broadcasts on Radio Moscow. He had been given a multi-channel radio as a Christmas present from his dad some years previously, which up to this point had only ever been on Radio One or Radio Luxembourg. Being utterly awake at half past three he discovered the Shortwave dial and messed about until he found the strangely American accented voice talking about marvellous wheat harvests and wonderful Soviet scientific progress. Countries he had never heard of were casually acclaimed as 'world leaders' and 'remarkable innovators'. They all seemed to be called the 'people's republic of' whatever. Somewhere called Georgia, which he had imagined was in America had had the best barley crop in fifty years and new towns were being built for the workers all over some place called Azerbash-something. According to the presenter, who sounded an entirely reasonable sort of a man, rockets were being hurled into space, new forms of vaccines were being discovered and politicians were being welcomed in tear-filled joy by the Great Soviet People every few minutes. One politician somewhere had died and his body had been paraded in an open hearse in Red Square – thousands of people came from all over the USSR to weep and wail. The presenter said he was a greatly respected representative of the people. Russian politicians were clearly very different to the ones at home then. He listened for an hour as feat after amazing feat was recorded interspersed by reports of decadent drunken riots and industrial unrest in the USA. The last he remembered hearing as he finally collapsed onto the living room floor was the sound of children in the People's Republic of Mongolia singing songs about a wonderful new dam project.

It was all very depressing. Here he was, nearly twenty years old and playing with dummies on the road whilst eight year olds at the other side of the world were into hydraulic power generation – something, somewhere was wrong.

Nate had things to do around the farm and didn't get around to looking at the old Wolsey again until well after lunch. When he eventually entered the barn a plastic bag was sitting just inside the door. A battery charger was inside it with a note from Nathan.

'Sorry, can't make it today, promised Mum I'd do the garden and stuff. Maybe see you next week? Got dad to leave this round this morning on his route. P.S. Give Lennie and Bisto a thump from me. Nathan.'

After clipping the charger onto the battery terminals he went back to work around the farm. Nothing much could be done until Lennie turned up with the petrol anyway.

It was after tea-time before Lennie got himself sorted out. He went down to the small garage in the village and bought two gallons of petrol in two old Castrol oil cans that he found in the garden shed. One still had a bit of oil in it but he hoped it wouldn't matter. After all, it was the same stuff – what was oil made of anyway? Whatever it was, petrol, oil; it was all sucked out of the ground wasn't it?

A police car was in the forecourt and he recognised Sergeant Gilmore from the local neighbourhood police unit. As the policeman got back into the car he nodded to Lennie who nodded back. It wasn't every day a policeman nodded at you and Lennie reckoned it was probably because he was nearly twenty – nearly twenty made you a man of note, a man of note who would soon be a highly successful business man.

It wasn't every day either that Sergeant Gilmore had a raw recruit under his watch. The sergeant was a man who liked to get his day's work done cleanly and efficiently; a probationer under his feet was a mild annoyance.

"Right, lad," he said to the young man as he started up the engine. "A presence about the place is what the locals like to see and a confident, capable presence is what you must learn to show. You're wearing the Queen's badge, lad – you represent the rule of law and order – don't you forget it!"

The young constable was nervous; being a policeman in Northern Ireland had its own unique dangers, the gun on his belt was evidence of that. In fact, the gun on his belt was playing on his mind and he risked a question to the stern sergeant.

"The guns… do we need them much?"

The older man turned an eye toward the thin faced youngster.

"I've been in the force twenty-two years son – I've never had to take it out of its holster except to clean it."

The answer calmed the young constable and he began to breathe easier. Weapon training had not been his favourite part at the depot – it sounded like he didn't have to worry too much about that then.

Bisto had looked more enthusiastic in his life. Lennie stood at his door looking expectantly as he stood in his slippers looking tired.

"Oh, right, do you need me then?" he asked stifling a yawn.

"Don't you want to see the van start?"

"Can't wait," replied Bisto but actually meaning he cared as much as a monkey in a glue factory.

"Well, come on then, get your shoes on," pressed Lennie. "It won't wait forever!"

As Bisto turned to get ready it occurred to him that a hearse was probably one vehicle that waited for everybody.

Nate was reversing a trailer into a silage shed when the other two arrived. Once again Lennie and Bisto marvelled at what skills their younger friend displayed in tractor driving. At the Presbyterian Annual Fair Lennie had watched him win the tractor slalom course, reversing a bale filled trailer back through cones every bit as fast as he had done it in forward gear. Of course farmer's sons are introduced to tractors at a very early age. By their second day of life they are surrounded by toy Ford tractors, balers, combines and slurry tankers in their little hospital cots. Farmers' sons' first blabberings are not mere sounds, they are the child's expert impersonations of a power-take-off on the back of a John Deere six series. Sitting on the back of the trailer was the dummy. Seeing them looking at it Nate said "I picked this out of a hedge this morning – doesn't say much does he? Can you put him back in the hearse?"

Bisto and Lennie poured in the petrol as Nate connected the radiator hose and filled the radiator with water. Bisto chucked the dummy into the back of the hearse and gave it a disparaging look.

Twenty minutes later the engine was ready to try.

"Here goes nothing!" called Nate from within the hearse. He turned the key on the dash and a big red light on the fascia glowed like a Belisha beacon. Another twist and the big straight four churned like a cavernous cement mixer. It didn't start.

"It'll take a while to get the petrol into the carburettor," pointed out

Nate.

Lennie nodded. He didn't know exactly what a carburettor was, but if Nate said it needed petrol then it needed petrol.

"We've already poured all the petrol into the fuel tank," said Lennie thoughtfully. "Will I go back to the village to get some more for the carburettor?"

Nate just looked oddly at the tall man and instead got out and poked about at something under the bonnet.

"Have you ever wondered what petrol actually is?" Lennie asked Bisto.

"No," said Bisto.

"You know, what is it made of? Why is it underground? If it's sucked out of the ground does it leave a big hole or something when it's all taken out? If they take it out from under the sea what's to stop the sea water rushing in and filling it up? Would that make the sea level go down? Did you ever wonder about that?"

"No," said Bisto again.

"Someone told me it is all ancient dinosaurs or something – that can't be right though – dinosaurs hardly change into oil, do they?"

"Hardly," agreed Bisto.

"Ah, I forgot to connect the coil!" exclaimed Nate from underneath the driver's side bonnet, "let's try it again."

After a few more churns the motor spluttered and coughed into erratic life.

"Timing's a bit off – a bit of a twiddle should sort that out," said Nate as he returned to the engine. The shed was now filled with smoke and Bisto pulled his jumper up as a mask. Lennie went to the doorway.

The next time the engine roared, gave a couple of loud bangs and settled into a thrumming beat of a big engine glad to be resurrected from the dead.

"She'll smoke for a bit until all the oil burns off. I had filled the cylinders with diesel to loosen her up," explained Nate to Lennie outside the doorway. Nate had retired from the building to let the car warm up – smoke billowed out in great plumes through the open doors. "Where's Bisto?"

When they pulled Bisto out of the smoke-filled barn his eyes were streaming and he was coughing like a forty fags a day man.

"What were you playing at?" asked Lennie. "Trying to get yourself choked to death? Sometimes I wonder if you're half sensible."

Bisto could think of plenty of replies but the coughing and wheezing left him in no fit state to do so.

"You wait here and get your breath," suggested Nate, "Lennie and I will take her for a short spin to see how she goes."

The big vehicle trundled out of the smoke; a prehistoric monster from a primordial mist. Nate gunned the engine and the whole body shook like a dog coming out of water. Lennie got in beside Nate and waved regally to Bisto who sat spitting on the grass. The light was fast falling and they were delighted to find the headlights worked.

"Not bad for seventy-five quid eh?" said Nate.

Lennie grinned and glowed in that superior attitude worn by those who have shown by their intelligence and cunning to be a cut above the common man – not in among the fray but looking down upon its bumbling affairs. Yes indeed, not bad for seventy-five quid at all.

Nate turned out of the lane and steered the car down toward Ballydoonan. The street lights were coming on, their dull red glow casting a pallid blush on the streets as they began to warm up.

At the corner of the village a small bunch of local lads hung around the wall that ran along the edge of the beach. The road widened out wide enough to allow Nate to turn full lock and return back the way he had come. The big car was not fast, but its engine was purring steadily as he heaved on the large walnut rimmed steering wheel. As he did so he caught a glimpse of a couple of the faces outside stare open-mouthed at the hearse as he drove by. More exactly, they stared open-mouthed at the back of the hearse.

Nate glanced in the rear-view mirror and saw what it was that had caught their attention – apart from the weirdness of seeing a hearse drive by at night. The dummy lay on the casket shelf in the back; they thought they were seeing an actual dead body in open display – not something you see every day. Nate quickly wound down the window and shouted out to a couple he recognised.

"Got a stiff in the back!" he called, laughing. As a street light shone in through the side windows, the small crowd grinned like Cheshire cats seeing the dummy in overalls lying rigid in the back.

"Has the dummy a licence?" called back a boy called Gibson who knew Nate had not. "Maybe you should get *him* to drive!"

Lennie was in the middle being diffidently superior and unattached to the world when the calls made him postpone disinterest.

"What? What was that?" he asked. They were already on their way back up the road.

"The dummy made them jump!" smiled Nate. "The car's going fine though."

Lennie turned and looked back down the road. "Here, I've an idea!" he said. All indifference had gone.

Back at the barn, when he heard the plan, Bisto thought it was a stupid idea and said as much.

"That's a stupid idea. What if some old woman takes a heart attack?"

"Now you're being stupid – like how many old women do you know hang around street corners?" asked Lennie. "You sit up front with the wreaths. It'll be a cracker!"

Bisto grudgingly went along with it – grudgingly because he actually liked the idea and it was bound to produce a laugh.

Nate brought out a couple of his dad's old jackets and ties from the house and recovered the chauffeur's cap from the glove compartment. Lennie pulled the dummy out and stuffed it into the compartment underneath the casket floor. He climbed in himself and lay down on his back, his feet towards the rear.

"You wear this jacket," said Nate to Bisto, putting on the other. "I could only find one black tie, this other one is blue but it'll do all right."

Bisto had warmed more to the joke and he pulled a long face.

"Let's take the dear departed on his last journey to his final resting place Mr McFadzean."

With Lennie lying solemnly, eyes closed and Nate and Bisto up front, Nate with the peaked cap, they trundled back down the road. In the back Lennie imagined himself a well loved hero of the USSR, expectant crowds lining the streets to weep and bemoan his passing. It was a pity you had to be dead to be fully appreciated. In the front seat Bisto sniggered and straightened his face again. All traces of non-involvement were gone – this was going to be a cracker.

"Ssshh!" said Nate, "we're nearly there!"

The group at the street corner watched as the hearse approached again, this time much slower and with what seemed to be a bigger dummy in the back.

"It's a person!" shouted a voice.

"A *real* person!" cried a girl's voice.

"What *are* they at?" called another in amazement.

As the hearse drew level, Nate nodded funereally for effect and Bisto made his face as long and grave as he could get it. As they passed, he tapped the glass partitioning off the back. At the signal, Lennie slowly raised his head and upper body and stared grotesquely at the small crowd. Whoops and cries rose in a wave from the footpath, along with faces full of shock, surprise, then delayed laughter with realisation that the corpse was very much undead. The improvised funeral rumbled on, the laughter and cat-calls following after it.

Instead of turning at the wide junction, Nate turned left and began driving out of the main street and along the coastal road. He wanted to give the car a longer run and intended to turn left up a road a mile out and back home via a detour. Unaware of this, Lennie lay back and prepared for the second pass.

Suddenly ahead a red light came out from the verge and began waving him down.

"Oh no!" exclaimed Nate, his heart missing a beat, "the police!"

Bisto looked across in mild panic at Nate.

"We're done for!"

In the back, Lennie was imagining a scene of weeping adoring crowds and dirges of the heart-broken Mongolian children. To die a hero, such a sweet bitterness. For such a sensation he was prepared to aim for supreme greatness himself – the fruit and veg business was how it would begin. He pictured the hordes of customers lined out behind buying his wares, waiting all day outside doorways for a glimpse of his coming. In his reverie he did not notice the hearse come to a halt – he was ruminating on the business side of his scheme.

He would need business cards, advertisements in the local press, maybe a photo shoot. He could see the headlines. 'Fresh new venture by local businessman – quality comes to the peninsula." After a while he could branch out – buy more vans, hire staff, maybe buy a farm – that way he could control the quality of the produce. He would buy more farms, become a major landowner – he would purchase houses for his workers, send Christmas presents to their children, advise them on their various problems, be their well-loved employer. He had heard of workers who called their children after their employers. Little Lennies and Lennettes would speckle future generations – maybe he would be sponsored for Mayor.

While Lennie drifted along in his sea of inflated imaginings, Nate and Bisto were sweating in the front seats as a policeman approached the driver's window. The glass partition prevented Lennie hearing any of the events unfolding in the compartment behind his head.

"Good evening Sir," said the policeman as Nate wound down the window. Nate merely nodded, no words of explanation or plea-bargaining had yet sprung into his head. What his dad would say was too demanding a vision.

"May I see your…" It was at this point that the dim red light of Sergeant Gilmore's torch glowed onto the face of the occupants of the car. What he saw brought him up short. Evidently he had flagged down two undertakers, pale-faced from their duties and returning from a scene of bereavement and sorrow. Suddenly he felt amateurish and unprofessional. It was his duty to serve the public, to ease the facilities of civilian life and provide the rule of law and order in a humanitarian setting.

And he had stopped a hearse! What was he going to do, check the tax and tyres? Sitting in the police-car behind him the young probationer sat watching his every move – he could afford no spectacle of bungling if he wanted to demonstrate and maintain proper standards. He stepped back and dropped his head in a token of deference to the duty of those who deal with the deceased.

"Pardon me gentlemen, carry on – I'm sure you have things to do. Goodnight."

Nate couldn't believe his luck! He fumbled about with the gear-stick and nodded again as he let out the clutch. Bisto stared out the front window like a rabbit caught in headlights.

As the hearse slowly pulled away a number of things happened at once.

Bisto, in unbelieving relief dropped his head back where it bumped off against the glass partition. As he did so, the young probationer police-officer looked out and saw something lying in the back of the hearse. At that very moment the sergeant's torch-light illuminated Lennie's long prone form and Lennie stirred and responded to the evident signal from the front.

Nate saw Lennie's shoulders fill the rear-view mirror and saw also the look of horror in the face of the diminishing policeman standing in the middle of the road. There was nothing else for it; he pressed the accelerator full to the floor.

"Hold on!" he shouted as he swung hard to the left and roared up a small road leading off and away from the coast road. Lennie fell over and the sergeant's senses collected themselves and did an immediate situation report.

"Right, lad!" he shouted as he jumped into the police-car's driving seat, "we've got a right one here!"

The probationer had been told on leaving the Depot that police-life was rich and varied. He had not imagined it stretching to chasing after resurrecting zombies. His mother had warned him about the Low Country. Perhaps the bank would have been a better choice after all.

"What are you doing?!" shouted Bisto as Nate flung the big Wolsey around the country bends.

"What do you think I'm doing? I'm getting us out of here! I've no licence and Dad'll kill me if I get caught at this lark!"

"He won't need to!" shouted Bisto whose expected life experiences had not included being hurled down country roads at seventy miles an hour in an ancient hearse. "*You'll* have us killed first!"

As Lennie was thrown about off roof and windows in the back – he was thinking of how soon that prospect appeared to be. Managing to grab hold of one of the guide rails, he began beating feverishly on the glass partition.

"Slow down! Tell him to slow down!" he yelled at Bisto who turned at the sound of the beating glass. With the sound of the racing engine, the squealing tyres and his own yelling, Bisto could not clearly hear the big man's cries, but it was obvious what he was complaining about. He was complaining about it himself, but Nate was not listening. He had seen blue lights in the distance behind them and he had no intention of getting a closer look.

"Pick up that mike and ask for another call-sign," barked the senior policeman. "Tell the station we are in pursuit of a possible stolen vehicle and need back-up."

The junior constable picked up the mike, he hadn't been permitted to use the radio before and he enjoyed the feeling of authority that suddenly came over him.

"This is Golf Delta seven-zero," he said, reading their own call-sign off from the dyno-taped letters above the radio. "We are in pursuit of a possible stolen car and need support… emm, over."

The radio crackled and a voice came back.

"Roger that, this is Golf Delta seven-two, can you give a position, over?"

"Heading West out of Ballydoonan on the…" what's this road called, Sir?

"Kilbride," snapped the sergeant as he swerved around evidence of some recent cow's passing.

"On the Kilbride road over."

"Roger, what is the vehicle description and occupants, over."

"Uh…" he looked to the older man beside him and saw he was busy concentrating on keeping the speeding car on the slippery narrow road – on reflection he decided not to take his attention from that particular task.

"A large black hearse with three occupants; one possibly dead... or... ahm... or maybe not, over."

Nate was driving like a man who was competing in a Formula One race. Dangerous enough though that sport is, doing it in an old Wolsey hearse with dozed cross-ply tyres and indecisive steering was considerably more so. In the back Lennie was frantically trying to kick open the back door – jumping out seemed to offer a greater chance of living than remaining in with Nate driving like a maniac.

As they approached a T-junction up ahead, Bisto threw whatever modicum of reserve he had left and screamed at the top of his voice.

"Noooooooooooooooooooo!!!"

At the same time Nate violently pulled on the handbrake and slewed the big car around, the back end swinging around to the right in a skidding handbrake turn. Lennie was thrown feet-first into the rear door and the door sprung open into a crazy smoking, screaming world of noise and rushing hedges. He immediately reversed his opinion that he had a chance of surviving a jump and hysterically tried to remain in the car – it wasn't easy.

Now on two wheels, Nate caught sight of someone departing the rear but had no time to do any more than simply observe it – the car was in danger of overturning and he wrestled madly with the wheel to get the car to right itself. Nate also saw that Bisto had fallen into the foot-well and was still screaming, his head in his hands, a wreath around his neck. Something about that seemed ominous.

Two hundred metres down the road and closing, Sergeant Gilmore saw the lights of the car ahead suddenly disappear and he became immediately suspicious.

"It's a trap, lad!" he shouted, standing on the brakes at the same time. The police car got a grip of the road and came to a stop in a remarkably short distance. It was also a very short distance from the probationer's forehead to the dashboard and it covered the distance in a remarkably short time.

"You all right son?"

"Uhhh… yes, I think so," replied the younger man rubbing his head.

"Good, stop the messing about then and come with me." With that the sergeant leapt out of the car and grabbed his torch. "You go out ten feet to the left in the field, keep in line and give me cover as I proceed up the road – if you hear me shout run to the road – you know how to use that thing I hope?" He pointed to the probationer's side holster with its nine millimetre Walther Pistol. He had already unclipped the fastener on his Ruger Magnum.

"Y…yes, I…"

"Good, keep your head down lad and your eyes peeled." With that he faded into the darkness, his torch off, his dark green uniform an invisible cloak. The probationer looked at the holster on his belt and wondered if his mum had kept the bank clerk application forms.

A dim figure stood vaguely outlined against the dark night sky. He appeared to be standing and facing the sergeant as he approached. Keeping down, the sergeant was sure he hadn't seen him yet. What was he doing? Where was the car?

At thirty feet off he gave a call.

"You, you there! This is the police. Stay where you are – do not move!" The figure remained where he was and made no motion. Patting the revolver at his side, he scanned the hedges. Nothing. He moved up closer and put his torch out at arm's length in his left hand. He flicked it on and pointed it at the man up ahead. The red-faced man stared back unblinking into the light as the sergeant approached – he seemed to have no shoes on and…

"Constable!"

The noise of his heart beating almost drowned it out, but he heard the sergeant's strident voice and ran to the hedge, his pistol held out straight in front of him in both hands. This was it then!

"You can put that away, lad," said the sergeant brusquely, "this fellow's not about to do much." He dragged a figure in overalls up to the hedge.

"One dummy – our hearse has got clean away. Do you think we can do this character with leaving the scene of an accident? Look, they've left their bumper behind."

After colliding off the earth bank, Nate had managed to regain control of the Wolsey, albeit with no lights since he had left a good bit of the front of the hearse in the hedge. He drove on but at a much slower pace, trying to guide the car between the hedges and expecting blue lights behind him at any moment. They never came.

At last they reached the McFadzean farm and Nate guided the car down to the shed. Turning off the engine he gave a sigh of relief and then suddenly sat bolt upright.

"Lennie fell out!" he exclaimed. A second later a voice at the window made him bump his head off the ceiling cloth.

"Lennie didn't fall out but no thanks to you, you madman!"

It was Lennie and he looked tousled and ruffled. Bisto's voice drifted up from the foot-well.

"Never, never, never ever am I getting back in this car. Never, never, never."

"I nearly fell out," added Lennie at the window, "I don't know how I'm still alive."

"*Somebody* fell out," said Nate, perplexed. "What happened?"

"That was that stupid dummy, it flew out and tumbled into the hedge. At least it managed to escape."

"Where'd the police go?" asked Nate.

"I neither know nor care," said Lennie. "I'm going home, and no, I don't want a lift." He turned to go but remembered Bisto. "Are you coming?"

"What about the car? It got a bit damaged," said Nate, "I'm sure we can fix it though."

"You can keep the car," replied Lennie. "I've gone right off fruit and veg – a person can only take so much excitement."

Bisto untangled himself from the ball he had curled himself into and shakily got out of the car.

"By the way, I wasn't screaming, I was just trying to tell you to look out for the hedge."

"Oh, right," said Nate.

"And one last thing," added Lennie as they turned to walk off into the darkness, "you really need to get a driving licence."

Nate sat for a few more minutes in the car and considered their narrow escape. The hearse would have to stay in the shed for some time now until the hullabaloo had died down. Thankfully apart from a chrome bumper and few bits of broken lights they had left no traceable evidence where he had struck the bank. In the meantime, perhaps getting around to applying for that licence wasn't such a bad idea after all; in fact, he still had the application in his overalls' pocket. He got out of the car and went to the shed door.

Now *where* were those overalls?

7.

THE LONG DISTANCE ROMANCE

Will Patterson's life was a misery. He was in love.

From what he had read in books and seen in films on TV, love was not supposed to be a misery, but he was in love and he discovered that it was not laughter and joy, birds twittering and flowers blooming – it was just misery.

The object of his love was not. The object of his ardour was beautiful, graceful and pain in the chest achingly unreachable. Liz McCutcheon got on his bus every day on her way to school; she was in fifth form now and he had had just left. He continued to travel on the same bus that had been his transport to education for seven years as it transformed into his means of getting to work. On leaving school he had got an apprenticeship with Shorts, a large aircraft factory in Belfast but he had gone from the world of education to the one of employment without losing any of his admiration for the dark haired girl who got on every morning looking as fresh as a daisy and as beautiful to him as it was possible for anyone to be.

Liz McCutcheon was not unreachable because she had spurned him, or rejected any of his advances – no, Liz was unreachable simply because

Will had made none. He would have loved to just take the seat beside her some morning and happily break into an easy conversation about things that would make her laugh and smile into his face. He longed to do that, he dreamed of doing that, but somehow the thought of a cold shoulder or an emotionless response from the girl he had come to think of as simply the most attractive and fascinating person he could imagine was too much to risk incurring.

He was not normally so retiring; in fact, Will was a cheerful and happy eighteen year old and no-one who knew him was aware of any of the turmoil that churned within him when Liz McCutcheon's slim and graceful form slid onto her seat and turned her slender neck towards the window. A couple of times some other boy had sat beside her and at those times Will would burn with envy and self recrimination. If he lost her, if someone else made the move, he had only himself to blame – his own inaction would have sealed his fate and he would live forever with the knowledge that he had loved and lost without even having fired a shot.

It was an absolute cliché, a scene from a Mills and Boon that happened one Thursday on the number ten bus heading up the peninsula. He had been sitting one seat behind the lovely girl that morning when, as she got off in Ards, she dropped something at her seat. She was off before Will had time to react, but when he leaned forward to see what had fallen, he saw it was a handkerchief. Looking around furtively and seeing that he alone had seen the event, he put out a hand and picked it up.

It was a dusty pale pink, with tiny blue flowers stitched in one corner and it was neatly folded and freshly ironed. Without thinking, he slipped it into his pocket and feigned innocence.

Of course, it *was* innocence but the possession made him feel oddly like a thief. What else should he have done, stopped the bus, chased her down the street? He knew that if someone else had seen it, for them it would have been a non-event – girl drops handkerchief – bus drives on – girl has no more handkerchief; but for him? He felt like he had engineered it – it wouldn't have happened if he hadn't wanted it so much. He was an intruder, a taker of things too valuable for hands like his, somehow it seemed too personal, too close, too intense, like peering in through her bedroom window and watching her sleep, like opening her mail and secretly reading her letters. This was not just any old handkerchief, this was *her* handkerchief.

At tea-break time in work he brought the soft and feminine little handkerchief out of his pocket and smoothed it with his fingers. A wistful smile grew on his face as he thought of its gentle owner. Raising it to his face he caught a fragrance that so vividly placed Liz's face right before him that he gave a small start. It came out of his pocket quite a few times the rest of the day. What a mystery was a girl – what a wonderfully different creature they were. What did they think of, what kind of things caught their attention, filled their thoughts? If only he could know, perhaps he would know how to speak to the girl who filled his own.

In school, Liz told her friend Belinda about dropping the hankie. It provided enough conversation for all of lunch-break and the whole journey home in the bus.

Will's bus journey home each night was a later one than the school bus so seeing Liz at night was a pleasure he never enjoyed. This night however Liz's brother Nathan had stayed late for Scripture Union and when he got on he came over and sat beside Will.

"Hi, Will," said Nathan. Nathan did not know Will well, but he knew him well enough to talk to.

"How's you?" smiled Will. "You're late tonight; kept back for blowing up the school again?" Nathan's episode with the fume cupboard was one of the highlights of the school the year before.

"I'm going to have to join the French Foreign Legion," said Nathan. "At least they'll let me forget!"

Will briefly considered giving Nathan his sister's handkerchief but quickly talked himself out of it. He could give it to him to return to Liz another day – maybe tomorrow, or the day after. Maybe he would even return it to her himself, he lied to himself, knowing it was a lie; he had guts like guts – soft and flabby.

"The Young Farmers are on tonight in the Masonic hall. You should come, you haven't been for a while," said Will, glad to have the opportunity to talk to Liz's brother; who knew? Maybe Nathan would mention to Liz who he had been talking to. He imagined his name being spoken in Liz's house – it gave him a tingle just to think of it.

"Hi Liz, I was talking to Will Patterson on the bus – you know, he's a right sort."

"Oh," Liz would say, her face brightening, "Will Patterson? He does seem a nice person, why don't you ask him round some Saturday? I'll make us all some tea."

Right. And pigs would roar overhead in Harrier jump-jets too.

"What's on tonight anyway?" asked Nathan. True enough, he hadn't been for three or four weeks and it could sometimes be good fun. He wasn't from an actual farming family himself, but then it wasn't a prerequisite for membership anyway.

"Banbridge are coming down for a debate. Ballydoonan is proposing the motion that the European Common Agricultural Policy is ineffective and harmful to farming. Banbridge have to oppose the motion. Fun, eh?" Will grimaced and then smiled. "You should come anyway, there's a quiz and supper afterwards."

Nathan ended up going. His dad was helping out in the Young Farmers' choir practise for some thing or other they were doing at the Queen's hall in Newtownards later in the year. Not doing anything else, Nathan took the lift and ended up sitting beside Will again. The Masonic hall had two floors – an upstairs and a downstairs. The upstairs was out of bounds and was where the Masons did all their secret stuff. Nathan had once peeked in through the keyhole of the locked door and saw what looked like a courtroom. Wooden benches faced a dock-like affair and dark curtains surrounded a lectern. He imagined bare-legged people killing goats, drinking blood and swishing great swords about. On reflection, that might have been what the Orangemen did and since he was never quite sure if they were the same sort of thing or not, it made little difference to him. He had a friend whose dad was in the Masons and he had told his friend to 'never join, son. I'm in and it's too late for me – but you keep well away.' His friend had told him that his dad had said the only way to leave was by being hanged and then cut into four pieces, but then the same friend had told him that he himself had been taken up by aliens one night into a flying saucer and mind-wiped. It made his testimony was somewhat suspect. He didn't doubt however that he had been mind-wiped somewhere or other.

The group debating and public speaking were actually events that Nathan enjoyed in the YFC. He had been in a few himself and the opportunity to present a case or take apart another's was like boxing except without the sore face afterwards. One team would propose a motion and the first of their three speakers would be given three minutes to present their case. The opposer's first speaker would then present the opposition viewpoint, being given the same three minutes. The second speakers would present further reinforcement to their arguments for half their time and oppose the opposition's first speaker in the second minute and a half. The last speaker would basically ridicule the whole premise of the other team's argument and finish with a resounding confirmation of their own. A well presented argument won applause and the corresponding club's spectators attempted to bend the judgment of the adjudicator by the volume of their appreciation. The debater was always assured of a rewardingly loud conclusion to their speech.

Nathan had once been first speaker on the proposal side of a motion entitled 'This house believes that Euthanasia is wrong'. Unfortunately he had got it into his head that Euthanasia was a country somewhere near Hungary and part of Russia. He had also given himself very little in the way of research time – he wrote the speech between tea-time and going to the club – about one hour. The bemused looks of the audience as he berated the other team for condoning communism, Stalin and state-run agriculture (a clever farming reference he had popped in) had not dawned on him until the opposition got up and proposed killing off old people. He knew communism was bad, but now they were really taking the biscuit.

That night's debate was nowhere near as malevolent but it didn't stop the debaters making it sound so.

"The C.A.P. is a financial disaster, a bureaucratic debacle and an Orwellian nightmare," Ballydoonan's Y.F.C. final speaker was saying. He had been busy with the thesaurus then.

"Any person who defends such an utterly discredited scheme demonstrates only that he failed to grasp any realistic hold on reason and common sense long ago or is making the argument merely in a vain and unconvincing attempt to win a debate for their club! I move the motion!" Uproarious approval from Ballydoonan, boos and hisses from the equally passionate Banbridge.

The trouble with having to defend or attack a motion was that you actually sometimes convinced yourself. Afterwards, during supper the antagonists continued the argument about the Common Agricultural Policy and had to be stopped by the sensible detached who hadn't listened to the actual discourse anyway. The Young Farmers' Clubs were more about girl hunting than listening to rubbish about who thought what about whatever. Unless you were a girl of course, then it was about boy hunting. And some farmers' daughters were pretty good at it.

As it happened one of the Banbridge girls had been sitting beside Nathan and Will during the debate. Now and then she had smiled over to Nathan who smiled politely back and quickly got back to the serious business of applauding his team's magnificent reasonings. During supper he had helped by pouring out tea from the enormous battered teapots that emerged from hiding on such occasions and again he got a coy grin from a girl he vaguely recognised as the one who had smiled earlier.

The quiz was a straight contest between the two clubs and each person on either club was asked one question each. The winning team was the one whose members had answered most questions correct. An independent Y.F.C. president asked the questions and she had an assistant who totted up the scores. Each club had all its names put into a hat and the person drawn next was the one asked. Ballydoonan had twenty-two members along that night and Banbridge sixteen, so the first six names were drawn from Ballydoonan's as an elimination list. Will sighed with relief as his name was called. Nathan groaned as the sixth was called; his was not one of them.

"Don't worry," said Will, "as long as you're not last nobody cares how you do. Besides, it's only a bit of crack." It was all right for him, thought Nathan, he was off the hook.

Four names were drawn from each hat and the eight protagonists took their seats at the front of the room. Nathan sat with Will and wished he had been called to get it over with.

"Geography," declared the Craigabride president, Mrs Wallace. "One question each; no conferring."

As Nathan listened, he grew slightly easier. He liked Geography, the questions weren't hard. Maybe it wouldn't be so bad.

"Name the capital of Argentina?" asked the portly lady.

"Buenos Aries," whispered Nathan absently to the person beside him. It was the grinning girl. She grinned again.

"Uh… Madrid?" The sigh of disapproval from the room that said 'What do you mean, you didn't know that?' only arose when the correct answer was given by the assistant.

Nathan wasn't in the next batch of four Ballydoonan brainboxes either, and he was glad he wasn't. The next round was 'Farm Health and Safety.' Like as if he knew what chemicals were produced in effluent. He hoped his subject would be more straightforward. He also fervently hoped he was not going to be in the last group.

The third group was made up of another four on each side, none of which was Nathan. He shook his head and looked forlorn. The score was still close enough for one or two marks to make the difference – maybe the next round would be 'letters of the Alphabet' or something his mildly panicking head could cope with.

As his name was called for the last round, he arose and felt a tap on his side. It was the girl again. In his perturbed state he did not pay much attention to her appearance but he saw her grin again and he turned to take his place. Will put his thumbs up and gave a wink. "Easy," he mouthed. Nathan prayed he was right. Not only had Nathan managed to get picked for the final batch, by the time he got to the stage the only chair left was the one in the position for the last question. It couldn't get worse, he thought.

He was wrong.

"This round is mental maths," announced Mrs Wallace with a big silly smile on her rosy-cheeked face. Nathan could have punched it.

Banbridge got to go first. Nathan waited to hear what level the maths was set at – not that any level was within the bounds of his mathematical abilities. Zero was a hard standard to get beneath.

"If a farmer digs a pond with a radius of eight feet, and he wants to build a fence totally encircling it at a distance of two feet from the water, what length will the fence be?" Mrs Wallace's face plumped out as her wide mouth grinned and pushed out her cheeks. Nathan did a quick calculation. He could possibly dash to the back door and be out in under four seconds. The Banbridge swot must have been some kind of a genius, for after a bit of forehead rubbing and face pulling, he got the correct answer. Nathan wondered if he could dive through the window – being torn to bits by broken glass was beginning to look preferable to the situation gradually looming in his direction.

Each question was worth two marks and one mark was awarded if you knew the answer to the opposing team's wrong reply. Banbridge had led most of the way but at their last question they got lost in an algebraic mist and Ballydoonan scraped back another point by knowing something about weight gain in a Hertfordshire bull calf. It wasn't enough though and with the score at twenty six to Banbridge, twenty five to Ballydoonan all eyes turned to Nathan.

He suddenly felt like a window cleaner who has accidentally walked onto the Pope's balcony in St. Peter's square and frozen as ten thousand faces turned expectant gazes onto him and his Windolene. The room hushed and Mrs Wallace brought her pudgy cheeks around with a smile of reassurance. The poor woman had simply no idea. Down in the audience Will tried to look encouraging but Nathan knew it was hopeless; he wondered if alien spacecraft flew by and mind-wiped people often. He would have gladly donated his brains to being sucked right out of his head at that actual moment – at least it would have given him some kind of an excuse.

"Just before I ask the last question, Miss Perry will tell us the scores," said the Craigabride president, a quite uncalled for remark Nathan thought.

"Twenty five to Ballydoonan, twenty six to Banbridge," said the assistant. Nathan felt the world lean on his head and he wished it would bury him.

"Last question for Ballydoonan and last question of the competition," announced Mrs Wallace. "If a poultry-keeper has two thousand laying hens and two thirds lay seventy five percent of the eggs while…"

That was as much as Nathan heard; there was no point in hearing any more. Basically a stack of chickens laid a stack of eggs and some kind of an answer was required. He caught vaguely that it was to be expressed in percentage terms but that was about as much as he understood. He became suddenly aware that the room had quietened and was waiting for him. In the audience he caught sight of Will Patterson shading his eyes as if trying to avoid Nathan's embarrassment. For Nathan there was no avoidance. The door could not be rushed at – the aliens weren't coming – it was all down to him.

In a sudden moment of clarity he devised a strategy – he would look as if he was working out the answer. Placing his hand beneath his chin he lowered his eyebrows and looked studious. "Mmm," he said.

What kind of a number should he say? Ten percent? Twenty three? A hundred and sixty five and a half? Who knew? He certainly didn't.

"Ahmmm," he continued. The room waited, breath baited.

"Well, I… yes, mmm, how many? Yes… right," A pin could have been heard just falling through the air, let alone hitting the ground. Sixty percent? Did that sound stupid? It was somewhere near the middle so perhaps it would do – besides six out of ten eggs had to be not too bad for an average chicken. Six out of ten what? What was the stupid question again? Oh stuff it, just say something.

"Ahmm… Sixty percent," he pronounced at last. The room opened its massed eyes wide and looked to the quiz mistress. She looked at her page and then back at Nathan. Nathan looked blankly back at her and she checked her sheet again.

"Did you say sixty percent?"

Did he? Was that what he said? What a twit.

"Yes."

"The correct answer is… sixty percent!"

There was a sudden eruption of noise in the room as the Ballydoonan Young Farmers cheered with agricultural gusto the maths genius in their midst. Ballydoonan had won the inter-club quiz against Banbridge for the first time in anyone's memory. Banbridge was given a round of magnanimous applause and Ballydoonan was given a burst of hand-clapping that must have brought the blood to every set of palms in the room. But the loudest and longest was kept for Nathan.

"You were brilliant," said Will trying not to look too surprised, "That was a really difficult question, for a minute I thought you were totally stumped. I don't know how you did it."

Before Nathan had time to reply, Mrs McKee, the Ballydoonan president appeared, face beaming and alive with excitement.

"Nathan McCutcheon! You are wonderful! How did you ever manage such a complicated piece of maths in your head? I had to use a pen and paper and you got the answer before me! Obviously you will have to be made part of the inter-county team, we could hardly do without that brain of yours now could we?" She smiled and looked approvingly at her protégé. "Well done again! Oh… give me a hug!" With that she grabbed Nathan and squeezed into him all her feelings of appreciation, pride and delight. After some more effusing and expression of gratefulness, she moved on to the rest of the room to bask in her own reflected glory. Nathan logged 'sixty percent' in a corner of his brain for future use. It might come in handy again – it was clearly a number that when grasped out of nowhere had the power to bring wonderful results.

Maybe he was better at maths than he had credited himself with.

Half an hour later the room had emptied as people left for home and farm. Nathan's dad pulled up outside and Nathan went to leave.

"Oh, I forgot!" said Will, who had waited with him. "I was to give you this, a girl from Banbridge gave it to me for you; probably congratulations for doing so well in the quiz – see you about!" Will headed off to his motorcycle and Nathan put the note in his pocket; it was too dark to read it now anyway.

Will waited to see if Liz was in the car and when it was clear she wasn't, he put on his helmet and kick-started his wee Suzuki – the handkerchief was still in his pocket.

Bob McCutcheon was always looking out for a bargain. Unfortunately, good and cheap were not often qualities he managed to get together in the one item. Mystery jams, soups without taste and biscuits like putty. The motorcycle was of the same ilk, just bigger. It arrived in the boot at the back of the bus.

Nathan had just arrived home from school one day when he saw the long blue and white Ulsterbus coming up the lane. At first he thought he had done something wrong and the school bus was chasing him up the lane, but as it turned into the yard he saw his dad's face at the wheel and reckoned there were a couple of interesting minutes ahead.

"Here son, give me a hand at the back," called his dad jumping out of the air-powered doors. Nathan followed his dad to the back where he had already got the rear boot doors open. Inside, lying on its side was a motorcycle.

"Whose is that Dad?" he asked curiously. His dad was already hauling at the front wheel.

"Ours, son," replied his dad. "I bought it from a man with one ear who sells sawdust near Newtownards." It was an entirely reasonable answer from his dad's point of view. Nathan just shrugged and grabbed hold of a rear shock absorber. It was soon out and his father began wheeling it quickly to the back shed.

"Keep an eye on the bus son, I'll be straight back." Nathan nodded and wondered what the bus was likely to do that it needed watched. The front door was still open so he got on board and sat down on the driver's seat. All of a sudden, an idea struck him and he looked carefully at the controls.

The bus was semi-automatic and had only two pedals – the brake and the accelerator. There was a short stubby gear-stick that ran in a tracked slot with three forward and one reverse gear. Behind the bus lay a long silage shed, empty now and big enough to reverse the bus into twice over. The bus was still ticking over and so it was a simple matter of paying keen attention to the mirrors, letting off the handbrake, engaging reverse gear and applying a little pressure to the throttle. The bus began to slowly back up and Nathan began to grin. By the time he had withdrawn back into the shadows of the barn he was laughing out loud. When his dad appeared and actually scratched his head as he looked around, Nathan whooped like a parrot.

When his dad looked suitably frustrated, Nathan blew the horn and revved the engine to get his attention. Unfortunately he had not disengaged reverse and the bus took a backward leap toward the rear wall. It was all Nathan could do to violently slam on the brakes and get the bus halted inches from the solid concrete. He let out a relieved gasp and at the same time heard a soft thud at the back of the bus followed by what sounded like a moan. It was too dark to see what it was but by now Bob McCutcheon's shadow fell over the doorway.

"What do you think you are doing?" he said, his face unsmiling.

Nathan grinned as a hopeful ice-breaker.

"You want to have seen your face looking for your big empty bus dad!" laughed Nathan. "I got you a good one there!" His dad put his hand to his forehead and spoke more loudly than Nathan reckoned he needed to.

"Sorry about that – he's young – a bit over enthusiastic." He then got back into the seat and glared at Nathan.

"What…?" began Nathan, realising slowly that his dad was not actually speaking to him. By now he had taken control of the bus and was driving it out of the shed. Light illuminated the rear of the bus where to Nathan's extreme surprise he saw two old ladies. They were dusting themselves off after an apparent introduction with the floor of the bus.

"Oh, I… um…"

"Quite," said his dad.

As the bus retired back down the lane Nathan remembered the motorcycle and went to have a look. His dad had locked the shed door but Nathan knew that locks only ever kept honest people out – he climbed in the window.

It was a Honda 90. It sat upright on its centre stand in the middle of the cluttered shed, the light from the window falling on its brown frame and cream plastic wind guard. The front wheel seemed to be oddly turned to one side and when he tried to straighten the handlebars it become evident that the front forks were bent and warped. Obviously the bike had been involved in a frontal accident. He wondered if that had anything to do with the previous owner's single-eared condition. Now what did his dad want with a crashed motorcycle? There was only one real answer – it must have been cheap.

Over the next couple of weeks Nathan pestered his dad to allow him to try out the bike on the lane. At first it was a definite "No".

"I got the motorcycle to ride to work in the mornings," he explained to the breakfast table one morning. The breakfast table waited to hear more.

"If I take the bike then Mum will have the car now and then. If it's too wet then I'll take the car. No-one *else* is to play with the motorcycle, or try riding it without my permission." The eye cocked accusingly at Nathan made it clear who the *else* was.

"Aw, but Dad, can't I even…"

"No."

"But I'll be really carefu…"

"No again."

"But…"

"Is 'no' a difficult word Ellie?" said his dad looking across the table.

"It is when you're a teenager dear," smiled back his wife. "They prefer words like 'Yes' or even 'I'll think about it.' Don't you remember being seventeen?"

"Hmmph," grumbled his dad. "When I was seventeen I'd been working for three years and was riding ten miles a day to work on a bicycle."

"Mmmm," replied Nathan's mum absently. "Distance increases with years removed from the experience I see. I seem to remember it being nearer two."

"Well, whatever," admitted the man who should have known better than to lay down the law when he was presenting dodgy facts. "I'll think about the bike."

Bob McCutcheon tried riding the bike once himself but quickly discovered that it was a lot less like a pleasant alternative to car transportation than he had imagined. For one thing, he was a bit wobbly at slow speed, so wobbly that he found himself unable to prevent himself from dribbling across the white line into the oncoming traffic. It was not an experience conducive to a long life of motorized cycling enjoyment. Another problem was the bike itself; it wanted to continually drive over the hedge to the left – not due to any actual malice on the part of the Honda itself, it was because it was badly out of line after its one eared sawdust seller's accident. Getting it fixed would have been the obvious answer but Bob McCutcheon had not bought a bargain to spend money on it. After his first and only test ride of the motorcycle, Nathan's dad rubbed his aching arms, sore from wrestling the handle-bars continually to the right and parked it unceremoniously in the shed. This time there was no locking – whoever wanted the darned thing was welcome to it.

So it was that by default the Honda 90 became the preserve of Nathan McCutcheon. His dad's unwillingness to share his motor driven bicycle now rapidly fading like the promises of a newly elected local councillor, Nathan took to riding the bike up and down the lane, up and down the fields and even up and down the quiet road at the bottom of the lane on quiet evenings. When nobody was about. With a scarf over his face. When it refused to start one morning despite everything Nathan tried to get it going, even he gave it the cold shoulder and shut the door on its wonky frame. For a time at least, the motorbike was forgotten.

It was a couple of days after the inter-club quiz that Nathan remem-bered the note. The other thing that reminded him was his mum taking it out of his pocket when washing his jeans. She asked Nathan about it.

"I see romance is in the air," she said suggestively to her son as he came into the kitchen for a biscuit.

"Oh," said Nathan uncomprehending. "Liz?"

"You're very cool about that," said his mother raising her eyebrows, "Nice name, mmm?"

"What?"

"This girl of yours," replied his mum, peering at the note in her hand, "it says *Linda* here."

Nathan looked at his mother whose mental capabilities had obviously just taken a turn for the worse.

"What girl of mine?" Ellie gave her son the piece of paper and Nathan examined it carefully. It didn't say much, just 'You were great tonight. Linda. Banbridge 3642.' The light bulb clicked – the girl at the Young Farmers' quiz.

"Ah, Will gave me that," explained Nathan reddening slightly. Liz had just walked into the kitchen in her dressing gown and slippers.

"Will Patterson? What about him?"

"Just a note," dismissed Nathan.

"Mmm, just a note?" repeated their mum.

"Is it…ahem. Is it for me?" Liz almost whispered, her chest suddenly feeling very strange.

"No, don't be daft, what would Will Patterson want to give you a note for? It's for me, but not from Will, it's… oh for goodness sakes, it's nothing, just a dopey note!" He turned and left the kitchen biscuitless and thoughtful. Ellie McCutcheon gave her daughter a furtive look. Liz was silent and looking thoughtful too – interesting.

It was all the note said. Just 'You were great tonight. Linda,' and then the telephone number. Nathan tried to remember the face of the girl who had written the note and found it a hazy picture. She had dark hair and… and that was about it. She might have been fat or thin, tall or short or a whole lot of things, Nathan just couldn't remember, he had been too busy worrying about the quiz. Maybe she was pretty? That would be nice; she had given him her phone number – he could always phone her but then that wouldn't tell him what she looked like.

"Hello, is that Linda? Nathan McCutcheon here from Ballydoonan. Just checking, are you fat and ugly or slim and pretty?" Not a good starting line he concluded. He decided to think more about it.

"If you had the chance to speak to a girl who you might want to well, you know, what would you say?"

Will looked across at Nathan and wondered at the question. Had Nathan guessed about how he felt about Liz? His stomach gave a quick jitter.

"What do you mean? To let her know how you feel?"

"No, let's say she already… what if she already seems to like you but maybe you're not too sure what *you* think?"

Wills stomach did a double jitter.

"Could you be sure she likes you?"

"Yeah, I think so," replied Nathan. Outside the bus window Strangford Lough passed by and thousands of Brent geese covered the wide tidal sands moving like a vast herd of bison grazing on the prairies. They came over for the eel grass – apparently in that few acres of sand waddled the greater proportion of the world's population of Brent geese. He wondered how girl and boy geese got introduced. Since they all looked the same to Nathan it was hardly a matter of liking the looks of one another.

Will was thinking. His stomach was jittering and at the other side of the bus the lovely Liz McCutcheon looked out the window and knew nothing of his feelings.

"Well, it would be up to you then. You must let her know how you feel. If you lose her now you may never get another chance. Just get up and speak to her, ask her if she'd like to go to see a film, or maybe come to your youth group with you some night. Don't just let it pass you by Nathan. *Carpe Diem.*"

"What?" Nathan had only been half listening. He was thinking that if an aircraft suddenly lost control and crashed right into the middle of the Brent geese, the species would be made extinct in a moment. Even the Dodo took a hundred years to achieve that.

"Seize the day. That's what it means. Just go for it." Having delivered his own advice, he also knew he was no nearer approaching Nathan's sister.

"Oh, right. Well, thanks Will. Here, you don't know anything about motorcycles do you?"

Three days later Liz was combing her hair at the front door and look-ing across the North Channel to the Galloway hills when she saw a motorcycle slow and turn up their lane.

"There's someone coming on a motorcycle," she called into the house to no-one in particular. Nathan's voice responded from his room.

"That'll be Will Patterson," he said, ridiculously calmly, Liz thought.

"What? Why… what is, why is he coming?" She speeded up her comb-ing. Will Patterson was coming to their house? Why? Surely not…? Oh her hair was a mess! Oh no! She had no shoes on!

Nathan strolled out into the hallway and passed Liz in her excited state.

"He's going to look at the motorcycle – he knows about bikes."

"But you never said… why didn't you say he was coming? Oh Nathan!" Liz flitted off into her room.

"I hardly think he'll care what you're dressed in if that's what you mean," said Nathan not realising just what a true statement he had made. "He's here to help me with the bike; he's hardly here to see you, is he?" 'Girls!' dismissed Nathan. They had absolutely no clue.

Will pulled off his helmet and gave Nathan a wide grin.

"Well, where is she?" he asked, rattling a small toolbox he had lashed on behind him. Liz was hiding behind the front room window and gave a small start.

"In the shed at the back," explained Nathan as he led Will around to the Honda. Liz ran around to look through the kitchen window and ran into her mum coming out of the bathroom.

"Where are you off to in such a hurry?" she asked.

"Oh, nowhere mum, just getting a drink of water."

"Mmm, is there a water shortage or something? Where did Nathan go? Who was on the motorcycle?"

"Motorcycle? Oh, *that* motorcycle. I don't know."

Liz's mum suddenly caught sight of something moving out in the back yard. She went over to the kitchen window and saw Nathan and someone else pulling the Honda out of the shed.

"Who's that with Nathan?"

"I don't know; Nate McFadzean?" tried Liz innocently.

"No, no, it's Margaret Patterson's son Will, isn't it?" Ellie glanced at her daughter and thought she caught a slight flush before she turned away.

"Maybe. Have you seen my denim skirt?" Without waiting for a reply Liz left the kitchen and returned to her room. She would strangle Nathan in his sleep some night.

Will would have preferred to have had a more difficult job of it. Unfortunately he discovered the fault quite quickly – it was a disconnected high tension lead from the coil to the spark plug. A longer job would have given some hope of seeing Liz around the place and maybe… who was he kidding, maybe nothing.

"It's a bit out of alignment, isn't it?" commented Will as it kicked into life. "What did you do to it?"

"That's the way Dad buys things, if it was straight it wouldn't be here, trust me."

"You do know how to get another eight or nine miles an hour out of these step-throughs don't you?" asked Will seeing by Nathan's expression that he did not.

"I've had it at about fifty-five," said Nathan, "you mean I could do over sixty?"

"Yep, all you do is take off that plastic knee guard, wind guard contraption. With the wind resistance lowered you'll be surprised what she'll do." Suddenly a call from the house made them both look up.

"Nathan! I've some tea and fruit loaf for you and your friend!" It was Nathan's mum calling from the kitchen window.

"So you're at work now?" enquired Ellie as the boys took their seats at the kitchen table. "And what are you working at?"

"I'm a trainee draughtsman at Shorts," replied Will.

"You design aeroplanes? That must be interesting," said Mrs Mc-Cutcheon impressed.

"Not quite," grinned Will. "At the minute I'm drawing a wing nut. Two weeks work and my boss says it looks like Plug out of the Bash Street Kids."

"Bash Street Kids?"

"Out of the *Beano* mum," explained Nathan, "and I've seen some of his drawings, they're really good."

"Thanks for the tea," said Will brushing off the compliment, "did you make the cake yourself? It's really nice." He was being quite genuine, he had never tasted fruit loaf like that before.

"Thank you, Will. Nathan just wolfs it down, I doubt if he even knows what he's eating, isn't that right, son?"

Nathan scowled. He would have spoken but his mouth was crammed full.

"Liz makes lovely tray bakes you know, would you like one?" She looked straight at Will and smiled.

"Oh, I, yes, that would be lovely, if that's O.K, maybe she has them for someone else?"

Ellie looked into a tin and shook her head.

"I hardly think so… oh! Dear me, we're completely out. Sure when you call again Liz will have made some more."

In the hallway where she was listening in to the conversation, Liz frowned at her mother's interference. Her mother was being so embarrassing – what would Will Patterson think? He probably thought he was in a house of nutcases. Girls didn't bake any more; they listened to pop music and giggled at boys. She felt so old fashioned. Will Patterson probably never even knew she existed.

Will Patterson was trying not to choke on a raisin.

"Thanks Mrs McCutcheon – anyway, I'd best get going soon, thanks again."

Ellie watched as Will and Nathan chatted and laughed in the yard. He seemed a right lad. Now, where did Liz go?

"Won't you stay on for a bit?" asked Nathan. "I've a track made around the field. We could time each other on the bike?"

Will laughed again. He really did have to go, he had promised his brother he would help lay some roof insulation in his loft and he was probably already waiting for him.

"Thanks anyway but I'd best head on, did you see my gloves?"

"Whose are these?" said Liz as she removed a pair of gloves from the seat she was about to sit on.

"Oh, those will be the Patterson boy's," answered her mother. "He and Nathan were in having a wee cup of tea a minute ago, nip out and give them to him before he goes will you?" Before Liz had time to think of a reasonable excuse not to, she found herself in the yard.

Will looked up and saw Liz come out the back door. Her long dark hair lay softly on her shoulders and she was slender and elf-like in her denim skirt and light pink long sleeved top. He had never seen a more beautiful vision. He was smitten and he knew it. Every time he saw her he felt a pang of longing. Longing in the sense that he longed to know everything about her. He wanted to be close to her, to catch the perfume of her presence, to hear the music of her voice. He wanted just to be near her, to protect and cherish everything about her. He had never felt like this before and he knew that he had got it bad. He also knew there was nothing he could do about it.

"Are these yours, Will?" she said holding out his gloves. Hearing her say his name made his day perfect no matter what else followed. He spurred himself to speak.

"Oh, thanks, yes, I must have left them in the kitchen, thanks."

As Liz handed over the gloves, a sudden pang of guilt stabbed him. He still had the handkerchief in his pocket.

"Em, actually, I have something of yours, you dropped it in the bus and I meant, I forgot to give it to Nathan to give to you, here, it's your handkerchief." With a twinge of loss overtaking his sense of guilt, he brought out the dusky pink handkerchief.

Liz looked taken aback for a second before she quickly composed herself.

"On the bus? Thank you. You got the bike going then?" Nathan had kicked the bike and it easily purred into life.

"Yeah, just a simple fault." He gave a smile and Liz smiled back. He was really nice. After a slight pause she turned to go.

"Bye," she said. Will smiled again.

"Yep, see you." It would have been a most unsatisfactory end except for one thing. She had not taken the little hankie. It still lay in his hand – in a moment it was back in his pocket.

Later that night Nathan turned the note over in his hand. 'Linda,' it didn't tell him much, he tried to remember the girl who sat to his left at the quiz. Dark hair, that was about it. Dark hair was nice though, he liked dark hair.

Bringing the phone on its long cord into his bedroom, he dialled the number and after a couple of rings a girl's voice sounded on the other end.

"Hello? Banbridge 3642, can I help you?"

"Hi," said Nathan, "is that Linda?"

"No, this is Emma."

"Oh, right, is Linda in?"

"Yes, can I say who's calling please?" The voice was young, probably a younger sister, thought Nathan.

"Er, could you tell her it's Nathan McCutcheon, from Ballydoonan."

Nathan heard the girl call out into the house.

"Linda! It's a bo-hoy! On the pho-hone!" There was a long pause in which he heard muffled giggling. He would have put the phone down except that a voice suddenly came on the line.

"Hello, Linda here, is that Nathan?"

The conversation went on for a few minutes and was about nothing in particular, what subjects each was doing at school, what Banbridge had to offer – the girl made it clear she thought that that was nothing. At the end of it Nathan found he had made a rash promise to come over to visit the following Saturday. Armed with her address and a vague idea of directions once he got there, he said goodbye and set down the phone.

He sat for a while and looked at the phone. He had thought arranging to see a girl would have been harder. It didn't quite occur to him that most of the arranging had not been done by him.

"So how are you going to get to Banbridge?" asked Nate McFadzean. "Do you even know where it is?"

Nathan had explained to his friend about the note and the girl when he was over helping Nate dig a hole during the week. The hole was for burying several very old rusty reels of barbed wire that had lain in the yard for as long as Nate could remember. His dad had asked him to clear up the yard and burying the coils of wire seemed as good a way of getting rid of them as any. In a couple of years he reckoned they would rust to nothing.

"I checked it on the map, once we get to Comber I take a bearing with a compass, 198 degrees South, South-West."

"We? Compass bearing? You sound like you have this all planned out already," said Nate who was still waiting to hear what plans he had for travelling the sixty odd miles – hardly by bicycle.

"I'll pick you up on Saturday morning," was Nathan's reply. "Trust me."

'Trust me,' is one of those phrases used by people who should never be trusted at all. It is usually said to people who are pointing out a weakness in an argument presented as infallible truth. The statement thus subtly removes the reasoned debate from a basis on facts to one based on the character of the proponent. The debate, being then focused on the moral character of the person is therefore irrefutable out of simple common decency.

Nate's common decency was fairly elastic, but it didn't stretch that far.

"Hah!" he laughed loudly. "That'll be the day!"

The day came in due course all the same, though when Nathan turned up at the McFadzean farm, it did not give any promise of being that day.

"Why have you got a football on your head?" asked Nate incredulously. Nathan stood in the yard looking surreptitiously around, his head sporting a white helmet along with a set of goggles and a pair of

Wellington boots on his feet.

"It's a crash helmet," he replied, "I made it myself, are you coming?"

"A crash helmet? It's a football! You've cut a crash helmet shape out of a football. How did you get here, did you come on your bike?"

"Uh, sort of, have you got a crash helmet?"

"Not like that I haven't," said Nate looking at his friend the way a person looks at someone who suddenly falls to the ground and begins barking.

"Well, you'll need something, hurry up, I've hidden it behind the outhouse."

When Nate saw the Honda he shook his head.

"You're nuts if you think I'm going behind you on that!"

Nate of course was quite nuts; after all, he was the boy who drove around licenseless in a hearse.

Soon he and Nathan were riding down the road, Nathan with his football on his head and Nate with his dad's riding hat. It was a white open faced skull-cap and Nate found a pair of sunglasses to finish off the appearance. Together they looked *interesting* to say the least. Nathan hoped they looked like two blokes on a motorcycle and any passing police would not guess they had not so much as a dog license, never mind a bike license, between them.

In under half an hour they were approaching Newtownards and Nathan pulled in at a hedge-covered laneway and stopped the Honda.

"What's wrong?" asked the dark-glassed Nate, "has it run out of petrol?"

"No," replied Nathan rubbing his left arm, "my arms are wrecked. The bike pulls to the left and it's like wrestling a bull at fifty miles an hour – I need a rest."

Riding through the town was exciting, nail-biting and hair-raising all at the same time. Not having had to comply with traffic regulations before, Nathan found it strange stopping at lights, indicating for turns and generally acting lawfully. 'Acting' being the active word. On behind, Nate tied to look as if he travelled this way every day. A lady in a car beside them at a junction eyed them strangely but Nate just put on a dispassionate and worldly-wise face. He looked at her straight in the eye and lowered his sunglasses until she looked away. He had out-manoeuvred her curiosity with his direct approach – he logged that as one to Nate and Nathan, zero to the world of regulation and restriction.

On the other side of town Nathan pulled in again.

"This is no good," he complained, rubbing again at his arm, "any more of this and my arms will fall off – have you any rope?"

"Yes, as much as you want," replied Nate.

"Where?" asked Nathan not seeing Nate deliver.

"At home. Want to go back for it?" said Nate with a wicked grin.

"Ha ha, No. Hang on, I'll take a look around." Nathan poked about for a few minutes in the hedges and returned a few minutes later with some baler-twine.

"Got some, let's see, now if I tie this off here…"

It was an unusual solution, but Nathan immediately felt the relief. He had tied one end of the twine to the right-hand handle-bar and given Nate the other end for his right hand. As they rode down the road, Nate pulled on the string and helped take some of the tug off Nathan's tired arm. Travelling like that, they trundled on through the mill town of Comber and a few miles out the other side. Here Nathan took a compass bearing and then gave the set compass to Nate. As they proceeded, Nate would continually check their direction against the compass. When Nathan was veering off, Nate would tap his shoulder and point the correct way.

The trouble with the roads and byways of County Down was that none of them had the foggiest resemblance to a decent straight road. The roads bent and twisted, curled and coiled around the hills and drumlins like devious snakes that had cleverly avoided Saint Patrick's best efforts. One minute they would be rumbling along due south, the next they had completely turned around on the corkscrewing roads and were heading east. Two hours after leaving Newtownards they were as lost as it was possible to be in a place as compact as Northern Ireland and they recognised none of the convoluted tongue-twisting place names. Nathan wondered for the first time why he had not thought to bring the map.

Pulling in beside an old building that had evidently once been a railway station, the boys got off the bike and Nathan checked the fuel tank under the seat.

"All this driving around the back-end of nowhere is using up petrol," he said peering into the dark filler hole. "You're not pointing enough."

"Not pointing enough? I've one hand dead with the rope wrapped around it stopping all the blood and the other feeling like the beak on a weather cock! Are we anywhere near Banbridge at all?" retorted Nate looking for some kind of reassurance.

"No idea," replied Nathan. Nate did not feel reassured.

"Tell you what, the next person we see, stop and ask directions," suggested Nate. Nathan nodded; it was as good an idea as any.

He was leaning over a fence when they saw him, he looked like he had been leaning on the fence forever – his old gnarled face appeared to have been made of the same ancient wood as the timber of the unpainted rickety fence. Behind him a donkey peered across at Nathan and Nate as they stopped and took off their helmets. Nathan's hair was wet and sweaty with having been under the polythene football for so long. The donkey didn't look impressed – in fact, it looked barely alive. The old man cocked back his flat cap and took out a battered and blackened blackthorn pipe from a permanent groove in his bottom lip. He pushed up his left eyelid with his left fore-finger and focused a grey eye on Nathan who stood upright in the motorcycle saddle beside him. The donkey pushed its hairy nose against the man's back and he made no movement in recognition.

"Hello sir," began Nathan respectfully, "I wonder could you help us?"

The old man nodded slowly.

"Aye lad, a wonder t'would be tae be sure."

Nathan looked back at Nate and got back a shrug.

"We're looking for Banbridge."

The old man scratched the back of his head. "Aye, that would be likely right."

"Sorry?" asked Nathan confused.

"Well now, if ye'd be in Banbridge already ye'd no be lukin' out for't." He put the pipe back in his mouth and let the eyelid resume its previous semi-closed position.

"Oh, right, thanks. Actually, we were wondering if you could tell us how to get there?" tried Nathan.

The pipe came out again and the eyebrow and lid was once again pushed up.

"Do ye know, I believe I cud dae that rightly, aye, you'd be right there now, ye're a cliver lad a'right."

"Ahem, well, would you mind, you know, actually *telling* us?"

"Ye'd be wantin' tae know the way by road, aye? I cud tell ye how tae get o'er the fields, but I'm thinkin' ye'd rather gae by road?"

"Well, yes, that would be good thanks," agreed Nathan.

"Wheel now, d'ye know where the Lagan crosses Edentrillick and Ballyvicnally?"

"Uh, no, sorry," said Nathan who had never heard of either place.

"Aye, thought you mightn't. What about Quilly or Edentiroory?"

"Are there signposts for them?" asked Nathan hopefully.

"Signposts? Din't be silly lad. Did ye pass Corbet? Oul Maginnis wud hae been out wi' his ugly oul bake gawkin' at the motors goin' by; a big silly lukin' face, like somethin' ye'd see on a merry-go-roun' – did ye see the oul devil?"

Nathan had seen neither the place nor the disrespected Maginnis; his blank look was reply enough.

"Dae ye know Tullylish? Din't tell me yez dinnae know Tullylish?"

"I'm sorry," said Nathan feeling entirely uninformed. How could he not have known Tullylish?

"Wheel, that's a'right then, for if ye's hae passed any o' yon places ye'd be right off track. Does ony o' that help you lads?"

Nathan was at a loss to understand how it could be. He said as much.

"No, not really, we just wanted to know the direction to Banbridge."

"Och, are ye boys must be from Belfast," the emphasis was very strong on the *fast*, as if the 'Bel' was a superfluous add-on, "for I'm thinking yez are as thick as tae planks set end tae end."

"Sorry," said Nathan feeling stupid for knowing so little, "We're from the Ards peninsula and we're a bit lost you see so…" Suddenly the old man's eye lit up.

"Low country boys! Well! Why did ye nae say so? Yez maybe aren't so stupid as yez are daft lukin' after all. Dae either o' yez come fra' Bal-lydoonan?"

This time it was Nate who spoke up.

"We both live either side of it, Ballydoonan's our village."

"Say yez are nae jokin! I've a brother married a lass who came from Ballydoonan, lovely girl – sweetest thing as ever breathed and as fair as the star o' the County Down. Boyso was I the green yin when he tuk and came back wi' that lass. Dis either o'ye boys have a lassie?"

"Not yet," grinned Nate, poking his friend in the back.

"Not a bad word did ever she say about onybody an' not a body ever had ocht but good tae say about her," continued the old man, his words now on the flow. "You know," he gave a little laugh as he looked back into the pictures in his mind, "she loved the chocolate... never got much mind, but it was her wee *thing*." He gave a smile deep into the past and rubbed a stubbly chin. "She gave him two strong sons before she burnt to the end o' her poor wee little taper."

"Oh, I'm sorry," said Nathan, was it long ago?

"Aye lad, longer than either o' the lives o' youse youngsters. Long ago... and, not so long ago. I helped my poor brother tae bury her ma' sell. Broke his big hairt, didnae dae mine ony good either. But she was a lovely lass, aye." He let his eyelid down and then fell silent and still. Neither of the boys felt compelled to speak in his sacred quietness. A curlew cried across the wet fields, far away a sheep called for her lamb and the donkey shuffled and dropped its head. On the rugged face of the old man a small tear glistened. In the stillness, Nathan and Nate lowered their heads not wanting to intrude on his private memories. Suddenly a leathery finger pushed the eyelid back up.

"Now, Banbridge? You boys just want tae keep on down that road – ye canna miss it."

Leaving the old man still welded to his fence with the donkey snuffling about at his pockets, Nathan and Nate rode off. Neither spoke, the meeting with the old man had affected them both in ways it was hard to put into words when you're seventeen. They hadn't gone four hundred yards when they passed a large blue sign to their left.

Welcome to Banbridge it said.

They were on the outskirts of the town and as the houses rapidly began to multiply on either side of the road, Nathan took the opportunity to pull into a disused garage to check his directions copied down from the phone conversation. After explaining the jottings to Nate, who was unconvinced that his friend understood his own scribble, they took off again, putting the 'we're just two guys on their bike, what's odd about that?' look on their faces. Nathan drove about for twenty minutes, and when he had thoroughly convinced himself he had no idea where he was going, he pulled in at an estate and beside a woman pulling a shopping trolley up a steep footpath.

"Excuse me, could you help us, we're looking for this address," he said showing the little round woman his notes.

"Two pints of milk?" said the woman narrowing her eyes at Nathan.

"Oh, sorry, wrong side, that was just where mum had… a message for…never mind, this is the address." He turned over the sheet and showed her the directions and address.

"Quilly heights? Top of the estate son, up there." She pointed up across the road to where the road ran up out of the estate and back into the country.

"Oh, thanks, that's great, bye."

"Son?" asked the woman, leaning back on her trolley.

"Uh, yes?"

"Why have you got a football on your head?"

Nate's voice quickly interrupted.

"I don't know him; I'm just here for the ride. Just pretend you never saw me; even better, just pretend you never saw him."

The woman took hold of her trolley and shaking her head set off up the remainder of the hill. Any hope she had left for the future generation had faded before she reached the top.

Taking the road the woman had pointed out, the intrepid motorcyclists rode to the top of the hill where Nate gave Nathan a jab in the shoulder.

"Stop at this shop," he said – Nathan pulled in again.

"Are you wanting to buy something?" he asked.

"No," said Nate, "*you* are. You can hardly go to a girl's house without some sort of a gift."

"A gift?!" exclaimed Nathan, horrified. Spending money was an anathema to Nathan. An event carried out in a dire emergency – a course of action only to be adopted when all the other options were exhausted.

"Yes, what are you going to do? You're hardly going to turn up empty handed?"

Nathan wondered what the problem with that was. He also wondered what he was supposed to buy.

"Get her a box of chocolates; girls love chocolates," answered Nate without being asked. "Come on, I'll help you choose them."

He also had to help him buy them. The wise precaution of bringing some money in case of emergencies had not occurred to Nathan – in fact, the thought of bringing money for any reason had not occurred to him. They pooled together what measly coins they had in their various pockets – Nathan found an extra ten pence that had fallen into his Welly boot, and went into the shop. Everything they had just managed to get them a box of milk chocolates – not a big box, but it was something.

The house had obviously once sat in its own ground and been a substantial farm at a time. Now the farmer seemed to be mostly growing houses for the outskirts of the estate was crowding around the paddocks and farm buildings around each side.

"Is this it then?" asked Nate looking around.

"Yes, I think so, the address is right. Do these Wellies look stupid?"

"Do you want me to tell you the truth and totally wreck your self-confidence or tell lies and make you feel like Cliff Richard?"

"Is one of those supposed to sound the attractive choice? Come on, stick by me here, this isn't easy you know."

They were standing now on the doorstep, Nathan with his arms hanging uselessly to each side, his DIY crash helmet still perched on top of his head.

"By the way, you remember what she looked like all right?" asked Nate.

The girl who stood at the door might have been her, it might not – it wasn't like Nathan had a clue. What he knew immediately was that he would much rather be back on his Honda and that said it all.

"Hello," she said.

"Hello… Linda?" tried Nathan, hoping it wasn't.

"Yes," said the girl, "Um… who are you?"

Imagination is a wonderful thing. Given time and a bit of free rein, it can produce all kinds of illusions. For Nathan, the girl before him fitted none of them.

For the girl, the football head in front of her was clearly something from another planet – a planet she had no intention bringing into her front room where her friends eagerly awaited meeting the good looking boy from Ballydoonan. She thought quickly.

"Um… actually, I'm Linda's sister."

Nathan felt a wave of relief flood over him. There was a way out, a subtle choice of words and he might be able to escape before he got in any deeper. Sisters looked like one another and he had seen enough.

"Oh. Oh well, tell her I called. Got to go, bye!"

He tried not to run from the door but was not altogether successful.

"Quick! Let's go!" he stage-whispered urgently to Nate, dragging him by the arm back to the Honda.

With his heart thumping like the Zulu drums at Rourke's drift, Nathan pulled back hard on the throttle and without a backward glance they escaped at speed down the road.

Back in the house one of Linda's friends giggled.

"Was that him?" she asked.

"Wrong address," lied Linda. "Fancy a chippy?"

Nate was confused. He had been dragged half-way across the country with a numb hand on a wreck of a motorcycle to visit a house where he got to stay less than a minute. Budding romance had clearly withered before it had even got out of the seed packet.

"What now anyway?" he asked his friend, "home?"

Nathan looked at him as if he had just turned into a trout.

"Are you joking? All this way and not even getting to see Banbridge? Let's ride into the town to see what it looks like – if I ever write a story about this someday, at least I've got to see the place."

"Aye, like that'll happen," said Nate shaking his head. "Well, watch out for police."

Following the signs for the town centre, Nate and Nathan trundled crablike along the road into the town. As they motored into the main area of the town centre Nathan took a double-take as they passed a statue with four polar bears below his feet. Banbridge was indeed an exotic contrast to Ballydoonan. He turned up into the hilly Bridge Street where either side of the wide street ran rows and rows of massive square concrete flower pots, all beckoning with colours of every hue. Behind the pots, multicoloured shops displayed their wares in their windows and footpaths. Ballydoonan seemed very small and plain in comparison with the bustle of business of the busy town.

At the top of the hill a bridge ran across the street with the centre part of the road cut to pass underneath while either side traffic climbed and turned onto the bridge itself. Rumbling under the bridge the Honda's engine echoed back and they were immediately out the other side and pottering back down the road and the other side of the hill.

Nate was looking straight ahead over the white plastic football helmet when he suddenly saw a figure standing in the middle of the road.

"Oh no!" he exclaimed out loud. In his panic he pummelled Nathan's back with a little more vigour than necessary.

"Look out! Police!" he shouted into his ear. Meeting the police while road-legally unprepared was beginning to become a bit of a habit for Nate and not one he had been planning to cultivate any further.

Unfortunately the shouting and the pummelling had unexpected results. One was that Nate suddenly released the baler twine that was helping to keep the bike running straight, another that the unexpectedly surprised Nathan let go the handlebars momentarily as he jerked in response. Suddenly the motorcycle, now liberated from its constant wrestle, leapt to the left and careered onto the footpath, miraculously missing two troughs filled with roses. Somewhat less miraculously, it rocketed straight into a narrow walkway between the shops. They hurtled down the path and straight towards a drop of fifteen feet down a series of descending concrete steps. Nate closed his eyes and prayed like only a man who knows he has only two seconds left to live can pray.

The bike went airborne and landed with a clatter. Nate waited for the angel voice of welcome.

Unbelievably, they were still alive and on the bike, its motor still running, both wheels on the ground. They had come to a halt on a roadway at the back of the shops. Opportunity for relief was immediately cut short however as an ominous growl suddenly sounded from their left.

Not ten feet away a foul looking Alsatian dog glowered at them, its hackles raised.

Seeing the arrival of 'meals on wheels', the Alsatian bounded straight for the two on the bike and prepared for its first chunk of leg. Out of the corner of an eye, Nathan's brain caught the dark blur of movement and sent an emergency message to his right wrist – 'throttle on full!' Unfortunately, as the bike leapt forward, Nate fell off the back.

Nate now did something that had the McWhirter brothers been watching, would have secured him a place in the Guinness Book of

Records. Immediately leaping to his feet, he bolted like a cheetah on amphetamines. Whatever speed Nathan was doing, Nate did more – becoming dog food appeared nowhere on his list of life's aspirations. Catching up with the Honda he leapt on behind, grabbing Nathan's middle with a grip born of desperation.

The sudden yank almost unseated Nathan from the bike, but hearing the guttural howls from the Alsatian ridiculously close behind, Nathan crouched over the handlebars and pulled back harder on the throttle. It briefly crossed his mind to check up later in the *Encyclopaedia Britannica* to see what was the top speed of an Alsatian dog. This one deserved at least a mention. He also guiltily wondered how much of Nate it had managed to eat.

The roadway ran parallel to the main road behind the shops which they had so merrily been travelling moments before. After a hundred yards it veered right and, still shell-shocked, Nathan followed it and popped back out onto the street.

"Turn left!" screamed a voice behind him. Nate had come alive again and realised they had come out the other side of the police officer.

Nathan needed no other encouragement. Hunched over the handlebars, he changed up through the gears and sped down the street.

Nate chanced a quick look back and as he did so saw something that made him look again. The policeman was still standing, arm apparently upraised in the middle of the road; except he wasn't a policeman, he was a war memorial. Surely not…?

"Quicker! Don't look back, he hasn't seen us yet!" he called into Nathan's ear.

Technically he wasn't lying, he told himself. Besides, it *might* have been a policeman – who knew, maybe there was one lurking about up the street somewhere. How was enlightening Nathan to his simple mistake going to help anyway? Yes, just forget it; he shouldn't be riding about without a license in any case.

Coming from Nate it was a pretty hypocritical justification but in the absence of any other it made him feel better all the same.

They had taken a left turn and headed out into the countryside where Nathan took whatever road came up next. After five minutes the bike slowed and came to a quiet halt at the side of the road.

"What's wrong?" asked Nate.

"Bike stopped – I think we're out of petrol," said Nathan shaking the bike and listening for the sound of fuel swishing about in the tank below him. "Hang on, there's a reserve." He twisted a small valve and waited a few moments for the petrol to flow into the carburettor.

"How far will the reserve get us then?" asked Nate suspiciously. "We have a long way to go and I've no money left – I know you don't have a bean."

"Don't worry, it'll be fine," said Nathan worrying. He reckoned the reserve was good for maybe ten miles but not much more. "Have you still got the compass?"

Setting out again they meandered along unknown roads and lanes, Nathan going easy on the throttle in an effort to conserve fuel. What on earth they were going to do when they ran out, he had no idea. At the end of the road he turned left again onto a road that was oddly familiar.

Suddenly Nate, whose hand was numb again already, leaned forward and spoke into Nathan's ear.

"Hang on, we've been here before!"

They had. They had obviously done a long U turn and were now back at the spot where they had first entered Banbridge. At least now knowing where they were, Nathan turned in the middle of the road and headed in the opposite direction. Thirty seconds later Nate thumped Nathan's back again.

"Stop, there's that old man!"

He hadn't moved, or if he had, he was back in exactly the same place where they had left him. Behind him the donkey looked up and flapped an ear at the new arrivals. The old man took the pipe out of his mouth.

"Youse boys back hmm? So what dae yez think o' Banbridge?"

Nathan turned off the ignition – there was no point wasting petrol; Nate took off his helmet.

"It's quite an exciting town actually," said Nate giving Nathan a secret poke in the back, "you wouldn't believe the things we've been at today."

The old man gave a wry smile and tapped his pipe on the wooden fence.

"Ye know, sez I tae maesell," he said thoughtfully, "'them boys are after chasing the girls'. Am I right, or am I right?"

"It's the girls in Banbridge do the chasing," complained Nathan. "The boys do the running."

"Ah," laughed the old man, "maybe the lassies at Ballydoonan arny so bad? Far off fields luk good from far off – that's *why* they're far off, close up's another thing eh?"

Nate and Nathan smiled back wonderingly at the old man. He wasn't as simple as he looked. Suddenly Nate thought of something. He reached into his coat and brought out a package. Turning it over in his hand he looked at Nathan and then back at the old man.

"These are for you," he said. "Maybe they'll help you remember another Ballydoonan lassie?"

The man raised a surprised set of eyebrows and took the brown paper bag. Putting in a big gnarled hand he brought out a box of chocolates. He held them in his hand and stared for the longest time at the box while the donkey behind stared at the boys. After what felt like a full minute he spoke.

"Ah'm thinkin' these are no for me," he said slowly.

"Well, actually," began Nathan, "they were meant for a girl who…"

"But thank ye no the less," continued the old man, "youse are a good pair o' boys and dinnae let ocht say otherwise." He turned the chocolates over in his hand and gave a far away smile. "Aye, her wee *thing*." His eyes glistened and after a slight hesitation during which he seemed to be considering something, he put the chocolates back in the bag.

"When I said they were no for me, I mean't maybe they were for samebody else. For Maginnis maybe. You'll be going back through Corbet, so here's a wee thing yez cud dae for an oul man…"

Maginnis was sitting on a beaten up wooden chair beside an old garage forecourt. It was one of those ancient long forgotten forecourts – just about enough room for one car, small garage windows advertising forgotten products in yellowed notices and a single pump with a large red shell on top.

"Mr Maginnis?" tried Nathan, taking off his goggles.

"If that oul skitter toul ye tae stap here and winge tae me about some oul rubbish, ye can tell him he's nothin' but an oul wizened up waster!" declared the man before Nathan or Nate could say another word.

"Well actually… how did you know we had been talking to that old man?" began Nate. He was interrupted by the man who was Maginnis.

"The oul skitter's forever sendin' me abuse through every passer-by as takes the time to listen tae his oul waffle," he said. "Well, you can tell him he's as ugly as the day his mither tried to drown him rather than have tae admit it was her ane wean!'

"Actually," said Nate nonplussed, "he asked us to give you these," he handed over the chocolates. "He said to tell you 'not to be so hard on yourself. You did all could be done.' I hope that means something?"

Maginnis took the chocolates and his face drained of its colour – for a minute he looked as if he was about to faint.

"The oul skitter… he sent these?" he asked quietly.

Yes, well, actually they were for him, but he said he'd rather you had them," replied Nate.

The man went very quiet and his weathered face looked suddenly even more old and frail. Countless years were inscribed in each leathery wrinkle, each one marking the passing of time and spent days.

Big hot tears welled in his rheumy old eyes as he pulled a ragged handkerchief from his pocket.

"Aye, well," he said simply, blowing his big red nose. "He hasna forgot then." Slowly rubbing his forehead, he closed his eyes and was for a moment no longer sitting on a chair, but somewhere else altogether. For a minute Nate thought he had taken a turn and was about to go over and check when he opened his eyes.

"Will ye take a bit o'tea or what? I can make yez a cup in the garage."

"We can't really stop," said Nathan excusing themselves, "but thanks anyway, we have to try and get back to Ballydoonan and we're nearly out of petrol."

"Youse boys are from Ballydoonan?" exclaimed the man. "Why didn't ye say so? Ye need petrol? Here, pull her up tae the pump and I'll give ye all ye need."

"Thanks," said Nate, "but we've no money."

"Houl yer wheest!" cried Maginnis, "did I say I wanted yer money? Bring her over now and stop yer gurnin."

He filled the Honda to the brim and as the boys remounted, the man gave them rough directions in the general direction of Ards.

"Have yez got that now? Dinnae forget now, if ever yez are back, call and see oul Maginnis – I'll no see ye stuck! And…and thanks for the chocolates."

As they prepared to head off, Nathan suddenly remembered a question he had been meaning to ask.

"By the way, what is the old man with the donkey called? He didn't tell us his name."

Maginnis looked at him oddly as he replied.

"What's his name? Sure it's Maginnis of course, what else would my brother be called?"

The rest of the journey home was uneventful, if long. With an aching hand and burning backside with sitting so long, Nate stretched and waved from the end of his lane as Nathan left him and turned and headed the last couple of miles home. It was well after nine and he was so tired he just went straight to his bedroom, starved though he was and fell asleep on top of the bed.

Nathan had to sneak into the yard to hide the fact he had been away on the bike all day. When asked by his mum where he had been, he simply replied truthfully, "with Nate McFadzean."

He too was tired and sore all over – his arms ached and throbbed with the struggle with the delinquent motorcycle. As he stuffed a couple of jam sandwiches into his mouth before heading, like Nate, to his bed, Liz entered the kitchen.

"Hi," said Liz, "where have you been?"

"Can I give you a piece of advice?" yawned Nathan. "If ever you take a fancy to somebody, make sure it's somebody nearby. Forget long distance romances – they aren't worth it!"

As Nathan passed her on his way to his room, Liz's mind went somewhere else. It was the first advice he had given her that she was well prepared to accept.

Nearby would be the most wonderful thing.

A couple of miles away a young man held a handkerchief to his nose, breathed deeply, and thought the self same thing.

8.

THE TAXIDERMIST

The Veterinary Surgery outside Ballydoonan had a simple name. Without deference to either subtlety or clever wordplay, it bore the name printed in not very tidy black text on one of the pillars to the entrance to the smallish bungalow that was the office for the Surgery.

'THE VET' it said. Doctor Angel – he was a Scotsman – did not truck with witticisms, innuendo or clever-dickery. Trained at Edinburgh University, he saw no reason to embellish what was a position unembellishable by smart words. He had studied for longer than a medical doctor; was intimately familiar with the internal workings of not one, but at least six mammals and operated without the backup of anaesthetist or assistant, being all in one, the complete professional, a man without need for clever names. His patients could not recount their symptoms or explain how they were feeling, no placebo could pacify unspoken pains and since any mistake was laid solely at his door, so was the glory of a job well done. Dr Angel did his jobs well and his skill was renowned even beyond the narrow confines of the thin strip of land that was the Ards Peninsula.

His work was almost exclusively directed towards farm animals or horses. When a Friesian cow had got itself into a bit of a jam by attempting to give birth to a wrongly turned calf, Dr Angel was called and his rubber-gloved professional arms were thrust into bovine places that resulted in safe deliveries and saved milkers. When a herd of sheep broke through into a field of cabbage and gorged themselves to the point where the gases within swelled them up like barrage balloons and gave them mere hours to live, Dr Angel was there with his special spike and professional skills. Sheep bursting was not an amateur job and Dr Angel was no amateur.

The bungalow itself was not the Surgery – it was only the building used as office and reception where his wife and secretary, Angela answered the phones and sent out the bills. Unlike Dr Angel, whose parents had chosen Edward as a first name thus causing no tension or conflict with his Christian name and Surname, Angela's parents could make no such provision for their daughter's eventual marriage appendage. She had fallen in love with the man, not his name; the other way about would have been a much greater misfortune – one she had to spend a lifetime with in sickness and in health – the other was just tough luck.

Of course, being that her husband was a vet, a fair bit of it was in sickness though unlike a doctor of people, a doctor of animals had less angst and doubt to trouble and recriminate himself over at night when the old demons of self-accusation prowled the minds of other concerned practitioners revisiting the events of the day. The absence of a human soul was a blessing for an animal – at least, it certainly was for the vet.

Behind the bungalow lay the farm of the McFadzeans and one of the outbuildings was rented by Dr Angel as the Surgery and operating theatre for his animal patients. The building stood apart from the farm and by using a secondary lane that ran up the side of the bungalow, the vet's was able to be a separate entity from the farm where Nate lived with his parents and brother.

Nate's brother's name was Winston and he was fifteen. Whether it was due to the close proximity of the vet or simply because he was a farmer's son, Winston McFadzean had a keen interest in animals. Not necessarily farm animals, in fact he had no interest in farming at all, leaving the driving of tractors and agriculture to his father and elder brother. His interest was in money, or rather, ways of making it. Animals seemed to Winton to be a little explored avenue in the pursuit of this goal. Various schemes had occurred to him at one time or another and not being a mere dreamer, he often put these schemes into action.

Digging up worms to sell to local fishermen had been one of his early ideas. Discovering in Biology class that the way to catch a worm was not in fact to be the early bird, but to pour warm soapy water onto the ground, he immediately set about covering the orchard garden in froth and bubbles. The worms did indeed come up by the bucket load and Winston counted the money in his head even as he gathered the slippery crop and prepared to find a market for his catch. Rooks watched hungrily from the surrounding trees as Winston's bucket squirmed with his wriggly produce though none dared to try a smash and grab robbery – the boy was a known shotgun user and rooks weren't that stupid.

The local hardware shop had seemed the obvious choice, but Winston was devastated when the owner bluntly pointed out that although the worms were indeed many, they were also now quite clearly dead; the wiggle was completely out of them. The fishermen did not want dead worms and neither apparently did the Biology teacher – not even when Winston offered them to her at a price half of what he had been hoping to get from the hardware shop. The bus driver likewise was unimpressed by the bucket on the return journey home, so much so that he insisted Winston empty the contents over the hedge before he travelled any further down the road. Thus empty bucketed, Winston considered his next commercial venture.

The spark came from visiting an antique shop in a neighbouring village with his mother. She had been looking for an oval mirror; all he saw was the eagle.

It was a stuffed one, in a glass cage. It was not on its own, but posed with some kind of a medium-sized mammal in its claws – possibly a rabbit, but remarkably like a piece of stuffed brown sacking with ears stitched on. The eagle however was magnificent. Its bright eyes scanned out through the glass and its semi-spread wings gave the impression that the bird was just about to take off, breakfast in its grip. Winston knew immediately that he had found his Eldorado – the money was all but in his pocket.

The local library was in Newtownards and after looking under 'S' for 'Stuffing' he was eventually redirected by a suspicious looking librarian to 'T' for 'Taxidermy'. The book he finally found was dusty and evidently little used, but he took it all the same and prepared to be educated in all things taxidermatological.

Winston was nothing if not methodical and after reading the book through not once, but twice, he felt he was if somewhere near an expert already in the art of animal mounting. The term 'stuffing' he discovered quite quickly was a term to be repudiated and one that the most eminent taxidermists eschewed with vigour. It also helped explain why the librarian had seemed to respond so oddly to his question; "Can you help me, I want to learn how to be a stuffer?" She knew more than she looked like she knew – librarians were like that.

Taxidermy it seemed, was no simple procedure of just pulling the insides of an animal out and pushing in a lot of cotton wool in the place of the guts. It was an art in its own right and great pioneers like Carl E. Akeley and William T. Horneday had developed talented and unique skills for producing anatomically correct and extremely lifelike specimens – or so said the library book. Although he read it twice, Winston had skipped over some sections where he felt his current understanding was somewhat challenged. There was a whole chapter about chemical preservation that eluded his mental grasp each time he read it. Fortunately his dad had studied chemistry to 'A' level standard or whatever it was called when he was young. Farming had been a second choice for his dad, one that he just sort of subsumed when his own father had taken ill and needed the farm taken over. ICI ended up the losers, but Nate and Winston's dad ran the farm with a calculating and intelligent hand – the 'A' levels never went to waste.

It was to his dad that Winston went for further advice.

"Where could I get Borax, Dad?" he asked him one night after tea. "Would the Chemist Shop keep it?"

"Borax?" asked his father, pushing his half-rimmed reading spectacles down his nose, "Sodium Borate, hmmm? What would you want that for, son?"

"Well, I was planning doing a bit of taxidermy – I got a book out from the library, it says you need borax to rub into the skin to preserve it – I wondered where I would get it?"

Mr McFadzean set down his Farmer's Weekly and changed his attention from fluke worm drenches to his son's next scheme.

"Taxidermy eh? It's not just a matter of stuffing a dead animal, you know," he said, taking off his glasses.

"I know, I've read all about it, I'm going to mount some specimens and sell them – not many people are doing it, it's a goer, Dad."

Mr McFadzean nodded slowly. His maxim was 'never stamp on enthusiasm' and Winston had plenty of it. He could have asked him where he intended getting his dead animals from, how he planned to dispose of the unwanted entrails and so forth, but he declined – his son would find out the pitfalls soon enough and it was better to come upon some things yourself – it made for better character building.

"You know, probably salt and wood ash would be as effective; the goal is to dry up the fat and preserve the skin, would save you money too."

Winston smiled. It was great having a dad who knew about chemical stuff. Some day he would have to find out how to make home-made fireworks. Nate came into the room half way through the conversation and listened before speaking.

"Taxidermy? What, like animal stuffing?"

"Specimen mounting," replied Winston, "and don't say it's just a crazy scheme," he added rising and heading out to the yard, "there's big money involved."

As Winston shut the door behind him Nate turned to his father.

"Specimen mounting?"

"Don't worry about it Nate, it just one of Winston's crazy schemes – harmless enough."

'Harmless' to whom he didn't say – not to the pigeons in the hay barn certainly.

The pigeons were the first candidates in the budding taxidermist's list. They weren't dead yet so Winston's first job was to facilitate a change in their current condition. From 'alive pigeon' to 'dead pigeon' to be exact.

The following day, Winston set to work. The old single barrelled shot-gun lay about in the working kitchen, propped in behind the Welsh dresser where it was deemed to be more or less safe as well as being available. Foxes and Rooks were its main targets, though an occasional rat met its nemesis from time to time; a sore shoulder for a McFadzean, a rather more life changing event for the rat.

Winston wasn't stupid, he realised that to fire lead shot at a pigeon would fill it so full of holes as to make it difficult to work with – a more intelligent method had to be employed. Taking a twelve gauge shell, he prised open the end containing the lead shot and emptied it onto the bin in the working kitchen. He then proceeded to chop up a blue eraser, the one with a white stripe running up its centre, into small chips. Mixing them with a small quantity of dry sand, he filled up the cartridge again, this time with his rubber-sand mixture – Sellotape finished the job and sealed the end. After adapting four cartridges in the same way, he pulled the single barrelled gun out from behind the dresser even as his mother walked into the room.

Anne McFadzean was an incredibly even tempered woman; nothing fazed her. Seeing her younger son preparing to go out with the shotgun did not please her, but neither did it bother her overly.

"Where are you going with that, Winston?" she asked, more because she felt she ought to than due to any actual concern.

"Oh, just out," he replied enigmatically, "don't worry, it's not like I'm going to murder someone."

"Oh, that's nice," responded his mother automatically. Having asked the question she was not particularly concerned about the answer. The boy had a gun, after all, he was a farmer's son – if they lived in a town it would as soon been a bicycle.

"But be careful," she added as an afterthought. Having given her maternal advice, she returned to the task that had called her to the kitchen in the first place; making soda-bread.

The pigeons might have fluttered about a bit to make it more sporting, but having seemingly adopted an air of fatalism, they merely hung about on a metal roof beam in the barn instead.

There were four of them altogether, huddled together and looking incredibly innocent and harmless. For a second Winston felt conscience stricken to what he was about to callously perform until he remembered the financial rewards. The conscience was easily cowed, especially when Winston told it that in fact he was giving the birds a kind of eternal life – these pigeons would live for decades, sitting in a place of ornamental importance on someone's dresser. In that regard he was practically their saviour.

Winston was not a remarkable shot, but at fifteen feet he could hardly miss. The very first shot knocked all four pigeons off their perch and onto a feathery heap on the straw at his feet. At this rate it wasn't even going to cost much in shotgun cartridges – the profits were mounting.

The pigeons were unmarked apart from pieces of rubber embedded into their feathers, which were easily removed. It occurred to Winston at about this stage that having acquired the pigeons, he was unprepared for the following stages. There was little point in gutting the things if he had not got the wires to make the internal frames that would replace the skeletons, or even a suitable filling to fill the skins with. With a potential delay of a day or two looming it seemed that temporary pres- ervation was the answer.

The old fridge freezer was one that had been sent over from America some years previously. Gordon McFadzean had sent it over as a present for his wife when he had been over on an Ulster Farmer's Union trip in the late sixties. Seeing it for sale at a knockdown price at Sears Stores in New York, he bought it straightaway and arranged for its exporta- tion through a friend who was a farmer in New Brunswick. The cost of exporting the machine cost twice what he paid for the fridge itself and took him the best part of a year to recover from; that part he somehow omitted to tell his wife Anne. In any case, the fridge had paid for itself a couple of times over. It had been built to last, and last it did. Those clever Americans made things to run and run. They also made them to run on electricity – lots of it. The first post-new fridge bills were a bit of a shock but he hadn't bought his wife a present to complain about it just because she plugged it in – some things just have to be borne in the pursuit of love and harmonious matrimonial relations.

Back home people either had fridges or they had freezers. Some had both, but they were always separate appliances. The American Fridgidair in the McFadzean's was unique in that it was both machines in one. The top third was a freezer, the remainder a normal fridge. In the days before that became the norm, the towering cooling edifice in the kitchen was like something from another world.

It was another world into which four recently alive and kicking pigeons were transported. Winston put them in a paper bag and stuffed them into a shelf in the fridge. To Winston the finer details of freezing had yet to present themselves to him and the important distinction of to which part of the fridge-freezer should the pigeons be placed was unexplored territory.

One of the agreed realities of the human condition is that for some people, out of sight is out of mind. Winston was one of those people. The pigeons, now safely deposited in the darkness of the fridge quickly lost their claim on the attention of Winston McFadzean. He was a boy of many schemes and now some of those other schemes claimed his attention, including one of continuing work on his tree-house – a long standing project that was approaching culmination in the winching up of an old van into the beech trees behind the house – though that is a story for another time. The upshot of it was that for the remainder of that day the taxidermy was postponed and the pigeons forgotten.

The pigeons were remembered on the following morning. Winston remembered them at about a quarter to eight. He was actually asleep at the time, but found himself very quickly awake by the sound. The sound that awoke him was his mother and she was screaming. They lived in a large three-storied house and Winston's bedroom was on the top storey, which impressed Winston all the more for the scream to have awakened him. The scream had come from the kitchen and it had something to do with him. He knew that because his mother screamed again, and this time it was his name she screamed.

"WINSTON!"

It did not sound a happy scream and something about it shook his mind into a quick self-examination of what it could be about. The pigeons in the fridge came high on the resulting list, though why she should seem so upset about it wasn't clear. His mother was a very quiet tempered woman; something was evidently bothering her badly. Biting the bullet, he quickly pulled on a pair of trousers and T-shirt and loped downstairs to face the music.

The music was very loud. In fact, his mother's volume switch was way beyond 'high' and somewhere near the 'you are about to die, Winston' level. Winston did not ask his mother why she was shouting; the answer to that was plain enough. The fridge door lay wide open and jerking and flapping about on one of the shelves were a couple of very not dead at all pigeons – the other two were careering around the kitchen itself, knocking over cups and pots, bouncing off the windows and dirtying over everything for good measure. It was a dramatic scene.

"Winston!" screamed his mother, coming down to about 96 decibels. "What ever do you think you're doing? Look at the state of this mess!"

Hearing his mother shout unnerved Winston somewhat due to its rarity and he struggled to reply. The shouting did not seem to calm down the pigeons much either and one knocked over a vase sitting on the window sill, sending it crashing to the black and white tiled floor – water, flowers and broken pottery covering the floor along with feathers and bird-droppings.

"But, but, how did that happen? They were dead yesterday!" explained Winston, explaining nothing.

"Well then obviously the last trump has sounded for unless my eyes deceive me, these pigeons are very much alive today," retorted his mother. "I'll leave it for you to tidy up then, Winston," she added giving her son a serious frown before leaving the kitchen and shutting the door on the pandemonium behind her.

From not having displayed very much in the way of life and vitality in the hay barn, the pigeons were making up for it in the working kitchen. They might have been easy to shoot on the roof truss; they were far from easy to catch in the house. Half an hour and an alarming amount of sloppy grey and white splatterings later, they were at last secured in a large plastic bag and Winston took them out to the greenhouse to return and clean the kitchen.

The kitchen turned out to be no small job; the pigeons had visited every part of the fridge before their release and had left ample evidence of their stay. There were footprints in the butter, feathers in the milk jug and anything that could be knocked over was. That, along with ridiculously copious amounts of pigeon poo, added to more work than Winston thought four stupid birds could contrive to engineer for a lad for whom cleaning up in the kitchen normally meant licking his plate.

The job eventually done, he headed out to and bumped into his dad.

"Hello son, you're up early for a Saturday, have you seen your mum?" said his father peering into the kitchen window.

"Yes, but mostly *heard* rather than *saw* actually; she was a bit upset with me, I may as well tell you."

"Your mother? Upset? Is everything all right?"

"Oh she fine," explained Winston, "I made a bit of a mess of the fridge and she got a bit annoyed about it."

"That's not like your mother," said Gordon McFadzean, scratching the back of his neck. "Because you left the fridge untidy you say?" His wife was the most peaceable of women, a few 'tuts' yes – upset? Strange.

"Oh you know women, Dad," said Winston, looking over his dad's shoulder toward the greenhouse where something was definitely moving, "probably a hormone thing."

As Winston moved on down the yard toward the greenhouse, his father looked after him and shook his head. What did they teach the children in school these days? When he was Winston's age he would have blushed even to think such a word, let alone let his father hear him say it about his own mother. He remembered the parent-teacher meetings the school held from time to time. He usually left it to Anne to go; maybe he would go along too next time.

In the greenhouse a second pigeon-recapturing episode awaited Winston. Had they been anywhere else he would have just gone and got the shotgun and fired unadulterated lead shot at them, but it occurred to Winston that the greenhouse was probably not the place to employ such methods. In the end an old butterfly net did the trick and this time Winston deposited the protesting pigeons one by one into an empty plastic Schermuly flares container he had found one day on the beach. The pigeons were having quite an adventure-filled day.

Coat hooks and kapok from an old sleeping bag used as a bed by Skeeter, their border collie, were the raw materials Winston eventually gathered together to begin his production. The one piece of business he had yet to address was how to do in the pigeons. He wasn't keen on wringing their necks and the whole gun thing had run its course as far as he was concerned. It was all very frustrating. What was the use of a conscience if it kept kicking in at the most inconvenient of times and places?

He needn't have worried – when he opened the flares container the pigeons were already dead, they had run out of air and simply shuffled off earth's mortal coil – their adventures were over. The few moments of self recrimination at killing unintentionally were quickly overtaken by the relief of not having to do so intentionally. Being brutally frank with himself, Winston confessed he had had his fill of visiting death upon the innocent and was perilously close to giving up the taxidermy idea. Fate swung its pendulum again and the stuffing was firmly back on the agenda.

It wasn't a pleasant job; respect for his mother grew considerably as he thought of her gutting and stuffing the turkey each Christmas. Mothers were a tougher lot than they looked. By the time he had messily removed the insides of the pigeons he was quickly becoming less attracted to the whole taxidermy thing altogether.

Skeeter seemed very interested though. So interested that when Winston returned from the house from where he had gone to get a radio to lend some distraction, the innards he had so recently removed from the pigeons were gone. The dog was doing an inordinate amount of lip smacking.

The problem of disposal thus unexpectedly remedied, Winston got on with the job of making steel frameworks on which to mount his specimens. It looked a lot easier in the book. Eventually having made shapes that he hoped would appear more pigeon-like once the bird skins had been pulled over, he set to winding strips of kapok and string around the coat-hanger skeletons. When he was happy they were substantial enough he began the awkward task of clothing them in the exoskeletal remains of the pigeons. A lot of pulling, pushing, yanking and even the somewhat frustrated use of a hammer later, Winston's first attempt sat on the table of the shed before him. The dog looked from the pigeon to Winston then got up and walked out of the doorway.

"The next one will be better," Winston called out to his retreating audience. It was a redundant sentence; the next one could hardly have been worse. If he had shot the bird at point-blank range, run over it in the tractor and stuffed it into a cement mixer for an hour and a half it would have looked better. How he had managed to get the head inside-out with one leg poking out above the left wing was beyond him. Still,

Winston was nothing if not a trier and he had three more candidates ready for his next attempts.

Attempt three was definitely bird-like and gave him the confidence to give number four the benefit of his mounting skills. This time he made every effort to ensure there was at least some anatomical correspondence to the creature, which had so recently inhabited the feathery shroud on the table.

It was a much better job, a bit lumpy around the gizzard and the neck was maybe a bit longer than he would have liked, but a pigeon it unquestionably was – a blind eyeless pigeon, but a pigeon all the same.

Nate was the first person Winston showed his creations to. The first two attempts were put out of the way and Winston had the third and triumphant fourth nailed onto two small logs when he ambled into the shed.

"Well, what do you think?" asked Winston with the warm glow of achievement attained by those who have done something outside the ordinary. Nate wasn't aware of the glow, but he was aware that he was seeing something out of the ordinary.

"Did you do that yourself?" he asked, hoping it would be taken as a fairly innocuous remark.

"Yep," replied his brother with a beam, "I've been at it all day – you wouldn't believe how hard it is to get them to look like this."

"I'm sure it wasn't easy," hedged Nate.

"You have no idea," replied Winston. "This is only the start though," he continued, lifting up one of the wobbling creations, "once I get the hang of this I'm planning on going into large scale production, when I get a name for myself I'll have people queuing up to buy."

"Oh, you'll make a name for yourself all right," agreed Nate, unsuccessfully trying to keep his eyebrows from climbing up his forehead, "what are you going to do with these two, em… specimens?"

"Sell them," grinned Winston, "I'm taking them down to Drysdale's – he'll sell them for me if I give him part percentage of the profit. I've it all worked out. What do you think? Pretty good eh?"

Nate was not a boy given to lying but neither did he like to be critical where it would simply offend. Thus juxtaposed in an impossible position, he took the easy way out. He side-skipped the question altogether.

"You should show Dad, he'll be really interested," he said instead as he turned to leave, "I'd better head on, I want to check the calves in the bottom field."

Winston bypassed the 'show Dad' suggestion and took the pigeons straight down to Drysdale's shop. Willie Drysdale had a fairly eclectic village shop; groceries, postcards, men's underpants and week old puppies all vied for place in and around the various corners of his shop. The one thing the miscellaneous objects within his shop all had in common was that they were all for sale. A story circulated that he once sold a pair of trousers to a passing tourist who had had an accident on the beach involving a washed up drum of oil and a crab, though those particular details were somewhat fuzzy. The one thing everyone agreed on, however, was that the trousers were actually being worn by Willie Drysdale at the time. To Willie, a sale was a sale. He got the money and the tourist got a pair of pre-warmed trousers.

Willie turned the stuffed pigeons over in his big gnarled hands and looked at Winston.

"I'll need half," he grumbled, "half to me half to you, how's that sound?"

It sounded a bit severe to Winston; he had been thinking more in the order of two to three percent. Fifty seemed steep.

"As much as that? I was thinking maybe a little less?" he tried. Willie Drysdale slowly shook his head at the boy.

"It's a matter of risk, son. The man who takes the risk gets a decent share. I have the risk. Who has to use up precious display space to show the customers the produce? That would be me, son. Who has to balance the stock between what I can afford to keep and what I can sell? That would be me too. Who takes the risk of customers being put off by the wrong kind of stuff in the shop? Don't answer; I'll tell you, it's me again. What risk do *you* take? None, all you do is supply me – I have all the risks – no, half is fair, trust me son, you're getting a good deal."

Winston left the pigeons for Mr Drysdale to display where he saw fit and cycled back up the road. At first he felt a little chagrined at the deal but as he mused over it his annoyance was eclipsed by the thought that once he was established other shops and dealers would be pleading with him to be allowed to run his line of products. 'McFadzean Anatomical Art', yes, he had to start somewhere, maybe old Drysdale was just using his business acumen – if it got him up and running he had to be thankful enough he told himself.

Dr Edward Angel FRCVS was having a busy day of it. He had spent all night with a Charolais Bull that had managed to get barbed wire wrapped around its neck and was in danger of cutting its own throat. Trying to get at the bull without being crushed by the agitated animal was an ordeal in itself. Cutting the wire out and suturing up the flaps of skin took the most of the night and Dr Angel was tired and wondering when he was going to get to bed. After four hours sleep he was up again with a suspected Brucellosis outbreak in a herd of Holsteins. It was a false alarm, but it did nothing for his vain attempts to get rid of his perennial tiredness.

"You need some help, dear," said his wife when she brought him out a cup of coffee that morning from the bungalow. "You have too much work on and if you keep this up you'll start making mistakes." She smiled, kissed him on his cheek and returned to the ringing phones. Edward rubbed his face and watched her retreating figure. She was a good wife, he could hardly remember a time when he had heard her complain – she worked at the rate of three and yet was concerned for him. Perhaps he did need some help; maybe a veterinary nurse who could assist Angela and help out with some of the paperwork. He logged the thought in the back of his busy brain and got on with the job at hand.

Although the practise dealt mainly with farm animals, from time to time Dr Angel had to work with pets. Cats and dogs mainly, but an occasional hamster or guinea pig slipped in as well. Although his main interest was with farms, he was increasingly finding that people were prepared to spend a lot of money on poor old Rover or hair-ball spitting Tiddles. It hadn't been his idea of a working vet's remit, but if that was what people wanted and they were prepared to pay and pay with a smile on their faces; well, he guessed he ought to be thankful for the lighter work.

Winston had checked every day that week at Drysdale's and every day that week the pigeons remained unsold. Winston had heard once that a market had to be educated to accept a new product. The Ballydoonan market by all indications was totally illiterate.

"No son," was Willie Drysdale's reply when asked. "There have not been queues of people waiting to purchase either of your pigeons and if they don't move by the end of the week I shall be moving them myself – out into the skip in the yard. Come down on Saturday next and if they're not gone you can take them away."

Winston was not convinced that Mr Drysdale was actually trying all that hard. The birds were tucked at the very back of a dark shelf, which had dusty fireside poker sets and coal scuttles for sale. Winston reckoned they had been for sale there since the outbreak of the Boer war and the whole shelf had some kind of invisible cloaking device activated on it that prevented people from even seeing it. Winston decided he was going to have to assist matters somehow. Jill McNarry was his solution.

"Psst, Jill!" he whispered across to the teenage shop assistant on the way out. Jill looked up and saw Winston beckoning to her from near the doorway. Winston McFadzean was a dreamboat and Jill McNarry could hardly believe her eyes. She looked behind her but saw no-one – it really was her he was calling over. She made her way over to the doorway – she would have run but too much enthusiasm was unladylike.

"Hello, Winston," she said quietly.

"Hi Jill," said Winston under his breath. Jill's heart gave a quick jump – he even knew her name!

"I wonder would you do a favour for me," continued Winston. Jill nodded slowly and expectantly. This was going to be interesting.

"I left two pigeons in last week."

"Pigeons?"

"Yes, you know, bird things."

"I know what pigeons are, I just wasn't sure you actually said 'pigeons'," explained Jill. This was not a good start.

"Well, there's two of them with the pokers and I was wondering if you would move them for me?"

"The pigeons have pokers?" She hadn't heard of that one before.

"No, the pigeons are over *with* the pokers. No-one will buy them if they can't see them. Who looks at pokers? Would you mind maybe moving them somewhere better? Somewhere where they can be seen? I'd really appreciate it, Jill."

There, he had said her name again. Jill smiled.

"Sure, I'll do that, Winston. Are you going to school on Monday?"

"Uh, yes," answered Winston wondering where else she thought he might be going.

"Me too," smiled Jill.

"Well… that's good. Um, thanks."

As Winston left, Hazel Johnston, a girl in Jill's class walked in.

"See you Monday then!" called out Jill as Hazel passed. Winston waved back, not sure if he had missed something.

"Winston just called by to see me," explained Jill to her classmate as she turned to get back to her work. One for Jill McNarry, zero to Hazel Johnston.

Now where were those pigeons? She knew the very place to put them.

The woman on the other end of the phone was speaking quickly and sounded as if she was in some kind of a rush. Angela waited until there was a gap and spoke into the receiver.

"You say the dog bit someone? I'm not sure we can really help, Mrs McCully, is the dog injured?"

"No," responded the lady, "the dog's all right, but that's the third time the thing has had a go at someone. It's mad. It'll have to be sorted before it ends up doing some serious damage, or even killing someone, God forbid!" She still hadn't made it quite clear what she wanted the Practice to do so Angela tried again.

"And what would you like Dr Angel to do for you then?"

"Put the brute down!" replied the animated voice on the other end. "If not, the police will be on to us and then what? Can Dr Angel do that?"

"Yes, I see, right well, when can you bring it in?" asked Angela. Putting animals down was not unusual for a vet; in fact it was all too common. Usually it was due to some disease or other; occasionally a court order necessitated it. It appeared the woman was merely acting before she was forced to. It was a responsible thing she was doing and Mrs Angel could why see had got herself so excited about it – she was probably wrestling with her turbulent emotions.

"I'll have to have it done before tonight," was the reply. "I'll be around as soon as I can catch the $@§/! swine."

Yes indeed, her emotions seemed very turbulent indeed.

It was his dad's suggestion that perhaps the vet next door could do with a bit of a hand. It was clear that Winston had no real interest in the farm – besides a farm could only really support one son in any case and Nate was the obvious candidate there. It had been a week since the pigeon escapade and it occurred to Mr McFadzean that if Winston was so interested in animals perhaps a part-time job with Dr Angel would give his youngest some clearer focus. Winston had never thought of it before and as soon as his dad mentioned it Winston was interested. Gordon McFadzean prepared the ground first by calling by with Edward Angel, and so that morning, Winston stood before the man of letters.

"Your father was saying you have an interest in animals." said Dr Angel as he wiped the blood off his rubber-gloved hands. He had just operated on a cat whose owner was tired of constant litters of kittens appearing every so often around the yard. This cat's days of progeny production were over. It would be a bit uncomfortable for a few days, but a week or two down the line it would be as right as rain and forever kittenless to boot.

"Yes sir," replied Winston, "all sorts… pigeons mostly at the minute."

"Pigeons mmm? Very good, well, I was telling your father, a splendid man, your father, I was telling him that I could do with a bit of help. The surgery has got into a bit of a state recently; Mrs Angel and I have been very busy, and if you would like to tidy up for me for an hour or two this morning it would very helpful, yes, very helpful indeed."

There were a lot of empty boxes, drugs and medical supply things that Dr Angel wanted disposed of and Winston gathered them and took them to the back of the farm where he lit a bonfire and soon had the a pile of boxes and rubbish burning brightly. Returning to the surgery, he continued tidying up and was soon making good inroads into sorting out what even Winston could see had become very disorderly indeed. It was while he was busy brushing the small room the vet used for the store that Mrs McCully arrived at the bungalow with the dog.

If Mrs McCully had seemed rushed on the phone, in person she was positively supersonic.

"He's in the boot, is the doctor here? Can he hurry up? This needs done straightaway! Can you help me get him out? Where's the doctor?"

Mrs Angel tried calming the woman down. She kept looking over her shoulder and down the road from where she had come as if expecting someone to suddenly arrive behind her. Angela began opening the fees book to explain the costs involved.

"Oh stuff that Mrs Angel!" dismissed the restless woman. "I don't care what it costs, just get it done quickly!"

Angela rang through to the surgery and let her husband know that the dog had arrived. As they waited for him to come through, Mrs McCully got a large stick out of the car and moved to the boot. A length of rope hung out onto the rear bumper from the shut boot-lid and she wrapped it around her left wrist with the stick in her right.

"You'd be as well to stand back," she warned. "I don't think he appreciated the drive over – he was trying to eat through the back seats."

From the back store Winston heard the barking, shrieks and snarling howls. It went on for some time before eventually quietening down. Whatever the vet was working at, it didn't sound like it was wanting it much.

What the dog wanted was to sink its teeth into something moving. The woman holding his leash was hard to get at – she walloped him on the head with a stick every time he went for her. The other lady, the one with the white coat was an easier target but she would insist on running about the place, making an awful noise about it and generally proving difficult to get a good grip of. When the man arrived it was manna from heaven and after one good bite on his leg he did something with an object in his hand that gave him a sharp prick in his neck. After that things just didn't seem to matter much and he decided to sleep on it. He would eat all three of them later.

Rubbing the antiseptic on his leg, Edward Angel looked at the woman who stood sheepishly holding one hand to her face and a stick in the other.

"Oh, I'm sorry Mr Angel, are you all right? I did tell Mrs Angel he was wild," she apologised.

"Not your fault," said Dr Angel shaking his head, "All part of the job. If I had a pound for every time I've been bitten or kicked I'd be a rich man." If you want to go into the reception with Mrs Angel, I'll take care of the dog."

When the women had gone into the bungalow Edward Angel turned to the large tan shape lying peacefully on the drive. Normally he would have taken the animal into the surgery and gently have administered the fatal injection; this creature had left him with no alternative but the quick stab before his leg was chewed off. In a way he did not resent the dog its attack. After all, it had died doing what it liked doing most and since he was the agent of death, did he not in a strange sort of fashion deserve the marks? "All's fair in love and war," he told himself as he wondered for the first time how he was going to move such a large animal. It had to be near seven stone.

"If you can give me a hand out the front," Dr Angel said to Winston, "I've a dog I need a lift with."

Winston trotted along behind the vet and when he saw the dog lying on the drive remembered the howls.

"Is it sick?" he asked the doctor. The dog was warm and he imagined it was sleeping or unconscious.

"No," grunted the vet lifting his end. "Just dead."

"Oh," said Winston as he lifted his, "I suppose that's a kind of sick."

"There is a sickness that leads unto death – this wasn't it," said the vet enigmatically. Winston thought he recognised something biblical in his words but wasn't sure. It was appropriate though.

"Oh," he said.

"The fourth seal was opened," added Dr Angel, "I was riding my Pale Horse."

Winston nodded knowingly. Knowingly on the outside only, on the inside he hadn't a clue what Dr Angel was talking about.

"Where are we taking it?" asked Winston, "to the surgery?"

It was a question Edward Angel had omitted to ask himself. Now it was asked he realised he hadn't really considered the answer. At the door to the surgery they put down the dog and he pondered the reply.

"Now that's a bit of a problem actually. It's a big dog; normally I just leave cats and the like out the back for the dead cart to collect at the start of the week. This being a Saturday, it'll be Monday before it gets lifted and…"

"Do you want me to bury it for you?" interrupted Winston with a sudden surge of eagerness in his voice.

"Bury it?" queried the vet, "where?"

"Oh, we've an old rough patch behind the tractor house where we burn stuff and that. I could bury it there. It'd be no problem."

The veterinary surgeon rubbed his eyebrow and slowly nodded his head.

"Yes, well, if that's O.K. with your father?"

"It'll be fine," replied Winston encouragingly, "just glad to help."

"And you say your husband doesn't know?" Angela asked Mrs Mc-Cully.

"Are you joking?" the woman replied. "If he knew I took his favourite dog to be put down he'd go berserk! He loves, well, *loved* that thing. Every free minute he gets he's out killing rabbits or ducks or some poor unsuspecting creature with it."

"He kills them with the dog?"

"Well, he shoots them and then the dog rips them apart. By the time they land on my kitchen table they look like something that's been swallowed and spat out."

"What will he do when he finds out?"

"Lord knows!" exclaimed Mrs McCully. "But it was the dog or me. I didn't want to give him the choice. Francis McCully is a hard man, Mrs Angel."

"Where is he now?" asked Angela.

"Out on the fishing boat. The fleet comes back into Portnaboggan at about six or so. I'll tell him then." She paused in thought for a moment.

"Actually, I might get his mother to tell him – he'll probably not hit her."

Winston could hardly believe his luck. Now he could really get serious. The vet had responded to a call from a farm to sort out a sick sow so he fetched a wheelbarrow from the greenhouse to move the dog.

As he wheeled his prize into the yard, Nate came out of the tractor shed.

"Bringing work home?" he smiled at his younger brother. He had a massive tan dog in a wheelbarrow and what he was up to he could only guess at.

"Sort of," replied Winston, "The vet gave it to me."

"The vet gave you a dead dog? I sort of imagined you'd be working for money. What is it, a Great Dane?"

"No, I think it's a cross between a Labrador, a Doberman and a Rotweiller – maybe a bit of some other stuff too."

"What are you doing with it?"

"Well, the vet wants me to bury it, but what a waste. I'm going to stuff it!"

Having witnessed at close hand Winston's efforts with the pigeons, Nate was somewhat surprised.

"What, *all* of it?"

"Yes, of course all of it. The pigeon's were awkward because they were small and birds. The book is better when it comes to dogs.

Nate hoped his brother was too, though he doubted it. He watched him wheel the dog into the bottom shed then turned and headed off. This was going to get interesting.

Whether or not the pigeon gutting had hardened him or not Winston could not be sure, but the skinning of the dog bothered him less. It was like peeling an orange, he told himself. He had stuffed some toilet roll up his nose to deaden the smell and that, along with the excitement of his first real taxidermy job diverted his mind from the actual bloody task that separating an animal from its skin actually was.

After a couple of hours the first stage was finished and a rumpled tan skin lay before him on the wooden table. The rest of the dog he put into a black plastic bin bag – he didn't want Skeeter recognising the form of a fellow member of the canine fraternity in such a horrendous state. Even dogs could get traumatised.

Winston had managed to sneak out a large bread knife from the kitchen and now he used this to begin the job of scraping clean the inside of the skin. A large tub of table salt sat below the table, also covertly taken out of the kitchen and a bucket of ash taken from the bonfire sat ready to be rubbed into the hide to help dry and preserve it. Winston was feeling very pleased with himself and so absorbed was he in his labours that he didn't hear Nate enter through the open doorway.

"You didn't waste any time with Fido did you?" he asked as he saw Winston scrape away at the hairy skin. Four legs hung off each corner and the shape of the head was clearly distinguishable, two ears flopping off each side with a lippy inverted grin smiling up at him from the table.

Winston started as he looked up to see his brother peering at the skin on the table.

"Fido?"

"The dog," said Nathan pointing, "I take it this is the dog you had in the wheelbarrow?"

"Oh, yes, though I doubt if he was called Fido," said Winston. "What do you think so far?" he continued holding up the skin. Once it dries I'll make a frame and start the filling. You won't believe your eyes when

I'm finished."

Nate shook his head and rubbed the side of his head with his fingers. "Can't argue with that," he replied.

When Francis McCully got home he was wet, tired and hungry. It was a mixture of states that rarely left him in good humour. The fishing had not been particularly good either and that, along with being boarded by the fishery protection officers off the Calf of Man had not made things any better. By the time they had inspected the catch and the nets, a good hour had been wasted and the skipper took it out on the crew. All the way back Skipper Coffey ordered the men about the boat like wee boys and McCully bitterly resented it. Francis was not the kind of man you took anything out on but Ed Coffey was the only man on two legs who held no fear of Francis McCully. If Francis was the terror of the village, the skipper was the terror of the seas.

With the simmering return from the fishing grounds behind him, Francis McCully was in no great mood and the one thing that calmed him down a bit was his dog. Other men took theirs for a walk; Francis wrestled with his and generally kicked it about a bit. Right now he had a good bit of kick in him and he wanted it out. Unlike other dogs, Bane didn't whimper or run off. Bane stood and fought back. Francis McCully had the bite marks to prove it and he liked that spirit in a dog. In his own distorted thinking the kicking was given as a grudging admission of care for the dog and the bites were the reciprocation. After all, man's best friend was his dog, Francis McCully and his dog just had a strange twisted way of demonstrating it.

"Bane!" he called outside the back door. There was no growl from the shed and when he went to check there was no dog either.

Returning back into the house he heard the front door close.

"Is that you?" he barked.

Joan McCully was in no doubt as to who 'you' was. The rare times he used her name was when he wanted something or inadvertently forgot to be gruff. She loved the man despite herself but it was a love that defied rational explanation. He almost certainly loved her too but had yet in all their years together been able to find a way of expressing it. If there was a softer, kinder side to Francis McCully it was buried deep. Joan was the type of woman who was prepared to dig long and with dogged perseverance.

He could have hardly noticed the dog missing yet she told herself, and when he did she would just tell him. There had been nothing else to do and she knew she was right. There was no need to get his mother to do the dirty work of telling him – she would do it herself. Francis was likely to go mad but it would pass and the dog would still be mercifully gone. It was worth it: so she told herself – right now however she was feeling considerably less confident in her reasoning.

"Yes," she replied with some apprehension, setting down the shopping in the hall. "Just home?"

"Aye," grunted her husband, "where's the dog?"

"Ahm… your mother called to tell you something, I think she wants you to call back."

Winston heard the tyres screeching from the shed but thought nothing much about it. It could have been Nate – his brother didn't have a licence but it didn't seem to stop him much. It was a funny thing, his dad was so particular about 'doing the right thing', about keeping on the right side of the law. Nate's driving liberties seemed to fall on a blind spot in his dad's otherwise impeccable outlook. Maybe his dad thought Nate had a licence. Maybe Nate thought he did. Winston knew otherwise.

There was the sound of someone shouting too, but Winston paid scant attention. The fields around about were full of dairy cattle and one of the things people did with dairy cows was to shout at them. The other thing was to milk them, but it was almost always preceded by a lot of shouting to get them out of the fields, along the roads and into the parlours. Cow language had few words. There was 'Heyuuup!" with the emphasis on the 'uuup!" – it meant 'come along there now cows'. There was 'awayon awayon!" which meant 'move along there, time's moving on' and 'gedawayoudathat!' which was a word used to discourage a cow which had strayed up a hedge or was heading in a beeline for an out of bounds garden.

Had Winston listened more carefully, he would have heard that the shouting from the road included none of those phrases, and were considerably more colourful altogether.

On the other hand, Angela Angel was getting the full benefit of every word. She could hardly have missed them. The man who was delivering the tirade stood not six inches from her face and was shouting each phrase with an energy that actually made her chest wall vibrate. The extreme volume at which the words were released mercifully disguised much of their clarity, though none of the meaning was lost. The man was angry. In fact, the man was actually gnashing his teeth, something up to that point Angela Angel had thought was a mere figure of speech. He was also foaming at the mouth – specks of spittle bounced around the corners of his mouth and broke off in flying suds in every direction, though mostly hers. In the middle of his screaming accusations she heard the words 'dog' and 'I'll kill her'. It was a poor introduction to the fisherman husband of Joan McCully.

"Is it about your dog?" she asked quietly. She had heard that an American president once said that the most effective approach to a tyrant was to speak softly and carry a big stick. Having performed the first she felt an urgent need for the second – preferably *very* big – with iron studs – sharp ones.

"Yes it's about my $@§/! dog!" shouted the man. "If anyone has so much as laid a hand on Bane I'll wring his $@§/! neck with my own bare hands!"

Edward Angel did not need to be summoned; he heard the ruckus from the surgery and came out to investigate. He likewise did not need to hear much to realise who the man was and what was his complaint. With considerable tact and encouragement he managed to get the man to follow him into the surgery where he explained the situation and the procedure used. Francis McCully listened and looked fit to be tied; Dr Angel wondered if his wife had had the foresight to ring the police. When he was finished pointing out that the dog had suffered in no way and in fact would certainly have been put down anyway by the police along with a sizeable fine to the owner of such a dangerous animal, Francis McCully shocked Edward Angel by suddenly dropping his head into his hands and letting out a loud sob.

"My dog, my poor Bane!" he wept.

As suddenly as it had started it was over. Raising his head and wiping the side of his eyes he looked into the face of the vet. Any softness that might have been expected after the sob was gone and a steely determination stared out instead.

"Where's he now?" he demanded.

"The dog?"

"Aye, where's my dog? I want to see my dog!"

Nate was in the front yard taking a link box off the back of the Massey when the vet from next door and another man appeared.

"Hello," said Nate, "are you looking for Dad?"

"Actually no," said Dr Angel, "I was wanting a word with Winston? He was going to bury Mr McCully's dog for me this morning, I was wondering if he's done it yet?"

The man from behind, obviously the Mr McCully, a man Nate recognised, though didn't know well spoke up. He looked angry.

"I want to see my @*@* dog!" He also sounded angry.

"Ah," said Nate. "I'll go and ahm… would you like me to go and see if I can find Winston?"

"Thank you," said the vet, "that would be appreciated."

"And I'm coming with you!" barked McCully as Nate began down the yard, "I want to see my dog!"

Nate's mind was working like a paper-mill. If the man discovered what had become of his dog he would surely break every bone in his brother's body. Maybe his too. Nate called down the yard toward the shed where Winston was ensconced with the canine cadaver.

"Winston! Winston! Mr McCully's here to see where you buried his dog!" It was louder than it needed to be and with a lot of emphasis on the 'buried'. Winston's head appeared from behind the open shed door.

"What?"

Nate walked towards him, his index finger pointed surreptitiously back through his chest toward the following Francis McCully. Winston's eyes popped wide as he took in the meaning behind Nate's words and the intention written all over Francis McCully's fuming face. He glanced back into the shed where the remains of the sought after dog lay spread out like a blanket on the table. Winston instantly felt utterly convinced it was not the way the man with the red face was aspiring to see his dog. Dead was going to be bad enough – dead and rug-like was a big no no.

"Oh, right, the big dog?" asked Winston quickly slipping out of the shed and pulling the door behind him. It wouldn't shut fully and a foot wide gap yawned open into the dim morgue behind him.

"Where's my dog?" demanded Francis McCully. It was a demand that brokered no ill thought out reply.

"Buried," replied Winston simply and with a suddenly dry mouth.

"Where?" ordered the man.

"Ah, well…"

"Out the back," added Nate quickly. He could see his brother was grasping wildly.

"Where out the back? I want to see my dog!"

"Right, O.K. um, Winston, lead us out to the back where you… buried the dog for Mr McCully."

"You never buried him for me!" snarled the fisherman, "but if there's a burying to be done I'm the man to do it."

With the ominous threat ringing in his ears, Winston led them blindly around to the field behind the shed. What on earth was Nate at? He knew the dog was lying as flat as a pancake on the shed table – what were they going to do around the back? Maybe Nate's idea was to get a good bit of flat ground in order to make a run for it.

Once at the rear of the building Nate spoke up again.

"Was it over there you buried it Winston?" he asked, pointing the rough bit of ground beside the now cold bonfire. "Yes, just over there near the hedge, yes?" He looked expectantly at Winston. Winston nodded back robotically.

"Uh, yes, just beside the hedge."

The last few yards Nate led the way. A couple of yards from the hedge he stopped and looked at the ground.

"Here Winston?"

Nate had taken them to a place where obviously some digging had indeed taken place. The soil was raised but it was evidently not all that

178

fresh. Leaves lay on the soil and Winston saw evidence of grass just beginning to take root. Before Francis McCully had time to notice much,
Nate kicked the soil about a bit.

"Hmmm, I suppose you buried him deep? You always bury them deep,
don't you Winston?"

"Oh yes, very deep, six feet, sometimes a lot more," nodded Winston
warming to the ruse. "The bigger the deeper. Big animals, I just dig till
I drop. Massive holes, monster holes. Sometimes I…"

"I want to see him!" barked the fisherman interrupting Winston's
flow.

"But…" began Winston.

"Get your spade – I'm taking him home!"

Francis McCully's mother came round to her son's house after talking
to him on the phone. He had not taken the news about the dog well
and she was concerned for her daughter-in-law. Maggie McCully was
a small biddy of a woman, quiet but with an inner strength that belied
her outward appearance. She was not one of those mothers who saw
sons through rosy tinted glasses. Francis McCully had picked up all the
bad traits of her late husband and not many of the good ones. What her
daughter-in-law had seen in the scoundrel she could not imagine but
she admired her all the more for that. Francis had definitely improved
a little with his marriage to the admirable girl, but he was still a bad
tempered, selfish brute at times.

"So, where's the monster," she said arriving at Joan's front door. "Skulk-
ing about in the back yard no doubt."

Joan smiled and brought her mother-in-law in. Many of her friends
complained about their interfering mothers in law. Joan would have

married Francis just to be Mrs McCully's daughter-in-law.

"He roared off in a temper; said he was going to kill the vet," she sighed. "I hope the vet sticks the same needle up his backside that he used on the dog."

"What we need here is to cool him down a bit," commented her mother-in-law, "it's hard to work on your man when there's so much heat and noise. What do you say you and me go to the shop, get something nice for tea and stew his head in undeserved acts of womanly kindness?"

Joan smiled, she knew what she meant. Francis' wind would be fairly knocked out of his sails if he came home to sweetness and light. Coals of fire upon his head – a loaded gun and a target of vapours and mist.

"I'll take you over to Drysdale's in Ballydoonan if you like," added her mother-in-law. "He has a good game counter. A bit of duck or something will leave his mouth open and his big stupid head right out of gear."

"You are one devious little woman," laughed Joan. "Pity I hadn't cooked the dog, that would have been a good one!"

The two McCully women headed out to Maggie's Morris Minor. Already the sting was out of what had been promising to be an evening of argument and bad temper.

Skeeter had watched as Winston, Nate and the angry man had headed around the back. Rising from where he had been lying on the grass, he stretched himself and ambled over towards the open door. There was something interesting going on in that shed and Skeeter decided the time to investigate had come.

Winston arrived back at the fake burial site with a spade. He looked first at Francis McCully whose return stare was a clear indication that he expected the digging to begin immediately. He glanced at his brother; his expression was one of 'don't ask me, I'm trying to become invisible'.

He began digging, wondering for the first time what actually had been buried there. The soil was easily broken into and had evidently been unearthed and removed some time fairly recently. Visions of a cow popping its big head out were not helpful.

After a couple of feet of silent digging, the spade became tangled in what at first Winston thought was a root; the more he poked about, the more was revealed. It was barbed wire.

"What's that?" growled McCully.

"Barbed wire," said Nate quickly.

"Barbed wire?"

"Yes," confirmed Winston, "barbed wire."

"Where's my dog?" snarled the man, "I thought you said Bane was buried here?"

"That's right," replied Nate.

"That's right what?" asked the increasingly suspicious ex-dog owner. "Is it Bane under there or barbed wire?"

"Both," said Nate. Winston watched the conversation with complete incomprehension. He was going to die, but it might have been nice to die knowing he had a half sensible brother, not some nut. What *was* he talking about?

"Badgers," continued Nate. Winston closed his eyes and waited the inevitable stranglehold from the fisherman.

"Badgers?"

"Yes," explained Nate. "Every time we bury something around here the badgers dig them up again. That's why we always cover the animals with loads of barbed wire, that way the poor things get some peace. Getting dug up again can't be much fun – don't you think?"

Francis McCully looked at the hole and then at Winston. He looked at the hole again then at Nate. Finally he just looked at the hole.

"Hrmph," he grunted, rubbing his forehead with a large powerful hand. He went silent for a minute, a silence which neither Winston nor Nate felt the compulsion to break.

"He *is* definitely dead?" he said finally, in a much less confrontational tone.

"Oh yes," nodded Winston hastily, "definitely – completely dead."

After another pause, something seemed to click in the man and he turned and began to slowly move off.

"Well, that's all right then. I just wanted... I just wanted to be sure. No point digging the old boy up, I suppose."

The waves of relief that crashed upon the shores of Winston's mind were so real as to be almost audible. He and Nate walked back into the yard, a pace or two behind the silent McCully. As they approached the shed door, suddenly Skeeter appeared with something strewn over his back. Something large, tan and rug-like. Something with four legs dangling at each corner. Catching movement to his right, Skeeter turned and saw the three approaching. He suddenly moved up a gear and loped up the yard and down the drive. Half way down, he turned and disappeared into the bushes. Francis McCully stopped short, raised his head and spun around.

"What was that?" he demanded.

"The dog," replied Winston without thinking. McCully's face began to change.

"*Skeeter* the dog," stammered Nate quickly. "He's our dog."

"What was that he had over his back?"

"Over his back?" stalled Nate desperately.

"Yes, what was that on the dog's back?"

"Oh, you mean his novelty coat? That's some old thing we put on him in winter. Stupid dog wears it all the time, doesn't he, Winston?"

"Oh yes, loves it," replied Winston, grinning stupidly.

The fisherman seemed to consider the information for a moment before shaking his head slightly and moving on to his car.

"Daft looking, you'd never get any of my dogs wearing anything like that."

As he disappeared into the vet's yard Nate shook his head.

"You'd be surprised," he whispered.

"I think I've finished with taxidermy," said Winston.

Francis McCully arrived home just behind the Morris Minor. He had half intended storming into the house and giving his wife a piece of his mind – only half intended; to be honest the passion was out of him by now. With his mother at home he resigned himself to letting it go. Some things weren't worth the bother. As he entered the front door he saw the women had been shopping; a couple of bags lay on the kitchen table.

"Where have you been?" he said to whoever felt like answering.

"Drysdale's," said his wife's voice. "We got something special for tea."

"Oh? Special?"

"Yes," she said, pointing to one of the bags on the table. "You haven't had this for a while."

"Had what?"

"Pigeon!" returned the triumphant reply.

Skeeter soon tired of his new toy. Taking the floppy thing into a field he did what he often did with unusual treasures. Finding a quiet corner he dug a hole and buried it.

9.

Marks in the Sands of Time

Nathan McCutcheon, not being a great devotee of education, had nonetheless a favourite subject in school. Favourite in the sense that, if he *had* to be at school, if once there he *had* to attend classes, if in those classes it really was necessary to be cognisant of what was going on around him, then English was his favourite subject.

It was a subject that allowed a certain freedom of thought denied by those other unyielding subjects such as Physics or Maths. It seemed to Nathan that those subjects were simply a matter of learning formulae, procedure and endless lists. There was no individuality in those subjects, no flair, no soul. They also took no prisoners. You either got the answers right or else you were wrong. What bothered Nathan most was that to get them right you had to study and spend time memorising and learning. Life was only so long, a finite experience – using it up in learning stuff he was never likely to ever have need to refer to again seemed to Nathan to be as useful as a chocolate fireguard.

That the same argument could have been applied equally to English never occurred to Nathan. He liked English, he did not see reading Thomas Hardy as study – that was something he would have done whether it was in the curriculum or not. It was the same with the others whose words curled around his mind when he spent long periods in their company. Robert Frost, D. H. Lawrence, Charles Dickens – they were all familiar companions to Nathan. Why some people professed to dislike English was strange to Nathan – the weirdoes who preferred Chemistry or Physics had clearly some mental aberration that meant they only used the hard crusty little parts of their brains.

He would have loved English were it not for his English teacher. Not that he didn't like the teacher – it was just that Mr Davidson was rarely there. Mr Davidson was a dark stocky man, an ex-rugby player who had escaped with normal ears and with a head of black hair just beginning to thin like a monk's at the top. His head was large and square with a dark shaven face and a Roman nose neatly running long and straight down the centre. His short legs propelled him along shiny corridors at an amazing pace, his arms swinging militarily by his sides.

He was head of the English department and apparently that meant that he had to be off sorting out problems in other teacher's classes every five minutes or so. In a forty minute period of English, Mr Davidson's class was fortunate indeed if he was actually present in the room for any more than ten minutes. His usual mode of teaching was to give the class a poem or chapter from a book to read, leave a few questions and tasks and promptly pop off to rescue somebody else's class. Somebody had to rescue his some day, thought Nathan, especially if he was to get to grips with blinking haiku poems. Some things from Japan were good. He liked Toyota cars; Honda had some very impressive motorcycles, but haiku? Why English classes had to include Japanese stuff was beyond him. He heard once that Japan had a similar population and land area to the United Kingdom but he hardly thought that merited it having its inscrutable poems imposed on an unsuspecting nation on the other side of the world.

So it was that when Mr Davidson took sick and was off for four weeks having some part of his body removed – it might have been an appendix – paradoxically English class improved dramatically.

Improved in the sense that with no teacher, they got a stand-in – a sub-teacher, Mr Godley.

He was young, keen and enthusiastic, tall and blonde, he had a vaguely Nordic appearance and in fact spoke with a hint of an accent that might have been German, or South African or somewhere out of the ordinary. Coincidentally at around the same time a new girl arrived in class. She was quiet and kept mostly to herself but seemed to like English. Nathan noticed she wrote a lot and seemed to do well in homeworks. She didn't laugh much, or even smile come to that, but then it wasn't like anybody laughed a lot in actual classes. She was in a couple of Nathan's other subject classes too and there too she kept herself to herself. Her name was Heather Woods and she was a girl. That was about all Nathan knew about her – just a girl new to their school.

With an actual teacher spending actual time in the actual classroom however, the class began to learn things about the authors they had been reading and the topics amongst which they had hitherto been cast adrift. Nathan had had a vague notion for example, that Mister Thomas Hardy Esquire was still alive and well somewhere in the place called Wessex – probably an old man, but alive all the same. It came as a bit of a shock to learn that he would need to be a very old man indeed to be alive; he had died in 1928 at the age of eighty seven.

"Hardy's Wessex was a creation of the author's," explained Mr Godley, "a semi-real semi-poetic artefact devised to contain the fatalistic life-view of the writer," he continued. The class were beginning to learn all right, but Nathan wasn't so sure he was liking the information.

"Excuse me, sir," he asked as Mr Godley began to move onto the naturalist movement. Some boys in the class looked impatiently toward

Nathan for his interruption, they thought they were about to hear about naturism, a very different subject altogether.

"Yes?" replied the teacher, his eyebrows raised. An interruption was not a bad thing but he nonetheless was not expecting one. The boy half way down the middle of the class probably wanted to go to the toilet. Why couldn't they just go during break? If he was re-writing the school rules he would make it a mandatory act – 'piddle time' he would call it. Now what did the boy want?

"Did you just say there's no actual Wessex at all sir?"

Mr Godley pushed back his long blonde fringe and set down his text book. He glanced at the roll book on the desk.

"No… *McCutcheon*, is it?"

"Yes sir."

"No, McCutcheon." Nathan's school was not one where teachers called the boys by their first names. That was the preserve of the girls – boys were another animal. "No, Wessex is a name Hardy sequestered from the old Anglo-Saxon Kingdom that once existed in roughly the same geographical area. The actual counties of Devon, Dorset, Hampshire and a few others were the setting for his novels. Wessex is a fabrication."

Nathan gave a slow nod and said no more. It helped explain right enough why his letters to Mr T. Hardy, Casterbridge, Co. Wessex, England, had never been replied to. That and the fact that he was dead.

"Thank you, sir," said Nathan in reply.

A *fabrication*? It was a bit of a blow to him actually. He had had an argument with his mother about the very same thing. She had come from an age where-in school children learned things by rote. His mum could rhyme off the capital of every country Nathan could care to remember the name of. When he challenged her to name the nine counties of Ulster she had laughed at him and recited all thirty two in

Ireland. When she reached Wicklow and stopped, Nathan told her she had forgotten Wessex.

"Wessex?" she repeated with a quizzical look on her face. "There's no county in Ireland called Wessex."

Immediately realising his error, Nathan laughed deprecatingly and shook his head.

"I know – I was just trying to catch you out. Wessex is in England."

"Wessex? Don't you mean *Essex?*"

"No, Wessex. It's a county down near the bottom of England."

"Wessex?"

"Yes, we're learning about it in English. Thomas Hardy comes from there."

"Thomas Hardy?"

"Yes, a famous writer. He's from Wessex – they mostly milk cows down there and breed sheep and stuff."

"There's no county called Wessex dear," said his mother thoughtfully. It was then that Nathan had turned on his 'I'm young and educated – I know, you don't' voice. For him it was as sure as pigs were dirty. His mother had just shaken her head and looked unconvinced but not sure enough to push the point.

"Trust me mum, I *know*." His mother gave a shrug and said no more. For Nathan that was a win.

But now Wessex was a *fabrication*? Some guy had just made it up? Was there nothing reliable left in the world?

"I have a homework I want you to do for next week," said Mr Godley, breaking abruptly into Nathan's thoughts. "Hardy explores the pointlessness of the human experience. Hopes and aspirations are almost never fulfilled in reality. Like entropy, man's experience is one of winding down, the weight of aimless fatalism grinding down even the most naïve optimisms to the final, purposeless dust of the grave. I want you to write a short piece in Hardyesque fatalism and sketched on a similar canvas of naturalism. About five hundred words or so."

It would have helped if Nathan had half understood the question. Discussing class work was a totally uncool thing to do but after his cool reception from his question in class, Nathan did not risk asking Mr Godley to explain his homework. At lunch he found himself sitting opposite the new girl who was sitting on her own on the other side of his dinner table.

"Uh, hello," muttered Nathan catching the girl's eye as she looked up, a far away look on her face. "What did you think about Godley's homework?"

The girl didn't seem to hear Nathan's question and instead looked over his head as if in a daydream. Nathan looked behind himself and saw nothing but a canteen full of noisy pupils eating and gossiping. He turned back and was about to ask the question again when the girl gave a small start and focused on Nathan.

"Sorry, what? Did you say something? Oh, I'm sorry… I was… sorry…"

"No, that's O.K." smiled Nathan, "nobody ever listens to me much anyway, I was wondering what you made of Mr Godley's homework."

"In English class?" asked the girl engaging into the conversation. "The one about Hardy?"

"The very one," confirmed Nathan. "I was sort of not very much listening and I might have missed what he said a bit." For the first time since he had seen her, Heather Woods gave a smile – it was slight but it completely changed her appearance. He had not thought about how she looked before, but her smile, though weak revealed a pretty face circled by long dark hair.

"I don't like it," she said with a small shudder, "I'm sorry, I know your surname is McCutcheon, but I don't think I know your Christian name? I'm Heather Woods."

"I know," said Nathan, "I'm called Nathan, I'm from Ballydoonan. Welcome to our school. Have you just moved here?"

"Yes," replied Heather, "we had to move from Fermanagh. I went to a girl's school there. Do you like English?"

"Actually I do," admitted Nathan. "Not sure what I think of Godley though. He's only been teaching us a week – came about the same time as you. He's only a temp; our real teacher is even more absent than usual. He's in hospital – that's if they can keep him there longer than five minutes. No, I just wasn't sure what Godley wanted us to write about."

"What he *wants* us to write about is death," said Heather quietly. It was all she said. There was a silence for a few awkward moments before she suddenly stood up and gathered her plates.

"I have to go," she said. "I've to see Mrs Ford the form mistress." With that she left and Nathan watched her thread her way through the tables, leave her plates on the canteen trays and carry on out through the double doors. Nathan shrugged as she disappeared.

"Death," he repeated. "What fun."

'Death' was the last thing on his mind that weekend. 'Exploration' was however. He had started reading a book on the race to the South Pole. Captain Scott and Roald Amundsen were the two protagonists whose fearless and awesome exploits in the icy grip of undiscovered land drove him to look farther than the woods at the back field. Finding an old map of the Ards in his dad's filing cupboard, he pored over it on Friday night and made his plans.

"Hey, Dad?" he asked his father as he sat reading something more about Perry Mason. There seemed to be a lot to learn about that man – his dad had about a million books with his name plastered all over the dust cover.

"Yes, son?" replied Bob McCutcheon without lifting his eyes from his book.

"Did you know there's a big piece of ground between here and the Lough and there's no roads crossing it? Do you think it could be almost unexplored? Maybe like a forgotten tract of wilderness?"

"Could be, son," replied his father absently. Perry Mason was just about to discover a motive for the foul murder of the rich heiress – Bob's mind was not quite on the question.

"That's what I thought," mused Nathan as he left the room. Tomorrow was Saturday and if the weather was good he had plans to prepare. What was he saying? Amundsen would be ashamed of him – he was going exploring, foul weather or fair. Amundsen used dogs, Scott used horses and even tractors for a bit – Nathan had his bicycle.

The 1/25000 scale map showed a long dotted line running into the otherwise roadless tract and it was to this line that Nathan decided to begin his assault. When he got there half an hour later it turned out to be a lane up to a bungalow on a low hill. It was an inauspicious start – he doubted if Shackleton or Franklin had started from bungalows. Of course, Shackleton and Franklin, Scott and Amundsen started with white empty sheets of paper for maps – they would doing the filling in the blanks as they went along. In Nathan's case, his map was just wrong – there was no bungalow on his dad's faded HMSO edition.

He would have given up at that point except that he decided to risk it and ride up the lane anyway and take a look. There was no-one around in the yard at the bungalow, which was just as well since were he asked he would have had no answer in hand as to why he was loitering about in a stranger's drive. 'Exploring' had the capacity to be entirely misunderstood.

What he did discover was that the lane did not stop at the bungalow, but continued on by, the single storey building obviously having been built on the lane long after the lane's creation.

Without hanging about, Nathan cycled on by the house and pedalled on up the lane. From here on, the hedges were thicker and taller and grass grew up the middle of the tarmac which itself petered out after a hundred metres or so into a bumpy stone lane. Two axle tracks carried on, the grassy strip running up the middle, ragwort tall and yellow and growing unmolested by the absence of traffic.

The bicycle shook and rattled with the bumps and holes and the lane wound over and around several hills and then through a bog with bulrushes holding up their heads like rats on skewers either side of the lane. About a mile and a half in there was a steep down hill, a ninety degree bend to the left and the lane climbed up a hill so steep that Nathan had to dismount and walk up it, pushing his bicycle along on the centre strip. Trees circled the top of the hill, rook's nests heavy in their boughs.

Cresting the ridge, a farm building suddenly arose on his left and he saw an orchard on the opposite side. Thinking he had stumbled onto a working farm he stopped and listened. He listened for a number of things; tractors, machinery, cattle, voices perhaps, but mainly he listened for dogs. A dog disturbed in its own territory had the ability to run remarkably fast. And bite at the same time. Nathan turned his bike on the lane and listened with one leg over the bar. Exploration also involved good preparation. Preparation to cycle like a lunatic was a particularly relevant preparation, Nathan thought.

It was an unnecessary precaution. After a few moments observing the rusting steel sheds and overgrown orchard, it was clear the farm was abandoned. The farm opened out on the left as he passed the first building – a decrepit hay shed. Creeping gingerly into the central yard he looked around at the silent scene. The square yard was framed behind him now by the hay shed while straight ahead and left low farm outhouses, their roofs caved in and windows covered in briars, stood quiet and still. To the right, the farm house, a tall Edwardian building, stood looming over the yard, a door framed by dark windows, small panes obscured with cobwebs within and mould and grass without. The house made up that corner of the yard, the L shaped building with the door on the main dwelling commanding the whole of the yard. Tall hexagonal chimney stacks towered into the sky; each stack of four lined with four black pots, some broken, others long and slender like prim ladies of clay, presiding over all beneath them. On the far side of the farmhouse, a lean-to shed housed an ancient tractor, so attacked by rust that its wheel rims were splayed open, algae-covered tyres half off and filled with oily water at the bottom.

Nathan set his bicycle against the wall at the yard door and peered in a window. Vague darkness without shape or form looked back. The door was nailed shut, long six inch nails roughly driven through the door frame making all access there a cold refusal. Leaving his bicycle in the lean-to beside the tractor, Nathan returned to the lane and made his way around to the back of the house. Here the house looked down onto the other side of the hill, a wildly overgrown garden making access almost impossible. Squeezing between the woody fuscia and the cracked plaster wall he got to what was actually the front door; a tall porch thrusting out into a garden, losing a war with briar and the uncontrolled fuscia which had forced through the rotten door and past the cracked glass on the high brick-arched porch windows. Although the door was rotted and useless, Nathan could make no impression whatsoever on it when he pushed. The fuscia stems were six inches thick and in thrusting through the timbers had wedged the door completely immobile in their powerful grip. He looked back into the garden and saw a monkey puzzle tree rising above the jungle of shrubbery and bushes. Entwined in a half-dead furze bush he saw the remains of iron fencing, even its metal permanence overtaken by the relentless force of nature.

It took a bit of hauling, but after five minutes or so of frenzied pulling, he managed to extricate a six foot length of fencing which he placed up against the wall of the porch.

A ladder now in place, Nathan got up to the window and easily removed the cracked and broken glass, dropping it carefully into the porch itself. Taking care not to slice something open that was not supposed to be sliced open; Nathan let himself in through the window and immediately fell through the floorboards in a puff of orange dust. The shock made Nathan let out a short cry, but the ground beneath the floorboards lay only six inches below and the sharp surprise was as bad as it got. The floor was completely wood-worm eaten and everywhere the smell of decay rose like a ghoul awakened from a long dead sleep. Moving more carefully and testing the floor as he went, he moved into the house and began to explore. Apart from his cry of surprise he made no other noise; the house itself seemed to forbid it, a quietness different from mere lack of noise seemed to fill the place like a shroud.

Nathan looked wide-eyed around a room to the right – the house lay furnished and complete as if vacated with every expectation of return. That no return had ever taken place was clear in the dust and decay that lay thick and grey, all colour having been drained as if in some final deadly transfusion. In a corner an ancient piano lay falling to pieces, its veneer almost completely peeled off by successive years of damp and wind and rain skirmishing in through the cracked panes of glass.

Peering at the odd lights draped in cobwebs on the ceiling, Nathan realised that the house had no electricity – the lamps were paraffin. Lace curtains covered the windows within, though when he went to push one back to allow in more light, it fell to shreds in his fingers. A small hallway led to a working kitchen, a great stove making the heart of the room, rusted pots and kettles hanging from metal bars above the long cold fires. Running up from the nailed back door was a staircase and taking care on the creaking carpetless steps, he ascended into what he imagined would have been the bedrooms. Darkness dropped like a heavy curtain as he ascended into a silent gloom lit only by moss covered skylights. As his eyes adjusted to the dim light, he saw that the bedrooms were unlike any bedrooms he knew. The main room at the head of the stairs was divided simply into two partitions by a thin wall. Gaps where the plaster had fallen off appeared to show that it was made out of strips of wood and mud. Each partition had two beds each but when he looked a bit further, a further double bed lay behind drapes of Hessian hanging from poles strung across the wall in the room to the left. He looked more carefully and saw that the beds were straw filled; the sheets were missing and the thin mattresses looked tired and worn out. Frail bedside furniture, all strength long since sapped by wood-worm stood at the beds, some with thin china vases, one with metal tongs and broken combs. Seeing the walls more clearly now, he saw that they were decorated with old sepia photographs in thin black frames. As he peered at the images, serious-faced individuals looked back at Nathan from an age before his and seemed to wordlessly demand who he was and what was his business. The photographs were faded like everything else in the house and contained nothing of much detail except the severe faces, but as he turned to return to the stairs, one particular image caught his eye and made him pause to take a second look.

It was a family photograph, but unlike the other studio posed images, this one was taken in the open, a house behind and white chickens in the yard. Tall hexagonal chimneys on the house made him realise the house was the very one in which he stood, but its gleaming windows and open door was a house at ease; a house alive.

The man and woman each held a child in their arms, the woman nursing a baby, the man with a child of perhaps one and a half. Either side they were framed by two boys, both about fourteen years old, each the striking resemblance one to the other. *Twins*, thought Nathan. Unlike every other face in the photographs, the boys were smiling – wide open smiles, smiles that hid no secrets, smiles that were pure and simple in every sense that was good and right and real. Something about their bright faces seemed vaguely familiar but like echoes from a dream forgotten, all that remained was the disjointed sense of something unknowable – a nameless lost experience. He stood and looked at the photograph for so long that, when he turned and readjusted to his surroundings, the contrast was like turning from life and peering into the grave.

The rest of the house was just as dead and dusty. Downstairs he saw light pouring through a door that lay ajar by an inch or two and when he pushed it open, he discovered a single story extension, its roof collapsed on a rubble mound on the floor. Here light and life was reclaiming the dying and green shining ivy grew along every wall while several young slender ash trees sprouted from the mound that had been the roof. Somehow it made the house's dying all the worse and Nathan returned the way he had come and climbed back out the porch window into the thicketed light of the long forgotten garden.

All the way back, Nathan felt as if something heavy had been placed on his chest. He felt as if he had lost something yet could think of nothing he had left behind. He kept thinking of the photographs in the bedrooms – because of where they were, photographs not intended to be seen by any but the family whose history he knew nothing about. He felt as if he had intruded, not just in an old house, not that kind of interference – but as if he had infringed on something private, some event of which he was a stranger and that forever.

Back on the road, he revived considerably with the return of the familiar and by the time he was cycling back up his own lane, less than an hour later and then into his own yard, the odd feelings of unidentified remorse had more or less evaporated.

On Monday, Mr Godley broke away from *Tess* to relate more of the author's viewpoint to the class.

"So you see, in *Tess*, whatever hopes you may have for the final salvation of the innocent are lost in the reality that Hardy saw life actually was. There is no happy ending – at least not by design. The nonsense of Divine Fate, or some vain hope in a god out there who makes things right in the end are demolished in the reality that the righteous are no more likely to know peace than the miscreant."

That's all very sobering, thought Nathan. Mr Godley seems to be ill-named.

"Don't you believe in God then sir?" asked a voice at the back of the class. All eyes turned back to the teacher at his desk. He seemed to think for a moment before replying, but when he did it was not usual impassionate teacher stuff.

"Do I believe in God? How can I believe in something I can neither see nor hear? Is there a God? I've never met him; I've never heard a big voice from the sky telling me what to do. Look, belief in God is romantic drivel, lazy thinking – the easy way out of facing up to life's difficult questions. I can scarcely believe that any semi-intelligent human being actually believes that there is an actual personal God out there and who has any relationship with people and their problems. Hardy certainly didn't and neither do I."

Another voice spoke from behind Nathan.

"Doesn't Hardy mention ghosts somewhere in his writing? I thought Hardy was into Spiritualism?"

"Hardy was a man of his time," explained Mr Godley holding out his pen like a lance. "Many writers of his generation were interested in the spiritual, but not in the sense of the Christian God. He wrote about supernatural forces that indifferently controlled the universe, as aware of humanity as you are of the dust molecules under your desk. No will exists outside of our own. Hardy only played with idea – inside he knew, like we all know, we are alone in the universe – there is no big daddy who's going to fix it all in the end. I mean, just look at the rubbish spouted in the hymn books. I heard somewhere once a hymn being sung with the ludicrous words 'Footprints in the eternal sands of time' or some such trash. Just think about it, how long do footprints last on a beach? I'll tell you how long; eleven hours and fifteen minutes at most. That's when the tide comes back in and erases every mark. In the end everything runs down – everything finally crumbles into final dust and returns to the nothing from which it came, blown away by life's capricious winds. The fact is that hard cold reason erases every argument in favour of the existence of god, or *purpose*, or whatever you choose to call it."

As he spoke, Nathan noticed Heather Woods, the new girl in the row to his right and one desk forward, lower her head and apparently close her eyes. Mr Godley set his pen on his desk and surveyed the class like a man with a machine gun regarding a small crowd of natives with sticks. Nathan put his hand up.

"Sir, Mr Hamilton says you should never get your theology from your hymn book." It was out before he had decided whether or not it was a sensible thing to say. Mr Godley turned to Nathan, a sardonic smirk on his face.

"Mr Hamilton?"

"Our minister, sir. He says most hymns are sentimental nonsense too. He's Presbyterian."

"Presbyterian? What's that got to do with it?" Mr Godley was mildly curious and at the same time unsure if the boy four desks down was just trying to be smart.

"Presbyterians didn't use to sing hymns. Mr Hamilton said they only used to sing Psalms; anything else was just man-made and not suitable for the, the ah… the worship of God. He said it contravened the first catechism." Nathan tried not to present the view as if it was his own – he was just pointing out another viewpoint, that was all right, wasn't it? – still, half-hidden sneers from others in the class made it clear he was not winning the 'coolest boy in class' award that year.

Mr Godley was fairly new to Northern Ireland. He had had a mixed upbringing, coming from a white family in Southern Rhodesia who, unusually, owned no land; they nonetheless were treated as rich foreigners and got out before the going got worse. They ended up in Holland where his father had eventually found work as a welder in a large engineering firm. When that firm had moved to England, the family had gone too and the Gottfried family changed country and name all in one fell swoop. Much of the culture learned in England had not transferred well into the land of grey steeples and green hills. As a teacher in a land where he had much to learn himself, Mr Godley was sometimes put off balance.

"The first catechism? Pray what is that, McCutcheon?" The class sniggered and Nathan flushed. Why couldn't he just keep his big trap shut once in a while? Nathan cleared his throat.

"What is man's chief end?" he asked rhetorically. Rhetorically as far as the teacher was concerned for he continued by providing the given answer. "Man's chief end is to glorify God and enjoy Him forever." That said Nathan went silent. Perhaps the bell would ring now.

"Hmmm," mused the teacher. He faced the class and looked around. "I'll tell you what. Apart from parroting words that you have heard and have not thought about – making them therefore irrelevant, I want you all to consider a reason for the belief in God. On Wednesday I'll ask you again and we'll see if any of you have come up with anything that can stand the face of a reasoned debate." The class gave a ripple of laughter; a laugh that made it clear the consensus was very much with the man called Godley. At that the bell rang and Nathan slunk out with the others as the class poured out to break. By chance, Nathan spotted Heather Woods' pale face as he headed down the staircase leading to the floor below and as he did caught a glint of something on her cheek. It was a tear.

As it so happened, the Reverend Hamilton called by on one of his pastoral visits that very evening. Bob McCutcheon wasn't in and, not a man to call when a woman was without her man in the house, would have left except that Nathan spoke to him at the door.

"Actually, if you have a minute, Mr Hamilton?"

"Well of course your English teacher is quite correct," said the minister, giving Nathan a bit of a shock. "I have never seen God, and He has never bellowed down in some thunderous voice from heaven to catch my attention either."

Nathan had hoped for something a bit stronger in the god-evidential department from his minister and he was substantially disappointed to say the least.

"So how do we *know* there's a God… well, I know there *is* all right," he stammered, "but how do you *prove* it?" The minister set down his tea and smiled.

"Well, he's certainly not going to walk into your English class and say 'Ta daa! Guess Who!'"

"Well, no, I suppose not," said Nathan, "but you'd think He'd do *something!*"

"Ah well, you see, that's just the point, He has. But it was expensive and He could only do it once. 'Once for all', Nathan. You know, the Russian Cosmonauts returned from space saying that they had been into the heavens and there was no God because they had seen no God there. C.S. Lewis said that was a bit like a man saying that there was no Shakespeare because he had read all of his plays and failed to find any person so named. Lewis was saying that God is more related to his work as an author than as a character. He exists, he exists absolutely and actually as a Person, but not in the way we might expect. When the author steps onto the stage, the play is over – the characters' little parts have finished. Those who wish to see Him might better think what they wish for.

"I see," said Nathan, not sure if he did at all.

"Think of it like this, what would God achieve by just stepping up to the lights?"

"Well, at least everyone would know that He's real," answered Nathan.

"Yes," nodded Mr Hamilton, "but that's not the kind of kingdom He's building, Nathan; not a kingdom just merely made up of people who simply believe in their heads He exists. God wants us to *know* Him; you don't get to know a person just by looking at them. His kingdom will be one where people have come to *love* Him and you don't truly love by mere sight. My wife doesn't love me because she sees my face every day; she loves me because, well, because she loves *me*. She trusts me, has faith in me, knows that I love her too – all those things – no, love comes through discovering who people really are – and one of they best ways to do see what they *do*. People believe in God when they discover what He has *done*. *'It is finished'* is action louder than any word."

On Tuesday Heather Woods was absent from class again, though later Nathan discovered she had been with Mrs Ford for one of her meetings. Female form mistresses were a strange breed. The boys only had chats with the male form teachers if they had tried to blow up the school or something – or in Nathan's case, when he had almost succeeded in blowing up the school. The girls met with their form mistresses for all sorts of stupid things – half of the girls in his year were forever moping off to Mrs Ford for headaches and stomach cramps – like, let a boy try that one!

On Tuesday night Nathan felt a big hand slap across the back of his head. It was a figurative hand – his memory had suddenly slammed the fact into his head that he had a piece of Hardyesque prose to hand in the next morning and his effort expended in that direction was precisely nil. For anybody else it would have meant getting down to a long night of writing and a mental vow to take homework more seriously. For Nathan it meant sharpening a pencil for the bus journey in the morning. Events however were to take a different turn. The world turned, the sun shone on another part of the globe and night time noises called across the woods behind the fields. In his bed, Nathan entered another world.

Nathan was a dreamer. Not that he had occasional dreams, or sporadic mixed-up dreams interspersed with the odd vivid one. No, Nathan dreamed *every* night. Every morning he would awake with quite clear recollections of the dreams of the night past. He used to recount them at the breakfast table but after a while the others tired of his exploits involving driving cars off cliffs or exploring the universe in silver spacecraft. Dream relating was not what people were wanting to hear when looking into the day to come. Actually, what people wanted to hear in Nathan's house in the morning, especially parent people, was the sound of cornflakes being eaten and doors being opened and closed with some sort of correlation to the impending arrival time of the school bus at the bottom of the lane. Nathan's dreams were just so many precious minutes wasted when teeth should have been being brushed. So for Nathan, the accustomed practise had become just to let the dreams fade away as the day warmed.

That night, Nathan dreamed a dream so vivid and realistic, he awoke staring at the ceiling – totally awake in a second, his mind a reel of 35mm movie film in full blazing Technicolor detail. Dim light from the eastern sky filtered in through his bedroom window casting fingers of light across the floor. Nathan's schoolbag lay at the side of his bed and he immediately leaned over and pulled out a jotter and pencil and began to write. He didn't bother with the bedside light; electricity had no place right now. This was one he had to remember.

At the top of the page he scribbled down a title, 'The Cross-Barred Gate', below that he wrote without stopping to think – he just unrolled the reel of film.

I dreamt I stumbled upon an old fallen down farm, through hedges thick with bramble and black thorn. Tall and stately its walls once must have been, but thick stony silence greeted me in the emptiness of its long lost roof.
Beams spanned the chasms from wall to wall and here and there crumbled holes in the masonry overflowed with ivy and long spindly arms of inquisitive briar.
How melancholy it looked, dreams and hopes long, long forgotten, and now a bitter memorial of stone, solitary and lost.

I crept out to the yard beyond and in the cold dank grey after-noon November light, crossed to where, at a corner of the yard stood a cross-barred gate. Though once its wooden frame led to a field behind, age here too had invoked the untended hedgerows to mingle and grasp it in its growth.

Looking over the wooden bars, I saw a sodden colourless sky with a water-logged and wasteland field, a corner no-one cared to remember. Still, I leaned against its gnarled bars when to my surprise, as if running on newly oiled hinges, the gate gracefully slid apart. Just an inch or two, but enough that gave me a sight that made my heart almost halt to take it in.

Nathan scribbled quickly, the words pouring out from his still vivid dream, pictures becoming words on the paper before his fuzzy eyes.

Through the chink, a blue, blue sky was beaming in summer abandon, low cotton clouds hung on the horizon and in the newly mown straw stubble, amongst the tied up bundles of straw played two boys, whooping and screaming as they chased each other around the sheaves.

My whole being ached to see, to drink it in, the tidy rows of hedge, fragrant with blossom of haw and blackberry, the musky odour of the straw, the laughs and freedom of the boys at play.

… and then, quite unexpectedly, the boys stopped and looked straight at me. From fifty feet away they stopped and gave me such a look of joyous recognition that even as their open mouthed faces broke into grins, even as they careered towards the gate, I knew for certain that I knew these brothers and as I forced my memory to recall, the gate, slowly on silent oiled hinges clicked shut, and gazing through the bars my desolation was mirrored in

the sodden colourless sky and wasteland field.

Returning, void and empty, I cast another gaze at the lofty walls.
What had these gables long looked out upon? On children, laugh-
ing as they grew, on strong and bronzed arms guiding ploughs
behind stocky horses. Whitewashed walls soaking in generations
of lives lived in their strong and safe shadows. And secrets held
within, quiet sobs in upper rooms, decisions taken and looks ex-
changed.

And now, looking at these solitary, silent walls, I think perhaps
they are not unspoken in loneliness, but heavy with remembrances
stored within each crack of plaster and it might be, deep within
its rich and secure masonry the fallen farm closes its eyes in the
quiet memory of what it once had known.

Later, after I awoke it crossed my mind that in this side of time,
where grey resides somewhere in everyone's vocabulary, the stony
walls of solitude bring me to press against the cross barred gate to
see beyond faces that I know, faces that await the day when grey
is gone and warm and happy arms wrap around and say —

"Didn't you know? Didn't you see it written in the very stones and
hidden in the world for all to find"?

He wrote without stopping, and when he finished he closed the jotter, lay on his back and stared at the ceiling below the roof above his head. For what seemed like hours he thought of life and death, angels and the human soul and also, after a while, how long he could hold on before going to the toilet. The last thought eventually won and he padded on the cold hallway tiles to the bathroom before crawling back to bed for the last hours before morning full and warm. Before he fell asleep he realised for the first time that the words Mr Godley had used about life being a passing, crumbling dust had weighed upon him more than he had guessed. He knew it because before he fell asleep he became aware that a kind of weight had been lifted off his chest.

"You were up early this morning," said his mother at the breakfast table, "everything all right, dear?"

Nathan marvelled again at the vast aural range of a mother's ear. Dads might possibly hear an articulated truck crashing into the house at ninety miles an hour with all its horns blaring and sixty bullocks roaring in the back, but mums could hear a pin leave the fingers before it hit the ground – amazing.

"I had a dream," said Nathan rubbing his teeth with his fingers – they didn't squeak, that was bad; they must need cleaned.

"Stop that," said Liz, "It's disgusting."

"What? Dreaming?" asked Nathan, genuinely blank.

"No, scraping your teeth like that... it's horrible, what are you looking for? No, forget I asked that."

"Was it a bad one?" asked his mother.

"No, just a rice crispy actually, or it might be a bit of carrot from last night."

"Oh yuk!" said Liz getting up and leaving her breakfast. She was never going to get fat while Nathan was her brother, that was for sure.

"No, did you have a bad dream last night, is that why you got up?" asked Ellie McCutcheon as Liz left the kitchen.

"No, just a vivid one. I dreamed about homework actually."

"You mean you haven't done your homework?" asked Bob McCutcheon becoming alive to the conversation from behind his morning paper. It was beginning to dawn on Bob that he was unlikely to be father to a successful millionaire son if he was going to continue getting such average marks in school. The homework word caught the attention of that part of his brain that knew it had to encourage his progeny in the pursuit of academia. The Liz part of the progeny required no such encouragement, Nathan was a different matter.

"Oh no," grinned Nathan. "I've my homework all done. It a piece of naturalism prose dealing with fatalism and stuff, do you want to hear it?"

"No, that's fine son, just see me if you have any problems." Bob McCutcheon understood about three words of what his son had said – the rest he reckoned he would be safer not knowing. He was never the scholastic sort himself but having done his paternal duty to be interested in his children's homework, he kissed his wife and left to go to work. Ellie smiled as he went and turned back to Nathan.

"Is everything all right, Nathan?" She looked him square in the eye. Nathan saw the look of the motherly detective and nodded.

"Yip, everything's fine, why?"

"Oh, just you and the Reverend Hamilton had a long talk last night… I just wondered."

"Oh, that? Naw, we were just chatting. Nothing much, really mum," he assured her munching into his toast. Ellie looked at her son and shrugged. Oh well, he seemed fine and if he seemed fine he probably was.

Mr Godley was leafing through the homeworks that had been handed in at the start of class as the class read aloud from Milton's *Paradise Lost*. It was heavy stuff and every sentence seemed to have about fifty unpronounceable words that entertained the rest of the class as each successive reader tripped over the old English. David Eccles was making a particularly woeful attempt and the class was in danger of beginning to descend into anarchy when suddenly Mr Godley held up a hand.

"Ah, I've just remembered," he announced, putting David Eccles out of his misery much to his relief. "We were to have a class discussion on the existence of God." Nathan squirmed in his seat and tried feverishly to remember some of the things Mr Hamilton had said. There was something about Shakespeare and astronauts – but what? What did Shakespeare know about astronauts? He thought like a cat in a spin-dryer but nothing was coming out in any sensible order. Shakespeare didn't know about astronauts which proved… which proved what?… Or was it astronauts who didn't know about Shakespeare? Maybe he could escape by asking to go and see his form master with a crampy stomach.

"First of all, I want any of you who actually believe in the Christian God – the so called God of love – I want those of you who believe in that God to stand up."

There was a faint murmuring in the class and the sound of chairs scraping as the class turned this way and that to see who was going to make a fool of themselves. Nathan had Shakespeare, Russian king-doms and spaceships running amok in his head and he panicked as Mr Godley narrowed his eyes in his direction. Suddenly there was the clear sound of a chair being pushed purposefully backwards and every eye turned and faced the corridor wall. Nathan turned and there to his right, standing erect and tall stood Heather Woods, alone and every face toward her. Nathan's brain sent a message to his legs to stand, but his legs were in rebellion and sent a very rude message back to his brain. 'Stand yourself!' they said. Before any more messages could be relayed, the voice of Mr Godley broke the silence.

"Ah! So, you believe in God then do you, Miss Woods?" Heather merely nodded. Mr Godley actually rubbed his hands and the class held its expectant breath.

"Can you show me God?"

Heather gave a slow shake of her head. The class turned to see what the teacher would say next.

"Have you ever seen him? I mean, can you describe what he looks like?" He gave an unsmiling grin. Again Heather slowly shook her head but remained standing. Nathan looked at her eyes. He could just see her left eye from where he sat and it was beginning to glisten.

"And I'm presuming you've neither heard him, smelt him or touched him either?" This time she just stood and made no response.

"So, if none of the above, how can you tell me you believe in God, a god for whom you have absolutely no evidence?" The class turned and waited to see Heather Woods wither and take her seat. She did neither – instead she took a breath, raised her head slightly and spoke quietly and in a slightly tremulous voice but clearly enough to be heard in the dead silent classroom.

"Because He loves me," she said simply. "My father loved me too, but he died when I was four and I can barely remember his face, or what he looked like, or what his voice sounded like. I believe he loved me because my mother told me he loved me. I believed my mother. I love God because He loved me first and because He never let our family down in all those years. Two weeks..." she paused for a moment as if collecting herself and then continued, though slightly weaker than be-fore. "Two weeks ago today mum... my mum... died. In these last two weeks I have never... I've never known such love as my dear heavenly Father has loved me with. At night I sing myself to sleep with 'Jesus loves me, this I know.' And I... I really do know it, sir. Without Him I..." She stopped and Nathan watched a tear run down her cheek. She raised her hand and gently wiped it away.

"That's all, sir," she said as she finished and sat down, her head slightly bowed, her eyes dropped now to her desk.

No-one spoke. There was no sound except the sound of the clock above the black board – a ticking Nathan had never heard the classroom quiet enough to hear before. No-one looked at anyone else; Mr Godley looked at his desk and said nothing. Nathan looked up and caught his eye as he briefly glanced at the class and in that moment he felt ashamed at his own cowardice even while his heart burned with admiration for the girl in the row opposite.

The class ended somehow shortly afterwards and dispersed into their various classes in the school. The following Monday Mr Davidson was back, whatever bits taken out of him duly removed and the man back to not be there again. Mr Godley's temping spell was apparently over but he had one more period to attend before he left and that was with Mrs Ford.

She called by to see him as he was marking the prose homework in the quiet room to the rear of the staff room. It was often used by teachers as a place to do odd bits and pieces and he looked up to see the slim forty year old form mistress enter and close the door behind her.

"This looks promising," he said as he grinned and set down the pages of prose as Mrs Ford sat opposite him.

"Mr Godley," said Mrs Ford, ignoring the remark, pressing back her narrow skirt and neatly folding her legs as she sat opposite him, "you're a young teacher, capable and enthusiastic. I hope you don't mind if I speak plainly?"

"How could I complain," replied the man, his smile uncomfortably close to a smirk for the form mistress' liking, "if that's the sort of thing you're going to say?"

"But perhaps you lack a little... wisdom?"

"I do?" asked Mr Godley, suspecting correctly that the girl in senior English class was about to be referred to.

"English is a philosophical subject, I don't deny that," she continued, "but wisdom dictates that those of us with great influence and power use it with care and discretion. Do you follow me?"

"I'm not... sure that I..." began the English temp.

"Come now, we know that a teacher to a sixteen or seventeen year old is an authority as near to infallible as it gets. I appreciate that like all of us you have your own particular views on God and that's your prerogative – no-one denies you that. Young Heather Woods however has just started coming through the most traumatic time in her life. Not only fatherless, her mother was hit by a hit and run driver and dragged up a lonely Fermanagh road for half a mile as she went to visit an old woman. That old woman was the mother of the man who years before murdered her husband."

"Sorry, you said the woman she was visiting was the mother of her husband's *murderer*?" asked Mr Godley incredulously. Mrs Ford nodded.

"One night Mr Woods answered a knock at his door and was gunned down in his own hallway – he was holding Heather's twin sister in his arms at the time. The little girl died in hospital two days later."

"What about the killer, was he caught?"

"Not by the law if that's what you mean. No, that man was himself murdered by fellow members of the terrorist group in whose name he killed some years later, leaving his old widow mother now without her only child. Mrs Woods showed the grace of God by caring for a woman who ought to have been her enemy. That same grace works in Heather. Put out of their tied home, a star pupil in her old school – head girl, winner of the laureate cup and holder of the 'winner in adversity' award she ends up living in a place she does not know, with an aunt and uncle she barely knows and a school to whom she is but a stranger. In all this her love for others shines like a beacon. Do you want to know one of the reasons why she was meeting with me? – To pray for her classmates and her English teacher. She prayed that you might discover like her, the peace of knowing a God who loves without bias and without condition. Was this really something so necessary for you to destroy? And re-place with what exactly? Sometimes we discover there are two realities – one that works and one that is merely a conjecture of disinterested doctrinaire. All of our so called reason falls flat or turns its bitter back when the traumas of life kick hard Mr Godley – pray God you never have to face something like that alone."

Mr Godley looked at his feet and then at the prose in his hand. *'The cross barred gate'* it said. It had been supposed to be prose written with a fatalistic world view but he hardly knew how to mark it. Looking up he expected to see a kind of anger in Mrs Ford's face and was surprised to see something quite different.

"Thank you," he said after a moment. "I suppose I ought to be more tactful in future."

"I'm sure you will," smiled the form mistress. "None of us gets it right very often – but only a fool fails to realise that. I do not think that you are that fool."

As she turned to go she looked back at the young man. "Heather asked me to tell you she thinks you're a good teacher and she'll con-tinue to remember you in her prayers."

Left on his own again Mr Godley gathered up the papers and looked around. It was a good school. He had enjoyed the classes and the teach-ers seemed to genuinely care. There was at least one lesson there. He looked at the prose on the desk before him, thought for a moment and slipped it into his folder.

It was in the canteen two weeks later that Nathan got his chance to speak to Heather. She had made a couple of friends now and he had seen her smile three or four times of times; it was like dawn breaking after a cold moonless cloudy night.

"Hi," he said catching her eye.

"Oh, hello, how are you, Nathan?" she said. Now that she had assimilated into the school she had been given her permanent English class and it was with Miss Winters rather than Mr Davidson – lucky her.

"Oh, I'm fine. I... I er, I wanted to tell you thanks."

"Thanks? Me? What for?" she asked quizzically.

"For standing up... you know... in English. It took guts."

"Ah..." she said realising what he meant. "Mr Godley. He wasn't the worst – he didn't know, that's all."

"Yeah, but you stood where others didn't – like me, I felt... *feel* ashamed."

Heather shook her head and lightly placed a hand on Nathan's arm.

"We all have good days and bad days – don't let that bother you. If Someone loves you they're not going to give up on you that easily." She smiled again and Nathan smiled back.

"Besides, I forgot," she said as she rummaged about in her bag, "Mr Godley sent me this last week – said I might like it – I see your name at the top. I did, it was good – death, but with hope at the end. Evidently Mr Godley liked it too – it's a photocopy." She handed him a wrinkled sheet of paper. *'The cross-barred gate'* it said at the top. "Is it about angels?"

"I don't know," stumbled Nathan, caught off balance by the strange reappearance of his prose. "It was just a dream."

Heather merely nodded and gave a knowing smile.

"Perhaps," she said.

10.

THE AVIATOR

Hamish Ferguson was the son of a man who was related in some far off connection to Harry Ferguson of the Ferguson tractor fame. On his mother's side his great, great-grandfather – or it might have been a great, great-uncle – no-one seemed quite sure, was purported to be Alexander Fleming, the discoverer of penicillin. It was a formidable ancestry, an ancestry filled with the genes of potential greatness - none of which stuck in any shape or form to Hamish Ferguson.

Hamish just got through life. Life passed along and Hamish just went with the flow. He had no particular skills, no remarkable abilities – he was just a normal guy, Mr Joe-average, all except for one thing - his name.

In Ballydoonan, girls had a variety of names. Everything from Abigail to Zelda was possible; a girl's name could have a bit of flair, a bit of the artistic air. Girls' names could be amalgams of other names – Wilamena, a girl whose parents were William and Ena; Robbetta, an unfortunate youngster whose enterprising parents were Robert and Netta – an odd name in itself for a woman in any other place but Ballydoonan.

For a boy, choices were pretty limited. Robert, William, James and

John were the staple diet. Using a bit of imagination, a child could leave the hospital with an Ian, or an Alan, but tucked away somewhere on that birth certificate would be a hidden William or Charles. Chancing fate with a boy's name was just a bit too daring – too risqué, there were the neighbours to think of, for goodness sakes! It had a lot to do with other boys actually. What mother would intentionally shackle a boy with a name that was going to get him teased and tormented to a pathetic wreck of a future mother-despising psychopath? No, there were precious few Valentinos or Enricos in Ballydoonan.

Hamish may not have been an Enrico, but then neither was he a George. Whatever strange air had blown through the village the day Hamish was born, it had obviously moved on quite quickly, detecting that it was perceived as nothing but an ill wind in the steadfast minds of the prospective parents of Ballydoonan. Hamish was as adventurous as it got – the Roberts, Williams and Hughs flowed on as ceaselessly as before right after his première appearance; a new baby tucked up in his Maclaren pram with a name like a haggis.

Twenty-eight years later Hamish Ferguson had reached the lofty pinnacle of Insurance Clerk in a local insurance office in Newtownards. He was happy enough in his job; it wasn't too demanding and left him with time and money to invest in the real interest in his life. Having an interest was an acceptable social more in the conservative outlook of the general consensus of the town. Some enjoyed fishing, taking their rods up to a variety of quarry holes that swarmed with rudd and roach. Others were active shooters, heading off early on a Saturday morning in thigh-height green waders and camouflaged jackets to add excitement to the otherwise mundane day of a Barnacle goose out on the Lough. Saturday was also a day for football and various local teams would meet at Ballydoonan playing fields where the away team would find a Ballydoonan welcome in the form of bruised shins and black eyes. In the local league football was very much a contact sport – rugby minus the BMWs in the carpark. None of these alluring temptations however were for Hamish; Hamish's interest lay in another direction altogether, an interest that was invested in a waistline twice that of any other man in the village.

Hamish's interest was food. Hamish loved to eat.

His singular devotion to all things food were challenged however when The Big Idea came to him one day at his aunt's house. She was relating at the time how her U-slim class had helped her lose six pounds in as many weeks. Hamish cocked an eye at his aunt and wondered from where the six pounds had gone. She didn't look any slimmer. In fact, Hamish was not convinced that she had lost any weight at all. She seemed to have little idea of how much she had weighed before the mysterious loss and certainly had no idea of how much she weighed now. At least, so she said. The six pounds was pure gospel though.

His aunt was a big woman, not as big as he perhaps, but he knew that he was just big boned and carried a rounded musculature. He had a *mobile* flesh tone. No, his aunt was fat and the more he thought about it, so were half the middle-aged women in the village. It was as he watched her puff around the house that it came to him. It was such a singular thought, so straight and true did it thud solidly into his mind as to be almost an epiphany. It was a revelation – a spark of pure undeniable truth. What Ballydoonan needed was a keep fit class. What Ballydoonan needed was a keep fit instructor. What Ballydoonan needed was Hamish Ferguson.

The average keep fit instructor is a person easily identified. They are the person you see running down the road in the rain when normal people are warmly wrapped up in the car wearing a scarf and the heater on full blast. Keep fit instructors are the people who buy a burger and eat only the lettuce and garnish. They are the individuals who chose

clothing on the basis of what finely honed bodily trait can be accentu-
ated by the wearing of it. Keep fit instructors are the people who are
built like Action Man or Barbie. Female Action Men and male Barbies
being less uncommon than might be reasonably expected. Keep fit
people, gym instructors, health professionals – they all have one thing
in common – an attention to the human form, a singular attention.
Health enthusiasts are slim, sometimes muscular and often of athletic
build. The one thing they almost invariably are not is fat. Hamish was
about to break the mould - smash it. Crush it with pure bulk actually.

When Kirkie told the long suffering Wilma that he was going to invest in a kit aeroplane she thought he meant an Airfix model or something similar. She did wonder why he seemed to think he needed her
consensus to proceed but Kirkie was unpredictable; maybe it was a big
model.

It was. With a wingspan of twenty feet and a fuselage of sixteen, it
was big by any Airfix standard – if it had been an Airfix – which of
course it was not. It was a home-build UW-1 Do-it-Yourself aircraft
– fully functional and capable of cruising at seventy miles per hour at
fifteen hundred feet. Kirkie had been researching them for some time
and when this one appeared at such a bargain price it was too much to
resist.

"I've to go down and see it with a view to purchasing," explained
Kirkie to his wife on Thursday night. "Why don't all three of us go
down – make a weekend of it and bring it back up on the Sunday?"

Wilma had never heard of model aircraft being taken quite so seriously. Dublin was a long way away and little David had never travelled
so far before.

"Is it in a box or has it already been made up?" asked Wilma. It occurred to her that bringing an already glued together model back up from over a hundred miles away was going to be difficult – especially if it was to sit in the back of the car beside the inquisitive David – she had taken some strange things out of his mouth lately.

"I think it's partly made up – I'll be taking the bigger trailer anyway so it shouldn't matter. If the worst comes to the worst I can always take it apart a bit, maybe unscrew the wings or something."

Wilma eyed her husband and came to a decision. She had learned early on in their marriage that if there was a niggle in the back of her mind about something her husband was up to then it was probably best to let him proceed alone. The niggling was making her hair curl.

"Maybe I'll just stay and look after David – it's such a long way. I'm sure if it's company you need some-one will be glad of the trip."

Kirkie nodded and didn't argue. Wilma was probably right enough; the wee fellow was still very young for such a long journey. Besides, if Wilma wasn't going, he knew just the person who would.

Nate McFadzean was changing the fuel filter on the backup generator when Kirkie drove into the yard in the old Fiat. He wiped his hands on a rag and went to meet his older friend. Theirs was a friendship built on the love of things mechanical – Nate was a dab hand at anything with an engine and Kirkie was an enthusiast in everything in the field of amateur engineering. Although his enthusiasm was without equal, Kirkie had some problems when it came to transferring that into something tangible. That was to say his expertise was flawless until he came to the point where he actually put theory into practise. Aspirationally he was a genius – unfortunately when it came to the realisation, the final results often let him down.

In this case, any thoughts of failure were a million miles away from Kirkie's mind. There was a plane to be bought – it would be bought – it might need some final preparation – it would be thus prepared - it was then to be flown – well, that would be dealt with later.

"Fancy a trip to Dublin and back?" asked Kirkie with a conspiratorial grin.

"Dublin?"

"Dublin."

"When?"

"Well, now actually," grinned Kirkie, "I'm going to collect something – that's what the trailer's for. I'll buy the grub – I know a nice chippie at Newry."

Nate shrugged. As it happened he hadn't much to do that day. A trip to Dublin and back in one day sounded like fun; maybe Kirkie would let him drive part of it.

"Hang on, I'll let Mum know."

He was back five minutes later, a clean pair of trousers on and a bag with a pint of milk and a couple of mars bars.

"Wagons ho!" called Kirkie as he drove out and turned left past the vet's. "Is one of those chocolate bars for me?"

In Ballydoonan, Lennie McClurg and Bisto Gillespie were chatting in Drysdale's shop. Bisto had gone down to get a loaf of bread and bumped into his pal who was paying for a magazine.

"What's the magazine?" asked Bisto peering at the colourful glossy below Lennie's arm.

"The future," said Lennie tapping his nose and giving a slow wink. Bisto briefly wondered at what kind of magazine Lennie felt he needed to give a slow wink about but quickly dispelled the thought. Drysdale's didn't sell stuff like that. In fact Willie Drysdale, although normally a vendor of anything that would sell, had stopped keeping *National Geographic* since they did a month all about Fiji. Willie Drysdale saw his position as local shopkeeper as being a social responsibility. Incurring the outrage of customers was bad enough, sniggering schoolboys at the back was taking the biscuit.

"*Aviation Monthly,*" added Lennie outside the shop. "Look, that's a Cessna on the front page – inside there's all sorts of stuff about planes and things – class or what?"

"Aeroplanes?" checked Bisto. "It's a magazine about aeroplanes?"

"Duh!" replied Lennie, "like what else do you thing a magazine called 'Aviation Monthly' is going to be about? – Bee-keeping?"

"But what do you want with that," asked Bisto ignoring the sarcasm, "it's not like you've got a plane… *have* you got a plane?" On reflection, Bisto recalled Lennie had once been an owner, though a brief one at that, of a hearse. Perhaps he had made another recent acquisition? Perhaps he had won the pools? Perhaps he should stop thinking stupid? What was he doing with the magazine?

"I'm learning to fly," was Lennie's smug reply. "It's the future."

As they passed through Dundalk, just south of the border, Kirkie gave his head a nod toward the car window.

"You know, down here it's a different world."

"Down here?" repeated Nate, not quite sure what Kirkie meant.

"Down here, in the Republic – it's a strange place. A different people – a different country. Look at the colour of that telephone box for example." They had just passed a telephone box that stood oddly slanted at the side of the road as if listening in to the traffic passing by. It had appeared to be like every other telephone box Nate had seen except in one regard – it was green.

"Just painted them over you know – when the South separated. You can still see the British crown above their doors. Then they have to go and write 'Telefon' on them in Irish. They just do it for badness you know."

"For badness? But this *is* Ireland, Kirkie," argued Nate, "it's not like they're going to write it in Italian."

"And look at that," continued Kirkie without seeming to hear, "why change all the 'Give Way' signs to 'Yield'? I mean… *yield?* What do they think we're doing, driving or wrestling? Not that there's much difference down here. I'm telling you, we've entered the Middle Ages. I never bother with all keeping to the speed limits or anything – what's the point? Nobody else does."

Just who the 'nobody else' was, was difficult to imagine – the roads seemed incredibly empty of any traffic. They were also unimaginably bumpy and pot-holed. Nate observed that even achieving the speed limit, let alone keeping to it would have been quite a feat. Suddenly a tractor appeared out of a field and drove straight onto the road in front of them. Kirkie let out a shout.

"Where'd he come from?"

The muck flying off the rear wheels in every direction was answer enough.

"That field," smiled Nate. Great clods of wet mud were landing on the road, on the Fiat's bonnet, roof and windscreen. Kirkie turned on the wipers, which promptly stuck on the mud on the first upright sweep.

"I'm not sure he didn't do that on purpose," said Kirkie, his eyes narrowing and boring into the back of the head under the flat cap in front of him.

The tractor had a small two-wheeled trailer on behind, one wheel almost twice the size of the other. In the trailer sat an enormous black face ewe, chewing idly and eyeing the car behind with a studied disinterest. In complete contrast, a mud-matted Border collie whirled around the trailer in quick bounds and leaps, looking from the sheep to the tractor driver to the road ahead and to the two Northern visitors in rapid circuitous bounds.

"Either that man's face is on fire or he's smoking something," mused Kirkie impatiently as smoke wafted around and over the man's head. As he turned to look at some fascinating twig or something in the hedge, Nate saw a pipe curling out of his mouth, smoke puffing out like an old steam engine on the pull. He appeared to be totally oblivious of the car behind for as he trundled along he wandered aimlessly from one side of the road to the other.

"Maybe if you gave him a small hoot on the horn?" suggested Nate. Kirkie was clearly taken with the idea for he immediately gave the steering wheel a sound thump. The Fiat had its horn on the end of a column stalk with an additional button on the middle of the wheel. When Kirkie thumped the steering wheel the horn sounded. It didn't stop. Kirkie gave the wheel another thump, then another. The horn paid no attention and blared away in vociferous Italian.

"It's stuck on," said Nate loudly. He tried not to laugh and ended up sounding like his voice was breaking. Kirkie looked over and saw the grin that Nate could not prevent and after a second began laughing too. The farmer in the tractor ahead turned neither to the left nor to the right. He was either stone deaf or wonderfully unconcerned by the impatience of people who were under the impression that five miles an hour was not a fast enough speed at which to pass through life.

Kirkie had it in his mind that when he pulled over and turned off the ignition the horn would go off. It didn't. They sat beside the verge, the blaring sounding ridiculously loud in the open countryside. Over the hedge a knot of sheep scattered and careered through a barbed wire fence at the far side. Nate winced.

"Stupid thing!" said Kirkie glaring at the steering wheel. The humour had faded as fast as it had arrived. "Stuff that! It'll probably wear itself out soon enough," he added as he started the car and drove off.

A mile down the road they passed the tractor as it turned off into a lane on the right. As it did, Nate saw the farmer raise a piped filled hand in recognition – he didn't bother to turn his head. Two miles and many fields of various scattered domesticated animals later, even Nate's temper had just about snapped. Had it been a British car it would have been a feeble monotone *parp*, which would have been bad enough, but miles of two-tone continental road rage was way too much. Kirkie pulled over into a lay-by.

"Right… well… do you think you could help me find the wire to the horn," asked Kirkie. Nate was below the bonnet before he had finished speaking.

Nate eventually found the wires that led down the inner guard and after a bit of fiddling managed to get them disconnected. The immediate silence was a drink of cold water to a thirsty man. Nate was more than thirsty though – he was hungry to the point that the grass on the verge was beginning to look attractive.

"I'll buy us something at the next village," he stated as a fact. Kirkie winced and scratched his face.

"What?" asked Nate bemused, "aren't you hungry?"

"It's not that," explained Kirkie, "it's just – well – I don't like the thought of giving the Free State good decent Protestant money. Dear knows what they'll do with it. Give it to the IRA, smuggle three legged sheep north, pay for nuns to go to America – who knows?"

"*Protestant* money? *Nuns*? You're winding me up aren't you? What were you going to buy the plane with? Be serious Kirkie, you're pulling my leg – tell me you're pulling my leg!"

Kirkie's jaw muscles hardened as he gripped the wheel and glared out into the road passing under the windscreen ahead.

"Aw Kirkie! I didn't think you'd be like that? Since when did you turn into Orange Billy?

"I still don't see how just buying a magazine with pictures of aeroplanes in it is going to make you into a pilot," stated Bisto.

Lennie gave him a withering look and tapped his forehead with his index finger.

"Knowledge," he said, "it's all about knowledge." He sat on a bench overlooking the harbour with the coastguard station beside them and began leafing through his magazine. A very intelligent and worldly-wise expression appeared on his face as he peered in a studious fashion at an article about air thermals. Rather, he looked at the pictures in an article about air thermals.

"What?" said Bisto.

"What?" replied Lennie looking up from his studies.

"What are you on about is what?" said Bisto. "Knowledge? You hardly know how to spell your own name, you big balloon. What knowledge are you on about?"

"Look, it's all very simple," said Lennie in a carefully studied manner. "Everything in life is about knowledge. If you know how to, then you can. Pianists play the piano because they know how to, doctors operate on people's kidneys and guts because they know how to. Famous brainy people, like that scientist man, Ein.. Eins... Ein-thingy, he knew a whole stack of things and it was because he studied and studied until he was just full of knowledge; it poured out of him like sweat from a pig. This magazine here is teaching me stuff about aeroplanes you have no idea about. When I'm flying over your house some day in a jumbo-jet I'll wave out the window at you as you sell dulse to the day-trippers." He paused for a second and then added, "And I do know how to spell my name."

Bisto shook his head and looked out across the Irish Sea. It was a beautifully clear day and the gentle peak of Snaefell on the Isle of Man was clear and sharp South-East across the water. Straight ahead, the fields above Portpatrick chequered the rough hills above a town as familiar to the Peninsula fishermen as Bangor or Newtownards.

"So what do you know then, you big loon?" he asked. Lennie passed over his magazine and rose to the challenge.

"Ask me anything, go on, ask me whatever you like."

"O.K. When did you last change your socks?"

"I mean out of the magazine, you burke!"

Bisto shrugged and leafed through the pages. Pictures of planes, all of which looked the same to him, adorned the glossy pages. One page showed a schematic diagram of a plane called a Piper J3 – Cub. The page on the other side showed a Piper Cherokee. Both had all their parts numbered and listed down the side.

"All right then, Mr Fount of all Human Knowledge, what is the back squiggly bit on a Piper Cub called?"

"The back squiggly bit?" repeated Lennie looking askance at his friend.

"Yeah, you know, the bit that flaps about on the very back?"

"You probably mean the rudder – it helps steer the plane."

Bisto raised his eyebrows and tried not to look impressed.

"Yes, well, that was an easy one, here try this; what are the big knob things beside the driver for?"

"You dope, it's the pilot's seat," sighed Lennie. "That's the trim control. It allows the pilot to control the lift and drag – there's no point explaining it to you, you wouldn't know whether I was right or not." He also hoped the magazine said no more about it – he had read the words but remained quite clueless to what they meant. In any case Bisto seemed satisfied with the replies and he handed back the magazine.

"Not bad," he admitted grudgingly. "But I'm sure there's more to flying than just reading about it all the same."

"Naw," said Lennie shaking his head, "I reckon a couple more editions and I'll know all there is to know. I saw this film once where a jet airliner was going to crash because the pilot knocked his head or had a heart attack or something. I can't remember why the co-pilot didn't take over – maybe he got stuck in the toilet or something; anyway, suddenly this passenger who's only started learning to fly a wee plane ends up landing the thing on his own with a radio talk-down from the control tower. Well, if it ever happens when I'm on board, I'll be that man. I probably won't need the radio though."

"My family came from Pettigo," explained Kirkie as he changed up through the gears, "do you know where that is? Never mind, it's on the Fermanagh-Donegal border. During the war my dad served on board the *Prince of Wales*, he was a radio operator you know, served on the Russian convoys – do you know what they were?"

Nate didn't and said as much.

"Supply convoys that sailed up to Archangel and Murmansk through the bitter Arctic Ocean and Barents Sea to help Russia survive the treacherous Nazi war-machine. All the way up the Norwegian coast they were bombed from the air and torpedoed from the sea. One convoy he was on, twenty-eight out of sixty-four ships were sunk and hundreds of men died. He saw his friends blown up, burned to death and horribly injured. There was no escape in the water either, one minute in those waters and a man froze to death. Every mile the U-boats followed them in packs. When they arrived in Archangel the Russians wouldn't even let the British sailors set foot on the dock. As soon as they had unloaded, the Russians refuelled them and sent them back on their long route home while the U-boat packs waited to pick them off like so many sitting ducks."

Nate was wondering what this had to do with his Protestant money, but Kirkie carried on speaking.

"For two years he never got home. He'd just married my mother a week before his ship was called up and for two years all he had were long out of date letters. When at last he got six days leave he made his way home to Pettigo and my mother. The local doctor lent them his car and they went to Donegal for a long awaited honeymoon. Everything went well until they went for a walk in Donegal town and saw the German sailors sauntering up the main street, smoking and joking with the locals. These were the same people who had torpedoed his convoy, the same Nazis who jack-booted all over Europe and slaughtered human beings like they were dogs. And there they were, all tucked up in bed with Eamonn De Valera. He and Mum turned right there, booked out of their guesthouse and never went south again the rest of their lives. My Father said he would never spend so much as a penny in a country that licked up to the greatest murderers of history – he'd turn in his grave if he knew I was here."

Nate listened and though he found the story compelling, couldn't help but think it was a long time ago.

"But wasn't Ireland neutral during the war?"

"They could afford to be – if Britain hadn't stood in the way Adolf would have eaten them like minnows."

Kirkie said nothing for a while and as they drove along, Nate wondered if part of the reason people couldn't get on was because they had such long memories. Holding the sins of the fathers against the children seemed a bit much – besides, how could people be responsible for the actions of a government? It seemed to Nate that governments did pretty much whatever they wanted, most folk just wanted to get on with their lives and generally do the decent thing. Apart from Francis McCully, he just wanted his dogs to eat people.

Liz McCutcheon loved to go on long cycle rides on her own. None of her friends were keen to join her at all. Girls of her age didn't go on cycle rides. Girls of her age were young ladies and bicycles were for children and boys. A boy on a bicycle was all right – a motorcycle was better, but girls and bikes? How could you show your better angles on two wheels? No, if you wanted to be ignored by a boy, or at least have him thinking you were either going out to look for cows or were just a very big ten year old, then you rode about on a bicycle.

Liz couldn't have cared two pence what anybody thought about her riding about on a bicycle. Her Raleigh took her down yellow gorse-lined hedges and along honeysuckled lanes. On her bicycle she could hear the cry of the curlew and the rasp of the invisible corncrake. Sparrows flitted along, chasing one another through the hawthorn and sometimes rabbits would dart across her way, making her start but laugh at their bobbing tails. On this particular day she had a reason to ride her bicycle. For her Domestic Science homework she needed custard powder and the tin at home was empty. Ballydoonan was only a couple of miles down the road, but there was a longer way and that was the route she took. It joined onto the Tubbernacreevy road eventually and followed it down into the village. It was as she freewheeled down the last stretch that she saw the man and the motorcycle.

The motorcycle was lying against the hedge and in the field beyond a man lay flat on his back – his helmet at his side, obviously knocked off by the force of the impact when he had crashed. Liz pulled on her brakes and came to a heart-thumping halt at the motorcycle. For a few seconds she hardly knew what to do, but seeing the unconscious shape lying on the grass knew she had to act quickly whatever she did – the man might be injured, or…

Leaving her bike on its stand, she passed the motorcycle, which seemed strangely familiar and made her way as fast as she could to the gate. Thankfully it was ajar – climbing with a skirt on was never easy at the best of times – and half ran to the prostrate man. As she approached she gave a call.

"Hello, are you all right, hello?"

Suddenly the man's legs gave a twitch and then he shook his head and sat bolt upright. It wasn't a man at all – rather, it wasn't just a man – it was… oh no!

"What…? I wasn't sleeping, I was… oh…" said Will Patterson quickly rubbing his blurry eyes and trying to focus on a girl who came to a halt six feet beside him. It wasn't? It was! It was Liz McCutcheon!

"Oh, sorry," her voice said, "I thought you were… that is, I em… are you O.K?"

Will felt stupid, dopey, simple and gutted all at the same time. On impulse he had stopped his bike to lie down for a few private moments to watch the clouds in the high blue sky and daydreamed himself right into a fast sleep. As if that wasn't a stupid enough thing to do in private, who happened upon his childish reverie but the one girl in the world he would least want to see him make himself a fool in front of? Liz McCutcheon, the star of the County Down if ever there was one. He was a clown and he knew it. Worst of all, now she did too.

"No, I… I mean yes… I'm fine… I, er… ahem… I was just…"

"Were you cloud watching?" asked Liz slowly. Any hope of escape was gone. You don't lie to the girl you would give your life for.

"The clouds? Watching them? Me?" He looked up and saw she had not run off laughing. She stood there, every part of her a picture of all that was graceful and feminine. She was dressed in her denim skirt again and a light blue blouse. On her feet her slender ankles swept into a pair of plain white sandals and she was beautiful. Since this was the closest he was ever likely to get to her, he burned as much of her shape and form into his eyes as to make a permanent impression.

"Yes… yes, well I was just… it's such a lovely day and I… I think I might have fallen asleep for a minute or two, I've been working long hours this week and I… I'm sure you think I'm stupid. I'm sorry if I gave you a shock, I suppose…" he looked at his Suzuki propped up against the hedge, "…I suppose you thought I'd fallen off? I'm sorry, Liz."

When he said her name, something inside Liz McCutcheon gave an involuntary jump. It gave her a slight catch in her throat as she replied.

"No, no… my fault, I didn't look properly… I… They are beautiful this morning though aren't they? The clouds I mean." She began to turn back for the gate. "I'm sorry I disturbed you, I'd better get back to my bike; I've a message to do."

Will was up in a flash and got to the gate before Liz. He opened it wide for her and smiled.

"I'm sure you think I'm a right spoon, lying there like that on the grass. I'm normal sometimes, you know"

Liz smiled back. She didn't know what to say. She felt as if she had been pushy enough already. He was really nice.

"Well, bye then," she said as she pushed back the stand on her bicycle, "I've to get custard powder." She winced inside herself. What did she say that for? *Custard powder?*

"Do you like cycling?" asked Will. He was partly stalling her to keep her from rushing away too quickly and partly because it was nice to talk to a girl who liked the simple pleasures of life.

"Yes, I love cycling," she confessed. For the first time she felt a slight embarrassment of appearing so unsophisticated.

"So do I," said Will smiling again. Liz smiled back and this time for a brief second they stood there smiling at one another while the world carried on doing whatever the world did when for others time held a short breath.

Liz suddenly lowered her eyes and flushed imperceptibly. She got up onto her bicycle and set her foot on a pedal.

"I like the clouds too," she said and with that, gave the bike a push and pedalled off down the road.

Will watched her go and part of him went with her.

"So, do you know where in Dublin we're headed?" asked Nate. Kirkie gave a nod.

"Rathfarnham," he said, "the address is in my wallet. An E. Thornton. I haven't spoken to him, but I sent a letter saying I'd be calling today at some stage. The advert said it was available for viewing all day."

The first part of Dublin they drove into was called the Finglas Estate. It was a large sprawling development of housing on the north of the city. Roads and streets ran in every direction. The names of the streets were in Irish and none of them said 'this way to Rathfarham'. In no time at all Kirkie and Nate were hopelessly lost. After half an hour of seemingly driving in circles around streets with tethered ponies and abandoned cars, they managed at last by pure luck to exit on the other side where after a mile or two more found themselves in a huge area of trees and grass.

"I think, this, yes, this is Phoenix Park," announced Kirkie like he had fully intended to arrive there.

"Is Rathfarnham near here?" asked Nate.

Kirkie mumbled something indecipherable and then suddenly pointed out of the window.

"Oh look!" he said, "the zoo."

It was indeed Dublin Zoo and it stood opposite the entrance to a large set of iron gates leading into some kind of government facility. 'Gardai Siochana na hÉireann' said a large gold sign on the wall. A Gardai officer stood tall and erect at the entrance.

"Hang on," said Nate, "there's a Gardai officer at that gate, do you want to stop and I'll ask directions?"

The Guard was very helpful, he not only gave very good directions - he also drew a map. Twenty minutes later they were turning into a very plush street in a leafy suburb with 'Dublin 12' chiselled into a grey granite sign at the mown grass entrance.

Bisto had promised Sarah-Jane Thompson that he would call up for a chat. When asked by Bisto to come up with him, Lennie had agreed. As they walked up the Tubbernacreevy road, they saw Liz McCutcheon, Nathan's sister, come riding down towards them on her bicycle. As she passed, she gave a wave.

"Hi!" she said smiling. The boys waved back and Lennie called after her.

"Your chain's flat!" he said.

Liz called something back, but she was freewheeling down the hill at a good pace and her words were just a posy cast into the warm day.

"She's got a bit seriously pretty that one," said Lennie as he watched her grow smaller down the lane. He had no interest himself, but he knew a pretty girl when he saw one.

Will Patterson was starting his motorcycle on the side of the road further up. Neither Lennie nor Bisto knew Will all that well, but in a small village like Ballydoonan, everybody knew everybody to some extent. Will was Lennie's age but they had gone to different schools. School was where lifetime friendships were forged. In school you were cemented into your place in time. The passage of years and the perspective of how life altered and affected others was a gauge written in the faces of those you started school with. Others grew and became adults and so, you would have to suppose, did you.

"What about you?" asked Bisto. Will was looking down the road over Bisto and Lennie's shoulders and appeared not to hear.

"You alright?" asked Bisto. Suddenly Will gave his head a small shake and focused on the two boys before him.

"Oh, sorry! I was just… I… Yes, hi, I'm fine, just checking the bike. How's you guys?

Lennie glanced back down the road and saw the far off shape of Liz McCutcheon disappear around the bottom corner.

"Good," said Lennie. "Seems the day for two wheels, eh?"

"Uh, yes, well, that's it sorted. Either of you two looking to buy a nice wee Suzuki?"

"What, are you selling your bike?" asked Bisto. "I thought you were umbilically linked to that thing?"

"Nope," said Will. "I've bought a Mini. The bike's for sale. If you know anyone looking, it's going at a good price."

"Not me," said Lennie. "I used to own a car myself – more into flying now."

"Flying? What, like *planes*?"

"Yip, probably aim for my pilot's licence soon – got most of the theory stuff sorted."

Will looked impressed.

"Class! Well, I'm moving up from two wheels to four. You're just moving up! If you're ever looking to give someone a burl in your plane, I'm your man! Getting to draw bits of them all day in work is O.K, but I'd love to actually go up someday." He gave the bike a kick and the Suzuki hummed into life.

"See you lads!"

"Good grief!" said Bisto as Will rode away, "now you own an aeroplane! What are you like?"

"Nobody ever drew a horse by painting a duck," said Lennie in as aloof a manner as he could manage.

"At least a duck can fly!" retorted Bisto. "Your head's in the clouds and that's about as much of you is ever likely to get there."

"Well," said Lennie folding his magazine under his arm and inspecting the horizon. "You'll never learn to swim on the kitchen floor. You may laugh, but I've got aspirins!"

"Would that be aspirations?" mocked Bisto.

"Whatever," said Lennie with a waft of his hand, "it's easy to take the mickey, but even Howard Hughes had to start somewhere."

"Hmmph!" grunted Bisto, "maybe, but I bet it wasn't Ballydoonan!"

"That's it!" said Kirkie pulling up at a large house sitting in its own grounds and surrounded by large fir trees.

"Nice house," whistled Nate, "probably got an airfield around the back!"

A small dainty woman answered the door. She was neatly dressed in a grey lamb's wool cardigan and black trousers. She had a screwdriver in her hand and peered curiously at the two strangers on her doorstep.

"Hello," she said, "can I help you two gentlemen?" her voice was polite and not unfriendly.

"Good afternoon," said Kirkie in his best telephone voice, "would Mr Thornton be in?"

The woman hesitated for a second before replying.

"To tell you the truth no, Mr Thornton wouldn't."

"Oh, I see," said Kirkie put off balance slightly. "Will he be in anytime soon?"

Again the woman hesitated before replying.

"I would be surprised if I saw him at all sir… did you know my husband?"

'Did you know'? A bell rang faintly in Kirkie's head but not loud enough to prevent him continuing.

"No, not at all – I wouldn't know him if he jumped up and bit me!" he quipped. "I was to meet him today – he said he'd be here all afternoon."

"He said that?" The woman looked curious, perplexed and slightly amused all in one.

"Yes, I'm here to see about his aeroplane – he's selling a UW-1?"

The woman seemed to remember something and gave a wide smile.

"I would think that he's no more thinking about selling his UW-1 than the man in the moon," she laughed mischievously.

At her declaration Kirkie's face fell into a dumbfounded miscomprehension that the lady did not let endure for long. Nate had guessed what had happened and was confirmed correct in her next statement.

"Mr Thornton died four years ago sir. It's myself who is doing the selling. It was Mrs E. Thornton you corresponded with!"

Mrs Thornton welcomed the two Ballydoonan travellers into her home and insisted on making a cup of tea before speaking one word about the plane. Kirkie's remonstrations fell on deaf ears.

"If you're thinking that I would speak business to gentlemen who've travelled half the length of Ireland to see me, you've a poor conception of a decent woman."

The house was furnished in dark expensive furniture and dark wooden floors. Large paintings hung on the walls and thick drapes hung heavily by the windows. It spoke of an opulence of an age past, a slower, more purposed age, when time was measured in weeks, not seconds. A large grandfather's clock ticked ponderously in the wide hall and stairs swept up to a mezzanine landing, girdled by dark twisted balusters.

She led them into a large room with high-corniced ceilings and in-vited them to take a seat. Old Edwardian leather chairs welcomed them easily as they sat and watched her depart for the kitchen.

"I'll be a couple of minutes," she called back. "Make yourselves at home; you might like some of the pictures."

The walls were furnished with a great many paintings and photo-graphs. Kirkie loved history and was keen to look at the old black and white photos. Nate preferred the paintings.

There were no prints – all of them were originals and many were of horses. Not horses in fields chewing grass – racing horses – some standing with Grecian styled backgrounds, others in full flight, mus-cles straining, nostrils flared. Below some the names of the horses were engraved in small brass plates; dates were printed beneath. 'Kenmare's Pride - 1910' said one – 'Emain Macha - 1919' said another. Suddenly Nate heard Kirkie give a small gasp.

"What's wrong?" asked Nate.

"Look!" he said pointing at a photograph on the wall. It was a photo-graph of three men standing on steps outside a large building. 'A. Griffith, E. De Valera and W. T. Cosgrove 1923' it said beneath. The man on the right was wearing a silk top hat.

"We need to get out of here," whispered Kirkie quickly, "It's a *republican's* house!" His face looked like thunder and he would have headed out the door straight away except for the arrival of the lady with a tray in her hand.

"Fruit cake all right? I'm sorry, I've nothing plain. You've been looking at my pictures then?" She set down the tray and began handing out the cups.

"I see you like horses?" said Nate hoping Kirkie's sudden coolness wouldn't be noticed.

"Not really," she smiled. "That was more William's interest. I like the paintings though – they look so alive. Funny to think they're all dead now after looking so full of living."

Kirkie remained quiet and the silence was very obvious.

"Maybe you'd prefer a little biscuit?" said the lady after glancing at Kirkie's untouched plate and saucer.

"No, that's fine," said Kirkie abruptly.

"Did I see you looking at the photographs?"

Nate cringed. There was no steering out of this one – it was a one-way street.

"Yes."

"You like Irish history? I never met an Ulsterman who hadn't some interest in the past. Why don't we go out to the back garden and have a bit of chatter there – the garden is always the best place for conversation you know. William used to say the closer to God you are, the more honest your words will be and sure isn't the garden about as close to Him as you can get anywhere?"

Nate's heart fell. 'Honest words?' There was definitely going to be an argument, probably a shouting match. Orange and Green in a no holds barred wrestling match.

Kirkie scowled and, looking like a man fit to explode, went reluctantly out with the lady to the garden. Nate excused himself and remained behind; he wanted to stay close to the front door. If there was going to have to be a hasty exit, he didn't want the additional embarrassment of hearing the quarrel that led to it.

It was a full hour and a half later that Nate looked up from a book on Mechanical Engineering he had found on the bookshelves and heard approaching footsteps. It was Kirkie and Mrs Thornton at last – and there had been no shouting at all. In fact, they were both smiling.

"Mary's going to show us the UW-1 now," grinned Kirkie. He seemed entirely happy and all at ease. Nate blinked hard and stood up. *Mary?*

The garage was dark, but after fumbling about for a bit, the lady found the light switch and the darkness flickered and fled. There was a small red car and shelves with paint pots and the usual garage property. Nate saw no plane.

"It's at the back," said Mary Thornton.

Behind the car, which had been reversed in, was a space of about ten feet between the rear bumper and the wall. A series of large boxes lay in disarray on the floor.

"He never did get around to actually building it," said Mrs Thornton, "but all the bits are here – he was very particular about keeping things together."

Nate shook his head in disbelief. Kirkie's face went through a gamut of emotions. It started with a vague disappointment, moved quickly to acceptance and thence rapidly to positive challenge. It was in bits – Kirkie would build it. Also, an unconstructed plane was a cheap plane.

Kirkie never did tell Nate how much he ended up paying for the UW-1, but it must have been cheap – he grinned like a Cheshire cat all the way to Drogheda. Nate wasn't about to ask him how much money he had parted with but he did ask him about the transformation of relationship after an hour or so of private conversation. Had he convinced her of King Billy's honourable cause? Had she promised to send the Pope a nasty letter of resignation from his club?

"You know, some people are too quick to judge," pointed out Kirkie. "People are people wherever you go – just because a man doesn't stand for 'God save the Queen' doesn't mean he's a bad person." He nodded his head purposefully at Nate as if to make sure he had taken that in.

Nate hardly knew what to say in reply – whatever he and Mrs Thornton had discussed, it had certainly had an effect on Kirkie's thinking. After a period of quietness, Kirkie spoke again.

"Did you know the weather reports that cleared the way for the D-day landings came from County Mayo? Ireland was neutral during the war and technically that was aiding the Allies."

"No. I didn't know that," replied Nate guessing that Kirkie was passing on part of his conversation in the Rathfarnham house.

"De Valera allowed planes to fly across Donegal from Castle Archdale too you know," said Kirkie. "It was one of those planes that spotted the Bismarck. My father was involved in the action that ended up in the Royal Navy catching her and sinking her." He shook his head thoughtfully.

"Did Mrs Thornton tell you all this?" asked Nate. He wondered how she knew.

"Yes, and other things too - it's funny, you know, you never really know as much as you think you know."

"How did she know, about the weather reports and all?" asked Nate. He was curious now – it didn't sound like common knowledge.

"Her husband told her. Seems he was an officer or something in Irish Intelligence. She said he worked closely with the British during the war. The South was bound to follow certain rules having declared neutrality

– from what she told me, his job was to find ways around them."

"I heard you tell her that De Valera sent a message of sympathy to the Germans on the death of Hitler. Is that true?" Nate had heard Kirkie's impassioned accusation as he had been trying to escape in the hallway. He hadn't heard the woman's reply.

"Oh yes, that's true enough – that was pure stupidity. The funny thing was though that his personal support for Jewish refugees ended up with a forest being planted in his name near Nazareth in Israel by Dublin's Jews. See what I mean? You never know half of what you think you know. It's not that the goose isn't a goose, just that it's not the goose you thought it was."

In Ballydoonan Liz McCutcheon was home again after finishing her Domestic Science homework. Outside her bedroom window she watched Nathan as he fiddled about with something on their dad's old Honda. His hands were oily and so was his face – the bike seemed to be the only thing that wasn't oily. Boys were funny. Why would you want to mess about with a dirty old thing like that? Did they do it for fun? She thought of Will Patterson. His bike didn't seem to give the same bother – she wondered if he spent much time working on its engine – he had nice hands – strong, broad hands. She thought about him lying on his back looking up at the clouds and wished that she had not been so foolish as to rush over like that. If she had just taken a minute to look before acting, she would have seen who it was and seen that he was only sleeping. She could have stopped and watched him for a minute – that would have been something – to watch his chest move in and out as he breathed and dreamed of what? Maybe of a girl? Maybe that girl was… no, that was foolish – though it was a pleasant enough foolishness to dwell on. She looked at an unfinished maths homework sitting on her bed and for the first time ever Liz McCutcheon thought of it as an uninteresting and boring chore. Other things were in her thoughts.

Four months passed, four months during which William Mungo Kirkpatrick had been busy. The various boxes containing the parts for the UW-1 were slowly emptied as Kirkie persevered in his new-found skill as aeronautics engineer.

"Stupid idiot," complained Kirkie as he stormed into the house one Friday afternoon. Wilma looked up from the kitchen table, a spoon in one hand, and a baby-food plastered face beside her in its high chair. Feeding young children was more of a job for a plasterer than a mother at times. Getting the bland puree of what the makers laughingly called 'tasty carrot and roast beef dinner' into the infant's mouth was very much a matter of trial and error. The mouth was such a small target to aim for – especially when it was firmly closed shut. Once Wilma had managed to get the spoon by the outer defences of erratically whirling arms, it seemed a terrible waste to return the spoon to the jar without at least emptying it somewhere in the vicinity of little David's mouth. The face was the inevitable repository.

"Sorry dear, what did you say?" asked Wilma, vaguely aware that her husband had entered and made some kind of noise.

"Those stupid idiots who design self-build planes. I doubt if one of them has ever had a screwdriver in their hands. Some spotty eighteen year-old who thinks because he can use a protractor that he's qualified to design an operational aircraft. Oh yes, these boys could tell you the square root of an orange but wouldn't know how to peel one!"

"Oh," said Wilma poking some tasty carrot and roast beef out of David's ear, "won't it go together for you dear?"

"Oh it's going together all right – after I change things around a bit. It's as well I know what I'm doing – if I followed the instructions that thing would never be built."

It seemed an ominous sentence and Wilma decided she wanted to know no more about it.

"The lights aren't working in the bathroom again, dear," she said changing the subject.

"Did you step on the door saddle again?"

Wilma couldn't remember – there were so many things that caused secondary events in the house. The washing machine only worked if the kettle was unplugged, the toilet continued to flush if the handle wasn't pulled back up, the picture on the television disappeared every time Kirkie was working at something or other in his shed.

"I don't know, I don't think so," replied Wilma. It didn't seem normal that just because she stepped on the bathroom door saddle the lights would go out, but Kirkie had said he would fix it someday. Someday she would lose some weight too. There was talk of a keep fit club starting up in the village; it might be worth inquiring about.

"An aeroplane?" repeated Will, "he's building an aeroplane?"

Nathan had passed on the information that Nate had told him about Kirkie's plane and the journey to Dublin and back to get it.

"Yip, actually I'm heading over with Nate tomorrow to see it; Nate says he's getting near finished."

Will shook his head and looked at the stage for a few moments. He and Nathan were at the Young Farmers' Club and Mrs McKee was pointing out sections of a bull drawn on an old roller blind, showing what to look out for on the upcoming cattle-judging contest.

"Has he had the final air-worthiness test then?" asked Will.

Nathan shrugged. "Don't know. What's that then?"

"Well, every aircraft under construction has to have regular inspections by the Department. If every Tom, Dick and Harry just built planes like they were making go-karts then just imagine what would happen if one of those things fell into the street, or a house because of some silly mechanical oversight. No, every plane, DIY or commercially built has to have an air-worthiness certificate. I'm sure your friend has it all sorted though."

Nathan scratched the back of his neck. He tried to visualise Kirkie filling in all the forms and making sure everything was done to the letter. It was a difficult image to picture.

"Yeah, I'm sure he has," he said. No point muddying waters in which he had no reason to put a foot. "You should come over and take a look too," suggested Nathan suddenly. "What with you working in Shorts and all, I'm sure Kirkie would appreciate your knowledge."

"My knowledge?" laughed Will quietly. "So far I've drawn a torque nut and a wheel rim – trust me, I'm no Wright brother!"

"So, have you got that all stored away in your heads?" interrupted the voice of the Ballydoonan president. "Remember – we came second last year overall and we want to aim for the skies this year!"

Nathan smiled absently at no-one in particular. He wondered how many seats were in Kirkie's plane.

On Saturday morning the purple Zephyr burbled down the back lane as Nate and Nathan headed down to Wilma and Kirkie's house.

Nate used the back lane so that his dad did not see him leave. The driving about the countryside licenceless was a purely Nate McFadzean performance – if Gordon McFadzean had known the extent of his son's misdemeanours the purple Ford would have been well decommissioned. For an intelligent man, Mr McFadzean missed a lot going on around him.

Kirkie was in his workshop and when the Zephyr pulled up he came to the doorway and waved the boys over. Getting out of the car, Nate and Nathan saw that the older man was smiling – a good sign.

"You're just in time," grinned Kirkie. "She's near finished. Come on, take a look!"

The UW-1 sat in the middle of the large workshop and indeed it did look finished. It was a small thing, although the wings spanned the entire width of the shed. The cockpit was open with a curved Perspex windshield wrapping around the front seat. The front and only seat, Nathan noted with a mild pang of disappointment. Two small wheels on thin stalks stretched to the ground from under each wing with a simple skid resting on the ground at the tail. The engine compartment lay open, a shaft sticking straight ahead and a large nut on its end.

"Just the prop to put on," explained Kirkie, "but I need to give the engine a run first. Blinking engine cost as much as the rest of the plane. Rotax you know, air cooled – light but powerful."

Nate looked impressed and went to poke about at the engine. Nathan headed for the cockpit.

"Not much room in there," commented Nathan looking into the tiny cramped space that was the pilot's seat. The plane was very narrow and the width of the cockpit seemed ridiculously tight.

"Hmm… thought that myself," said Kirkie. "The actual plans and supplied parts were wider, but I made a few improvements. It was far too wide – never would have flown. Try sitting in it, I've an air-filled cushion on the seat – lighter than a normal seat."

Nathan prised himself into the cockpit and held onto the joystick between his knees. His legs lay flat straight out in front without support.

"What do you do with your legs?"

"Legs? Oh, I see, you put your feet on the pedals, don't you feel them?" Kirkie rubbed his chin and tried to peer in past Nathan's feet. "Further down, put your legs further down."

Nathan tried, but what with his hips jammed in the narrow confines of the compartment and the distance to the pedals, he couldn't manage it.

"Flip! You need long legs for this carry on," grunted Nathan, now firmly stuck with his head just about visible over the side of the cockpit. Kirkie appeared concerned and tried to see beyond Nathan's waist. "Mmm, you really can't reach the pedals?" he asked. Nate looked up from the engine.

"I take it you are able to reach them all right?" he asked. Nathan was as tall as Kirkie but considerably thinner. He wondered how Kirkie had been able to fit in when Nathan was finding it so tight.

"Well… not exactly, at least, I didn't have a problem… haven't had a problem. Actually, I haven't got around to getting in yet."

With a bit of pulling, Nate and Kirkie managed to extract Nathan from the skinny cockpit. It was clear that with Kirkie's adjustments there was little chance of Kirkie even fitting into the plane, let alone flying it. Kirkie was by no means downcast.

"No problem. I could do with losing a bit of weight anyway. Besides, I've a few things to get sorted before getting this bird up in the air. Time enough to worry about tomorrow's problems, eh lads?" Kirkie gave a grin and rubbed his hands. Nathan smiled back and rubbed his thighs.

One of the few problems that needed sorted out was how to get the

UW-1 out of Kirkie's shed. The wingspan was almost twice the width of the door opening and was no more going out the door than King Kong was going to get into Audrey Hepburn's' little black dress.

"Ah," said Kirkie with dawning realisation when Nate pointed out the obvious, "I knew there was some reason to leave the wings to the last." Unfortunately he had not left it to the last enough.

If nothing else, Hamish Ferguson was an organiser. Working in the insurance office gave him the ability to sort out administrative tasks without much difficulty. Preparing adverts for his upcoming classes used up some lunch breaks and helped prove to himself if no-one else, the dedication and commitment he was prepared to invest in his project. In the local newspaper an advert ran for four weeks. *'Join HUF and PUFF off the pounds'* it said. Smaller text at the bottom gave the venue and times. *'Hamish's Ultimate Fitness – Ballydoonan Presbyterian Hall. Mondays at 8pm. Every age, shape and size made welcome'*

The start day was a fortnight off and Hamish prepared himself physically by taking to wearing trainers and loose-fitting jogging bottoms in his forays around town. At home he commenced a drastic food regime change by leaving some chips uneaten each night on his plate of fish supper and pastie with cheeseburger. It was not an easy transition and he did not succeed every night. The nights he did leave four or five chips he treated himself with a congratulatory packet of chocolate digestives. 'Success needs to be rewarded', he told himself.

The other piece of pre-class preparation was done at the library. Here he browsed the shelves and came home with a book that had much to do with fitness. With some adaptation, Hamish planned his classes from the pages of the dusty book, *A Condominium of Military and*

Civilian Fitness and Health 1919. It's author, a certain 'Lt Col P. M. Basenthwaite – (retired)' had most likely not foreseen its future use as an encouragement to personal fitness over sixty years later, but Hamish felt sure the doughty old soldier would have been proud to be a part of the transformation of the good people of Ballydoonan.

Hamish sat with his new silver and red trainers propped up on a stool as he ate a sugar-coated doughnut and leafed through the pages of the thick paged book.

'*The undeniable veracity of scientific evidence demonstrate clearly to the organised mind the direct relationship between the growth of the British Empire and the fitness of its Imperial subjects',* it began. Hamish pulled in his stomach and nodded seriously. This was no mere commercial enterprise he was instigating – this was a matter of serious gravitas. There was honour in this – duty even.

'*Scientific anthropometric studies estimate that in 1905 approximately ten percent of recruits for the British Army were judged as unfit for service. By 1913 that figure was over twenty percent and up to twenty five in the more affluent southern shires.'* Here some reader had pencilled in a note in the margin. '*Sixty percent in 1979. Official Home Office Statistics.'*

Hamish finished his doughnut and gave a tut of dismay. What was the world coming to? Everyone is born for their time, thought Hamish, a time when they can make a difference. This is mine, he nodded to himself seriously. He would do it for free if he had to… theoretically speaking. Lifting the book again, he flicked through to the illustrations of vested men in heavy trousers, puttees and boots. Each picture gave a demonstration of how to use a rifle or a spade as a tool for fitness, Men were holding rifles out at arm's length; others were squatting with spades held behind. Adaptation, that was the key. Hamish reckoned he was probably going to have to leave out the guns.

Will Patterson called up at Nathan's house in the middle of the following week. Nathan and he had arranged to meet at Nathan's place from where they were going to head over to Kirkie's. Nathan had wanted Will to see the UW-1 and Will was glad of the excuse. The McCutcheon house had a certain and very particular strong attraction, though he was disappointed when on arrival Nathan was out in the yard and ready to go.

"I've a helmet," said Nathan coming over to the Suzuki, "do you know where Nate McFadzean lives?"

Will had to take a second look at what Nathan had on his head. It was a very odd-looking crash helmet; unlike one he had ever seen before – it looked a lot like a football.

As they hummed down the lane, Liz looked out through the net curtains while combing through her wet hair. Who was that Nathan was away with? It looked like… it was, it was Will Patterson! Will Patterson, and he had just turned up and driven off. She sighed and returned to the mirror. She looked at her own reflection looking glumly back. They stared at one another for a minute; both deciding that they had looked better and it was just as well Will Patterson had seen neither of them. Not that it was all that likely he would have been looking anyway.

Will headed out towards the McFadzean farm kicking himself for turning up late at Nathan's. If he had come earlier Nathan wouldn't have been ready and he might have got to see Liz. Not that she would have cared to see the cloud watcher anyway.

"This is Will Patterson," said Nathan introducing Nate to the motorcyclist as he climbed off the back. Nate smiled and nodded.

"Hi, yes I know, I've seen you about. Your mum's Margaret Patterson?"

Will nodded. Margaret Patterson was well known around the area. She was just one of those people whom everyone knew. She was a widow; Mr Patterson had died some years previously in an accident of some kind. Nate didn't know how it had happened except that there had been a massive funeral. Mr Patterson had evidently been well regarded as well. If Will was like his parents he would be a right sort.

They headed over to Kirkie's in the Zephyr; Will was impressed with the big car.

"Nice motor," said Will. The three of them sat in front on the single wide red leather bench seat. The back seat was filled with all kind of things – drive shafts, a radiator, empty sheep dip containers. The car was too old to have seatbelts fitted and they slid around on the shiny worn leather as Nate went around corners like they didn't exist.

"No such thing as corners," he grinned, "just bendy straights!"

The gear stick emerged from the steering column and it seemed pretty much a lucky dip as to whether the gear selected next was the one intended.

"This old thing's done anyway," said Nate as they approached Kirkie's, "what I really need is a bike – cheaper to run than this heap."

Will looked up.

"A bike? I'm selling the Suzuki if you're interested."

Nate's highbrows shot up. He was.

A surprise sat out in front of Kirkie's shed. It was the plane.

"How on earth did he get it out?" exclaimed Nathan.

"Probably chopped the wings off and stuck them back on again!" laughed Nate. Nathan laughed and explained to Will how they had been unable to get the plane out of the shed. All the same, Nate and

Nathan did wonder how he'd done it.

"I sawed the wings off and reattached them," explained Kirkie when he emerged from the workshop and heard their questions. Will's eyes widened involuntarily even though he tried not to look shocked.

"This is Will Patterson," said Nathan, nodding towards Will.

"Patterson? Nothing to David Patterson?"

"Yes, that was my dad," replied Will.

Kirkie nodded slowly. "A good man, David Patterson, a very good man – we were friends you know."

Will smiled and appreciated the comment. Over the years many people had said that kind of thing in recalling his dad; he never tired of them and liked to hear people remembering his father. He was twelve when the accident had happened and had many memories of his own but the supplement of other's reminiscences stopped it fading into irretrievable past; made his father seem nearer somehow.

"Did you build this yourself?" he asked the slightly disorganised looking man.

"Almost," replied Kirkie, "Nate screwed on the air speed indicator glass."

"*Two* screws," added Nate.

"You didn't really cut off the wings though, did you?" asked Nathan. Will stood beside the plane and looked down at where the wings ran along and under the fuselage. Two large aluminium plates were bolted across a split in the wing and were driven through to two similar plates underneath. Aircraft construction was a specialism; the materials had to be light, strong and of the best quality. Kirkie had used dirty great spouting bolts.

"Actually, it was just as well," said Kirkie, "I hadn't thought about how I was going to transport her, now I can simply unbolt the wings and slide them up the sides of the trailer." Will tried to stop his eyes opening any wider – he was afraid they might fall out onto his cheeks.

"Have you worked out how to get into it yet?" asked Nate, "have you widened the cockpit?" It didn't look any wider.

"No need," pointed out Kirkie, "there's more than one way to skin a cow."

Will turned his head. A cow?

"What? You're going to hire a dwarf pilot?" exclaimed Nate.

"Nope, I've enlisted!" pronounced Kirkie.

"Enlisted?" repeated Nathan without further enlightenment.

"In the new Keep Fit classes on Monday nights. Wilma told me about them. I'm going to lose weight! It all makes sense; the lighter I am the better the plane will fly anyway. Lose a few pounds around the spare tyre," he patted his belly and then pointed to the aeroplane seat, "and I'll slip in there like a foot in a slipper. Just as well I made those few adjustments after all, eh?"

When Kirkie heard where Will worked he was like a dog with a new bone. Will was shown every nut, every bolt. As he pointed out the various parts he would explain he difficulties or challenges he had had with that particular bit. There seemed to have been a great many challenges.

"I mean! High tensile 3mm cable? Where on earth are you going to get something like that around here? The way I see it it's only to steer the rudder so why not improvise? I just used some plastic coated washing line wire – probably better job anyway."

Will nodded and was impressed. He knew next to nothing about building aircraft himself, but this man seemed to be put off by no obstacle.

"And the inspector passed all your alterations?" he asked innocently. Kirkie's face darkened suddenly.

"He passed what he saw, what he didn't see won't hurt him," he replied in a lower voice. Nonetheless Nate overheard the remark.

"The man with the clip-board? Has he been out again?"

Kirkie grunted and made no comment.

"I thought he had to inspect every stage in the construction. He *has* been here since you put together the aircraft frame?"

Kirkie had had a bit of a run-in with the certification inspector. He was supposed to pass every stage of the building programme and at the end give the required airworthiness certificate in order to allow it to be flown, but after he had come back five times and each time had made Kirkie change a type of rivet or informed Kirkie that the floor pan was poorly spot welded, Kirkie had had enough. There were words spoken, words that called into question the intelligence of the inspector and generally equated it with certain animals of the primate family. Kirkie very rarely lost his temper – Nate had never seen it happen, but when he did he tended to colourful metaphor. The inspector had threatened to condemn the project if Kirkie didn't conform to his instructions. Kirkie was close to threatening the inspector with something else but had caught himself on at the last minute; he wanted the plane more than he wanted the inspector chucked off the harbour – just.

"You know, give some people a position of power and they think they have the right to treat other people like they are simple or something. That boy needs someone to cut him down in size a bit. Do you know he had the cheek to tell me he had a University degree? I told him big deal – I only didn't become a nuclear physicist by failing one simple exam. That shut him up." Nate looked to Nathan with an impressed expression – Nathan returned the same.

"What exam was that?" asked Will with some interest.

"The eleven-plus," replied Kirkie.

"Well, what did you think?" asked Nathan as Will left him off home later on. "Do you think it'll fly?"

253

Will wasn't sure he liked the way he was being treated as the expert. It was like asking the cleaner at Queen's University what he thought about Higher Radical Criticism.

"He's put a lot of work into it. He never said where he's going to fly. Is he going to take it to Ards airport?"

Nathan shrugged. He didn't know.

"I wouldn't mind seeing it flying. If you know when the maiden flight is give me a shout will you?"

Nathan agreed but didn't know that Will's main reason for asking was to find some reason to return to the McCutcheon house again. Although seeing his friend's aeroplane was interesting, seeing Liz Mc-Cutcheon, speaking to Liz McCutcheon, sitting on the lawn and chatting with Liz McCutcheon, maybe working up the courage to ask her out even would have been better than seeing Concorde loop the loop over the harbour and land on the beach. He sighed as he rode off. The Concorde scenario was the more likely of the two. Why was he such a wimp when it came to that girl?

Hamish's first class started promptly at eight. He hadn't been at all nervous about it until the last minute. It was then that he had a mild panic. What if no-one came? Worse, what if only one or two came?

He needn't have worried, when he walked onto the stage he looked down and saw the large hall filled with women of various ages and sizes, many only there out of curiosity right enough, but there all the same.

Seeing the crowd, Hamish's nerves immediately vanished and he took command of the nervous hubbub below him.

"Hello, ladies!" he began. "Welcome to Hamish's Ultimate Fitness!" He flicked a switch on a cassette player behind the curtain and a heavy beat boomed out of distorted speakers. As he had practised at home, he immediately snapped to a single star-jump and then bounced across the stage in a series of highly energetic jumps, punching the air as he did so and calling out in time with the music.

"Get it up! Move and jump! To the beat! Po-wer feet!"

Two dozen sets of awestruck eyes watched as a very overweight man dressed in red tracksuit bottoms and a white sleeveless T-shirt bounded across the stage like some crazed hippopotamus while the stage lights shook and reverberated with alarming vigour.

"Up and down! Move those pounds! Fighting fit! Get to it!"

He had crossed the stage and back and already he had worked up a sweat. He stopped and as the music wound towards its end, stood with his hands on his hips, or rather, on the fat that covered his hips, and gave a long wide smile to the initiates below. He would have said his opening remarks at that point but he was too busy desperately gulping in air between his grinning teeth to speak. Thankfully the music ran on for another ten seconds or so and when it finished he was able to get words out in short sentences. In between he sucked in air like a commercial vacuum cleaner. This was going to be harder than it looked in the book.

"Welcome ladi*eees*!" he began in a voice as excited as boxing ring commentator's. A chuckle went around the hall as most of the women turned and looked at an individual standing in the middle row.

"And gentleman!" added Hamish with equal enthusiasm as Kirkie returned a nervous wave. The women laughed louder. Hamish hadn't really expected there to be any men, actually, he hadn't really known what he expected, but it was all the same to him – he was going to transform the shape of the village and there was no obstacle to his self certitude – Ballydoonan wouldn't know what had hit it.

Another male face he didn't see in the lobby peered in through the glass doors. The photographer from the local paper had called in to see if anything was worth recording for the following week's edition. Local flavour, that was what people liked to see – the bursting leotards and shapes of every imagined proportion would fill the Ballydoonan section very nicely. He would come back toward the end and see if the organiser would like a group photo to be taken.

"Now," Hamish continued scanning the faces below him, "first of all, my guarantee to you. Now you have enrolled on the HUF programme, the very least that lies ahead is an exciting prospect of a new you! That old fat frump of the old you will be a thing of the past, the old wheezing pot-bellied person you used to be will be nothing but a bad memory. In a few short weeks you will be fitter, faster, stronger, slimmer and feel better about yourselves as you watch the pounds drop off like droppings from a crow's nest. No more frumpy freaks – it's bubbly babes from here in!"

The room gave an audible sigh of uncertainty and Hamish quickly moved on.

"But let's not just talk about it – let's gooooo!" He clapped his hands and waited for the cheers of enthusiastic agreement. What he got was a lot of suspicious looking women (and one man) who were not sure they liked all the talk about frumpy from a man who was twice the size of any one of them in the room. Also it all sounded more athletic than many were prepared to engage with.

"Warm ups!" cried Hamish. "Just follow me." He turned on the cassette player again and as the music of Don Williams singing the slow beats of *I'm Just a Country Boy* began crooning across the stage, Hamish began a series of weird and unusual movements with his arms. He wiggled his hands out straight in front and clenched his fists, then he wiggled them back again and did it all with the look of a constipated man. It looked like nothing so much as if he was simulating pulling the gizzards out of a turkey. The audience had no way of knowing that it was an adaptation of Lt Col P. M. Basenthwaite's *'Lee Enfield Rifle Drill for stronger forearms.'*

It was all done extremely slowly; Don Williams didn't do anything that required musical activity more energetic than a casual strum. The keep-fitters began copying the odd movements, looking at one another with bemused bewilderment. Even before the energetic introduction, some had worried that the classes were going to be away above their capabilities. Maybe this was going to be something they could do after all?

The energetic introduction had been a one off. Hamish had had no intention of continuing at such a frenetic pace - not without a cardiac ambulance parked outside the front door. Hamish reckoned that movement was the key – the rapidity and quantity of it was irrelevant. For a man whose average nightly movement rarely exceeded moving from the television to the kitchen and back, the turkey gutting was impressive indeed. By the time he had moved on to the two steps forward and two steps back with a ten second breather in between, Hamish was convinced he had been right with the rest of his music selection. Bing Crosby's *Dreaming of a White Christmas* was next in line, followed by Elvis Presley's *Falling in Love With You*. By the time he had the class swaying their hips in a particularly unenergetic fashion to the tones of Bach's *Sleeper's Wake*, most of the women in the hall needed no more convincing in their own minds as to where they would be the following week - back in Hamish's Ultimate Fitness class. Why, this was nothing like those nasty sweaty shows on television – this was fun!

It was also extremely easy. Although it seemed to suit most of those in the room, two people were not too happy at all. One was Kirkie – he wasn't stupid, at this rate it would take years to lose any weight at all and most of that in getting in and out of the car on the way over.

Kirkie's thin hips plan was quickly evaporating into as much thin air.

The other person who was not content was Hamish himself. The sweat was running down his face, down his back, into his trainers and onto the stage. This would never do – next week he was going to have to slow things down.

It was Will who first suggested Lennie.

"Lennie McClurg?" exclaimed Nathan. He had met Will down at Drysdale's when he had cycled down to get bread and milk. Will was coming out of the shop as he was going in.

"Yes, you know him don't you? Big tall guy; hangs around with Bisto Gillespie…"

"Yes, I know Lennie, I know him pretty well actually, but how can Lennie help Kirkie?"

"You said Kirkie told you guys the only thing preventing his plane flying was that he needed a pilot? Lennie McClurg's a pilot – or he's learning – I think he said he had a plane, or was taking lessons. Anyway, he seemed to know a fair bit about flying. I thought he might help, he's thin enough and those big long legs of his are bound to reach down to the pedals."

It was news to Nathan that Lennie had any such skills at all, but then he had discovered before that the most unexpected people could some-times surprise you. He had known Nate for years and yet had only discovered within the last couple of weeks that he could play the pi-ano, and play it well – he had passed his grade six piano exam recently. Strange to watch someone you think you know do something you had no idea they could – like discovering a secret room in your own home, a room you never knew was there until one day you discovered the hidden door behind a wardrobe.

Lennie's flying skills were a very well hidden door indeed; still, it might be worth mentioning to Kirkie all the same.

At that actual moment Kirkie was standing waist deep in the Irish Sea with a pair of binoculars trained on his own front window. His house sat on the road on the other side of the coastal road just outside Ballydoonan and at low-water, the house and the tide were about a third of a mile apart. He had been in the water now for about twenty minutes, fifteen minutes more than he had planned and he was very cold. Honesty sometimes drove a hard bargain.

"Right, Wilma," he had explained to his wife an hour before, "you phone this number and ask to speak to Mr Richardson the airframe inspector – just tell him that tomorrow's inspection will need to be delayed by three weeks." He handed her a piece of paper with a number and a list of suggested replies to any questions she might receive from the other end of the 'phone.

"But why don't you just speak to him yourself, dear?" asked Wilma who hadn't yet quite got the import of Kirkie's cunning plan.

"Because then he'll know I'm just putting him off and dear knows what the nosy parker will demand next. Look, just tell him I'm not on these shores at the minute. Got it? 'not on these shores'. It's not a lie – I'll be watching you from the beach. Tell him I'll call him in three weeks when I'm back ashore – he's not to know I've only been at sea for five minutes – and that's it – all sorted and no lies told!"

"But, but wouldn't it be easier to wait till the tide's in? I could just call across the road then?"

"No, Wilma," said Kirkie patiently. "Technically I'm still on land unless I'm standing below the low-water-mark. I'm not about to start telling lies now. Honesty is always the best policy; liars always come a cropper in the end." He said the last part with such indignant conviction that Wilma decided to argue no more about it. All the same, she would keep her fingers crossed when she was on the phone.

Eventually Kirkie saw the curtains flutter; the agreed sign that the call had been made, and he dragged himself out of the water and squelched heavily back up the beach. When he entered the back door, his whole body was shaking and his teeth were clattering so violently off one another that Wilma gave a start on seeing him and pulled little David out of his way in case he accidentally got in the way. A jerky husband and a half-chewed child would be hard to explain to the social worker.

"W-w-w-what t-t-took so l-l-long?" chattered Kirkie. Wilma didn't feel that the time was right to explain how she had picked up the phone, fully intending to 'phone the department but had as a matter of habit 'phoned her mother instead. Mother was hard to get off the telephone.

"Oh, you know, by the time you get connected to the right person and all," she said dismissively. Her fingers remained crossed behind her back.

"O-o-oh, I s-s-see," nodded Kirkie, "all s-s-s-orted then?"

"Yes, he just said he'd hear from you in three weeks. He said he had a few things he wants to bring to your attention?"

"A length of f-f-four by two is what I'd like to b-b-bring to his attention," muttered Kirkie as he disappeared up the stairs. He had had quite enough of that inspector.

Will had the Mini going beautifully. It gleamed in the sunshine as he stood back after to admire it after polishing its orange paintwork and chrome trim. He knew just where to take it for its first run out.

Nathan was in the yard when he heard the engine. He had been fixing a puncture for Liz on her bicycle when he looked up and commented.

"Oh, that sounds like Will Patterson – he said he might call by today – here, you were saying you would like a go on a motorcycle some day?"

Liz looked up from the grass verge where she had been watching her brother and saw the distant shape burble up the lane.

"Oh, yes, but I, I meant on *your* motorcycle – I couldn't, why it wouldn't…"

"Don't be daft, Will won't mind – the old Honda's knackered anyway – go on, get into those red overalls, you can't go whizzing about on the back of a bike with skirts on."

Before Liz knew what she was doing, she had slipped into the kitchen and pulled on the clean pair of red overalls. They were ones Dad had got Nathan somewhere that week and they fitted him like a racing driver. They drowned her.

In the kitchen she couldn't see as the Suzuki pulled up outside the front door, but she took in her breath and told herself to be sensible as she went to the door. She mightn't have gone any further except that Nathan's voice called.

"Liz! Come on, Nate's here!"

Nate? Liz stumbled out of the door and saw Nate McFadzean astride a bike that looked very like Will Patterson's.

"Oh, hi Nate… I thought you said…?" she began as her brother finished the question.

"…that it was Will? No, good old Nate here has bought Will's bike. Cool eh? Hey Nate, it's taxed!"

Nate laughed and looked down at the disc on the front forks.

"And insured – and I've got a provisional licence! Hey! What do you think of that then!"

"Aren't you supposed to have 'L' plates?" quizzed Liz suspiciously. When these two got together there was always something not quite right.

The question was ignored as Nathan spoke up.

"Liz here wanted a go on a motorcycle – would you give her a quick spin up and down the lane?" he asked Nate. Nate got off the bike and went to pass the handlebars to Liz.

"Sure, the gears are one down and four up. Just watch the brakes, they're a bit…"

"No," interrupted Nathan, "Liz can't ride, I mean just give her a ride on behind."

Liz wished she had waited before getting changed into the silly overalls. The whole idea was stupid – she had thought it was Will Patterson - she didn't want a ride on the bike at all now but barring being ignorant about it how was she to avoid it?

"Oh, well, if you just hop on behind," said Nate as he pointed out where the footrests were, "and hold on to my waist, I'll go to the bottom of the lane and back."

There was no avoiding it so Liz got on and held on lightly.

"Hold on!" cried Nate as he turned and accelerated out of the yard and down the lane. Liz's light grip instantly became a fierce one.

The hedges whirled by in a green blur as tears from the wind ran across her cheek bones. If she had been unsure of riding pillion behind Nate before, now she was utterly convinced she had made a big mistake in getting on behind a madman.

As they approached the bottom of the lane Will Patterson indicated left in his Mini and turned in. He just had time to slam on his brakes as a motorcycle braked even harder and swerved to avoid him. It was a blue motorcycle. It was his Suzuki he'd sold to Nate McFadzean. Nate was riding it and on behind was… his stomach fell like a lump of lead and thudded into his feet. Liz McCutcheon was clinging onto Nate's waist. Life went suddenly grey. Nate McFadzean had stolen Liz from below his big stupid slow nose and he had used his own bike to do it.

Getting out of the Mini he went over to where Nate had managed to stall the bike at the edge of the road.

"Are you two all right?" asked Will. It had been a close enough thing.

"Sorry about that," said Nate with a stupid grin on his face, "I was going a bit hard there. Bike goes well though. Are you O.K., Liz?" He looked over his shoulder in time to see Liz slip off the back and step away from the bike.

"No, I'm, I'm…!" she looked up and saw Will standing with some concern on his face.

"I didn't see you two," explained Will, "you were fairly shifting."

"I'm not getting back on that bike!" she said simply. Nate shrugged guiltily as Liz turned and began walking back up the lane.

"Not like it was my idea anyway," muttered Nate below his breath. Will shot a look at Nate. '*Not his idea*'? What did that mean? He looked back towards the retreating Liz and watched her for a moment before getting into the Mini. She was poetry in motion. Pure unfeigned beauty. Every signal of feminine charm that he was wired to respond to. As she walked up the lane her movements within the loose overalls made every hair in Will's head stand on end. It wasn't *fair*! She did it to him every time!

He started the car and trundled up beside her.

"Jump in," he said, "I'll take you up to the house." He would have bought the car if only for what happened next. She smiled, came round and got in.

"This is a lovely car," she said. "Is it yours?"

He nodded as he drove as slowly as he could up the lane. "Yip, it's a Mini Clubman. Today is the first I've had it out. You're… ahem…

you're the first person to sit on the passenger seat. Some folk don't like the Clubman's square front."

"I think it's really nice."

No matter how slow he drove, the lane was only so long and after half a minute the tyres crunched into the McCutcheon yard. Ellie McCutcheon stood with her son at the front door.

"Whose car is that Liz is in?" she asked Nathan as the Mini drew to a halt.

"That's Will Patterson's. I forgot he'd got a car now. He must have brought Liz up from the bottom of the lane. Nate took her down – here he comes now," he said as Nate hummed to a halt beside the Mini.

"Thanks," smiled Liz to Will as she opened the door and got out. With an audience of three it was about all she could do. Ellie watched her daughter carefully as she headed into the house and eyed the tall boy as he slid easily out of the car.

"Hello, Will," she said. "You look very happy this morning."

"So would I if I had a car like that," added Nathan. "Hi Will, nice car!"

"Yes," said Ellie smiling and leaving the boys to open bonnets and look at bits of engines, "Two very happy faces," she mused to herself.

"So, did you say to your friend about Lennie McClurg?" asked Will after they had seen enough S.U. carburettors, oil pumps and high-lift cam housings.

"No, not yet, though actually Nate's the boy to say," pointed out Nathan.

In response to Nate's bewildered look, Nathan explained about Will's proposal to use the long skinny potential pilot.

"Lennie McClurg?" exclaimed Nate. "Lennie McClurg as in 'what end of a nail do I hit with a hammer?' That Lennie?"

"Apparently he knows a lot about flying, doesn't he, Will?" said Nathan. Will nodded.

"Seemed to know what he was talking about to me," admitted Will, "though I don't know him all that well."

Nate shook his head, and pictured the long tall shape of Lennie McClurg flying a plane and actually knowing what he was doing. It was not an easy image to hold for very long. Still, imagining Kirkie flying a plane and actually knowing what he was doing wasn't much better.

"I suppose we could see what he says," he replied eventually.

"What an excellent idea!" enthused Kirkie. When the Mini appeared and disgorged the three boys he wondered at first what was up. There had been a certain look of intent about their manner. When he heard about the tall thin pilot, it was to him a solution so glaringly obvious as to require no further scrutiny. Certainly two sessions at Hamish's Ultimate Fitness was enough to persuade him that any further pursuit in that direction was a pointless exercise. Hamish's second class had finished up with cream buns all round as reward to the hard working class. The first half of the class had comprised of each of them lying flat on their backs and thinking 'thin thoughts' to the music of Fats Domino. The whole night no-one had been required to move at a speed faster than a drowsy sloth and with an energy roughly equivalent to that needed to lift the needle off a record.

"When can he come over?" He asked.

"Lennie, your day has arrived!" blurted Bisto as he blustered into Lennie's kitchen. Lennie yawned, he had been up a good bit of the night restocking the shelves at the Stewart's store in Newtownards and he was tired.

"My what has what?"

"Your day – this is it! I was talking to Nate this morning and he say's you are the man! Lennie old friend! I thought all that stuff about aeroplanes was just so much waffle, but you've been spotted!"

"What on earth are you blubbering about?" asked Lennie with half of a mouth of Cornflakes still churning around his mouth, "spotted by who?"

"I'm not sure, somebody up in the aircraft factory in Belfast reckons you know a thing or two about flying and you're the man being asked for!"

Lennie's initial excitement at being head-hunted was tempered somewhat when he saw who was waiting outside in his Zephyr to escort him to his interview.

"What's going on here?" asked Lennie as Bisto bundled him into the front seat.

"This is your big day," grinned Nate as he ground about for some gear that would impart forward motion. "Hold on, the brakes packed in on the way over."

On arrival at Kirkie's house, Lennie found his hand suddenly grabbed and pumped up and down by an enthusiastic Kirkie.

"Thanks for coming, I'm sure you'll want to see her before we do anything else, so come on and I'll take you to her – she's just around the side."

Before he had time to ask any questions he found himself taken to where the UW-1 sat with its wings detached at the side of the shed.

"First things first," said Kirkie as Bisto and Nate watched with interest. "See if you can fit in."

Lennie still was far from sure as to what exactly was going on, but he slid into the cockpit and squeezed down till his feet rested on the rudder pedals. He pressed each one in turn and nodded with some aplomb as the rudder moved. It seemed he was there to give some comment and so he did.

"Very nice," he said approvingly as he pulled out the throttle and pushed it back again. He tapped a clock in front. "Hmmm, altimeter? This then would be the air-speed indicator?" he added pointing the second and only other clock.

"What do you think of her?" asked Kirkie. The wings are in the shed, a few minutes will reattach them."

"A fine machine," said Lennie slapping the sides with some ceremony. "Rotax engine?"

Nate's eyebrows nearly took off – Bisto nodded with appreciation. He always knew his friend just had his niche to find in life – this was evidently it.

Mr Richardson the aircraft inspector was at home having his breakfast and reading his newspaper when he nearly choked laughing.

"Are you all right?" asked his wife.

"Would you look at the state of that!" he chortled. "Ballydoonan has a fitness instructor and if that fellow isn't in mid coronary then your mother's a saint."

Mrs Richardson ignored the derogatory comment and looked at the photo. It was a picture of an alarmingly large man in mid bounce in front of a group of good sized women. The photo had been taken from behind the instructor and missed nothing of the sheer enormity of his backside.

"Those daft women," laughed Mr Richardson, "imagine paying to be told you're fat by Mr Blobby himself."

Mrs Richardson decided it was time to stand up for the members of her poor maligned fellow sex.

"Not all women – look, there's a man off to the right."

"Oh, yes, so there is, what's he doing there…?" he looked again and pulled the paper up close to his eyes. "Hang on a minute! What *is* he doing there?"

William Mungo Kirkpatrick had just been spotted and he was very much ashore.

Not even when the UW-1 had been fully loaded onto the trailer did it dawn on Lennie just how large a part of the forthcoming proceedings were falling upon his own shoulders. Mr Kirkpatrick seemed to appreciate his positive comments concerning the fine quality of the aeroplane and how well everything seemed to work on it. Lennie seemed to have become quite the centre of attraction and the money spent on Aviation Monthly was paying dividends in the respect he felt had so long eluded him.

Nathan and Will were waiting for them down at the beach when Kirkie's Fiat pulled off the road and down the track to the sand.

"All clear?" asked Kirkie getting out. The tide was well out and a full mile of broad flat sand ran from there to the village.

"Yep, just a couple of folk out for a dander," replied Nathan. "Will was saying that the Wright brothers first flew on a beach – where was that again, Will?"

"Kitty-hawk," answered Will, "they were very quiet about the whole thing, didn't even invite the press or anything."

"Just like us then," grinned Kirkie, secretly kicking himself for not thinking of it earlier.

The assembly of the wings took less than half an hour and when all was complete Lennie gave the port wing a slap and looked around.

"So, what now?"

Mr Richardson didn't bother to ring ahead. He just got into the car and headed down to Ballydoonan. It was a forty-five minute drive and the whole way all he could think of were Safety Violations and the repercussions that would land on his head if a build he was supposed to be accrediting ended up injuring someone. He would have put his foot down, but he was a safety inspector after all.

"What! Me?" protested Lennie. "Have you gone out of your tiny little mind you pea-brained twit!"

Bisto had taken him to one side when he had expressed similar reservations to the others.

"Look, you big burke! This is your chance! Didn't you say you could fly a passenger jet in an emergency? This is only a dopey wooden crate with an engine in front and a couple of wings stuck on the side – what can possibly go wrong?"

Lennie slowly craned his neck around to look full in the face of the smaller swarthy face.

"How about the engine dies and the wings fall off just for starters! What kind of brain-dead zombie did you take me for? Fly? I can hardly stay up on a scooter for goodness sake! No, I'm out of here, you can go

269

and visit the goonie shop – I'm an historical event on this beach! I'm gone! Get out of my way!"

Bisto threw in his last ditch attempt.

"Lennie, these people trust you. You may not trust you, you may doubt what you are capable of, but look, these guys are putting their hopes on you! Look at Mr Kirkpatrick. He's broken-hearted because he can't fly the plane he's spent his life building. Look at Nate and Nathan – when their friend needed a champion who came immediately to their thoughts? It was *you* Lennie. Ballydoonan is a village waiting for its hero – its own Wright brother. You have come to a moment in your life that if you don't grasp now Lennie, may never come your way again. This is your day, Lennie – seize it!"

Lennie looked down and saw that Bisto was kneeling on the sand, a tear welling in one eye. Gosh, he was serious. Maybe… if Bisto really thought…

"Well… maybe I'll just try taxiing it up and down the beach then."

Bisto jumped to his feet and slapped his friend on the back.

"Well done, I knew you had it in you!" As Lennie loped hesitantly off toward the waiting cockpit, Bisto pulled the broken limpet shell out of his knee and wiped his eye. Wow, that was sore!

When the inspector turned up at the house, initially he thought there was no-one at home. Going around the back he saw someone in the kitchen vacuuming the floor. He gave the back door a loud knock and the vacuuming stopped. A few moments later the door opened and the lady of the house stood on the step.

"Hello, can I help you?"

"I was looking for Mr Kirkpatrick?"

"Oh, he was in the workshop. Take a look if you like – if he's not there he might have gone down to the beach – I heard him discuss it with some friends an hour or two ago."

Thanking the lady, Mr Richardson went to the shed and discovered it empty. There was no-one about. There was also no UW-1.

"That's it!" called Kirkie across the ear-splitting crackle of the Rotax engine. Just steer with the rudder pedals, there's a skid on the tail. Now, open her up, but not too much, that's it… how's she feel?"

Lennie was very nervous but keeping a cap on it. Kirkie and the others were driving alongside him in Kirkie's car as Lennie taxied up the beach in the plane. If this was as bad as it was going to get then perhaps it wasn't so bad, but the prop was kicking up so much sand that it was like advancing in a sandstorm. The thick glasses Kirkie had given him were quickly fogged out with swirling sand whilst his face was stinging like he had stuck it in a sand-blaster. He was fast approaching the point where he felt duty and honour had been fulfilled.

"I'll just turn and give it one last run!" he shouted across the car. It was what he said; it was not what he did, nor what happened next. He pulled the throttle back in order to gun the engine a little for the turn – he was only trundling along at a good walking pace and it needed a little extra to execute a bend on the sand. Instead of the throttle stop coming out a few extra millimetres, the whole thing came out from the cockpit fascia. He grasped the cable and tried to push the stop in to knock off the revs altogether – nothing. In a rising panic he did what, on reflection was the last thing he ought to have done – he pulled it, cable and all, as hard as he could. In response, the engine roared into a new found pitch of life and Lennie found himself pushed back in to the seat.

"There he goes!" cried Kirkie, "he's got the hang of it now all right – look, he's laughing!"

The UW-1 gathered speed as it bumped down the beach, as it did so, pieces of the fuselage began to loosen and fall off – the Perspex windscreen was first to go as it whipped out over the top of Lennie's head and tumbled along the sand behind the bucking and bouncing aircraft. Lennie was yelling at the top of his voice, trying by sheer force of volume to call in some kind of rescue from what he saw as certain doom.

"I'm not sure he is actually laughing," suggested Bisto as the Fiat tried to keep up. "He doesn't normally laugh that loud."

Lennie hadn't shut his mouth since the plane had taken a mind of its own and his throat was quickly filling with sand and debris. He coughed and spat and looked around blindly for the others but could see nothing but a blur.

"I'd better pull back," said Kirkie, "he's checking for clearance before take off." He let the Fiat fall back as more bits fell off the UW-1.

"Uh, is that supposed to happen?" asked Nathan as the rudder separated from the tail and bounced by the car window.

The faster the plane went, the more fell off it; now it was careering down the beach at forty miles an hour and the wings were flapping up and down as if it were some huge goose trying to break free from the ground.

"I don't think this is going to work," suggested Will pointlessly as the wings simultaneously disconnected and flew up into the air and over the roof of the car.

"Oh no!" shouted Bisto, "there's someone on the beach – Lennie's headed straight for them!"

Hamish Ferguson, now that he was locally recognised as the fitness professional of the village, felt that it was his duty to be seen pursuing a healthy lifestyle. A short walk along the beach would be a good example to the good people of Ballydoonan and help foster the new air of personal health that he himself had initiated. Also, he had seen his picture in the paper, and although the cameraman had obviously been using a wide-angle lens with a particularly bad distortion, still his backside seemed to fill an awful lot of the picture. A short walk would do him no harm.

He had only walked a quarter of a mile and was about to turn for home when he saw it coming straight for him. Actually, he heard it first. It was some kind of a vehicle, and it was roaring straight at him. There was someone in it and they were yelling like something singularly intent on killing something. Hamish froze as he suddenly felt the complete assurance that he was that something.

He froze, but only for a second – in the preservation of life and limb, Hamish turned and ran.

He ran like a man possessed – he ran with a speed and acceleration unheard of in a man of his generous proportions. His legs went into a flurry of action as they pummelled the ground like a steam-driven pneumatic drill. They were a blur of motion, a whirlwind of movement. Now he had got his substantial bulk up to unheard of velocity and it would have taken a steam engine coming in the other direction to stop him. Not that it would have been heard, what with the wail of doom uttering forth from Hamish's tortured lungs. It was only matched by a similar wail coming from the cockpit of the UW-1. Hamish had ceased hearing that though; a single word was screaming through his head – a scream for survival, 'RUN!' it yelled.

Off the beach, some villagers looked down from the square and saw Hamish Ferguson cover ground like only Malcolm or Donald Campbell had ever done – though Donald had had the advantage of the 5000 horse-power turbine-engined Bluebird. It was surreal: like watching a sumo wrestler win a hundred metre Olympic race in double quick time.

Jacob Cully the harbour-master took his pipe out of his mouth and pushed his cap back on his head.

"Sheesh, for a big lump of a lad, that Ferguson fella can fair go when he puts a mind tae it," he said with some wonder. The couple of cronies with him nodded in agreement.

"The missus goes tae thon keep fit carry-on o' his. I thought it was only a bit o' hooey. If she ends up runnin' like that I'll need tae watch ma'sell," said one. It was only then they saw the machine racing behind him. The picture of a bacon slicer and a runaway pig was a difficult image to avoid until suddenly the UW-1's wheels collapsed and the propeller bit hard into the sand, sending chunks of the beach flying in a flurry of churning sand and seaweed.

The plane, now inches behind Hamish slowed and pieces of propeller splintered dangerously all over the flat sand. With a final lurch, it nose-dived into the ground and came to a sudden and complete stop. Hamish fell hopelessly to his knees and would have let out a prayer of thanksgiving and pure unfeigned gratitude except that he was sucking air like a snow blower in reverse and had neither mind nor capacity for any other thought or action.

Lennie let his head drop forward onto the fascia and coughed out the parts of the beach that had ended up in his mouth. He coughed a lot – a good proportion of the beach had managed to get there.

Ten seconds later the Fiat rolled up and Kirkie jumped out.

"Stupid plane!" he shouted at the wreckage. "Months! I spent months on you, you useless piece of wood and tin! And this is how you repay me? Fall apart even before you get two wheels off the ground? You stupid, stupid plane!"

As the others watched with alarm, Kirkie went to the boot and returned with a sledge-hammer. Without pausing he went straight to the front of the UW-1 and began laying in with fervour.

"Take that and see how you like it!" he yelled. He smashed the sledge down into the engine cowling and glared at his work. "Fall to bits on me will you? You piece of southern rubbish, I should have known it was nothing but a Republican plot!"

"We'd better get your friend out of the aeroplane," suggested Will to the others. "That sledge doesn't seem to mind where it's hitting."

It was a timely suggestion. They quickly pulled the groggy Lennie out of the wreckage and dragged him back a safe distance from the deranged Kirkie. As they did, Nate looked up and saw someone cross the beach from the village and come in their direction.

"Who's this?" he asked the others. They shrugged. No-one knew. They watched him as he walked right up to Kirkie and wait as Kirkie stopped whacking the plane.

Mr Richardson stood looking at the shambles on the beach. He looked up and caught Kirkie's eye.

"Mr Kirkpatrick?"

Kirkie set the sledgehammer down.

"Yes?"

"I had some safety alterations I needed to bring to your attention concerning the seating rivets on the UW-1," he began, adjusting his glasses and pointing to a clipboard in his hand.

"What?"

"You know, with the inspection procedures on your…"

"Inspection? *Inspection?*" Kirkie's voice raised a level. "Here, you four-eyed interfering twit – inspect that!" He raised the sledgehammer and buried it deep into the cockpit where Lennie had been sitting one minute previously. "Will that fix it?"

The inspector pushed his glasses up his face and looked startled.

"Well now Mr Kirkpatrick, if you're not…"

"Say nothing!" interrupted Kirkie raising a palm. "I'll give you something to inspect!" He went to the boot of the Fiat and returned with a can of petrol, which he sprinkled liberally over the remains of the aircraft. Tossing the can to one side he pulled out a match, lit it and threw it onto the soaked fuselage. The UW-1 burst into orange flames while Mr Richardson leapt back in fright.

"There! Inspect that! Ha ha ha! What are you going to write in your stupid little book now? Ha ha!"

The inspector could see that the requirement for him to continue any further with the project was well and truly finished. He closed his file, tipped his hat to Kirkie and walked off the beach. Letting country bumpkins build aircraft had always been a mistake anyway. At least this was one he wouldn't have to worry about falling onto someone's house anymore.

Kirkie looked into the orange flames and after a few minutes of saying nothing, turned to the others. He seemed completely calm again.

"Do you guys want a lift back?"

"No thanks Mr Kirkpatrick," replied Bisto, "Lennie and I will just walk up to the village from here – thanks."

Kirkie walked over and grabbed Lennie's hand.

"Thanks son, you did a grand job. You had her off the ground for a minute – well done!"

Lennie smiled. He was alive – the plane was gone – the world was wonderful.

Will took Nathan home in the Mini, which was parked up at the track, and Kirkie drove Nate back to his house to get his Zephyr.

"You know, that thing's not safe, Nate, and I suppose you've still no licence?" said Kirkie as Nate started the clattering Ford.

"I've got a bike now," replied Nate, "all taxed and insured."

"Good," nodded Kirkie approvingly, "you can never be too safe where machines are involved. Thanks for the help today."

"Sorry about the plane," said Nate sympathetically, "you put a lot of work into it."

"Forget it!" laughed Kirkie, "Mistakes are for learning from. Next time I'll build a two-seater and I'll get you up eh? I think it was the rivets in the floor pan – next time I'll put in double the amount."

Nate drove off and by the time Kirkie had got to the back door, he was whistling and remembering he had seen second-hand silk parachutes for sale in the Exchange and Mart. Paracending could be done from a long rope behind a car. Now there was an idea.

"Are you O.K?" Bisto asked the crumpled heap that was Hamish Ferguson. Hamish tried to stand but found his legs had been turned to jelly. He wobbled uncertainly and reached out for support.

"Not really," he admitted. "Could you just help me up the beach? Thanks lads."

"I've never seen anyone run so fast in my life," said Bisto as they inched up towards the village. "You can really run!"

"That was the first and last – the first and last," wheezed Hamish. "I feel my life has just taken a serious readjustment. Some things in life are not important enough to be caught doing while you're dying."

"Oh," said Lennie whose recent experiences had made him sensitive to such feelings, "like what?"

"Like running," replied Hamish. "When I kick off these clogs at least let me have a smile on my face. Here, point me towards the bakery will you? Have you ever tried their chocolate and cream filled fingers? No? Good - they're on me then."

"So your sister and Nate aren't umm… you know…" asked Will in the Mini.

"What? Going out together? Don't be daft. He hardly knows her. Besides, who would want to go out with my sister – do you know she actually likes homework?"

"I suppose she likes doing well at school?"

"I know, weird isn't it? Anyway, this is her last year – she's enrolling as a student nurse at the Ulster Hospital in September. She'll be seventeen then, I think. She'll probably end up marrying some doctor or other – that's what student nurses are for – wife material for doctors. Pam's a staff nurse there and her boyfriend's a doctor."

Leaving Nathan off, Will turned the small orange car and drove dejectedly back down the lane. The welcome news that Nate was no threat had been quickly overshadowed by Nathan's summary of his sister's inevitable future. Of course in a couple of years some doctor would snap her up. Doctors weren't stupid. They would probably end up fighting one another for her – scalpels at dawn, masks drawn. He was stupid – stupid for ever entertaining ideas about Liz, stupid for allowing his stupid imagination to ever hope for impossible stupid dreams. As he drove out of the lane he determined to allow no more hopelessly unattainable pipe dreams take root in his head.

It might have seemed a straightforward and well intentioned thing telling his head such things, but Will Patterson's heart wasn't listening.

11.

TO THE ENDS OF THE EARTH

Nathan looked up from the final words on the page and was half surprised to see the garden outside the window devoid of icebergs, howling winds and sledge dogs. He felt as if he had been in the very tent as Oates turned to Scott, Wilson and Bowers and said his immortal words. 'I'm just going outside, I may be some time.'

What a story, what heroes, these men who faced the unknown and pressed forward into inhuman conditions in temperatures fifty below zero to strive to stand at the mysterious unknown South Pole. Captain Scott and his hardy men, alone against elements totally alien and vindictive, a zeal for Country, for glory, for a place in history, gaunt figures in a desolate landscape of white emptiness. And then to arrive at last and discover the glory gone after all the bitter struggles. A Norwegian flag flying and a note from the intrepid Roald Amundsen and his skiers. The disappointment, the defeat, and then the long slog back. Broken men already, and now without the warmth of a glory attained, to stumble and fall and in the end to close their eyes; utterly spent, totally beyond hope, completely exhausted and worn to skeletons of men. Broken men in a canvas tent, ripped and battered by winds and the screaming storm outside while food and rescue lay but eleven miles distant. Eleven impossible miles.

Nathan wondered how he would have fared, could he have made the supreme effort for those last few miles? Would Shackleton have done it? How did Amundsen do it? He read again 'Birdie' Bowers' final letter, a note to his mother. He was most likely the last to die and his sad little note was the epitaph of a man who had done all and prepared to lay his head to final rest that fateful day in March 1912.

'...my trust is still in Him and in the abounding Grace of my Lord and Saviour whom you brought me to trust in... I should so like to come through for your dear sake. It is splendid to pass however with such companions as I have... There will be no shame however and you will know that I have struggled to the end... Oh, how I do feel for you when you hear all, you will know that for me the end was peaceful as it is only sleep in the cold.'

Nathan set the book on his bed and decided that exploration was how a man proved himself. To climb the highest mountains, to cross the greatest deserts, to go where no foot had ever been placed, to uncover vast wildernesses, descend unplumbed depths. Exploration – that was what made a man. He turned and caught sight of the side of his face in the mirror. He narrowed his eyes and looked into the determined reflection – a plan was forming in his mind.

Willie-Joe's suspicions were seemingly confirmed when, hiding in his father's wardrobe during a game of hide and seek with Joyce, he saw the uniform. Not so much a uniform as a pullover with military symbols and badges. Willie-Joe was no expert in uniforms but this looked like an RAF one except that the letters ROC were emblazoned on the shoulder along with wings and some rank markings. It was true! His dad was in some kind of secret army – probably fighting the Russians at night when he was in bed sleeping and innocently believing his dad was just a washing machine fixer man. But who else knew?

He decided to give the hide and seek a rest and he emerged from the wardrobe making sure he wasn't seen. He didn't want to blow his dad's cover and who knew who had binoculars trained on their house. Mr Woods the farmer lived nearby and Willie-Joe had always had his suspicions about that man anyway. His nose for one thing. He had a nose that didn't look like a normal nose – it was big and bendy and looked as if it had been to Russia. Normal people had noses that just sat on their faces and looked like all they did was breathe and smell things. Mr Woods' nose had a sneaky look about it, a nose that was far too interested in what was going on in front of it for its own good. No, the more he thought about it the more he decided that he would act completely normal when he saw Mr Woods again. He would give him no reason to point his nose in their direction – he had a dad to protect, a dad who was obviously up to his armpits in big important secret army stuff – stuff that would have to be kept secret with the last drop of his blood. Boy, he couldn't wait until he told Miss Carlisle!

When he eventually found Joyce, she was lying on her bed drawing horses. It seemed a funny way to play hide and seek.

"That's thirty five minutes and you still couldn't find me!" declared her brother, standing in the doorway, hands on hips.

"You're too good." replied Joyce without looking up, "Is that a record?" She finished drawing the tail on the horse.

"No," said Willie-Joe, "last week I hid for an hour under the settee and you didn't find me." He watched as Joyce began drawing eyes on the head. "You *were* looking for me, weren't you?"

"Oh, all over the place," said his sister quickly.

"Where exactly?" asked Willie-Joe suspiciously. It seemed strange now he thought about it that he found Joyce where he had left her counting when he had dashed off to hide.

"Up and down, here and there, really Willie-Joe, you should be in the secret service or the commandos – you are so good at that game." Suspecting that she was about to be caught on, Joyce used her trump card – approval of Willie-Joe's abilities using a soldier-type metaphor. It worked, Willie-Joe grinned from ear to ear and turned to leave, a glow of military pride in his chest.

"Oh, by the way, what do you think about Dad?" he asked suddenly.

"What?"

"What do you think about him? Does he seem a normal dad to you?"

"What are you talking about, Willie-Joe?" said Joyce, leaning over on one elbow and eyeing her brother strangely.

"I mean, he goes out every day and fixes washing machines and stuff – does that seem normal to you?"

"What do think he should do, get into his spaceship and fly to the moon or something? Willie-Joe, you do know you're totally weird?"

"No, I just wondered… what you thought and all… it's nothing, forget it." He turned again and left leaving Joyce shaking her head. Boys were so weird – all dirty knees and heads full of rubbish – if she had children she would ask the stork or whoever you spoke to for only little girls.

Willie-Joe made his way outside and went to his thinking tree at the top of the lane. Joyce might look stupid, he thought as he settled into his familiar perch, but she knew something all right. He hadn't even thought about astronauts – a *spy* astronaut. Some of the things Dad said were washing machine parts didn't look very washing machinery to him. Motors and belts and stuff? He would keep his eyes wide open from here on in.

"What, and walk for four days? No harm on you Nathan," said Nate, "but walking for a hundred miles and camping out on the hills is not my idea of fun, who else is going anyway?"

"Oh, maybe Lennie and Bisto, I was going to ask Will Patterson – he likes walking – at least he's forever walking by the bottom of our lane, he might like to come."

Nathan was a little disappointed at Nate's reaction to the expedition he had outlined – a hike from Ballycastle at the North Western tip of Northern Ireland all the way back to Ballydoonan. It was about ninety-five miles and he reckoned four days would be plenty of time to do it.

"Well, thanks for asking anyway," replied Nate, "Dad would need me around the farm in any case – would it not just be simpler to do it in the train? I think there's a train comes right down the Antrim coast, there's one goes to Portrush anyway, you could go there instead – I heard Barry's Amusements has a new big dipper."

Nathan shook his head; Nate didn't get it at all. It was a matter of grit and pushing oneself to the limit in difficult circumstances; fighting the elements, mastering discomfort and turning your back on easy living. Throwing up on a big dipper was a different kind of thing altogether.

When Anne McFadzean asked Winston what he would like for his upcoming birthday, Nate's ears perked up when he heard his reply.

"I'd love a rucksack Mum, you know, for camping and hiking and stuff like that."

Mrs McFadzean simply nodded and noted it in her head; Nate turned at the table and looked at his brother.

"Where are you going to go camping?" he asked.

Winston shrugged and set down his fork.

"I dunno, but if I had a rucksack I could carry food and a tent and maybe go to the Mournes or something."

Nate suddenly remembered the conversation with his friend Nathan a few days previously.

"Nathan McCutcheon is planning a hike, he's calling it a 'yomp'. He might take you with him – I think he said he's planning on four days."

Winston sat up straight and looked at his brother. "Four days? Class! Ask him if I could go would you?"

Anne looked up from the kitchen sink and addressed Nate.

"Where is he going? Is he taking anybody else? Four days is a long time Nate, a lot could go wrong in four days."

"Don't worry about it Mum," Nate replied, "It's only over the Antrim plateau, it's not like he's going to the North Pole."

"You will ask him, won't you?" said Winston again. He was immediately and definitely interested.

Lennie McClurg was definitely not.

"Four *days*? What, like outside and all? What if it rains?"

"That's all apart of the crack. We bring waterproofs and push on through," replied Nathan grandly, "just imagine, wind beating off our faces and us leaning into the storm and conquering everything thrown at us!"

Lennie looked at Nathan the way a man looks at a boy who has just chucked a cat over the harbour wall.

"Are you nuts?" he said. "The only people you're going to want coming on a walk like that are the sort of people who are normally locked up for their own safety. What on earth would you want to go wandering about on empty sodden hills for? And I bet there's no chip shops up there either."

"Of course there's no chip shops," sighed Nathan, "that's the whole point – never mind, I'll ask Bisto, he might fancy a challenge."

Lennie nodded. "Yes," he said, "Bisto is just the sort of burke would agree to do something like that."

"What! Like sleeping in a tent and all?" said Bisto when Nathan mentioned it to him outside church on Sunday morning. Nathan nodded.

"Yep, and we carry all our own food and sleeping bags and things. I already have the maps and a compass. We'll light campfires at night and cook beans and sausages and wake with the larks. Up on the hills the stars will shine like beacons and we'll tell stories and it'll be brill."

Bisto was definitely interested. He had no tent or sleeping bag, but Nathan assured him those were small details. The desire to go was more important than the means; the second could be sorted whereas the first was a matter of the soul. Bisto seemed convinced.

"Can I ask Lennie?" he said.

"You can ask," laughed Nathan, "but I already have, he really wasn't interested."

"Rubbish," exclaimed Bisto, "Lennie doesn't know what he wants. He just needs someone to tell him. You can count on us both."

When Nathan called around to the McFadzean farm about a week later, Winston made it very clear he was enthusiastic and incredibly interested in the hike.

"I could bring a tent and all; Dad says I can borrow an old one he used to use when he was younger. Do you have maps? I can get maps if you want?"

Nathan was glad to have someone at last who was as enthusiastic as himself. Winston was thin and lithe. He could be Captain Oates. He himself was Captain Robert Falcon Scott of course. Things were definitely shaping up.

"We probably need a planning session," explained Nathan, "you know, to arrange our route and food supplies and that. When would suit you?"

"Anytime – next Saturday? Sure why not meet here at my house – I'll get notepads and pens for us all and we can lay out maps and all on the kitchen table. Just like planning for an Antarctic expedition eh?"

"Just the same," said Nathan, "preparation and planning – 'start right and you'll finish right', my dad always says. You know," he said, his voice a conspiratorial whisper, "this might be tough."

"The tougher the better," replied Winston seriously.

"And we'll be on our own, out on the bleak hills."

"Bleak is good," nodded Winston with much gravitas.

"Maybe even danger and peril," added Nathan who was really getting into the thing with a fervour.

"Peril and danger – hikes are rubbish without them," agreed Winston, his lips pursed in steely determination.

"And it's a 'yomp' – hikes are what wimps do," corrected Nathan.

"Yomp?"

"Yeah, it's an army thing. We're not just a bunch of kids out for a dander – this is survival!"

Winston nodded and rubbed his chin purposefully. It was getting better by the minute.

Willie-Joe knew they were rat traps. At first he thought they were absolutely enormous metal mouse traps but the stencilled words on the base corrected his guess. *'Killit' Rat Trap* it said. No beating about the bush there then.

Willie-Joe had been poking about in his dad's store, a shed he normally kept locked across the yard. Finding his father had left it open;

Willie-Joe decided to see if he could find any more evidence of his dad's clandestine activities. There were several appliances in various states of disrepair and parts in plastic bags hanging from nails on the wall but nothing that was clearly a gun or a rocket launcher. Of course, people in secret jobs like his dad would know how to disguise things to look like everyday objects – things that with a few twiddles and adjustments would become something very different altogether. The rat traps were highly suspicious now he thought about it. Why did his dad need six of them for one thing? And why were they still in their boxes, cardboard boxes that were faded and crumbling? Holding a trap in his hands he tried arming the spring – it took all of his strength to pull it back and lodge the metal bar across and under the tilt-bar that would hold the bait. Experimenting further, he set it on the earth floor of the shed and prodded at the trap with a pencil he found on the bench.

Thwack! went the trap as it leapt into the air and shattered the pencil into more bits than Willie-Joe felt inclined to count. He let out a gasp and immediately saw what it really was.

"A man trap!" he murmured aloud. It was obviously some part of his dad's spy kit. Probably he would set traps out to catch counter-spies or double agents who were onto his trail. Boy, was his dad brave! Being chased by hundreds of Russians and his dad caught them like rats in a trap – exactly like that actually.

It crossed his mind that he would like to try them out. In fact, it was probably very important that the traps were checked out to ensure they were working properly. If he was to try them out a bit, it would almost certainly help his dad who was likely so busy doing his other secret stuff that he hadn't had time to test them much lately. A son like him was a real asset to his dad – he would take care of the testing and his dad would not be sneaked up on by some bendy-nosed Russian without being nabbed by a thoroughly tested man-trap.

The old quarry at the bottom of the lane and along the road a bit was used by Mr Woods as a place to dump chicken droppings from his farm. He dumped all kinds of things there actually; there were old hen houses, rubber tractor tyres, fence posts, dead things – all manner of waste and spurious material was emptied from the back of Mr Woods' trailer from time to time. Willie-Joe had seen rats scurrying about in the mounds of smelly rubbish and so with his old canvas school bag filled with four of the traps, he headed out on his mission.

The sausages he sneaked out of the fridge were uncooked, cold and surprisingly unappetizing as Willie-Joe stuck them onto the traps. The rats would have to be desperate to want to have a go at this yuck, thought Willie-Joe as he laid the *Killit* Rat Traps out around a mound of old chicken dung. Still, given a choice of old tractor tyres or un-cooked sausage meat, maybe the rats would be tempted after all.

Willie-Joe retired to an old wooden hen house dumped about fifty feet away and hid inside. It was a pretty disgusting hut on the inside, but he sat on his haunches touching nothing and prepared to wait and watch through a small wire covered opening at the side of the door. He didn't have long to wait.

Mr Woods and his wife didn't often have a lot of time to themselves. Running a farm was a busy life and left leisure time very far down on the 'things to do next' list. However, the odd evening, when the milking was done and the animals fed and bedded down, he and Agnes enjoyed a quiet saunter along the narrow road as the noise of the day faded and the countryside quietened and prepared for its evening rest.

It was on just such a dander that they met the young McCutcheon boy heading towards them, obviously on his way home. As he approached, they saw that he looked very pleased with himself about something; he was grinning fit to burst.

"Hello, Willie-Joe," said Mr Woods as the boy drew near, "out picking blackberries eh?"

"Hello, Mr Woods," replied Willie-Joe, "hello, Mrs Woods – uh, blackberries?"

"Well, it's just that your bag seems full and they look like they're leaking." He smiled at the young lad – he hadn't picked blackberries in years but the memory of long late summer evenings as a boy stuffing himself and coming home black-mouthed and smeared with purple was a happy one. The joys of remembered childhood were days of long hot summers and careless endless afternoons turning to orange and red painted skies. It was nice to see those days lived again in youngsters like his neighbour's son.

"Oh!" exclaimed the boy pulling his bag off his shoulder, "I see what you mean... no, actually I wasn't picking blackberries Mr Woods; wait till you see what I've got!" With a flourish of achievement and pride, Willie-Joe spilled the contents of his crimson bottomed satchel out onto the road. Half a dozen limp and very dead rats flopped out and lay in a disgusting heap at his feet. Mrs Woods took two steps back – two very quick steps.

"I caught these, Mr Woods, all by myself!"

There was a second during which the pictures of blackberries and innocence evaporated out of Mr Wood's pleasant reverie and were replaced by a very present mound of large dead rodents.

"What on earth are you doing with those?" he said with considerably less affection in his voice than a few seconds previous.

"Taking them home Mr Woods," replied Willie-Joe simply, "I was going to show them to Mum."

"You're going to take rats home to your mother?" exclaimed Mrs

Woods aghast, speaking for the first time. "Is she expecting them?" Mr and Mrs Woods had never had any children of their own and for the first time in her life it occurred to her that this might have been a blessing in disguise after all.

"Oh no, Mrs Woods," grinned back the boy, "she'll be really surprised – I bet she didn't know I could catch six rats all by myself!"

"Willie-Joe," said Mr Woods firmly and with some resolution, "those are dirty creatures, disease carrying and filth covered. Do not even *think* of taking them home. Throw them into the dyke right now and when you get home, get rid of that bag and go and immediately wash your hands – in fact, take a bath!"

Willie-Joe's smile suddenly wiped off his face and he looked at his booty on the road.

"What, all of them?"

"Every single one – do you want to end up with Leptospirosis?"

Willie-Joe didn't like the sound of the word that the farmer had used and he also reckoned that no, he probably didn't want to end up with it. Reluctantly he helped Mr Woods kick the sausage-filled rats into the verge and down into the roadside gully.

"And get your Dad to burn that bag when he comes home," added the man as Willie-Joe left and slowly began walking up towards his lane.

Willie-Joe was a fluster of emotions. Feelings of lofty achievement had suddenly been overtaken by a sense of stupidity and embarrassment. Now he thought about it, maybe his mum wouldn't have totally appreciated his efforts. Come to think about it, she didn't even like mice. The time he had put one in his shirt pocket and it went and stuck its head out during dinner was a case in point. Mum had not been very happy about that at all. Still, Mr Woods had suddenly changed from being very nice to quite sharp. And what was that big word again? As he turned into his yard it dawned on him. It wasn't even English –

caught out in a moment of surprise Mr Woods had let down his guard – he had spoken *Russian*!

Margaret Patterson was a mother and like mothers everywhere she had a sixth sense as far as her children went. Her two sons had been a tower of strength after David's death, they were sons to be proud of; sons who were a constant reminder of the man she had loved for over twenty-five years.

Johnny was well settled, having married a lovely girl a couple of years earlier, but Will had not been himself of late and she couldn't quite put her finger on it.

He was a young man who rarely demonstrated wild swings of emotion. Even as a child he had shown early signs of constraint and self assurance, a boy who could control himself and was able to stay on an even keel when events around him were a long way off calm.

It was this that Margaret noticed was different. Now, instead of his usual steady manner, sometimes he would arrive home in the Mini and appear either agitated or quiet. In anyone else it wouldn't have been noticed, but Will didn't do mood swings and something was affecting him to the point where he would come home whistling and laughing at the moon one day, morose and silent the next. She was concerned about him but didn't know what to do about it. She was due at Johnny and Beth's for tea that night, perhaps she would ask him – if anyone knew Will it was his older brother.

Will was at that very moment talking to Nathan McCutcheon. Will had gone for a long walk and ended up on the big beach to the south of the village. It was here that he met Nathan who was approaching from the opposite direction, all waterproofs, hats and gloves, a pair of big boots on his feet and an enormous rucksack on his back.

"Leaving home?" smiled Will as Nathan pulled up beside him, his face streaked with sweat and his hair clinging to his forehead.

"No, just practising – actually, I was looking for you," replied Nathan breathing heavily.

"Oh, what for? Not to help you carry that massive backpack I hope?"

"Naw," laughed Nathan, "though, do you have a backpack by any chance?"

As Nathan explained his upcoming expedition to Will, Will shook his head and apologised.

"Sorry, that sounds like a bit of crack all right, but I've no time off work to take at the minute. At least not until the winter week – I'll have to pass on that one. Thanks for asking anyway. By the way, what have you got in that backpack?"

"Forty-eight pounds of rocks," grinned Nathan. "I reckon that I need to get used to a bit of hauling before we set off. That's what I'm practising for – I've planned on about twenty-five miles a day and there's no point planning without preparing."

"Good point," agreed Will with some admiration, "so how far have you gone today?"

"Five miles," replied Nathan, "and I'm knackered!"

That night Nathan, Winston, Bisto and Lennie met at Winston's house to make arrangements. Winston's home was a large farmhouse and there was no problem finding an empty room in which to lay out plans and make notes. The back dining room had a large circular table and the protagonists sat around it like members of the cabinet thrashing out government policies.

Nathan had brought his maps of the Antrim coast and they covered the entire distance from Ballycastle to Ballydoonan on 1/25000 scale. Laid out on the table the distance looked formidable.

"Right," began Nathan, "first of all, it's about ninety odd miles if we take the direct route…"

"Did you say *ninety*?" asked Lennie suddenly. "Did you mean *nineteen* and say the wrong word?"

"No, it's about ninety to ninety-five miles, less than eighty as the crow flies but…"

"Ninety-five? Miles? Ninety-five as in 'almost a hundred'? That kind of ninety-five?" Lennie looked seriously shocked.

"Don't be a wimp," interjected Bisto, "it's not like we're crossing Africa."

"No, Africa's warm," agreed Lennie sardonically, "and it's got elephants."

"Elephants?" exclaimed Bisto, "elephants?"

"Yes, you dope," sighed Lennie, "obviously you catch an elephant and ride on its back – duh!"

"Well, anyway," said Nathan continuing, "that means we'll walk about twenty-five miles a day, we should manage that easily enough."

"On an elephant maybe," muttered Lennie under his breath.

"No, if you think about it," said Winston joining in, "there are twenty four hours in the day, you sleep about eight and allow say, another two for stopping to eat and stuff and that leaves twelve hours walking time. If you march hard you can cover four miles an hour, but we only need to do two, so we'll be practically crawling – it'll be easy."

Nathan doubted that easy was the word for it, but put like that it did sound less daunting. Actually, daunting was closer to what he was hoping for, but Lennie seemed put at ease to some degree by Winston's calculations.

"Yeah, well, I'm only coming because you lot need a mature head about the place. You teenagers need direction in your lives, a steering hand. What about food?"

"Mum's bringing us toast later on," said Winston, "and hot chocolate too."

"Your mum's coming?" asked Bisto with incredulity.

"No, I mean she's bringing toast to us in this room tonight, I'll let her know we're ready for it."

As Winston nipped out of the room to speak to his mother, Lennie shrugged.

"Actually, I meant food on the hike, though I didn't like to interrupt him. Mmm… toast and hot chocolate!"

The supper loosened them all up a bit and soon they were planning as if for 'D' day. Lennie had no walking boots but Winston knew some friend of his dad's who had size twelve feet too and a note was made to ask about them. Nathan had a two-man tent and Winston offered to bring the other. They planned how they would share out the weight and agreed that they should carry their own food, as no-one was quite sure what or how much they would need.

At the end of the night Nathan was satisfied that most things had been covered; it was Bisto who asked about transport.

"How do we get back?"

"Back?" repeated Nathan without understanding.

"Yes, once we get to Ballythingy. How do we get back?"

"We don't walk *to* Ballycastle," explained Nathan, the misunderstanding dawning on him, "we walk back *from* Ballycastle. That way, when things get tough we'll know that every step is a step towards Ballydoonan. Determination will drive us – the push for home!"

"Like Scott of the Antarctic!" pronounced Winston with fervour, "we'll be men versus the elements – the human will pitted against impossible odds!"

Lennie's sanguine attitude so recently achieved dissolved before his eyes and Nathan looked with surprise to Winston.

"You know that story?"

"What, about *The Race for the Pole*? It's my favourite film."

"I've just read the book, it changed my life," said Nathan with sudden seriousness.

"Class!" exclaimed Winston, "we'll be just like them – pressing on to make the last few miles, thinking of our loved ones, battling everything nature throws at us!"

As Nathan joined in with further dramatic determinations, Lennie looked at Bisto and shook his head.

"I am a nut. If I hadn't said I would go already, I would be sneaking out the back door and looking for the men with the white coats. Just remind me Bisto, how did you get me to agree to this?"

"I gave you half my Mars bar – it wasn't that hard."

"Has Will been down with you recently?" Margaret asked her son. Johnny, Beth and she were chatting around the table after tea and Margaret was keen to discover if either of them had noticed any change in Will's behaviour.

"Yes, he was down on Thursday, wasn't he, Beth?" replied Johnny looking to his wife.

"After the Young Farmers' club, yes, he had just left his friend home and called by for an hour."

"Why do you ask?" asked Johnny "is everything all right?"

"Yes, yes I think so – his friend, is that Ellie McCutcheon's boy?"

"Nathan, yes, he's been up at his place a fair bit recently. There's a bunch of them all messing about with motorcycles and engines and things. Actually, he was telling us about an aeroplane Mr Kirkpatrick had built… you know Kirkie Kirkpatrick?"

"Oh yes, I know him well, he was a good friend of your father's. David never had anything but good to say about him. His wife is a lovely girl… Nathan? What's he like?"

"Nathan? Oh he's spot on – Will's been taking him to Young Farmers, though I would think it's more the girls they're interested in than the cattle judging!"

"Girls? Mmm," mused Margaret. "He never mentioned any girls to me. You see, I think he's been a bit quieter than usual lately – well, actually, that's not quite true – sometimes he's as happy as a lark then next day sullen and silent, but that's just it, you know Will, he's normally so laid back. I just wondered if you'd noticed anything?"

Beth got up and began to clear the table. Margaret pushed back her chair and prepared to join in. Johnny took the teapot and milk back into the kitchen as the two Mrs Pattersons came behind.

"Have you ever seen Nathan's sister, Liz?" asked Beth casually as they carried in various plates and dishes to the sink.

"Long black hair, very pretty?" said Margaret in reply.

"Yes, very pretty. Smart too, she's wants to be a nurse I've heard."

"Isn't the eldest girl, um… Pam, yes, isn't Pam a nurse?"

"Yes, she's a theatre nurse in the Ulster – engaged to a doctor there. Liz is about seventeen now – she helps out with the crèche on Sunday mornings with me. She's really nice."

It was all she said and they moved on to other topics quite quickly. Margaret enjoyed chatting with Beth, she was so glad Johnny had married such a lovely girl. She was easy company and welcomed her into her house like a friend more than a mother-in-law. It was always a difficult relationship to gauge, that of a mother-in-law and daughter-in-law, but with Beth there was no barrier and she truly felt as if she had gained the daughter David and she would have loved to have. It was a pity her husband had never got to meet her.

It wasn't until she was lying in bed that night after turning out the light that the mention of Liz McCutcheon came back into her head. Now why did Beth mention her name?

In another bedroom in the house another mind was occupied with the same person. For the twentieth time he leaned over and took a small dusky pink handkerchief out of his bedside cabinet and turned it over gently in his hand. He felt the tiny blue flower embroidery with his thumb and caressed the soft cotton. Bringing it to his face he took in the fading scent. The picture of a slender girl in oversized red overalls sitting beside him in his car filled his senses and he gave a distant smile, sighed and returned the handkerchief to the drawer. Lying on his back he looked up at the ceiling and felt the power that from generation to generation had moved and broken men like earth before the inexorable plough.

To his shame a tiny tear appeared at the edge of an eye and he quickly wiped it away.

"I love you, Liz McCutcheon," he whispered aloud into the stillness and felt the relief and the burden of the words spoken fall upon him all at the same time.

Turning into the pillow he lay open-eyed in the darkness and discovered that eyes open or closed the image he saw remained.

At last, as he slipped into sleep, the beautiful girl who would not leave looked into his face and smiled from her eyes deep into his and he knew both misery and joy.

Willie-Joe was restless and slept fitfully. In his dreams enormous rats were chasing him across the fields, strings of sausages wrapped around their necks. Just as one would almost catch him from behind he would waken and stare into the darkness, convinced that they were hiding in the shadows, waiting for him to nod off again. He turned on his bedside light and discovered the rats were good at hiding. As he lay on his bed he heard noises coming up from downstairs and guessed his mum and dad had not yet gone to bed. Drowsily pulling back the sheets, Willie-Joe gingerly stepped out of bed, hoping that any rats hiding under the bed would not dare attack with the lights on and slipped out onto the landing. When he got to the head of the stairs he heard his parents voices waft up from the living room. The door to the living room was ajar and light spilled out into the downstairs hallway as Willie-Joe caught the conversation from below. He hadn't intended to eavesdrop, but the words he heard made him hold his breath and listen.

"Please be careful Tom, do you have to go tonight? It's so late and the whole thing worries me so."

"I'll be back in the morning," soothed his father's voice, "and there's nothing to worry about. The whole thing is about keeping us all safe – it's for the Country, for peace. The Soviets know about people like me and what we do, that very knowledge makes an attack highly unlikely."

"But what if something ever did happen when you up there, what would we do? It's an awful thing to even think about, it reminds me of that Cuba crisis, I thought it was the end of the world."

"Hush now Isobel, it really is nothing to even think about. It has to be done and someone has to do it. There's no good us sitting here expecting someone else to do it. No, I see it as protecting our family. Willie-Joe and Joyce sleep safer at night because of these things – that's enough reason for me to spend a few hours a month underground. I'd best get on – I'll be back before you waken – God bless."

There were a couple more mumbled farewells and Willie-Joe heard the back door below the landing open. Moving quickly and quietly to the window, he peered out and saw his dad leave. It was hard not to gasp as he saw his father dressed in his blue uniform and cap leave with a bag over his shoulder and head out into the fields behind the house. In a couple of seconds he was swallowed up in the darkness and he heard his mother lock the door.

Diving back into bed Willie-Joe quickly turned out the lights and rewound in his head the conversation he had heard downstairs. It was true, it was really true! His dad was a secret spy going out to fight the Russians at night – in the darkness, a bag of hand grenades on his back. His heart pounded with loud heavy thumps in his chest as he lay frightened and scared and also a little bit proud on his bed. His dad! Boy! Was Mr Woods in for a shock! Suddenly a thought struck him. What if Mr Woods knew? What if he knew and his dad didn't know he knew? What if his dad had no idea that the farmer next door was a Russian spy who spoke big Russian words by accident when you got him cross? He suddenly closed his eyes and did the one thing he could think of doing.

"Dear God," he prayed, "please look after Dad and don't let the Russians catch him. Especially Mr Woods, God. Please don't let Mr Woods chase after Dad tonight and fight him with guns and bullets and things. And if he does God, please let Dad shoot him first… Amen."

It helped. He immediately felt better. Tomorrow he would find some way of warning his dad about the farmer and his bendy nose. Turning onto his side he was soon fast asleep. All thoughts about rats had gone completely.

When Nathan explained to his dad about the planned walk, Bob Mc-Cutcheon was impressed.

"That's some walk, son," he said with a whistle. "How are you getting to Ballycastle? Would you like me to take you up?"

"That would be great Dad; we're going next Friday at the start of the term break. Would you have room for four of us and our packs?"

Bob was pleased that his son seemed to have got a plan in his head and the wherewithal to execute it. It showed independence, a strong spirit. Ninety-five miles was no mean feat. He applauded Nathan for his enthusiasm and imagination. He was always thinking, always using his head.

Friday soon came around and with a very early start Bob's car was soon filled with the prospective long distance walkers. Winston and Nathan chatted continuously as Bob headed north. Plans were still being finalised and the drop off point was only agreed as they drove through Broughshane and began heading north-west for Ballycastle. The tall Lennie was fairly quiet though Bisto occasionally joined in with Nathan and Winston.

"Look at that hill," said Winston pointing out through the window. Rising out of the softly rolling countryside a hill like one scribbled by a child rose from the west. It was almost a perfect semicircle and looked odd in its singular position on the horizon.

"That's Slemish," said Nathan's father.

"Slemish? St Patrick's mountain?" queried Nathan.

"Yes, as a young slave he looked after pigs there."

"Must have been some fit pigs," said Lennie, "that's a steep looking hill."

"I've always wanted to stand on its summit," said Bob wistfully, "but just never got around to it. Are you coming back this way? You should go up if you get a chance."

"What about the pigs?" asked Lennie.

"Oh, they'll hardly bother you," smiled Bob, "they'd be about fifteen hundred years old now."

Everyone laughed and Lennie joined in. Inwardly however he filed away the new piece of information. He had no idea that a pig could live that long.

The drive North took over two hours but finally they were approaching a sign that said the small coastal resort of Ballycastle was four miles ahead.

"Take this next road on the right Dad," said Nathan, a map spread out on his knee. Bob slowed down and turned into the minor road.

"This is a dead-end son," pointed out Mr McCutcheon seeing a sign at the side of the road.

"That's O.K. Dad, it goes to a carpark at the end. About four miles I think. You could leave us off there if that's alright – that's where we're starting from."

The road was little used and grass sprouted in a long thin line along its centre. At the end a small gravel car-park marked the conclusion of the road and Bob pulled in to a halt.

Pulling the back-packs out onto the roadside, the four lads all felt the excitement of the unknown trail before them. It was still only ten in the morning and fulmars wheeled above their heads as gannets crashed into the swell surging up onto the rocky beach beside them. The sky was a cloud filled blue and the sounds of the sea and screeching gulls filled the air. A small cottage lay on the path ahead and a waterfall flowed freely out of the rocks above into a cascade of rainbows in a crystal clear pool before running out to sea. The air was electric with the abandoned scope of the wild outdoors after the confinement of the car.

"All the best lads, if you get into any problems just find a phone and give me a call," said Nathan's father as he pulled the car door shut behind him.

As the car crunched back along the road and finally disappeared Lennie's voice broke the stillness.

"This is nice up here, isn't it?"

The others looked and saw that he was grinning widely and looking with interest at their surroundings. The sea pounded in from the Atlantic on one direction, grassy cliffs rose from the land.

"But no point in hanging about lads," he continued with some import, "we have miles to go before we sleep, miles to go before we sleep."

"Robert Frost!" laughed Nathan at Lennie's new found enthusiasm.

"What?" exclaimed Bisto.

"That's Robert Frost – *Stopping by Woods on a Snowy Evening*. Lennie's gone all poetic!"

"No point standing *talking* – these legs of mine are up for *walking!*" said Lennie with a grin.

"What happened to 'Mr Grumpy man'?" asked Bisto.

"There you are standing there," replied Lennie airily, "glad I talked you into coming eh?"

The coastal path wound along a boulder strewn strip of ground between the sea and the cliffs. A fresh salty wind blew steadily over their heads and climbed up the basalt walls behind them. Life was in the air and the four young men felt invigorated and ready for anything. Winston pulled a notebook out of a pocket and pencilled some words. *The long walk. Log; Day one*, he wrote with a flourish on the clean white page.

Nathan grinned at his friends behind – things had started well and his skin tingled with excitement and anticipation.

Half an hour later dark rain clouds began building up overhead. As the first spits of rain started to fall some of the excitement retreated and Bisto tried hard to remember if he had brought a coat.

"Did I ever tell you about how your dad first asked me out?" Margaret asked her son at the breakfast table. Her son left for work early and since she had always been an early riser Margaret enjoyed taking breakfast with him before he headed out for the day. It was a good time to chat and make arrangements if any needed to be done.

Will looked up. It wasn't that often that his mother talked about herself and his dad. She would often mention things about him of course – telling Will stories about what he said or things he had done but stories about the two of them and their life together she largely kept to herself.

"Sure I was there, don't you remember?" said Will.

"Ha ha," dismissed his mother dryly. "You know, your dad was very shy when he was younger."

"Shy? Dad?" It wasn't a concept that fitted with his memory of a father who seemed to know everything and baulk at nothing. His dad was his hero. His dad could do anything – put an engine in a car, repair just about anything that was broken – he had built the house they lived on practically all by himself. When his dad was with other men, it was his dad who was the natural leader. He was an initiator of ideas, a rock of stability and his dear beloved dad. It was still hard to believe he was no longer there to make things right.

"Oh yes, Mr 'I can do' watched me for years and all the time I thought he barely knew I existed. Everybody knew David Patterson, he was into just about everything that was going. I was just a girl who looked from a distance and felt small and only a shadow in his life."

"So what happened?"

"Well, I had no more clue about it, but all the time I thought he hardly knew my name, in fact he was writing love letters to me, beautiful letters telling me how much he loved me, how I was the most beautiful girl in the world, that his heart was and only ever would be mine to own."

Will would have been embarrassed at any other time to hear his mother speak so candidly, but he had a personal interest here, a resonance rang within his own understanding at what his dad had gone through.

"But… how could you think he didn't care if…"

"He never sent them to me. He just wrote them and hid them away. All the time he just let on that nothing was happening and I got on with my life."

"But he must have done something about it?"

"Long before that I started going out with another young man. I don't know why, he just asked me and I said yes. Your dad was distraught."

Will nodded. He bet he was.

"It was his own father who caught wind of what was going on. He gave your father some timely advice."

"Granda?"

"Yes, your grandfather Patterson came across a letter or sussed it out himself, whatever – he was a gruff old man, men weren't expected to be affectionate or compassionate in his day, it was seen as soft and weak, but he loved his son. 'David,' he said to him out of the blue one day, 'if that Robinson girl's the girl for you then what's somebody else holding her hand for? Be a man, son. It's your life and her life too and you're shilly-shallying about. Nobody else is going to live your life for you. Some things are too important to dawdle about with.' It was a pretty direct message and it shook up your dad. If his mother had still been alive she might have been more diplomatic, but that was your granda. Anyway, it set a resolve in your father."

"So what did he do?" asked Will who had forgotten his breakfast by now and was completely taken up with the account.

"He took my boyfriend aside one day and asked him how serious he was about me because he was going to marry me."

"He what?" laughed Will in surprise.

"That's what he did. Full scale assault. Faced with that, my boyfriend withered and said he wasn't sure he was that serious, the way was clear for him."

"What happened then?"

"Well, the first I knew my boyfriend called by and told me that he and David Patterson had spoken and he was breaking up with me. I was in tears – I thought David had told him I wasn't good enough for him or something, I had no idea. Next thing your dad turns up at my door with a bunch of flowers and asks my dad if he can court his daughter! Needless to say he had no idea what was going on, I had less."

"What did you say?"

"I was flabbergasted. I was busy thinking he was the worst creep in the world when suddenly he's at my front door telling me he I am all he thinks about!"

"Wow! What did you say?"

"I told him to get lost and slammed the door in his face!"

"So much for Granda's advice!"

"No, you're wrong. I was just angry. Over the next few weeks he showed me every kindness and I saw that he was actually very genuine. He asked me twice more, the second time I said yes, and well, as they say, the rest is history. If he hadn't done something, even though it was a bit unconventional, well, who knows? What's for sure is that your father and I were made for one another – it was a marriage made in heaven. God supplies, but he sometimes He hands us the oars and asks us to row the boat for a bit."

Will suddenly caught sight of the clock on the kitchen wall. He was ten minutes late and hadn't even noticed the time pass.

"Wick! Sorry Mum, got to go." He got up and grabbed his car keys. "Thanks for telling me all that, it's nice to hear about Dad. He was a great dad wasn't he?"

"The best," nodded Margaret quietly.

As Will left and the back door closed behind him she spoke in an almost whisper to herself.

"And a wonderful husband."

Miss Carlisle was not as smart as she looked. Willie-Joe had imagined teachers were all brain boxes, the things they had to know about all sorts of stuff. She could tell the class how flowers pollinated and never make mistakes in big hard multiplying sums but when it came to understanding the menace of local undercover Russian spies she was as thick as a plank.

"I'm quite sure Mr Woods is no such thing, Willie-Joe, and for the life of me I can't think how you could come up with such a crazy idea."

The proof as far as Willie-Joe saw it was overwhelming. The way he was always driving about in his tractor and looking all around himself for information to send back to Russia – the way he had broken into Russian that night a week before – they were proof enough for any sensible person. Then there was his wife. She was able to step backwards with the agility of a Russian gymnast even though she was an ancient old hag – she was probably getting near forty or something! Then there was the dump at the old quarry. Mr Woods often had bonfires down there and absolutely everybody knew that spies were forever burning secret documents and stuff to keep their cover hidden. And as for the nose? All on its own the nose was enough for the police to throw him into the cooler. He wasn't actually completely sure what a cooler was, but he had heard Paul Newman mention it on a film on TV. It sounded like a place for people like Mr Woods all right whatever it was. A good old cooling, that's what he needed!

In any case, even though a normal person would have nodded seriously and taken notes to pass on to the police, Miss Carlisle seemed to think that the nine times table was more important. Just wait till the Ruskies were tramping all over her garden and pushing her into coolers! Then she would know a thing or two but then it would be too late. His dad would be out in the fields being killed all over the place and Miss Carlisle would rather talk about sums? Crazy!

He didn't tell Miss Carlisle about his dad's secret identity in the end. A woman who couldn't tell the difference between an honest nose and one filled with badness was unlikely to be a person to share such secrets with after all. Instead he got on with his tables and tried to remember what the trick was about the nine times table. It was something about the answer adding up to nine, but what was the use of that if you didn't actually know what the answer was in the first place? One times nine was easy enough, after that things got tricky.

With the discouraging response from his teacher, Willie-Joe was slower in sharing his discoveries with his dad. He began to think that the best way to help him was to keep a secret watch on his back and if anything suddenly happened, to alert his dad to it at the right moment. In the meantime he would be the secret watcher.

He also became a secret poker-abouter. When the coast was clear he poked about in the trousers that hung with his dad's uniform. He didn't see it as being sneaky or underhand in any way. If he had to protect his source, he had to know something about him. At first he thought the pockets were empty, but as he prodded about suddenly something moved and glinted as it fell to the wardrobe floor. Picking it up his eyes opened wide when he saw that it was a large key on a fob with the letters EWS printed on it. It was a Yale key and their house had no locks like that – they were all the old fashioned type. This was significant. It was clearly a key for something to do with his secret work. Suddenly he remembered the plane that had crash-landed in the field the year before. Was that an accident at all now he thought about it? What if his dad had shot it down by mistake because it had violated secret airspace? What if the key was in fact a key to a fighter plane that dad kept hidden out in the fields somewhere?

Willie-Joe carefully replaced the key in the trouser pocket and shut the wardrobe door. He had a lot of thinking to do and so to the thinking tree he went. Up there he would make sense of it all and put together some kind of a plan. One thing was for sure, he had to watch his dad carefully, maybe even follow him. He nodded to himself as he felt the burden of duty lie heavily upon his young shoulders. Yes, if he knew where he hid his plane then he would be able to help. After all, dad wasn't always at home and who knew when Mr Woods the Russian would happen upon its lair. He had to be ready to stop that happening.

The rain came to nothing and it petered out as pathetically as it had arrived. It was something Bisto was immensely glad of since he realised that although he had brought a coat it was now making its way back to Ballydoonan in the back seat of Mr McCutcheon's car. Not so handy really.

The small cottage at the side of the road at the start of their walk had proved to be something that Nathan and Winston insisted in getting all interested about for ten minutes as they stopped to read a brass plaque pinned beside its door.

"Marconi's cottage!" exclaimed Winston who had an interest in things scientific. "This is very cottage where Marconi sent the first transatlantic Morse code from in 1901!"

"Not Marconi!" exclaimed Lennie. The others looked at him and waited to hear more.

"Whoever he is," he added.

"Marconi? Only like *the* famous radio pioneer Guglielmo Marconi," said Winston with an air of incredulity. "Work done at this cottage started the new technology of telegraphy that trapped the murderer Dr Crippen half way across the Atlantic when he tried to escape to Canada."

"Cribben? Isn't that a crab?" said Bisto who was still half thinking about his erstwhile coat.

Nathan turned to Winston as they moved on and whispered across to him.

"That's amazing. How did you know all that?"

"It was printed at the bottom of the brass plaque on the cottage. I thought Marconi was a make of TV actually."

The path they were following soon petered out as effectively as the rain had done. The strip of coastal ground now became increasingly boulder strewn and walking became more of a climbing exercise. Some of the rocks were as big as buses and the rock-faced cliffs became sheer and grassless.

Ten minutes later and less than three miles from the car-park Nathan finally admitted to himself that getting around the headland was going to be next to impossible. He decided to call a halt while he worked out their options.

"How many miles is that then?" asked Lennie.

"Um, about three," replied Nathan studying the map.

"Only ninety two to go then eh?" grinned Lennie.

"Maybe," said Nathan peering at the contours on the map. They got considerably steeper ahead – it looked as if the coastal strip disappeared altogether and left only cliff or Atlantic.

"Maybe?" queried Bisto, "what's *maybe* about three from ninety-five?"

"Where's that?" asked Lennie looking out to sea. A large island sat brilliantly green with surf beating on its rugged shores not five miles out.

"That's Rathlin," replied Winston.

"Rathlin?" repeated Lennie.

"Yes, Rathlin Island. Dad was there once on a walking holiday before he got married. People live out there, they don't have electricity or anything."

"Doesn't Rathlin have something to do with spiders?" said Lennie scratching the back of his neck.

"Um… spiders?"

"Yeah, what do they farm out there?"

"Hardly spiders," shrugged Winston.

"Robert the Bruce is who you're thinking of," broke in Nathan who was still peering at his map.

"I think I can tell the difference between a spider and a man, especially a king-type man" dismissed Lennie.

"You can?" said Bisto with a laugh.

"Yes you dope. For one thing, a man has two legs and a spider has six… or is it eight?… or is that an insect? Whatever, although now I think about it, there was something funny about that Bruce boyo, I think… "

"No, no… what I mean," interrupted Nathan, "is that Robert the Bruce hid in a cave on Rathlin. It was there he saw a spider."

"Some way to go just to see a spider," grumbled Lennie. "what's so wrong with Scottish spiders?"

"Don't you remember the story? He was in the cave and had given up his cause but then he saw the spider trying to get up the cave wall. As he watched the spider kept falling but it didn't stop trying until it finally succeeded. Robert the Bruce was encouraged and decided to do the same thing."

"Oh," said Lennie thoughtfully. After a moment's hesitation he spoke again. "What did he want to climb the wall for?"

Bisto shook his head and looked at the others.

"Some people just have to have it all spelled out for them don't they?"

"Like you could spell!" retorted Lennie.

"Look, what Nathan means is that the spider just didn't give up, so neither did he," replied Bisto in an air of patronising patience.

"So why, Mr big bulbous brain head, did he want to follow the spider?"

"You burke – he didn't want to just follow the spider!"

"He didn't?"

"No, he was probably hungry, hiding in that cave and all – he wanted to eat it!"

As Lennie and Bisto clarified in their minds the historical realities or otherwise of the Scottish hero, Nathan showed Winston the map and the problem ahead. After a while Bisto caught on something was adrift and prised his neck out of Lennie's grip.

"What's wrong? Did you say there's something wrong?"

Nathan explained about their lack of forward path as he studied the map and at the same time examined the cliffs to their right.

"You mean we need to go back?" exclaimed Bisto. Lennie's voice answered him. He was all reason and benign condescension.

"Now now Bisto, we came to walk, no point complaining if we have to do a bit more than we planned. This is a *yomp* after all!"

"What? What are you an about you big lump? You were the one who thought ninety-five miles was a trip to the moon and back!"

"Me? I was just making sure we all knew the risks. I *am* the oldest you know. I *do* have moral responsibility for you lot."

As Bisto and Lennie argued, Nathan pointed out a feature on the map to Winston.

"There's a gully in the cliff a couple of hundred metres ahead. *Grey man's gully* it's called. If we get there we might be able to get up above the cliffs."

"Do you think it'll be hard? Maybe dangerous?" asked Winston.

"Could be," admitted Nathan.

"Good stuff!" grinned Winston. "Let's give it a go then – I brought a rope."

It was hard and it was dangerous. Without the rope they'd never have done it. Nathan and Winston went first and hauled up Lennie and Bisto one at a time. The gully was a cleft cut into the otherwise impassable cliff. Loose stones clattered down on the others as each ascended the sodden channel filled with wet moss and loose clumps of grassy earth. At one point as Winston and Nathan hauled the sprawling Lennie awkwardly up the gully Nathan suddenly had a vision of them all falling a hundred feet to their deaths on the boulders below. He shuddered involuntarily and blanked out the picture of personalised blood and bones from his mind.

When they all eventually collapsed with heaving chests on the field above the sea cliffs, life was all the more precious for its new appreciation.

"Well, that was fun," Lennie's voice said after some minutes, "and I mean that as sure as I'm riding this bicycle."

Nathan had to make a few adjustments to his pre-planned route on the map but when he did so he discovered they had actually saved themselves a mile of walking. It was a small compensation for having ascended the north face of the Matterhorn but Lennie and Bisto seemed appreciative enough.

"Mind you, if you've any more shortcuts like that I'll be happy enough to go the long way," suggested Bisto.

"This is the start of the plateau," said Nathan. "From here we begin ascending up through forestry and glens."

"How lovely," said Lennie, "do we stop anytime soon for something to eat or do we just walk till our bones stick out?"

Nathan had thought no more about eating but realised it was a good point.

"Why don't we head for those trees over there?" suggested Winston, "that's the way we're going anyway isn't it? There'll be shelter in case it rains and it's only about a mile or two."

Half an hour later they entered a strand of Rowan and Birch. Further in the trees darkened into Spruce and other Fir.

"There's no bears in Ireland, sure there's not?" said Lennie peering into the quiet darkness.

"No, nor snakes!" laughed Nathan.

"Good old Saint Patrick!" quipped Winston.

"Here, do you know what Patrick said as he was driving the snakes out of Ireland?" asked Bisto.

"What?" said Lennie.

"O.K. lads, enough chat, get those seatbelts on back there!"

A sod of moss bouncing off Bisto's head was answer enough to what the others thought of his joke.

Throwing their heavy back-packs onto the pine needle covered ground, Primus stoves and hexamine cookers were soon flaming brightly with sausages sizzling in butter and tins of beans bubbling in aluminium pots.

As Lennie sat watching his bacon he looked up and saw Bisto eating something out of a plastic pot.

"How come you're eating already?

Bisto grinned and tapped his head.

"That's where a bit of brains makes all the difference," he chuckled. "Pot-noodles. Just add hot water, none of that messing about with cooking. No dirty pots to clean either!"

"Waster!" muttered Lennie while wishing at the same time he had thought of it. He wasn't having a lot of success with his breakfast strips and watching them shrivel into hard little black bits of charcoal in front of his eyes was doing nothing for his culinary confidence.

"What else did you bring?" asked Winston.

"Else?"

"You did bring something else? You're hardly going to exist on Pot-noodles for breakfast lunch and tea for four days, are you?" said Nathan joining in.

"I'm not?"

Bisto looked back at Nathan and Winston's returning incredulous expressions.

"What? I *did* bring different flavours you know. I'm not *that* daft."

Lennie had got fed up waiting for his bacon and although he planned on eating it with beans and smash, hunger got the better of him and he just dropped the hot spitting strips straight into his mouth.

Very hot spitting strips.

"Ow! Ow! Ow! Ow!" he cried jumping up and sucking in vast amounts of air in an attempt to cool off his burning mouth. "Wadder! Wadder! Hath anyone god wadder!"

"I have, but…" began Bisto as Lennie hurriedly grabbed a pot half filled with water out of his hand and downed it in one gulp. He immediately let out a yelp that would have awakened the dead and probably scared half the life out of them all in one go.

"WAAAAHHHH!!!!"

"…but it's hot water," said Bisto finishing the sentence. As Lennie pranced about the tree trunks like a berserk grizzly bear uttering words that appeared in no dictionary known to the others, Bisto gave an apologetic shrug.

"It was the water left over from the Pot-noodles. It was for a cup of tea. I was kind of looking forward to that tea."

Nathan wondered if Captain Scott had that sort of bother with his fellow adventurers. The grizzly bear was still leaping about amongst the trees and he hoped that it would calm down soon. At least Scott's companions waited towards the end of their expedition before they started dying on him.

The distraction had taken his mind temporarily off his sausages and when he returned to them they were cooked to a 'T'. Pulling out his plastic plate he added the beans and tinned potatoes he had already heated. Altogether his meal looked a very attractive one. Bisto looked over and found that the wonderful innovation of dried food paled somewhat in the presence of pork sausages freshly cooked in butter. Still, it was chicken and mushroom flavour for lunch – chickens were tasty things too.

With the absence of Nathan, Will was left without an excuse for calling up at the McCutcheon house. Two days passed and the most he saw of Liz was her house up on the hill as he passed each day on his way to and from work. His next big chance was on Sunday morning when with any luck he would see her at church. She normally sat with her folks near the front on the right side of the Presbyterian Church in Ballydoonan while he sat upstairs in the balcony on the very back seat. It was a privileged position, yearned after by small boys for years until the older boys finally married or moved away due to another stage of life kicking in and allowing the seats free for the coming of age ritual that was a seat on the long bench seat.

Finally getting there after years of admiring the big lads who so confidently posed on the bench was like suddenly awakening one day to find stubble on your chin, pimples gone, a voice booming in bass confidence and girls giggling in your direction. It was Arrival. It was the end of teenage limbo and the beginning of true male adulthood. Leaving it to sit 'accidentally' a row behind Liz McCutcheon was as utterly impossible as utterly impossible could get. He may as well have painted a big flag with 'I'm in love' on it in large red letters and paraded up and down the aisles. Even aching hearts did not totally dispense with some residues of prudence and self preservation

In any case, on Sunday morning, his high vantage point of the congregation below showed him that Liz was not sitting with her family that morning. Will reckoned she was probably at crèche. He knew she helped out there regularly along with Johnny's wife Beth.

As Reverend Hamilton preached a sermon from Philippians chapter four, Will looked down on Liz's vacant seat and pondered an idea. Johnny would probably be going around to the hall at the back when the service ended to meet up with Beth. No suspicion would be aroused by his brother walking casually around with him. While there, who knew? He might get a chance to see Liz, maybe chat for a minute, maybe even… well, whatever. He might see her anyway.

"And so," said the minister, "the end of verse eight continues with a similar exhortation, *"whatsoever things are pure, whatsoever things are lovely, whatsoever things are of good report; if there be any virtue, and if there be any praise, think on these things."*

Will's eyebrows lifted. 'Whatever things are lovely? Think on these things?' That was *all* he was thinking about! He took a greater interest in what Mr Hamilton was saying and in doing so the minister caught his eye and gave a small smile as he continued in his sermon. The lads who sat in a long row at the back of the church could sometimes be a problem. They weren't noisy or very badly behaved but up there they were in a world of their own and seemed to spend as much time whispering to one another as paying attention to what was going on in church. Sometimes he wondered if any of them ever listened to a word he said. Suddenly he became aware that one lad was staring right at him and listening avidly. Maybe they took more notice of what he said than he imagined.

At the end Will casually broke away from the other lads and made his way quickly down the wooden spiral staircase in the bell tower. He caught up with Johnny as he was going out the front arched door.

"Hi bro'," said Will as nonchalantly as he could. "Heading home?"

Johnny slapped his brother's back and shook his head.

"Not yet, just going to get Beth. She's in crèche. How's work?"

They walked around to the rear hall together and in through the back door. Johnny thought no more about his brother being with him as he waited outside the door to the room where the children were having coats pulled on and got ready for their parents. When the door opened Beth was there, a line of small children behind her and laughter and squeals flooding out in torrents. Seeing Will with Johnny she smiled and called them over.

"You two have come at just the right time," she said, "one of the children managed to break a window with a wooden block, can you do anything?"

Liz was inside sitting on her knees consoling a small boy who was crying. She had his head on her shoulder and his chubby little arms were stretched around her slender neck, his hands buried deep into her thick dark hair. Will stopped for a moment and felt a pang of admiration as he heard her voice tell the sobbing boy what a soldier he was.

"There's a great wee man," she was saying, "Mummy will be here in a minute and you can tell her all about your sore knee and how you hardly cried at all." As the boy stopped crying, Liz brushed away his tears and smiled into his face. A lady suddenly appeared at the door. "There now, and look, there's Mummy!"

As his mother came in Beth looked back and caught the direction of Will's attention. She gave a small inward smile as Will suddenly became aware he was being watched. He quickly moved over to the window behind Johnny and studied the broken glass along with his brother.

As Liz walked to the door with the little boy's mother, Beth whispered in her ear.

"See who's here this morning?"

Liz at first thought she meant a child or parent but as she looked back into the room saw the two young men at the window. Johnny was side on so she saw him clearly enough.

"Johnny?"

"And his brother!" said Beth tilting her head and opening her eyes wide in an expression of shared secret knowledge. Liz looked back quickly and knew immediately who it was. Her heart missed a beat and she went from easily assured to jumpy and nervous.

"Don't you say a word!" she whispered back, terrified Beth would make some jokey comment. She hadn't actually ever told Beth how she felt about Will Patterson, but it had somehow become an assumed knowledge they shared without actually putting words on it. When Beth occasionally teased the younger girl about boys Liz always strongly refuted the accusations… almost always. One time she had mentioned her brother-in-law and that time she had blushed and tried hard to hide it.

So it was that there were occasional knowing smiles and kindly meant nudges from Beth when Will was around. It wasn't often by any means but they were smiles Liz sometimes returned, glad of having someone believe Will Patterson would ever think about her.

"Here's some Sellotape," said Will seeing a roll on the piano, "we could stick on some hardboard or something – it would do to keep the rain out until the church can get it sorted tomorrow."

"Hello, Liz," said Johnny seeing her as he went to get the tape. "Keeping Beth from killing the children eh?" he laughed. "I remember seeing some old cardboard boxes around here, you haven't seen them?"

"Upstairs above the stores cupboard," replied Liz, very much not looking at Will. "I couldn't reach them though."

"That's O.K. Just show me where they are and I'll get them and…"

"Actually, I need you for a minute," interrupted Beth before Johnny could finish or anyone else could speak. "Will, would you mind?"

"No, er, that's fine. Upstairs you say?"

"Yes, Liz you don't mind just showing Will there?"

As Liz led the way and Will followed, Johnny looked quizzically at his wife.

"Is everything all right?"

Beth sighed and laughed. Men had no idea. No wonder God had made Eve. Adam would have named animals all day long and not thought to introduce one ram to a ewe the whole time he was at it.

"So… ahm, any word from Nathan then?" Will said to Liz as she led him up the stairs.

"Nathan?"

"Isn't he away on his walk?"

"Oh yes!" laughed Liz, her blue eyes bright. "When I asked him where he was going he said, 'to the ends of the earth and back again'. Dear knows where he is now. Phoning home would be a confession of failure."

"And… and how are you?" continued Will who, like Liz, was not really thinking of talking about Nathan or anybody else more than six feet away for that matter.

"Oh, fine, I'm fine," replied Liz, her skirts giving a small swirl as she turned right at the top of the stairs. "How's work? You must be busy; we haven't seen much of you recently." She immediately flushed and hoped Will wouldn't think she was being forward. What sort of a stupid thing was that to say?

"No, I, I er, yes, I've been busy. I… I um…you like crèche?"

Liz smiled and stopped at a tall built in cupboard.

"I love it. The children are so funny sometimes. That's the cupboard. There's some boxes on top."

Will was just about able to reach to the top where he saw a box pushed to the back.

"I suppose if you become a nurse you'd like to work in the children's ward?"

Liz hesitated in surprise as she realised Will knew more about her than she could have guessed. How did he know she was…?

"I think nursing would suit you perfectly. You were great with that little boy."

"Oh, I'm just, he had, his knee… anybody would… you saw me downstairs with wee Peter?"

At that point he would have loved to tell her that she was just about all he saw. That she filled his dreams and inhabited his hopes and heart. Instead he looked at her and thought of no words that would come out and not destroy any tiny hope he had. One foolish sentence from him and he might know that she thought as much about him as Jack Spratt and his stupid fat. She would say it gently he was sure, she could not be hurtful, but hearing his hopes dashed forever by the beautiful girl's tender rebuttal was too much to contemplate. Instead he stood with a crisp packet box in his hand and felt like an idiot.

Liz saw no such idiot. She saw Will hesitate as if he was about to say something and for one wild and crazy moment allowed herself to almost imagine it might be something her heart desired above all else. The two or three seconds of silence were somehow without embarrassment and awkwardness but they were suddenly shattered by another voice.

"Oh good," said Johnny, "you found one. Mr Hamilton's downstairs. Come on and we'll tape up the window then."

Mr Hamilton thanked them as they finished the job and thanked them again as they left. He recognised the Patterson boy as the lad who had shown an interest in the talk that morning. Making a note to see about the window on the Monday, he also made a note to call up and see Margaret Patterson and her son that week. Margaret was a wonderful woman and he was convinced that he learned more from her that she could ever do from him. It would be good to see how Will was getting along too. He seemed to have something on his mind just now. Probably just the window.

"You'll have to call by for tea some time," said Beth to Liz in a voice she was sure her brother-in-law following along behind could hear.

"That would be nice, thanks," said Liz, glad to be asked to visit Beth whom she saw as the epitome of female maturity. She was still at that age too where she visited with her parents and being asked because of her own friendships was a pleasant innovation.

Beth left it at that. She had done enough effecting of events for one day – too much or too noticeable and the protagonists involved would go all defensive and that would never do. One thing she was convinced of. Will had not come around to crèche to say hello to his sister-in-law.

Two meals later and Bisto had eaten all his noodles but one. He hadn't planned on eating so many each time they each time they broke for grub, but out in the open air and walking so far and so long, one hardly dented his appetite. He had eaten two for breakfast, three for lunch and still managed to gulp down four for tea. By the time Nathan pronounced they were stopped walking and just looking for somewhere to pitch their tents, all that was left was a single portion in beef curry flavour.

"We'll put up the tents before lighting a fire, that way we can get our rucksacks stored away and really wind down," suggested Nathan.

"Wind down?" exclaimed Lennie, "Wind down?! I wish someone would wind me up! My legs are wrecked, my back is broken – I think my spine is in at least six bits, my feet are blistered with blisters on top of blisters, my shoulders feel like someone's been whacking them with sledgehammers and my nose is running! The only bit of me that's not sore is numb and when that wears off it'll probably be the worst of all. This is why we invented civilisation!"

"It's not that bad, said Winston, sitting down and scribbling something else into his log book. You'll feel better once we get the tents up."

"Once *you* get the tents up you mean," said Lennie. "I'm lying down and waiting for the paramedics in helicopters." He flopped to his knees and then rolled over onto his back, his backpack still attached.

"I'm sure that's not comfortable," said Nathan seeing the big man arched over the pack.

"Where I'm at it is not possible to get any more uncomfortable. Throw stones at me if you like – my poor broken body won't feel a thing!"

"What have you written in your log so far?" Nathan asked Winston as he unpacked his rucksack. Winston passed over the little red notebook and Winston read the first entry.

Arrived 10:20hrs. Men restless. Fifty percent cloud cover. Wind, 8-10 knots, veering South. Cloud type, Alto-stratus.

This is the beginning, and how we will come out of this will mark the rest of our lives. We go in as boys, we will emerge as men!

1033: Following behind Lennie. He has purple pants.'

Nathan shook his head as he smiled and turned the page.

'1050: 1.1miles. I saw a frog.

1150: The worst one and a half miles of my life. 1:3 slopes, rocks every-where. Lives hanging in the balance.

1155: Saw a sheep.

1156: Another sheep. Lovely.

1158: This is the life!'

There was more of the same on the following pages. The episode about the gully filled a whole page on its own. Words like 'terror' and 'death-defying' cropped up frequently; some with up to six exclamation marks.

Bisto's efforts at raising his tent were so woefully pitiful that Winston and Nathan did actually erect their ridge tent in the end. The spot they had chosen was not so much a good site as the least bad. There had been no more walking left in any of them and they selected an area where the tussocky grass rose in mounds like giant mole hills. The pegs disappeared into the grass and Nathan hoped they could be found again in the morning.

Winston had brought his dad's old tent as promised and as they un-folded it Nathan was impressed at how small and light the package was. The impression did not last long. When he and Winston had it finally erected the reason for its light weight immediately became apparent.

"There's something missing!" said Nathan.

Winston had not thought to check the tent before taking it with him, it was a tent... what was there to check?

The flysheet apparently. In its absence the thin cotton inner tent flapped weakly in the wind. Winston grinned apologetically.

"Oh well, it could be worse – it might have been raining."

The rain started at three in the morning. Winston knew it was three because he had not slept a wink since they had damped down the fire at ten and retired to their tents. The fire had been a hot one. It had also been an extremely short one since as soon as they had lit it, it had been ridiculously obvious that the entire hillside of dry tussock grass was threatening to burn along with it. Only by beating wildly at it with their sleeping bags did they manage to knock it down before they were reduced to four crispy human remains. Winston's cheap flower print nylon bag was not entirely adapted to its new function as a fire beater and it quickly developed large burnt patches which did nothing for its thermal qualities when the temperature dropped to almost freezing that night. They were all exhausted and this left Winston alone and awake as all around him in the stillness the snores of his companions sounded across the hills and probably the sea as well where the residents of Rathlin Island were awoken to the last woman and child to run about the island naked and terrified. Possibly.

The rain withstanding properties of the flysheet-less tent was somewhere between zero and nothing. Water soon began dripping in from the ridge above their heads and added wet to already cold and holed Winston's bag. Nathan was much better off having been given an army down-filled waterproof sleeping bag complete with sponge mattress. Captain Scott knew better than to venture into the Antarctic without a cosy sleeping bag.

Half an hour later Nathan stirred and vaguely became aware of a voice speaking in his dreams. It was a sad voice, a pitiful voice and it was speaking to itself. He gradually wakened and the voice remained.

"I'm c…c…cold," it said, followed by a groan of woe.

"Is that you?" whispered Nathan. The voice continued on seemingly unhearing.

"S..s…so c…c…old."

"Winston?"

"Y…y…es?" replied the weak pathetic little voice.

"Are you all right? Who are you talking to?"

"No, I'm freezing. My bag is wet and I've never been so cold in my life."

Nathan found his torch and flicked it on. The sight of half an inch of water lying at the bottom of the tent surprised him, especially as he was as dry and as toasty as a bug in a rug. Winston's plight was immediately clear.

"Here, take this," said Nathan pulling his sponge mattress out from below himself. "It's heat reflective. Lie up along my back; it'll help a bit too."

The rain eased at about five in the morning and as Winston began to warm slightly he managed at last to get some broken sleep.

Only some – at half six Lennie's voice boomed across from outside the tent opposite. He had discovered the dawn and a good night's sleep had erased the pains of the night before. The morning was crisp and the air was a heady drink of freedom and adventure.

"Wakey wakey campers!" he cried. "Rise and shine! It's a *lovely* morning and I feel like *singing*!"

"Oh no," groaned Winston. But it was too late; the great Caruso opened his lungs and guldered into the Antrim hills.

"Oh what a beautiful M…O…R…N…I…N…G!"

"Shut *up*!" shouted three voices in complete unison.

'Day two,' wrote Winston in his book. *'Ominous start.'*

Willie-Joe made his move when his dad drove down the lane to see someone's twin tub that had gone funny. With his mum busy iron-ing, he sneaked back up to his dad's wardrobe and ferreted out the key from his pocket. Wherever his dad was hiding, whatever he was hiding, he had headed out across the back field to it and so, after telling his mother he was going out to play, he slipped out and over the gate that led to the sloping field beyond.

A hedge running along to his left led down to the bottom of the field where a deep drain was bordered by impassable black thorn and gorse. Arriving at the drain he pondered his next move. A vague pad seemed to be worn in the grass that followed the unseen river to his right so he went that way, examining the hedgerow as he went.

Soon he was farther away from the house than he had been before and enjoying the sense of adventure. He was a secret partner in his dad's dangerous hidden life – an invisible set of eyes watching and aware of everything.

Unfortunately his invisible eyes were not aware of the cow dung he managed to step into right up to his ankles. Secret agents had to battle with all kinds of difficulties and this was just one of many he reckoned. It was as he wiped his feet on the long grass at the edge of the sunken drain that he spotted the gap in the hedge. Going over he discovered that the gap led to an ancient overgrown stone bridge that stretched across the drain to the other side.

Looking down into the drain from the bridge for the first time, Wil-lie-Joe wondered what lived down in the slate-sided depths. Monsters no doubt. Big web-footed prehistoric scaly things that had survived the last ice age and lurked with sinister intent for passing boys to leap upon and pull into the dark waters. He quickly crossed the bridge and came to a fence on the other side with a stile built in. On the other side a freshly cut barley field climbed steeply ahead of him. Checking his bearings so that he would know his way back, he began to climb the hill, a feeling growing that he was nearing his goal. As it so happened he was not far wrong.

The day before Willie-Joe's crossing of the bridge, the four adventurers were pressing on over the Antrim Plateau. The glens and hills were beautiful in their wildness. Rivers often crossed their paths and here and there the occasional waterfall cascaded clear crashing water onto smooth stones in deep pools of refreshing water. Not that the boys saw a lot of it what with the sweat blinding their eyes and the pains and aches creaking in their backs and legs. Nathan had soon realised that their target of twenty-five miles a day was an optimistic one indeed, especially with backpacks that felt like mobile purgatory.

"If you see any more mountains like that last one you dragged us up, would you be so kind as to go around it?" said Bisto. "It's not a crime you know. What was it called anyway, Everest?"

"Oghtbristacree actually," replied Nathan fingering a contour on the map.

"That sounds more like a disease of the armpits," said Bisto, "I hope there's not too many more like that!"

"It was less than thirteen hundred feet you know," defended Nathan, "you would need over twenty of those on top of one another to be anywhere near Everest."

"Mmm… you mean if we climbed that hill twenty times we could say that we've climbed the height of Everest?" asked Winston, rubbing his chin.

"No, you could say that we climbed armpit hill twenty times, though why I say 'we' I don't know," said Bisto, "I certainly will not ever be up there again. Can't we just stick to the flat bits from here on? Here, can I see that map of yours?"

Nathan passed him the map and Bisto studied it carefully.

"What are the green bits?"

"Forestry," replied Nathan.

"And the blue lines? Rivers?"

"Yup."

"So what's the pencil line you've drawn? Is that our route?"

"Yes, the x marks along it show where we've got to at different stages – the last one is where we are now."

"Right… I see… and what's all the brown land we're going through… some of it is darker than the rest… you have us going through some very dark bits."

"Ah, well… dark and light brown sort of gives an idea of how high the ground is… it um…"

"For someone who knows so much, you know not very much at all do you?" interrupted Lennie glaring down at Bisto in a superior manner.

"What, and I suppose you know?"

"You don't get to my stage in life without learning a few things," replied Lennie, casually inspecting his nails.

"So what's with the colours?"

"It's the thickness of the soil. Dark brown – thick soil, light brown – skinny sort of soil."

"*Skinny* soil?"

"Yes, the higher you get the skinnier the soil gets. That's why high mountains have no soil at all. Anyway… shouldn't we be getting going, Nathan?"

Nathan was glad to concede that they should and with the debate raging along behind them, Nathan and Winston led off.

"Those two go on a bit, don't they?" said Winston.

"Yeah, but it's just noise. They're the best of mates really."

"You'll be nobody's mate when they discover you've planned a route up every high piece of ground on the map," chuckled Winston.

Nathan laughed back but as they walked on he pulled out a pencil and made a few subtle adjustments to the line on the map. Mutiny could be a nasty business – no point inviting it.

They walked all that day and the rain thankfully kept away. It did not stop them getting wet feet however. Parts of the plateau were like walking on an enormous sponge; their feet were continually squelching over their ankles in soft moss and heather that formed a mere skin over a sodden landscape.

"Hey! Look at this!" cried Winston at one point. He jumped up and came down with a heavy watery thump on the heather. To their surprise they felt themselves lift as if on a wave as the ground itself rippled with the impact.

"Wooohh… "exclaimed Lennie, "don't do that, I get seasick. This place is a floating marsh. Look at my feet!" Lennie's boots were filled with water, when he raised his leg a river flowed out of his boot. "How am I supposed to stop that happening?" he complained.

"Don't lift your leg," suggested Bisto.

"Sorry, Lennie," apologised Winston, "those boots I got you aren't all that good. My dad said they were very old right enough. Did the Dubbin not help then?"

"Dubbin?" queried Lennie.

"Yes, the tin of beeswax for waterproofing the boots. Dad's friend sent it with the boots."

"Is that what that was?" replied Lennie remembering the tin. "I thought it was cooking fat."

"Cooking fat? No, it was for rubbing into the boots. Do you still have it?"

"Um… no, not now," said Lennie, with a slightly worried expression on his face.

"What did you do with it?" asked Winston hesitantly.

"I fried my breakfast strips with it yesterday. No wonder they burnt black and tasted like old socks."

Nathan shook his head and turned to walk on. If he could just get them home before they began dying on him then maybe he wouldn't get the blame. That was the success of Scott's failure. He died with his colleagues and nobody could give him a hard time about it.

Personally, he hoped it wouldn't come to that.

When they broke for camp they were once again utterly spent. They had managed by Nathan's reckoning only twenty eight miles since Friday morning, having had to descend into countless glens and valleys before inescapably having to ascend the forested hills again on the other side. His estimate of twenty-five a day was well out – at this rate they'd be lucky to see Ballydoonan before the next ice age. He had planned on taking them over the summit of Trostan, but even Nathan had lost his adventuring edge with the hard going dragging the legs out from beneath him as the land slowly passed below their feet. The humour was completely off them all and only the thought of food and rest kept them going till they reached somewhere to pitch their tents.

As the others got out their cookers and tins of food, Bisto sat on a rock and watched, a glum look on his face. He was out of completely out of Pot-noodles and therefore by default, completely out of food. He was not however out of ravishing hunger. When the others realised what had happened they scrambled about in their bags and donated what bits and pieces they could.

"Sorry about that," apologised Bisto.

"No worries, it could happen to the best of us," said Lennie magnanimously.

"Thanks," said Bisto, humbled.

"And the biggest plonkers too, you dope!" added Lennie.

That night they camped on high ground overlooking Glenarriff glen. A gently curling river burbled beside them and the ground on its banks was soft and dry.

"This water safe?" asked Lennie peering into the river as the light rapidly fell.

"Better than tap water," assured Nathan, "I'm drinking it in my tea."

Soon they had finished and bringing out their sleeping bags, lay on them and listened to the sounds of far off home-bound birds and the distant dim cry of the sea.

As the stars appeared one by one and began speckling the darkening sky. Winston lay on his back and rubbed his sore legs.

"This is the life. When I grow old and think back, this night will be the night I will remember most of all." As if to underline his sentence, a streak of light scored across the sky towards Trostan, a meteorite marking the velvet blackness with its jewels behind.

The heavens gradually revealing their incredible vastness and sparkling wonder, the four fell silent and cast their eyes up and beyond themselves to gaze into the eternal scale, a measure that reduced them to grains of sand on an everlasting beach, grains struggling to understand land beyond the unseen horizon.

Nathan wondered if Scott and his companions had lain on their backs in the snow at the ends of the Earth and considered the same heavens and knew then, like he knew now, that their lives were but the flower of grass – so brief and fleeting in the everlasting turning of the wheels of endless time.

Winston lay, mouth open in awe and felt minute and infinitesimal under the uncountable billions of clustered stars. His mind expanded and stretched to conceive what it was to look into eternity.

He also thought about spiders. Spiders could be crawling about all over the place he thought as he quickly shut his mouth.

Leaving camp the next morning, they began to follow the river and hadn't gone twenty feet when Winston pointed at something in the water.

"What's that?" he asked going over to take a closer look.

It was a dead sheep. A very dead sheep. A very dead, horribly rotting, in the water dead sheep.

"Yuck!" said Winston. I hope none of you guys used any of that water last night. Just imagine drinking a mug of tea with a mouthful of *that* in it!" Nathan and Lennie looked at one another. Nathan paled, gave a weak grin and hoped they wouldn't get sick. Lennie just had murder on his mind.

They moved on, Nathan leading and thinking a lot about every twinge, real or imagined, in his stomach. Winston and Bisto followed behind with Lennie moodily taking up the rear. Having throttled Nathan at least twenty times in his imagination he decided instead just to look wounded and aggrieved for half an hour or so. This had several advantages to manslaughter, one being that it allowed the required sense of righteous indignation without the prison sentence.

An hour later, as they plodded on over heavy clumps of heather and along streams that appeared out of nowhere and disappeared as quickly, they came across a rise in the ground with a lightly worn grass pathway leading up to it.

"Where's that lead to out here?" asked Lennie who by now had thawed off significantly. He had voiced the question the others were pondering inwardly.

"I don't know," said Nathan, "there's nothing on the map."

They followed the path without dissent and after a few minutes stood at the top of the small hill. A couple of concrete constructions protruded mysteriously out of the ground. One had a padlocked manhole cover on top with metal vents around its low walls. Beside it a metal pole led up to a bracket and ten feet behind that, another concrete vent, this time without a cover.

"What is it?" asked Bisto, "something to do with the forestry?"

"Maybe a water collection point or something," said Winston pressing his ear to the vents. "Can't hear any water though."

"Weird if you ask me," put in Lennie. "What nut would stick an underground thing out here, unless it's the clubhouse for the end of the world club?"

"I think Lennie's guess is closest," said Nathan, suddenly remembering something.

"What, the end of the world?" said Bisto doubtfully.

"Well, near enough. My uncle is a volunteer in the Royal Observer Corp. He has one of those bunkers to look after."

"What's he observing... worms?" asked Lennie.

"It's an Early Warning Station. Apparently they're all over the place. He has to go up and practise taking readings in case there's a nuclear war."

"You're joking!" exclaimed Bisto.

"No, really. Down in there," he said pointing at the manhole, "there's a whole lot of instruments and stuff. Uncle Thomas sleeps over in it some nights I think. If there was a nuclear war, all the volunteers would be able to tell where The Bomb had landed and report back to wherever what was happening at their location."

"What? Your uncle would be under the ground in his bunker while everybody else is being killed by atomic bombs and radiation and all?" exclaimed Bisto. "You're winding us up! There's no such thing... you *are* winding us up aren't you?"

"I saw a programme about that once on T.V." said Winston. "You know, the Cold War and all. It was pretty scary, sirens going off and people hiding under tables and things. Your uncle? Cool!"

"Cool?" exclaimed Lennie, "it's terrible! I thought all those 'end of the world' films were just made up... I can hardly believe there are actually bunkers and radiation counters and all... and there's one at Ballydoonan? What would the Russians bomb Ballydoonan for?"

Lennie was shocked. To think he had listened to Radio Moscow and all the time those blinking Russians were planning on sending bombers to obliterate his village. Probably using his radio as a direction beacon too. He would make sure his radio was off at nights from now on.

"It does make you feel a bit creepy, doesn't it though," said Winston. "Here we are, you may as well say at the ends of the Earth, and the end of the Earth is right here in front of us."

It was all very esoteric and after hanging about at the ominous bunker, all four felt the need to move on. The subject was horribly attractive to talk about all the same, and for the next hour they exchanged stories about the various apocalyptic films they had seen and books they had read. Lennie's final contribution that 'Humpty Dumpty' gave him the shivers finally ended the discussion as they all fell about laughing and the conversation veered instead to what nursery rhymes they could remember. Some of Bisto's raised a few eyebrows. Certainly Nathan had not remembered 'Hey Diddle Diddle' having a piddling dog when he was in P4.

The sky ahead seemed to be darkening as Nathan took a bearing off a hill on the map. The highest peak was a low mountain called Collin Top and their way lay along its Eastern flank and on to hills and another glen beyond. Winston made a few more notes in his log as walked along at the back.

'Nearly all food gone. Men pushing hard. This is tough – asked Bisto if he was hungry – he gave me a very funny look. In bad situations men can resort to cannibalism. Walked up beside Nathan. Put penknife in outside pocket.

1855: Heard Lennie do a fart. Unbelievably loud. Said it wasn't him.

1859: Everyone agrees. It was him.'

It was less than an hour later when a grey ghostly mist descended from the south-west – shadowy riders with dull silver armour – cold vapour on grey steeds.

"Uh, this is a bit grim," said Lennie. "How do we know which way to go? I can hardly see you Bisto and you're not six feet in front of me!"

"Maybe we should wait for a bit," an echoless voice said from the greyness ahead.

"Who said that?" asked Lennie.

"Me," said Nathan, "if we wait a few minutes the fog should lift."

An hour later and the fog had thickened. The freezing damp clung to them all like a shroud and Bisto was cold and shivering. It didn't help that he had no coat and was clad in a fertilizer bag Winston had found and adapted for the purpose. Although it mostly kept the rain off his torso, his arms were cold and wet and he wasn't getting warmer standing still.

"Maybe we should just head on the way we were going," suggested Winston. "When we begin to descend we'll probably get below the fog."

The others agreed and Nathan checked their bearings and led off.

"Where are you going?" asked Bisto.

"One hundred and forty eight degrees south-east," replied Nathan, "it's our course."

"Your bum it's our course!" remonstrated Bisto shivering, "we need to go this way, away over to the left!"

The others found themselves agreeing with Bisto – Nathan did seem to be veering off to the west. Nathan himself was unsure, though the compass seemed to be working all right.

"I don't think so…" he said, "I set the compass and I haven't moved it or anything."

"I've heard of hills so full of iron that they act like magnets," said Winston, "maybe it's something like that?"

"Maybe…" said Nathan hesitantly, "but… but I don't think so… I think the fog has just disorientated us. I think we should trust the compass."

Lennie drew close to Nathan and peered at the instrument in his hand.

"That little squirty wee needle's right and we're all wrong… is that what you're saying?"

"Well, we'll have to choose one way or the other or Bisto will die of cold," said Winston seeing the once swarthy face beside him pale and looking like death warmed up. Bisto was now too cold to speak.

"Which way then?" asked Lennie. Winston looked to Nathan and Nathan felt the pressure of leadership press hard upon his shoulders. It was at times like this that leaders made choices, choices that affected outcomes, outcomes that affected lives. Captain Scott had had to do the same thing and in the end history decided whether or not he had made the right choices. Nathan felt the pangs of self-doubt and made a conscious decision. 'Stuff the Antarctic. There's no place like home.'

"I really think we should trust the compass. If it's wrong, it's the first time ever."

In the end they went with the bearings on the compass. An hour later they were descending in bright sunlight into Glencloy – an hour or so after that and they were into Glenarm and making mental notes to always trust compasses above intuition – even group intuition… especially group intuition.

In the distance tall chimneys towered above the horizon.

"That's Larne," said Nathan, "and if we can get there before too late I've got an idea you might be interested in."

Willie-Joe reached the top of the barley field and stood looking at the strange edifice at the top of the hill in front of him. He had no idea what it was, but it had a raised concrete plinth with a manhole cover and vents and a metal pole. The padlock on the manhole invited a key and it was a key that Willie-Joe brought out of his pocket. To his increasing excitement, the key fitted and the lock turned easily and clicked open.

The cover pulled up with some difficulty but he managed it all the same. A deep hole with a raking ladder leading down into the darkness lay revealed below him. Down there lay his dad's secrets, secrets that if Willie-Joe knew, he could help protect. He could almost hear his heart beating as he nervously climbed up onto the plinth. Without looking around he stepped onto the steel ladder and began descending.

Willie-Joe had intended to leave the cover open but as he waited on a rung for his eyes to adjust to the darkness, suddenly he heard a noise from outside. It was a voice.

He listened and heard it again. It was Mr Wood's voice!

"Here boy, here!" shouted Mr Woods to his border collie. He had been out looking for a bullock that had broken out of a field earlier in the day and decided to head up to the high hill above McCutcheons' to scan the surrounding fields. As he approached the top he saw that the door to the warning bunker was open. He walked up and peered down into the entrance hole. Darkness peered back. Lowering his head, he gave a call down into the bunker.

"Hello! Is there someone there? Thomas? Are you down there?" There was a resounding silence.

Hugh Woods had always wondered what it was like down in the nuclear bunker and for a moment he considered climbing down and taking a quick look. He thought the better of it however; it was a government thing and none of his business. Instead he pushed the cover down and replaced the padlock. Thomas McCutcheon must have left it open accidentally – the next time he saw him he would mention it to him.

A tractor with a trailer stopped when the farmer driving it saw the four lads thumbing on the small road above Carncastle. Soon they were bumping along the road, feet hanging over the back and lying back on the packs. Off to the south-west Nathan saw the rounded summit of Slemish peer over the cloud. It could peer all it liked, thought Nathan wearily. Climbing it could wait till another time, it wasn't like it was going anywhere.

"Isn't this kind of cheating?" asked Winston who seemed to have a capacity to forget pain very quickly.

"No, sure didn't Scott take tractors to the Antarctic?" pointed out Nathan. Winston nodded. Right enough, in the film, tracked vehicles were used to haul some of the gear over the ice shelf. They also all broke down.

The Ford tractor above Carncastle didn't have the rigours of minus fifty degree temperatures to contend with and half and hour later the farmer dropped them off outside Larne. From there they walked the last mile and a half into the town where they asked a woman for the way to the train station. Ten minutes after that they had pooled what money they had and were heading to Belfast on the nine o'clock train.

"I've never been on a train before," said Lennie, looking out the window as Belfast Lough passed by.

"You're joking," said Nathan.

"Neither have I," mumbled Bisto. He was tired and not quite warm enough yet to feel actually comfortable. Still, he had never been on a train and he might as well say something. He hadn't spoken in a couple of hours.

"Me neither," confessed Winston. "How many times have you?" he asked Nathan.

"This is my first too," yawned Nathan. There was a silence for a few minutes before Winston spoke.

"This must be cheating," he said.

They managed to make the connection with the last bus out of Belfast for the Peninsula and at half past eleven they stood on a crossroads, seven miles from Ballydoonan. They were by now the walking dead, all banter was drained out of them and Nathan felt like he was living in a half world between consciousness and the sleep of the dead. The others evidently felt the same way since no-one had spoken since they had got onto the bus in the city forty minutes before.

The last seven miles to home and comfortable beds was the goal, but as they pushed on unspeaking, Nathan seriously doubted they had the strength left to do it. Winston was working out in his head how long it would take them and didn't like the figures. In fact, any figure over ten minutes seemed utterly impossible. Even he had had enough of the endless trudging. The film was good to watch – starring in it was another matter.

Three hours before the arrival at the crossroads, Isobel and Thomas McCutcheon realised that Willie-Joe was not coming home. Convinced now that he was lost or something worse, Thomas began ringing round his neighbours and friends in the hope they had seen his son. Twenty minutes after that he phoned the local police station.

Will was at home when Mr Hamilton called by to speak to his mother. He seemed anxious about something and when Will explained his mother was still not back from visiting an old lady she often checked up on, he went to head on.

"Is everything all right Mr Hamilton?" asked Will as he saw the Presbyterian minister to the door.

"No, not really," admitted Mr Hamilton. "It's Thomas McCutcheon's boy. He's gone missing and a search party's been organised. I was just checking in case your mother had seen sight of him. You haven't by any chance?"

Will hadn't, but when Mr Hamilton left he scribbled a quick note for his mother and grabbed the Mini's keys. Thomas McCutcheon was Nathan's uncle. Probably the family could do with all the help they could get. It would be getting dark soon and he imagined the family would be getting increasingly worried.

He drove straight to Nathan's house and found Bob McCutcheon preparing to get into his car.

"I heard about your nephew. I came to see if I could help," he said jumping out of the Mini. "I have a torch with me."

"Good lad!" exclaimed Bob McCutcheon thankfully. "Actually, you can help a lot; we're heading over to my brother's house now, do you know where he lives?"

"No, I'm sorry, I…"

"That's all right,, I'll get Liz to go with you, Ellie is coming with me."

Just at that Liz and her mother appeared at the door to the house. Liz was surprised to see Will but her father explained the situation.

"Ellie and I will head up to the house. To save time, you and Liz check the full length of the road below their lane. Check the hedges, the ditches, everywhere along the road. If you find anything... if you find Willie-Joe or you're sure he's not there, come up to the house and someone will tell you somewhere else to look. Thanks again for coming' son."

Bob and his wife wasted no time and ten seconds later they were gone, tail-lights braking as they slowed for the turn at the top of the lane. It was a serious and troubling situation but Will and Liz stood awkwardly either side of the Mini for a moment, embarrassed but knowing they had to get going.

"If you don't mind, I'll drive and you can direct?" said Will breaking the impasse. Liz nodded and hesitantly got into the car. She pushed her embarrassment to one side and explained to Will how to get to her uncle's house.

"Yes, I know where that is," said Will nodding. Liz gave a weak smile, she looked worried and tense. "I'm sure he'll be found all right," he added gently, "don't worry."

It was four miles to the small road and Will slowed straight away and began scanning the fields.

"If you search right, I'll look left," he suggested. Liz nodded and peered out through the window.

Ten minutes later they had driven the full length of the road. There was no sign of Willie-Joe.

"Maybe we should get out and walk?" suggested Liz. "If he's... if he's over a hedge or something we'll never see him from the car."

Will agreed and parked up in the old quarry. Getting the torch from the back seat he opened Liz's door and looked around as she got out.

A gate opposite the quarry opened into a field and the two of them

341

climbed the gate and began searching the back of the hedge.

"Willie-Joe!" cried Liz as they moved along. There was no reply and the sky began to darken making the evening feel oppressive and frightening in the context of what they might find. Will watched the slender shape of the girl moving along the hedge and felt burdened for her. He wanted to be able to make things right, to fix it all, just for her. He would have loved to hold her, protect her, to somehow bring things right for her family. Instead here he was, probably embarrassing her with his stupid presence in a family crisis. He'd have been better staying at home.

Something made Will look up to the hill above them at the other side of the field and he suddenly had an idea.

"Liz, if we go up to the top of that hill we might be able to look around a bit before it gets much darker. I could call out for your cousin from up there. My voice would carry a long distance in the still night.

"Yes, yes, that's a good idea," she agreed. "He could be wandering about lost; up there we might see better right enough."

The light was beginning to fade rapidly now and as they made their way up the hill, Liz kept close to Will. Wandering about at dusk in the open was not something she was used to and keeping close to Will made her feel safer. She sighed inwardly as she realised he was never going to be interested in her now. She would be the girl whose family lost their children. He probably pitied her but it was not an emotion she felt glad to have directed her way from Will Patterson. It suddenly occurred to her then that she expected Willie-Joe would be found. The thought that something bad had happened to him struck her like a hammer on an anvil and made her shudder. She was glad to have Will near at hand.

Willie-Joe was initially terrified when the cover above his head slammed shut. When the farmer had called for his dog, he had slid down the twenty feet to the bottom of the ladder and backed into the darkness. After Mr Woods had left he fumbled about for the ladder and returned to the top where it did not take long to realise he had been locked in. It was an awful moment and the tears flooded down his cheeks as he cried and called for help. No-one heard and no-one came.

Ten minutes later the tears eased and Willie-Joe returned down the ladder and stood in abject darkness. It was a darkness like no other he had ever experienced and not knowing what lurked around him did not help. Realising that a place like this had to have some form of lighting, he began feeling about for a light switch. He seemed to be standing at a doorway and after a few seconds of feeling about, his hand felt what was definitely the shape of a switch. He flicked it and immediately a yellow glow illuminated his surroundings.

He was standing at the bottom on a shaft with the ladder leading up to the locked manhole cover. In front of him a small room big enough for a dry toilet and little else stood in shadow. To his right, from where the weak yellow light burned was a room no more than twenty feet long and about eight feet wide. At the far end was a simple metal bed and two mattresses, to the left was a bench with a seat tucked under it. On the bench sat all sorts of strange instruments and what appeared to be radios and telephone-type things. On the wall were posters. 'Fallout!' said one. 'Signs of Radiation Sickness,' said another.

A gas mask sat on the bench and a newspaper beside it. Apart from a cupboard with tins of food and electrical switch boxes on the wall, it was all in the room. The only exit was the shaft behind him. Crossing the room he sat on the bed and stared at the ground. His dad was a secret atomic bomb man. He fixed washing machines by day and fired off atomic bombs at night. It was a weighty thought.

Sitting on the bed he wondered how often his dad visited the bunker. A calendar on the wall bore only occasional ticks each month, which was another weighty thought. He could be here for weeks – weeks during which time Mr Woods would have strangled all his family and escaped back to Russia where he would press big red buttons and send atomic bombs back to Ballydoonan. It was terrible. Willie-Joe did the only thing he could. He buried his head in his hands and wept.

All four had their heads down now. Nathan led them through a wooded estate and dialled a direct bearing into his compass straight for Ballydoonan. Every yard seemed to matter now and just to head straight for home was the only way he could persuade himself to keep going.

Lennie's socks had disappeared down into his boots and although it was uncomfortable he was long past caring. Bisto trudged wearily in front of him and tried hard to think of nothing. It wasn't easy and his mind insisted on thinking of pain. Pain in his feet, pain in his back, pain down his legs, pains anywhere he thought about and some places he didn't to boot. Misery was his first name and he would have complained and told Nathan to stop except he didn't have the energy.

Winston was behind Nathan, suffering silently and telling himself that he would be a better person for it all. He would work harder around the farm, he would help his mother more, he would remember to buy Nate a birthday present from time to time, he would pray for world peace and smile more at small children in prams. He would also clean his teeth more often. Altogether he would be a better person.

Nathan was thinking about the last eleven miles to one ton depot. Captain Scott's team had just burned out. The last eleven was a million miles. At last he understood – Ballydoonan was less than five miles away but the way he felt it may as well have been on the far side of Jupiter. In his bones he knew they weren't getting there that night. The thought of putting up tents however was the far side of Neptune. No other idea was even in the solar system.

So he dragged one leg after the other and waited for a miracle.

Liz was right beside Will now, so close that she brushed against him as they neared the top. The darkness meant he could not see her face but he felt her touch his arm when a curlew gave a cry in the darkness and a thousand volts of electricity shot through every fibre in his body. She was right beside him; her breathing was the air of angels. He had to struggle to get his mind back to the task in hand – a young lad was lost – thinking of his own tortured feelings was totally out of bounds.

At the top Liz stayed close. It was clear now that nothing could be seen now the night had fallen, but he could still call.

"I'll give a shout – Willie, isn't it?" asked Will. Beside him a pale face looked up.

"Willie-Joe," said Liz, "it's actually not his real name but it's all he's ever been called."

Will nodded and held his hands up either side of his mouth.

"WILLIE-JOE!" he shouted. Liz wasn't quite prepared for the volume and she gave a start.

"Sorry," said Will, "didn't mean to make you jump."

"No, shout away," said Liz with a small laugh. It's just the silence, it's kind of oppressive; a voice seems an out of place if you know what I mean."

Down in the bunker Willie-Joe heard the unmistakeable cry of his name. He sat up on the bed and listened as the voice shouted again. In a flash he was up and climbing the ladder.

"I'm here!" he cried, "I'm under here!"

"Listen!" said Liz holding Will's arm. "I heard something!"

There was the definite sound of a voice coming from just behind them. Will called again.

"It's muffled," said Liz, "it's coming from that square object… what is it?"

At the Early Warning bunker, Will and Liz looked quizzically at one another and Liz gave a call.

"Willie-Joe? Is that you?"

"Is that you, Liz?" came a broken voice from the concrete box.

"Willie-Joe, we've come to take you home, are you all right?"

"I'm locked in this underground thing," said Willie-Joe through the vent, "the Russian spy locked me in. Has he strangled Dad yet? Where's Mum? Is Joyce still alive? I wanted to say sorry for not playing shops with her."

Liz soothed her cousin through the vent as Will tried to see if he could force a way in. It was clear it was hopeless.

"Who has a key, Willie-Joe?" asked Will.

"Me," said the muffled voice.

The vents were blocked with a gauze filter on the inside and after trying it was obvious the key inside the bunker was going to play no part in Willie-Joe's release.

"Where's Willie-Joe's house from here?" asked Will. Liz looked up and pointed across the valley to an outside burning less than half a mile away.

"That's aunt Isobel's house there. Do you want to go and get help?"

"What about you?" asked Will. Leaving her on her own seemed wrong, and yet Willie-Joe was frightened too.

"I'll stay with Willie-Joe," she replied. "You'd better take the torch too, it's dark down in the gorse."

Unwillingly Will agreed. She was right of course. The house was directly across the valley – it wouldn't take long if he ran.

Ellie was with Isobel when a knock came to the door. Ellie opened to a breathless Will Patterson.

"We've found him!" he exclaimed. "He's all right!"

Thomas was up in fields in the opposite direction; Will soon found him and told him where Willie-Joe had been found.

"You said he had a key?" checked Thomas McCutcheon with amazement as he jogged alongside the younger man in the direction of the house.

"Yes, but we can't get it out."

"I have a spare," said Thomas. Will thought that strange but said no more. What *was* that bunker anyway?

Thomas wasted no time unlocking the padlock and throwing back the metal cover. Willie-Joe's pale and frightened face looked out. In a second, Thomas McCutcheon reached down, pulled his son up to his chest and hugged him.

"Are you all right son?"

"Yes Dad... I'm sorry, I think the Russians know all about you. I'm sorry." With that he began crying again and Thomas McCutcheon hugged him and gave a shrug to the other two.

"He's in shock I think. Thanks... I'm sorry... I can't remember your name?"

"Will," replied Liz, beaming in the darkness, "Will Patterson."

Thomas made his way back to the house, Willie-Joe at his side. There a weeping welcome with kisses and hugs from his mother, sister and aunt awaited him. Bob would return and the police would stand down. For Willie-Joe all was well. The Russians were foiled after all.

Will turned and went to return the other way to the quarry where his car was parked.

"Will?" said Liz hesitantly. It was all she said, nothing else would come. Thanks she wanted to give but it was more than that and…

"Yes?" said Will. She had not gone with her uncle and had chosen to stay with him. Will's mind was whirling rapidly but getting no clear answer to his questions.

They were standing facing one another in the darkness with the torch turned on but set on the bunker, its light beaming away from them both. She was right in front of him. She was right there, her slim and beautiful shape undimmed by the gloom. She was inches from him and, as if in a dream, he made an almost unconscious decision, reached forward and took her hand in his. To his wonder she did not resist.

"Liz… Liz, I…" Liz remained there unmoving, her eyes intently fixed on his in the pale reflected light.

He said no more and gently pulling her to himself, he leaned down and kissed her soft face. She leaned forward, closed her eyes and lovingly put her arms around his neck with her cheek upon his chest. The sweet scent of her hair drifted into his nostrils and he placed a hand behind her head and kissed her lips. Her returning embrace said more than his wildest dreams had ever hoped. Heaven had descended to Earth and two hearts beat beside one another, each the complete and willing slave of the other. The world was not big enough for Will's swelling heart and if he could have burst into song he would have. Love had lost all of its misery and the two smiled in the darkness and held one another, disbelieving and happy beyond measure. Words would come later. A lifetime of words.

A few minutes later Nathan raised his weary head and saw less than fifty metres away a light shining on top of the hill they were curling around. In front of the light a couple stood, arms entwined as they kissed, laughed and picked up the torch before heading down the other side of the hill. Ten seconds later they were gone. Thirty seconds after that the four stood on the same spot and saw the open door of the bunker with the pale inviting yellow light coming up from below.

It was less than three miles to go, but the Ballydoonan four had come to the end of themselves, to the end of it all. Winston volunteered to look below and a minute later he emerged, a smile faintly stretched across his face.

"There's beds!" he said

They slept that night in the bunker so recently the scene of an imagined treachery, a family crisis, and a new beginning. Knowing nothing of that, Lennie, Bisto, Winston and Nathan slept the best night's sleep any could remember. The mattresses lay on the floor and with their sleeping bags and mats all were warm for the first time in three days. Outside the moon appeared from behind a silver cloud and smiled on the scene below.

A month from now they would remember what a great walk they had had together. Friends' marvelling at the distance they had managed would enlarge their recollections of the wonderful time it had been. No-one would ever mention the tractor, the train or the bus.

But that was the future. For now they quickly fell asleep one by one, aches and pains not near enough to stop the inexorable demand for rest. Three miles. The irony of being so close and yet so far was not lost on Nathan but then, as he drifted off to beautiful sleep he realised he cared as much as a waggle of a duck's bottom.

Outside Liz's house a little orange Mini happily purred down the lane as a dark haired girl stood in the porch and smiled, her heart as clear and happy as she could ever wish it to be. The boy driving home in the mini was no less so and his smile remained on his face and did not fade even as he fell asleep, a small pastel pink handkerchief with blue embroidered flowers held softly in his hand.

Dear Reader

I don't know how you came by this book – maybe it was a present or maybe you bought it in a bookshop – in which case I'd like to thank you for choosing this particular title.

Obviously I hope you enjoyed reading this book as much as I did – and if you did, why not tell someone about it?

Personally speaking, facing the myriad of books in a typical bookshop, it's always hard to know where to start but having a book recommended by a friend is always a help.

So why not spread a little happiness today and tell someone about Ballydoonan!

Timothy S Johnston

PS: While you're at it, why not visit our website where you can chat to authors on the discussion groups, tell others what you think about particular titles, see the other books we publish and avail of a constantly changing range of special offers.

You can find us at: **www.cottage-publications.com**

BALLYHAY BOOKS

Laurel Cottage
15 Ballyhay Rd
Donaghadee
Co. Down
N. Ireland
BT21 0NG
Tel: +44 (0)28 9188 8033